'NOW THEN,' SAID THE ANCIENT. 'WE SHALL TALK . . .'

'Of your actual meeting with the dragon, if indeed you reach him, I will say nothing, for that is still in the realms of conjecture. What I can say is this: in order to reach the dragon you have a long and terrible journey ahead of you, one that will tax you all to the utmost, and may even find one or other of you tempted to give up, to leave the others and return; if that happens then you are all doomed, for I must impress upon you that as the seven you are now you have a chance, but even were there one less your chances of survival would be halved.'

'I can see by your expressions that you have no real idea of what I mean when I say "perils and dangers": believe me, your imaginations cannot encompass the terrors you might have to face—'

'And if we don't go at all—if we decide to go back to—to wherever we came from?' I persisted.

'Then you will be crippled, all of you, in one way or another, for the rest of your lives.'

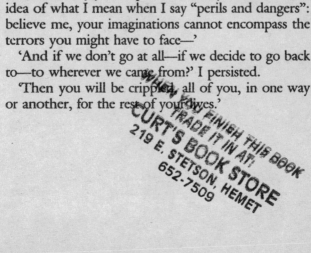

BAEN BOOKS by MARY BROWN

The Unlikely Ones
Pigs Don't Fly
Master of Many Treasures
Strange Deliverance
Dragonne's Eg

THE UNLIKELY ONES

MARY BROWN

THE UNLIKELY ONES

This is a work of fiction. All the characters and events portrayed in this book are fictional, and any resemblance to real people or incidents is purely coincidental.

A Baen Book

Baen Publishing Enterprises
P.O. Box 1403
Riverdale, NY 10471

ISBN: 0-671-57844-8

Cover art by Gary Ruddell

First Baen printing, November 1987
Fourth Baen printing, December 1999

Distributed by Simon & Schuster
1230 Avenue of the Americas
New York, NY 10020

Library of Congress Catalog Number 86-10598

Typeset by Windhaven Press, Auburn, NH
Printed in the United States of America

To the then of 'C' and 'Ly', my father and my mother and the now of Christopher, their great-grandson.

Acknowledgements

My thanks as usual to:
My husband, Peter;
My editor, Paul Sidey;
My typist, Anne Pitt.
Especial thanks to the author A. C. H. (Anthony) Smith,
Without whose encouragement this book would not have been written, and
Finally, last but not least,
Love and thanks to 'Wellington',
Once again my companion and also this time
Invaluable referee on the peculiarities of animal behaviour . . .

THE BEGINNING

The Thief in the Night

THE CAVE itself was cosy enough as caves go: sandy floor, reasonably draught-proof, convenient ledges for storing treasure, a rain/dew pond just outside, a southerly aspect and an excellent landing strip adjacent, but the occupant was definitely not at his best and the central heating in his belly not functioning as it should. Granted he must have been all of two hundred and fifty years old but that was merely a youngling in dragon-years, measuring as he did a man-and-a-half (Western Hominid Standard) excluding tail, and at his age he should have been flowing with fiery, red health.

He was not. He was blue, and that was not good. Dragons may be red, scarlet, crimson, vermilion, rose-madder at a pinch, purple, gold, silver, orange, yellow, even certain shades of green—but not blue.

He lay in a muddled heap on the cave floor, not even bothering to arrange his tail into one of the regulation turns, hitches or knots, listlessly turning over and over the pile of pebbles that heaped the space before him. The dull, bluish-purple glow that emanated from his scales illuminated only dimly the confines of the cave but made mock-amethysts and sham-sapphires of the grey and white stones he sorted: a semiprecious illusion. Nothing could transform them into a ruby from a sacred temple of Ind, an emerald from the rainforests of Amazonia; a diamond from the Great Desert, a sapphire from the Southern Seas or a great, glowing pearl from the oyster-mouth of the grey Northern River. And that was the trouble: they were pebbles, nothing more, the insulting substitute left by The Thief . . .

1

For the three thousand two hundred and fifty-fifth time or so he went over in his mind that dreadful day, some seven years ago, when he had sallied forth all unsuspecting for the Year's-Turn Feast. Over the few years previously spent gold-and-silver-gathering in this retrospectively accursed, damp, boggy, sunless island, he had made the cave his principal headquarters and had twice-yearly, shortest day and longest, received his tribute of roast mutton, pork or beef from the village below (after he had explained that raw maidens were not in his line). He had good-humouredly tolerated the current yokel dragon-slayer brandishing home-made spear, sword or some-such who insisted on defending a symbolic maiden staked out in front of his feast; he even retreated the regulation ten paces in mock-submission before insisting on his roast. He had flown forth that day secure in the knowledge that he need only wait for the better weather of the equinox to return Home with the assorted extras of gold helm, breastplate, mail, dishes, brooches, bowl, buckles and coin (there was too much silver to carry) and the glory of the necessary jewels, and was urged on with a healthy hunger for his last tribute. The side of beef had, he remembered, been slightly underdone, and he had had to barbecue it a little himself to bring out that nice charred flavour that added scrunch to bones and singe to fat. He remembered, too, that he had obligingly restarted the damp, smoky fire on which his rather unflattering effigy was regularly cremated, and had even joined in the dancing and jollification that always succeeded his surrogate demise, and so it had been well after midnight when he had returned to the cave, replete, sticky and tired, to find—

The end of his world, and a heap of pebbles.

His quest had been specific: one each of ruby, emerald, diamond, sapphire and lastly, the pearl. And any incidentals by way of gold or silver, of course. The ruby had been an easy snatch-and-grab, but the emerald had required travel at the worst time of year over seas grey and wrinkled as an elephant's hide; the diamond had proved troublesome and the sapphire fiendishly difficult, but one expected a gradation of difficulty in all quests, and he had been well within the hundred-year limit when the fresh-water oyster had yielded the final treasure, his personal dragon-pearl beyond price, the largest and most perfect he had ever seen, mistletoe-moon-coloured and perfectly cylindrical.

And now? And now he remembered as vividly as ever his return to the furtive sweat-smell of excited theft in the night, an unidentified shadow that left only a silhouette of the sorcery that had accompanied it. He had roared out into the dark, his whole body twisting into an agonized coruscation of shining scales whose thunderous passage through the gaps between the mountain and the hills had left a rain of split rocks and splintering shale cascading in a black torrent to the valleys beneath. But there had been no sight, no sound of the thing he sought, only the taint of a thing that crawled, that flew, that walked, that ran; a shape intangible, a sniggering darkness that fled faster than he could pursue and left no trail to follow. And this—this Thief-without-a-name—had stolen his jewels, his quest, his very life, for he could not return Home without those precious things. The gold was still there, true, but it was merely incidental: every dragon collected gold as a child might gather shells from the shore, but the jewels were special. They were the confirmation of his maturity, the price of his transition from Novice to Master-Dragon, and without these proofs of his quest, the badges of his success, he was condemned to die. Oh, not a sudden execution, that perhaps he would have welcomed: rather an exile's slow withering, an embering and ashing of the once-bright fires, a shrivelling of scales from calcined bones, a fossil's hardening in the remorse-less silt of the years. And if he attempted to return without his treasure there would be the turned shoulder, the stifled snigger, the, in itself, mortal loss of face that would be death in life. And he could not bear that: better to die a suicide of wasting, cold and hunger on this wretched Black Mountain far from home; better to suffer the slow pangs of winter and starvation than to return disgraced.

For a moment his tired brain flickered with pictures of his bright egg-brothers and sisters, a remembrance of sky-soaring flight, of play among the circumscribed cloudlets of his youth; once again he saw the heaven-turn of pagoda roof, heard the dissonant tonk of temple bells, felt the yellow sun of the yellow people gild his scales, tasted fire in his mouth, smelt sandal-

3

wood and cedar, and all at once he let out such a howl that for the first time in many, many moons the peasants in the village some two miles below heard him quite clearly; a cry of such piercing despair that it slunk under their ill-fitting doors like the keening of hound condemned to out-kennel in the worst of wolf-pelt winters. And those hearing crossed themselves, touched lucky charms, threw placatory offerings on the smoky fires, whichever pleased whatever God, gods or Fate to which their superstition turned. Then they cursed the dragon, near-forgotten in the years of silence, and at the same time were glad he still lived, for he was their very own living legend. They wished him gone and they wished him come, wished him dead and wished him living, all at one and the same time, like all disconcerting, uncomfortable, prestige-making myths-come-alive that they could neither control nor explain.

But this time the echoes of the dragon's despair went farther than the confines of the little village beneath the Black Mountain. Something of it travelled, thinner and more attenuated the farther it went, and eventually reached an ear just waking from sleep, an ear that had been seeking a diversion such as this. The owner of the ear thought about it for a moment, weighed the pros and cons, and then bestirred himself to look for a miracle.

And found it, in the unlikeliest septet imaginable . . .

THE GATHERING: ONE

The Unicorn and the Prince

HE WAS bathing in a rainbow, the rainbow made by the long fall of waters, and the colours shone in bands of coloured light across the white screen of his hide. Long mane and tail rippled like silver seaweed in the clear waters and the golden, spiralled horn flashed and sparkled in the light. Tender pink of belly and gums assumed a rosy glow, the long white lashes were spiky with water and the cloven hooves stamped the spray with sheer enjoyment until it splintered into mist. He was a splendid creature, at the height of his powers, all white, pink and gold except for the dark, deep, beautiful eyes which held a colour all their own that none had been able to name, but that reminded some of the sky at night, others of dark, new-turned earth, a few of the tender greening spring slips of fir and pine.

The falls dropped hissing to foam about his hooves, the sun flickered and shone on the tumbling waters, a crowd of gnats danced in crazy circles above the ripples, a dragonfly, iridescent green and purple, darted away to the tall reeds on the left; a silver fish clooped a lazy arc downstream, not really caring that the mayfly were out of reach; kingfisher flashed blue to his nest in the bank and an otter drifted by on its back, paws tucked up on its chest, creamy belly-fur warmed by the sun, ruddered tail lazily steering. All was right with the world, all was beautiful, all was high summer and yet, suddenly, like the shadow of a bird across the sun, black and fleeting, an alien fear touched the unicorn and he knew that something unknown threatened his world.

Flinging up his head, the droplets scattering like diamonds from his thick, floss-silk mane, he snuffed the air through

5

flaring nostrils, the long, pointed ears with their furred inners laid back against the small delicate head. There was no strange sound or scent, yet still a feeling lingered in the air. As he stepped from the stream, the waters flowed away from rounded shoulders and back to trickle into the plumed fetlocks above the bifurcated hooves. A green-white shadow, he slipped into the forest, bending in and out of the drowse-leafed trees, his hooves leaving no trace on the soft turf. Then, leaving the deciduous fringes for the quiet corridors of conifer, he heard it. A thin sound, a catch of music as plainly faery as himself, that stole like mist through the silent, bare trunks of the trees. Hurrying now, desperate at what he would find, he brushed heedlessly through the forest until he came to the clearing where he had left his prince, and the sudden sunlight shone upon a scene so unexpected, so bizarre, that he checked back violently on his haunches, hooves skidding on the grass.

In the middle of the open space between the dark avenues of trees a young man, no more than nineteen or twenty, was dancing. At first sight this was a beautiful thing to see: he moved so lightly, so gracefully, his whole being responding instinctively to the music—

The music? This appeared to come from a harp, played pleasantly by a pretty young girl seated on a hummock on the opposite side of the glade, but the unicorn had the eyes of faery and what he saw struck sudden fear to his heart. He saw the young maiden, assuredly, but she was merely an ephemeral outline, a deceiving frame for the evil thing that crouched within. A naked witch mouthed there, her wrinkled, sagging body twisting and turning within the illusionary young body that covered it like a second skin, her face alight with malice as she watched her prey dance himself to death. Already, even as the unicorn watched helplessly, the beautiful face of the prince aged some five years, and the lithe, lissom figure hesitated as it attempted a twisting leap into the air. But the music quickened, drove him on and on, and the movements of his dancing body grew more and more frenzied as his proud countenance tautened and paled.

The unicorn started forward, neighing his distress, and for a moment the music faltered and the young prince stumbled and slowed, but then the tune grew louder and more insistent and

6

he danced on, his face now turned imploringly to the great white animal, his arms extended in entreaty while his body and legs turned and twisted to the infernal music. The unicorn reached his side by tremendous effort of will, it seemed, his body for the moment a shield from the witch, and the prince stopped dancing and laid his trembling hands on the curling mane, whimpering, 'Help me, help me!' The great horned animal turned his head to gaze deeply into the distressed blue eyes so near his own, at the sweat pouring down the beautiful, ageing face, at the sweet mouth imploring his aid, felt the slim hand shaking as it clutched at his mane and the young/old heart racing close to his, and bent his head to nuzzle the damp tangled-gold curls.

'Trust me,' he breathed. 'I love you more than life, you know that . . .'

He turned to face the witch. And the birds of the forest fell silent, the small creatures were still, the wind held its breath and no cloud crossed the sun.

That very sun was declining behind the trees when at last the unicorn had to admit that he was beaten. The witch and her music now lay in an enchanted bubble that no hoof could break, no charging shoulder shift, no tooth pierce; he had blocked the tune effectively enough for a while by throwing a magic sound barrier round his beloved but the music had shifted, crept, sidled, turned about his shield and the prince was now lying exhausted on the grass of the shadow-lengthening glade and the unicorn dared not look into his face for fear lest all youth, all beauty had fled. Runnels of foam dripped from the animal's muzzle, flecking his neck and forelegs and the great head was lowered, the dark eyes full of pain. After a while the spiral horn on his forehead touched the ground in his exhaustion, sending a sharp pain through his body and jerking him fully upright once more. At once he knew what he must do. The magic horn, that which confers enchantment upon all unicorns, was irreplaceable; if it became damaged or broken he was no longer immortal. But he knew there was no choice—for the love he bore was greater than his fear of death and he lowered his head once more, giving himself no time to weigh the chances, and in that last moment before his magic horn pierced the bubble that encapsulated the witch and her killing music he at last saw fear in her eyes.

The bubble burst with the noise of a great crystal palace shattering around his ears, and the ringing and clattering echoed the great pain that suffused his head, his whole body. He knelt on the grass, his flanks heaving, a stink of singed flesh and horn in his nostrils, and knew without mirrored confirmation that his proud golden horn was no more. He was nothing now, a white horse with cloven hooves and no magic, but at least his beloved was safe and young again and beautiful, and would weep tears to heal the broken place where the horn had been, and together they would flee this horror, and find a kind of peace—

Not so. As he turned, he saw with dismay that the witch had escaped the destruction of her bubble and and stood, tall, dark-cloaked and menacing over the senseless body of his prince. Even as the unicorn started forward to challenge her, the pain in his mutilated head receding to a dull, bearable ache, he heard her begin to chant a spell of such malevolence that he started back again, his great eyes wide with distress, realizing too late that without the magic horn he was impotent. The darkening forest seemed to close in against the reddening sky as between him and the witch there appeared a deep pool: not of water, but hard as diamonds and as clear, with the illusion of plants waving in invisible currents in its depths. And there, at the very heart of it, resting on a bed of pebbles, grey, blue and white, lay the prince, eyes closed, legs and arms flung carelessly as though he slept on some feather bed.

Vainly the unicorn stamped and pawed at the unyielding surface of the magic pond, neighing his distress. He turned once more to the witch and she answered his unspoken questions.

'Why? He refused me, that's why, even though I made myself young and beautiful as he: I was not to know he was a freak, a creature-lover, was I?' and she spat. 'But no, he is not dead, he lies in spelled sleep. And the only thing that can save him—' and she laughed shrilly, confident in her revenge '—is a whole unicorn, who will sacrifice himself and his horn to pierce that sleep! And you—' she pointed derisively, '—you are hornless!'

And her shrieks of laughter pursued him like demons as he fled despairing into the forest.

THE GATHERING: TWO

The Knight and a Lady

SHE WAS the fairest lady he had ever seen: eyes like sapphires, lips ruby-red, diamond-fair hair flowing down her emerald-green dress, skin translucent as pearl. Although the fire on which he had toasted the rye-bread of his supper had burned low this jewel-creature seemed to carry her own light and her voice was soft and caressing as she crossed the clearing towards him, her robes making the faintest susurration in the long, dry grass.

'All alone, fair knight?'

He rubbed his eyes, convinced he must be dreaming. Sure his eyes had been closed but a moment—too short a time for sleep—but what else in the world could this apparition be but a dream? This one must come from a towered castle somewhere in Germanica; she should live in pillared hall on the slopes of the Middle Sea; she would not have been out of place in a screened harem in the Great Desert; she could have come from anywhere beautiful, faraway, exotic: all he knew was that she did not belong here, on the scrubby edges of this shabby forest hundreds of miles from the nearest towers, halls or harems.

He pinched himself, half-hesitating even as he did so, for if this were indeed a dream, he would be fool to wake just as everything seemed to be going so nicely. The pinch hurt and she was still there so she must be real, and indeed now she was standing a mere foot or so away and her heady perfume flowed out round him like a bog mist, a miasma, near-palpable in its form. All at once he became conscious of the sleep in the corners of his eyes, his two-day stubble, untrimmed mous-

9

tache and crumpled clothes. All else, sword, armour, purpose were instantly forgotten: she was all that mattered.

'I—I—' he stammered, for coherence was gone also.

'I—I—' she mocked, and laid her cool hand on his wrist, where it burnt like fire.

'L—Lady,' he stuttered then recalled, by a tremendous effort of will it seemed, the courtesies and protocol demanded. Knights were always respectful and courtly; ladies, in return, gracious and yielding. The men were allowed a little flattery and boldness of the eye, plus a little twirl or two of the moustache and from the women one expected a fluttering and dimpling, a casting-down of eyes and an implied admiration. But of course at first one had to go through the preliminary ritual of polite verbal exchanges—How the hell did it go? Ah, yes . . .

'Lady, I am at your service, and with my sword will gladly defend you from all perils and dangers of this night.' (When he had been a mere squire there had been the usual ribaldry with his fellows as to the true connotation of the 'sword' and whether it was 'night' or 'knight'.) 'And if you will inform me of your desire, I—'

'Tu,' she interrupted. 'Tu es mon seul desir . . .'

Somehow her use of the Frankish tongue made this all much more difficult. Although he could not fault her courtly language, yet the words were in the wrong context: they were the words one would use to one's affianced or groom, and this one looked neither virginal nor a bride . . .

He found himself trembling, hot desire running like siege-fire into the pit of his loins. He gritted his teeth: this must be A Temptation, sent to test him; he had heard They sometimes took fleshly form, the better to ensnare and seduce. Sadly, Goodness usually came wrapped plain in everyday clothes and required effort of a different kind: a dragon slain (only nowadays there were none left), the routing of wolf or bear or somesuch. Anyway, This in front of him now, clad in shameless importunity and little else, was not Good, so therefore must be Bad, coming as It did in the middle of the night, that lonely vulnerable time when a man's strength is at an ebb and his resolve at its weakest. Still, if It were A Temptation, all one had to do was to summon up the required Formula, step smartly away, and deliver the words with clarity and feeling, and after a moment the temptation would disappear. Simple.

Pulling free of her hold he crossed himself.

'Begone, Foul Fiend!' he said, in capitals, and crossed himself once more, to be on the safe side. 'For I Know You For What You Are . . .'

Initially he could not have wished for a more gratifying result. She hissed and drew back, her silken locks seeming to writhe like a nest of blond snakes, but before he could even draw breath for a sigh of relief that he had been right, everything was as it had been a moment since, only worse, for he found himself gazing, with a lust he found increasingly difficult to control, at a long, perfectly formed leg, bare to the thigh, and pointed, rosy-tipped breasts that spilled out like forbidden fruit, from a suddenly diabolically disarranged dress. These delights invited a more intimate examination than the eye alone could give, caressing hand or tongue or both, and he had to concentrate very hard on knightly vows, candled altars (priapic, phallic candles; bare naked, unclothed crosses—No! dear Lord, no . . .), hard, penancing stone floors, the weight of mail, the chill of steel at dawn (better . . .), chanting monks with tonsured heads, cold water and thin gruel, hair-shirts and such, before his rising excitement cooled sufficiently for him to be able to stand comfortably again. It did not help that instantly he wished to relieve himself.

Resolutely he drew his sword.

'Thou art an Evil Thing, a witch, and ere you suborn me further I shall set good Christian steel to your flesh . . .' It was all excellent stuff, learnt from *The Knight's Manual*, but unfortunately it seemed to have little effect on its intended victim. The manual had not provided for laughter, for disdain, for a flying-off of all clothes, for a moving forward until bare flesh was pressed skin-tight against his suddenly disarranged wear. Neither had it dealt with seeking hands that drew out a rebellious prick and caressed it unbearably sweetly.

If that had been all, then he would have been lost indeed, but even Evil makes mistakes.

'Swyve me, soldier-boy,' she said.

Instantly his prick shrivelled like a salt-sprinkled slug and he

11

felt as naked and cold as a fowl plucked living in a snowstorm. It was the words that did it. During his military service it had been an almost universal and convenient phrase that was accepted in all the stews and bordellos; it was used by the sluts on the quaysides, the wenches in the hedge, the girls (and boys) of the back streets all over the world, the preliminary to quick bargaining, the passing of coin, and even quicker release. It was a phrase become meaningless with time that nevertheless came trippingly off the tongue, alliteratively used as it usually was with other words than 'soldier': sailor, sweetheart, sire, sugar, saucy, sheikh, sahib, sergeant, signor, senorita . . . But a lady would never say it, never, not even in extremis.

The court ladies he had known, in reality quite as randy as their stew-sisters, if not more so, were all brought up to use polite euphemisms. 'Put the Devil in Hell' was a popular one, as was 'Sheath the sword', and the less flattering 'Pop the coney down its burrow'. All these were perfectly acceptable, and the very words gave the actions a superficial respectability, so that the lady could ask whether the Devil found it warm enough yet, or the gentleman assure his partner that the scabbard was a perfect fit without blush staining either's cheek.

So, for the second time that night his proud prick took a tumble, for the words had dampened his ardour irretrievably. It was just like being asked to drink nectar from a piss-pot.

She sensed his withdrawal, and for an instant she seemed to him to flare and grow taller, then her face crumpled, her bosom sagged and she spat in his face from blackened, broken teeth.

'You will pay for this, my fine gentleman, you will pay!'

Considerably frightened, but more scared to show the fear, he recalled the torn edges of his dignity and neatly sewed them straight with the classic line: 'Do your worst, foul hag: I am ready for you!' And perhaps he thought he was.

Stepping back, the once beautiful hair now a greasy grey thatch, she raised her left hand and pointed the index finger at him, the nail curved and blackened. She started to curse him, roundly and fluently. Shrinking back in spite of himself he forgot to cross himself: afterwards he wondered if it would have made any difference; on balance he thought not.

'I hereby curse you, and call the trees that stand and the stones that lie, the sun that rises and the moon that sets, the wind that blows and the rain that falls, the sky above and the earth below, and all creatures that walk, run, crawl, fly and swim betwixt and between to bear witness to the same . . .'

As if in answer there was a sympathetic growl of thunder: it had been a hot, sultry day.

'I curse you waking, I curse you sleeping; I curse you standing, sitting, lying; I curse you by day, I curse you by night; I curse you spring, summer, autumn and winter; hot or cold, wet or dry . . .'

So far, so good: it was the Standard Formula, nothing specific, and easy enough to be lifted by a bit extra to the priest and a few penances to the poor. The knight wondered if, after all, he was going to get away with it.

'And my special and irrevocable curse is this: may your armour remain rusty, your weapons blunted, your desires unfulfilled and your questions unanswered until you ask for the hand in marriage of the ugliest creature in the land!'

He started back, appalled, but before he could interrupt she went on: 'May she not only be ugly, but poor, twisted and deformed as well! And may you be tied to her for life!' And she laughed, shrilly, exultantly. In a blind rage he snatched up his sword again from where it had fallen during the cursing and sprinted forward ready to run her through in his anger, female or no, but came bump! up against some invisible wall that snapped off his sword some three inches from the hilt and bloodied his nose. He went hurtling back as if he had been thrown in a wrestle, to lie on his back on the ground, his head ringing and the broken sword blade embedded in the turf an inch from his left ear.

When he finally rose to his feet, pale and winded, she had gone, leaving a foul, decaying stench that made him gag and pinch his nostrils. Gone, too, was his horse, probably miles away by now, to be appropriated by some grateful peasant in the morning, who would have great difficulty in persuading a fully trained warhorse to submit to the plough. He peered at his heaped armour; already small spots of rust, like dried blood, were speckling and spreading on the bright metal.

There was only one thing to do.

Falling to his knees he prayed: long, angrily and in vain.

13

THE GATHERING:
THREE, FOUR, FIVE, SIX, SEVEN

The Slaves of the Pebbles

ONE MOMENT our little world was predictable, safe, ordinary: the next we were nearly immolated in a welter of flame.

Predictable, safe, ordinary: I suppose those words could be misleading. Perhaps I should explain that 'predictable' meant that we knew tomorrow would be as miserable as today; 'safe' meant housed and tolerably fed without outside interference, and that 'ordinary' meant just that. It meant an existence we had always known, as far back as faulty memory would take us; it meant a crouching, fearful, nothing-being, prisoned, chained and subject to the whims of our mistress. She should have a capital letter: Mistress. There. For that is what we called her, the only name we knew, slaves as we were, and woe betide any who even thought of her with a small 'm' for she would know, or pretend she did, and punish us, and we were so accustomed to her domination that we believed she could read all our thoughts, sleeping and waking.

We? Us? There were five of her creatures in that small hut on the edge of the forest. Slaves, I should say. I was the only one ever let out of the hut, and that for necessaries alone—a sack of flour, tallow for dips, herbs from the hedgerow—and then I was spat upon, ridiculed, even pelted with stones upon occasion by the superstitious villagers who called me her 'Thing', her Familiar. Even those intermittent forays were no freedom, for the stomach cramps hit me even worse when I was from her side, only easing when I returned, so it was no wonder that people only saw me as a humped, ugly, deformed thing. I could not even speak properly, for the only tongue I

14

heard was an occasional command, spells and the words of my friends, the others who shared my thrall.

There was Corby, the great black crow, Puddy, the warty toad, Pisky the little golden fish and kitten-cat Moglet, and though we conversed quite freely amongst ourselves when the Mistress was out, it was a language of squawks, hisses, spits, bubbles, and more thought-communication than human speech. I told you I was held near my Mistress by stomach-cramps, and the others, in addition to cages, strings and bars were held in the same fashion, by a pain that increased by degrees of hurt the farther we were from our jailer. The origins of all these hurts were concrete enough; small pebbles or stones that clung to our bodies as though they were part of us. For me it was a sullen red stone that stuck to my navel like a crab; for Corby it was a blue chip that stopped the stretch of his right wing; for Puddy a green rock on his forehead that gave him headaches; for Moglet a crippling glass piece that was embedded in the soft part of her left front pad and for poor Pisky a great moon-coloured pebble that quite filled his starving, round mouth. Why not pull them out? We had tried and all we had got was an intensification of the pain, till it grew too excruciating to bear and we had to stop.

Perhaps the worst part was that we could not remember them being put there, nor coming to this place nor, even, who we were. Yet there were tantalizing remembrances for us all of another life of freedom without pain, in another place, another time: yet so fleeting was this recall to all of us, swift as the space between puff and candle-out, that it was only when the flame dipped and wavered and bent a little before expiring that one remembered a swoop of wings, a cool stone grotto, the rasp of another tongue on one's fur, a gnat at twilight and—another name, clash of swords, warm arms, crying . . . We all had these moments, yet even as we snatched at memory, like a snowflake on the tongue it dissolved and all form was lost. Some things we could remember, though: apparently Corby remembered us all coming, except himself; Puddy remembered me, Moglet and Pisky; I remembered the last two, but Moglet remembered only Pisky, and he not even himself. The interval between arrivals none could judge, so it could have been seven hours, days, weeks, months, years between first and last. Neither did we know why we were held thus, nor would She tell us, and all questions were answered by laughter, blows or the scorn of silence. Seasons meant little to us, cabined as we were, for we saw and felt little of sunshine or storm, light or dark, rain or warmth—the inside of the hut was always cold, a meagre fire kept burning and the one window shuttered fast, so that day or night, summer or winter were much the same to us. Sometimes birds whistled down the chimney or a hedgepig would pause on the doorstep when She was out, but always these encounters were reported to Her on her return by her Creature-in-the-corner, the broom that was her real familiar, and we were beaten for encouraging curiosity. Once, I remember, I asked a martin resting on the thatch whether it was spring or autumn, and when she heard of this from the sly, crackling spy, she had it beat me senseless.

Yet this Broom-Creature was not only violent towards us, for sometimes when the air, even inside, was sticky and hot, and it was difficult to sleep, She would take the thing into her arms and whisper to it and push the smooth, knobbed end under her skirt and it would jerk and throb until she cried out in what seemed pain and would thrust it from her, its tip swollen into the thickness of a man's fist and all glistening and wet with what looked like blood . . . But it was not real as she and we were. It was only a piece of wood bound with dried stems and twigs and she had to use words to bring it alive, the same sort of words she used to bring things into the hovel, things that were shadows so thin you could put your hand through them like smoke and yet which threw writhing coloured patterns on any surface they touched. These apparitions floated and gestured and whispered in an obscene language only she could understand and always after they had gone she became increasingly short-tempered and restless, and sooner or later would come the time when we would be caged and tied and she would begin the preparations for a Shape-Change.

In some ways I looked forward to this, for it meant that I was let out to gather plants and herbs for her spells: mugwort and valerian; comfrey and stinking hellebore; bryony and monkshood; oak galls and liverwort; fly agaric and penny-royal. All the ingredients She used I did not know, for she had others in bottles and jars and boxes I was not allowed to see, locked away by magic words in cupboards and a chest. And of the mixing we saw little for She would go behind a curtained-off alcove at the other end of the hut when she was ready to begin. Then all we would know was the stink of dried, crushed and powdered ingredients in the smoke that rose from the blending of her concoctions, a stench that invaded every corner, lending foul odours to the dry bread we ate, the cold water we drank. We could hear a little of the muttered spells and incantations that accompanied all this and we were allowed to see all the transformation: I think having an audience for this somehow fed her overweening vanity, even of small account as we were.

She would come out from the alcove and stand in the middle of the hut, and gradually her whole appearance would change. First she would untwist her body and grow taller, then her greasy grey locks would untangle and grow lighter or darker, straighten or curl as she desired. Even as we watched she took breasts that rose firm and round, instead of flapping around her waist like empty goat-skins; her stomach flattened, her legs and arms grew shapely and hair-free; her skin whitened and discarded the liverish brown spots, the crooked, dirty nails on fingers and toes became pink and the dry, split pouch at her groin would rise, mounded with curling, moist hair. Lastly her face would take on the lineaments of a beautiful woman: gone the warts, the beard, the moustache and come rosy cheeks, sparkling eyes, white teeth and full, red lips. Then she would laugh and stretch her arms wide and her voice would come sweet and rich as she called from the air silks and fine linen to clothe her nakedness. Then she would beckon Broom, her creature, and sit astride, call on the roof to open and fly out into the dark.

But She would not forget us, oh no. The very last thing would be a spell to bind us faster than the rope, cage, chains and bars that already held us. But once She had gone we would breathe freer and stretch a little and talk, and that is when we practised conversing without the usual constraints of her presence, exchanged hopes and fears, ideas, what little we remembered of the past, and endless speculation on the immediate present. Talk of the future held small part in all this, for I found that my friends had very little conception of what it was, and I was afraid even to think about it.

Perhaps I should qualify 'talk', for it was not the sort ordinary beings would recognize, let alone understand. When I had first arrived I had talked wildly in human speech to Corby and Puddy, and they had understood nothing except the terror and distress, but in their different ways they had tried to soothe and reassure and gradually I had come to understand a little of what they were trying to communicate, and had tried to copy. It had become easier when Moglet and Pisky arrived later. Communication of the simplest kind was usually by noise; more complicated ideas were expressed by bodily position, movement, odour—in this I was way behind the understanding, let alone the expressing—but the most refined, and to me eventually the easiest to understand and adopt, was thought. A simple dialogue between Moglet and myself would use all these processes:—

Moglet:— A loud, attention-seeking mew, on a particular pitch that meant 'I'm hungry!'

Me:— 'Mmmm?'

Moglet:— Body position tight, paws together: 'And I've been waiting ages . . .'

Me:— 'Have you?'

Moglet:— A thought, like a ray of light penetrating my mind, giving me a memory-picture of what happened, cat's eye level, of course: 'Breakfast was the last meal and that was only gruel and it was a long time ago when that slant of sun was over in the corner and the fly buzzed up the wall and I caught it but Puddy ate it . . .'

Me:— 'Mmmm . . .'

Moglet:— Left eye blinking twice. 'You're not even listening straight!'

Me:— 'You'll have to wait . . .'

Moglet:— Eyes glancing sideways, to the right. 'Don't want to wait.'

Me:— 'Will a small piece of cheese rind do, for the moment?'

Moglet:— Blink with both eyes, lids returning to halfway. 'Yes.'

Me:— 'Was that nice?'

Moglet:— Tail flat out behind, tip gently vibrating. 'Very nice . . .'

18

Me:— 'What do you want now, then?'

Moglet:— Tail gently swished from side to side, right, left, right. 'More, please . . .'

Of course it was not all as easy as this. Abstract ideas like 'fear', for instance, were most difficult to express, for they did not use words for these, rather a thought-impression of what frightened them most, and it was easy to get an actual picture of our Mistress approaching the hut mixed up with an impression of her doing so, which might approximate to, say, Corby's idea of fear. None of this came naturally to us: it was just that we were thrown together in such close proximity that we formed a sort of alliance of misery—and in some queer way I believe our burden of pebbles brought us and our understanding closer together. And so gradually I forgot my human speech and could barely mutter my requests in the marketplace: my mother tongue became almost a foreign language.

Instead I would listen while Corby would tell of the grasping of sliding air under the fingertips of his wings, or soaring heights and dizzy drops; then there was Puddy reminiscing of cool grottos, buzz of fly and crawl of worm; Moglet half-remembering a warm hearth and dishes of cream, a substance none had tasted save Her, which sounded rich, thick and delicious; Pisky recalling the silk-slide of summer waters, the bright shoaling of his kin. While I held a dream of an armoured warrior, a fair lady and someone singing—but who was to say that all these were not just imaginings, for none of us could recall a place, a time, nor indeed how or why.

These respites together were all too short and sometimes not worth Her absence, for twice latterly she had returned in daylight and a foul temper, screaming at the air, the times and us. The first time she had contented herself with kicking out at whoever had been nearest, joggling Corby's perch till he fell off and emptying most of Pisky's water till he gasped. But the second time was worse. Usually she returned in the garb and looks in which she had departed, losing them only gradually, but this time she dragged herself back with the dawn in her accustomed evil form and there was a slitting to her eyes and a slavering to her mouth that boded ill. At first she had laughed shrilly and pointed at me.

'I thought of you, you ugly thing, when I cursed him! Yes, I

19

tried to think of the worst fate I could for the accursed fool, and then the thought came to burden him with the dirtiest, most hideous creature I could imagine and you came to mind, you filthy little obscenity! Twisted, monstrous, revolting— Thing—that you are . . .' And I had shrunk back, for the venom in her voice frightened me more than anything she had done before. 'Yes!' she had howled, 'I cursed him, for he refused—' but she suddenly snapped her mouth shut and seizing her Broom, proceeded to beat me so hard I could not help but cry, despite my determination never to let her see how much she hurt me either physically or mentally. Then she seized Moglet and tried to throw her on the fire, but I snatched her back and hid her, mewing pitifully, under my cloak. Thwarted, she kicked Puddy out of his crock and stamped down catching my hand instead, for he had jumped into my pocket for protection. Poor Pisky was next, for she threw his bowl against the wall where it smashed and he lay helpless and flapping on the mud floor till I stretched forth my uninjured hand and popped him into the leather water-bucket, drawing that also under my cloak. Then came Corby: she snapped the fine chain that kept him to his perch and pulled and twisted at his neck until he pecked her and spiralled down helpless to join the rest of the creatures huddled under my cloak. Then she seemed to go mad, and though she now made no attempt to touch us herself, she shrieked a curse that made all the pebbles we were burdened with hurt as they never had before. And then her Broom was beating and beating at my bowed head until the blood ran . . .

That seemed to calm her, the sight of my blood, for she called off her minion and I heard her whisper, as though to herself: 'No, no not yet: They must have a living home, a living body, or He will seek them out . . . Hide, hide, my precious ones, till I find the formula . . .'

For a while after that She had stayed at home and life had resumed its monotonous sameness, but I never forgot that moment of utter terror when she had lost control and we had seemed to face extinction; nor had I forgotten how my friends, for that is what they were, had all sought refuge under my cloak, as though I were in some way responsible for them all.

This action seemed to bind us all closer together in a way we all secretly acknowledged but never mentioned, which appeared to make our lives together easier and more hopeful in the days that followed.

And now came this day, the day that was going to change our lives irrevocably. The preceding night She had left the hut just before moon-high, and the whole of the two days preceding had been taken up with Shape-Changing. It was early autumn, for she had sent me out for a few heads of saffron which I had found easily enough and then lingered awhile at the edge of the forest gazing down at the village below. Two-wheeled carts laden with the last of the hay and straw creaked down the muddy street; children played with top and ball, their happy squeals and shouts loud in the still air; men trudged back from the fields, mattocks on their shoulders from breaking up the earth ready for the winter sowings; a woman beat out a rag rug and farther off they were burning off stubble, for the smoke curled up thin into my nostrils and stretched them wide with the acrid, sad smell that is the ending of the year. At last an extra-sharp twinge in my stomach reminded me of my Mistress and I hastened back in the blue twilight, snatching a handful of blackberries from a bush as I went and eating each bleb separately to make them last longer. I had been almost happy for a moment or two that afternoon, but there had been a cuff for my tardiness and another for my betraying, juice-stained mouth and I had gone into the corner by the fire and turned my face to the wall. And so, in a fit of the sulks, I missed that last change to beauty, with all its preenings and posturings, which to the others at least broke the monotony of their drab days. So once I heard her split the roof and disappear I was surprised as snow to find a beautiful lady return by the door some two minutes later, to fling Broom at my head with the remark to it: 'No point in taking you, after all: it's not far. There'll be no point in the binding, either,' and with a few words she loosened the invisible ties we were bound with, like a soaking in warm water softens dried meat. Broom hustled up next to me and rustled and chattered, so I moved away from my corner to join the others by the fire. Our Mistress paused once more before she left by the conventional door, swirling her long, purple

21

gown: 'I shall not be late,' she warned. 'So, quiet as mice and no tricks or I shall have you all with the cramps when I return . . .'

She looked very beautiful that night, with long brown hair the sheen of hazelnuts hanging down her back and eyes the colour of squirrel-fur. I wondered what it felt like to be beautiful.

It may seem strange that we never queried her Shape-Changing, nor questioned where she went in that guise, nor why, but it was so much a part of our lives that we just accepted it, I suppose: I do not remember puzzling over it—I was just glad that she was not there. Afterwards the reasons became clearer, but at the time we all took it as a sort of Holy Day, and relaxed. That night I rustled up some nice bone broth I had hidden away and ate it with freshish bread, sharing it with Corby and Moglet, and shaving a sliver of new-dead moth and slipping it with agonizing patience round the moon-pebble in Pisky's mouth, giving the rest, wings and all, to Puddy. I was comfortably dozing, back against the angle of the fireplace, when the door was flung open and she was back.

I could see that this time it was going to be different from any time before. She seemed to glow, to expand, to fill the whole room with a musky odour of femininity that scared me. Her eyes were sleep-puffed, satiated, and her lips full as a wasp sting and red as new-killed meat. There were scratches on her bare arms and legs as though she had run through bramble and her gown hung open on her breasts. But she seemed in a singular good humour and did not even ask whether we had behaved but whirled about the room in her ruined dress like the wind in a pile of new-fallen leaves.

'Now there was a man!' She sighed and yawned. 'A village yokel maybe, but hard as iron and full of juices . . . This time there will be a child! And then you, my pets, will be superfluous . . .' We shrank back, for even in the un-accustomed mellowness of her tone there was an implied threat, even though the others could not clearly understand what she said. 'I may decide however to keep you as you are for a while, slaves and servants, for Thing there at least is sometimes useful.' She ran long, still-beautiful fingers through her hair, for the magic had not yet slipped away. 'And of

22

course the babe will need a nurse . . .' She mused. 'I shall have to see . . .' and such was our awe of her that I believed in the immediate appearance of some infant witch, a smaller version of herself, and even peered into all the corners when one did not immediately materialize. I told the others what she had said and we huddled round the cheerless fire, trembling at this new threat, but she did not appear to notice and went into her alcove from whence we could hear her chinking glass and pouring liquid. She came out at last and drained a green, smoking mixture with every indication of enjoyment, but as she set down the drinking-flagon a couple of drops spilled on the oaken table and crackled and fizzed in the dark wood, leaving two shallow, smoking depressions.

She, however, looked more beautiful than ever, and as soon as she had drunk her fill she went over to her couch under the shuttered window. 'I shall sleep long during the next few months, Thing, and you will have to keep the place tidy and provisioned. I want no disturbances, no undue noise, and I expect the stock-pot full if ever I wake and am hungry.' She reached beneath her pillow for some copper coins and flung them to the floor, watching me scrabble in the dirt. 'That should last till the turn of the year, if you are careful. Buy the cheapest you can find, remember: I am not made of money. Gruel and bones will do fine for you,' and she yawned and lay down on the couch. 'I shall want you to go out at first light in the morning: there is one more mixture I have to complete. Bring me ten drops of blood from a boar; three heads of feverfew and twelve seeds of honesty. Oh, and six fleas from a male hedgepig not more than six months old. You may wake me when you return,' and with that, perfectly composed, she closed her eyes, her beautiful lips parted, and she started to snore as she usually did.

We looked at one another, afraid of being vocal, concentrating on thought, but were too frightened, too confused by the turn of events for the refinements we had so carefully practised. All I had from Corby was: 'Oh Hell! Hell! Witch brat—that's all we need!' Puddy said 'Shit!' and nothing more, but he was never a quick thinker. Moglet mewed that she was frightened and Pisky rushed round and round his bowl, talking to himself backwards, the thoughts and sounds bubbling up in

23

little pops through the gaps between his stretched mouth and the moon-pebble. I tried calming thoughts for them all: grass, trees, lakes, rivers, wind, sky, stars, dark, sleep . . . And gradually they quietened and we settled into an uneasy doze.

As first light pinched through the edges of the shutters I blew the embers of the fire into a blaze and swung the gruel pot over the flames; it needed no salt, for as I mixed the oatmeal and water the miserable tears dripped from the end of my nose. I sensed change in the air and did not want it, for always change had been for the worse. My little friends stirred in their sleep; Corby creaked and hunched his feathers; Puddy glugged, his yellow throat moving up and down; Moglet stretched and mewed in the stretch as though her muscles hurt, but her eyes remained shut; Pisky's tail waved, once. In that quiet time, apart from my silent tears, I suppose we were at peace.

I went out while the dew was still on the grass and spiders' webs hung with diamonds. I found the pearl plates of honesty and harvested the black seeds, one from each pod; withering head of feverfew, with its pungent leaves, grew near the hut; an obliging hedgepig curled from his coat of leaves in the roots of an oak, only too glad to lose a few fleas at hibernation time. I tickled his coarse, ticked fur stomach and rolled him back into his hole with thanks, then set off for the village since wild pig were uncertain at the best of times, even though now was acorn-harvest, and I should have better luck with one of the domestic ones. A quick and relatively painless nick on the ear should do the trick and I had a pocketful of beechmast and acorns for sweeteners: in my experience one never took without giving, for that would upset the balance we all lived by. As I crept down the narrow path to the village I took care to keep well out of sight, for as I said before the peasants mistrusted me as a representative of my Mistress and would not hesitate to harm me if they could, especially if I was not buying anything. I found a convenient sty and struck a bargain with the boar, for my time with the others had given me a primitive understanding of all beast-talk and certainly enough to bribe a pig. I nicked his ear neatly enough and dripped the blood into the little glass phial I carried. The drops were slow in coming for it was a cold morning and I fed the pig a few more acorns to keep him still.

He whiffled contentedly. 'Mmm . . . make a nice change, these do. What's your old woman been up to then? They say as she's gone too far this time . . .'

'How?' I questioned. Six drops; better make it seven.

'Seems as she rogered young Cerdic to death last night. Sprang on him and tuckered him out in five minutes . . . Mind you, these humans ain't got no stamina. Now I, I could tell you a thing or two about that . . .' and he rumbled away for a moment or two about servicing the sows they kept for him but I wasn't listening.

'He's dead?' I remembered the lad, bonny and brawny in the fields at haying, from my lonely spyings. Was that what my Mistress had meant, with all her talk of witch-babe? Had She taken man-seed into her body and now hoped—but she couldn't: she was too old. But then, her spells were strong. And was this what had happened on those other times, when she had returned angry and frustrated? Was this because her spells had not worked on those others, whoever they had been? My mind was in a whirl; why had she to kill that handsome young man, especially when he had obviously pleasured her so well? 'Dead, you say?' I repeated.

'As firewood. Seems they're all cut up about it; say she's gone too far this time.' His fanged mouth nudged me, none too gently. 'Got any more?'

'Of course.' To retreat safely from these razor-backed horrors, a precarious domestication a few generations back having done little for their manners, always required a diplomatic withdrawal. I threw down the rest of the mast and nuts and scuttled back over the fence.

'Where have they put him?'

'Huh? Oh, the dead 'un. Square. There's a meeting. All there. Come again . . .'

Stoppering and pocketing the phial, I crept cautiously round the back of the houses till I could see, between the washerwoman's and the whore's, that rectangle of trampled earth they called the Square. Sure enough the place was crowded, and there was talk I could not hear so, not daring to approach directly, I made a leap for the thatch of the washerwoman's house, luckily only a few feet from the ground at this point, and crept up among the straw till I could both hear and see without fear of discovery. Glancing sideways at the next roof I was glad I had chosen the one I was on, for the whore's roof was all rotten grey straw and loose with it; I could see an old nest or two and the roots of sear vervain: it would not have held me for two breaths.

Below me was a lake of people, heads bobbing like floats, and an angry hum of voices, a hive disturbed. In a space in the centre was a bier, roughly fashioned from larch poles and skins and the body of Cerdic lay disarranged upon it. His clothing was rough, homespun of course, but the young face held an unworldly look of disillusion and, strangely enough, an air of peaceful exultation too, at odds with the rough, uncomprehending features of the villagers surrounding him. The talk confused me, for I was not used to such a babble, but the gist was of witchcraft and revenge. They led forward a young woman, pretty enough, and she cast herself down weeping by the bier, clasping the careless dead hand of the young man and carrying it to her mouth, kissing it feverishly, and sobbing the while in an uncontrolled burst of emotion that made me hot all over.

I moved away, sliding back down the thatch till my feet found the ground, and crept back home, thoroughly bewildered and with a horrible feeling that something nasty was about to fall on my head or leap out and bite my ankles. The air was very still, as if everything was holding its breath, waiting, and I found myself glancing over my shoulder every few yards; I couldn't get back quick enough.

Back there, there where we all belonged, I tried to tell the others what I had seen and heard but it was only Corby and perhaps Puddy who understood. 'Always like that when they turn the corner,' said the former. 'Turn a corner and see Death staring 'em in the face. Gets 'em all, one way and another. Know it's long past childbearing time but reckon a touch of magic might make the difference. Think they'll renew themselves. Seldom works, but I've heard tell of a deformed mippet born of an old witch. Nigh unkillable, too. Pity She couldn't keep it off'n her own doorstep, though; sounds as though she's stirred up a hornet's nest down there. Could mean trouble for us all . . .'

'Water,' said Puddy. For a moment I thought he wanted a

sprinkle from the water jar, but he continued his thought a space later, as was his wont. It was sometimes a little irritating waiting for a toad's thoughts, although they were usually worth having. 'Don't like it. That and fire . . .' He appeared to meditate. 'Best things for killing them off.'

A hiss from Moglet alerted me as the Mistress yawned, stretched and rose from the bed in the corner. She still looked remarkably young and beautiful, so much so that I forgot to duck as her ringed hand slapped my cheek.

'Well, where are they? The things I sent you for?'

Humbly I offered my gatherings. She picked them over grudgingly, then took them over to the alcove, where we could hear her chopping and pounding and mixing during a long afternoon, while we huddled together, not sure what the next hours would bring. Twice I tried to tell her what I had heard and seen in the village and twice she stopped me, the second time with a jar hurled across the room and a threat that she would get Broom to beat me if I disturbed her further. 'I am not interested in what those peasants do or think,' she said, so I held my peace.

When it was dusk within and near enough outside I lighted a tallow and stirred the omnipresent stew; putting bowls by the fire to warm, I opened the earth-oven and took out the day's bread, standing it on end to cool and tapping it to make sure it was cooked through, for the oven was very slow. I fed the others surreptitiously, with an eye to the alcove and ear to the mixings and a nose pricked against the unpleasant aromas. When they were satisfied I gestured them back to their boxes, crocks and perches, for all day we had been uncharacteristically free to move and I did not want her reminded we were comparatively free.

'Supper is ready, Mistress,' I said timidly, but as she came from the alcove I saw with horror that her beauty had faded by ten years while her smile showed that she had not consulted her mirror recently. What had happened to the magic she was convinced would keep her young forever now she was pregnant of a witch-child? And was she indeed? My eyes went to her swelling belly: she seemed some three or four months gone, and that in less than twenty-four hours.

'Nine days!' she said triumphantly, her eyes following my

27

gaze. 'Nine days, that is all! And then you will have a new Master, you miserable worm . . .' Her mood changed as she took the bowl and bread, well over half of what I had cooked. 'What do you mean by giving me these slops? My baby needs good, red meat and fresh vegetables and fruit, and wine to strengthen his blood! Why did you not prepare such?'

'But Mistress,' I faltered, 'you told me to—'

I got no further for her free hand shot out and gave me a stinging slap. Holding my hand to my reddened cheek I backed away.

'Go now, and fetch me a rich pie from the village and a flagon of their best wine.' She reached into one of her boxes and spilt coins, silver coins I had never seen, in a stream onto the floor. Scrabbling to obey I pocketed ten, twenty even. I knew my task would be difficult, or well-nigh impossible, at this time of the evening, for it was now dark and the villagers would equate me with the darkness and chase me from their doors—but which was worse, their vindictiveness or hers? And there was the dead man . . . I hesitated.

And even as I did so, everything began to happen at once.

There was a thump, as some large object struck the door and a crash as stones rattled against the shutters. Starting back I whimpered with shock and fright, my hand still tingling, for it had been on the latch when the door had vibrated under the blow. For a long moment my mewlings were the only sound in that confined space, then there was a voice outside; ragged, scared, but still truculent.

'Come out, Witch! Come out and meet your accusers!'

For a moment the stillness inside was intensified. Then my Mistress hissed like a snake behind me and, turning, I saw such a look of evil on her face that even I, inured as I was, cowered flat in terror. But her look was not for me, and her voice, when it came for those outside, was honey-sweet, though I could see her hair and fingers writhe like snakes.

'Who calls so late, and on what errand?'

'You know who's here, and why!' came the answer. 'You knows what you've done, there were those that oversaw. Time's come to pay for it!'

She hissed again, but her voice was beguiling still. 'I know not of what you speak . . . Has someone been hurt? Perhaps my medicines . . .' but even as she finished speaking she was muttering under her breath spells I had never heard even the echo of before. All at once the pretence of beauty was gone and her body resumed its usual hideosity—all except her belly. Her fine clothes dropped to the floor but her stomach seemed to swell visibly—a smooth, rounded mockery in that ancient frame. She caressed it with her fingers, still spell-making—the gnarled, dirty fingers were an obscenity against the youthful mound she touched.

'Grow, grow!' She muttered. 'Grow, my manikin! I give you my strength, my lust for life—Make it not nine days, nor even nine hours . . . Not five, not four, not even one! Less, less!' and her voice became louder with the repeated rhythms of some incantation in a strange tongue. 'Help me, help me, Master, and he shall be yours!'

Of a sudden it grew deathly cold and a foul stench filled the hut. I crawled back to the fireplace unregarded, to cower against the hearth where the fire now burned blue and heatless. Outside the clamour rose; more voices, more stones, and a flicker of flame blossomed behind the gaps in the shutters. They were firing the hut! Now there was a scrambling outside, another thump above our heads this time, and a tearing at the thatch on the roof and an ominous chanting.

'Burn the witch! Burn the witch!'

The smell of smoke filled my nostrils. There was a crackling, a flaming of tinder-dry straw roofing and the voices grew louder, a chant to rival my Mistress's mouthings.

'To the stake, to the stake! Burn the murderess, the witch!'

But my Mistress continued her spells, louder now and even louder till I covered my ears and shut my eyes, pressed back against the back wall of the hut as far as possible from threat and danger. It was cold; it was hot; flames shot up, smouldered down, till it all grew as regular as my pounding heartbeats and I was afraid as I had never been.

And there my life might have ended, choked by smoke and charred by fire, but for one thing—

THE GATHERING:
THREE, FOUR, FIVE, SIX, SEVEN

Death of a Witch

A MEW.

A small frightened mew from a small, helpless cat. All at once I stopped being so scared and gathered Moglet in my arms, soothing and caressing as I had done so often in the lesser bad times. At the same time I felt Puddy climb onto my lap and heard Pisky bubbling in distress and Corby thumped down from his perch, breaking his tie, to flap around my feet.

'Get us out, for goodness sake!' he croaked. 'You'll have us all cinders!'

Get us out, but how? For a moment or two my brain would not work, then Puddy nudged my knee.

'Back wall. Weak. Corby's beak . . .'

Of course! Corby had heard too and we both remembered where the stones had fallen away from the side of the fireplace last winter with the cracking of the Great Frost, and how we had repaired it with a temporary amalgam of stones and mud. Tumbling the others from me I took out my sharp knife and tried to remember where our botched repairs had begun. There it was. I attacked it at once with the knife and beside me Corby pecked away with his strong, yellow beak—both unheeding everything else except the desperate need for clean air, for outside, for life. I knew the villagers would not be on this side, for out there the ground dropped steeply away to the stinking ditch where we emptied the slops. Desperately I chipped and scrabbled at the caked mud, my fingers tearing at stones, my nails breaking on flints, while behind me the clamour grew louder. Glancing round for one terrified moment I saw our Mistress outlined by the flames from the burning hut, her belly grown monstrous and huge, her screams rending the air and in the corner her familiar, Broom, with fire creeping towards the tangled heathers of its feet. Suddenly my bruised and torn hands jerked forward into open air and without thought I picked up Puddy and thrust him through the hole I had made, careless of where he fell.

'Escape, quickly!' I thought-shouted, then reached for little Moglet: 'Run, my dear, run!' The hole was only just big enough for Pisky's bowl and I reached through the gap and balanced it carefully outside. But that was it: no way was the hole big enough for Corby, let alone me; the others would perhaps be all right—Oh Hell, however I hurt the bird must be given his chance, too! 'Keep pecking, you great black gormless thing!' I hissed, and together we renewed our attack on the crumbling wall. A sudden blast of heat behind me redoubled my efforts and all at once the gap was large enough for me to push the crow through, scraping his feathers against the stone unmercifully. 'Hop away, friend,' I muttered, 'and please push Pisky's crock down to the ditch; he may be able to find his way down to the stream. Help him, help the others . . .'

'Don't be so blasted silly!' came the hoarse croak from outside: 'Come and do it yourself! Get scraping: I'm not nursemaiding this lot. We need you . . .' And there was a gurgle, a mew, a glug less than a foot away. They were waiting for me, they needed me to look after them! Perhaps without the incentive of their responsibility I might have succumbed, let the now-choking smoke take my last breath, but the knowledge that I was needed gave me the spur that fear and exhaustion had blunted.

With the last of my strength, from the crouching position in which I found myself, I charged that hole in the wall; my head was through, one shoulder. Breathing the fresh air outside aided my efforts; I twisted, scraped, shoved, tore and wriggled and with a final heave fell free of the inferno behind me, to lie gasping on the steep bank outside, my head lower than my heels, bruised, battered and exhausted, smoke pouring from the gap behind me.

'Come on then, Thing,' they all cried. 'Come on; we're not free of her yet . . .'

* * *

31

We crept stealthily to the edge of the wood, me carrying Pisky's crock, and hid behind a great bramble-patch. The hut was ringed by fire, except for the back part where we had escaped, and even now flames ran around the corner to eat the dry grass at that side. Not only ringed but crowned, for hungry tongues of fire leapt like bears licking for honey up among the thatch and all around was the choking smoke. The noise was indescribable: although we hid in comparative safety some hundred yards from the hut, yet the clamour, both of shouting villagers and their barking dogs, the crack and crackle of burning wood and the screaming of our Mistress seemed but a foot or two away. The men were gathered in a semicircle about the hut, most armed with clubs, billhooks or scythes, but even as we watched they were retreating step by step from the heat of the fire, hands before their faces. And what of my Mistress? Thoroughly sickened by the mad screaming we heard, I almost determined to go back and try to get her out through the hole in the back wall, but Corby grabbed my sleeve in his beak.

'Wait! She's not done for yet . . .'

True enough: as we watched there was a sudden change to the quality of the flames. One moment they were hot-tongued, roaring with insatiable desire, the next they were cool and pretty, green and blue, burning with a delicate flame that decorated rather than consumed. The hut now looked as if it were dressed for an autumn Maying, the scorched timbers and charred thatch hidden by the green leaves and blue flowers of the flames, and as we watched the whole place blossomed as the thatch burst asunder. The sudden flowering created a seed-pod burst as the witch, our Mistress, black and ripe and full, thrust from the roof, borne astride by her faithful Broom.

I picked up Pisky and with one accord we fled deeper into the forest as She swooped and shrieked among the villagers who cowered and ran from her as though she were a hornet, stinged and deadly. There was a path that twisted and turned away from the holocaust behind us, and at first the fluttering Corby was well ahead, with Moglet running behind, but before long they lagged back, crippled wing and foot hampering, so I stopped, gathered Moglet in my arms with Pisky's crock slopping water over all of us, perched Corby on my shoulder, pocketed the tired Puddy and scuttled as fast as I could, not even sure why I was except that somehow we all knew we had to get as far away as possible as quickly as we could. The trees grew denser and I halted, out of breath and lost, and in that moment they came again, those terrible pains near the seating of our pebbles so that I cried out and doubled up. I heard Puddy's moans and Moglet's mew, Corby's screech and Pisky's demented bubbles and realized that we were still in terrible danger.

'She wants us,' breathed Moglet. 'Wants us still . . .'

'Watch it,' said Corby. 'She's not going to let us escape if she can help it . . .'

'Help, help, help!' bubbled Pisky.

'What can we do?' I was screwed up in agony. 'Oh, the pain . . .'

'Lake,' said Puddy. 'Head hurts . . . Left and down: hates water.'

His words stuck in my fuddled, paining brain: 'Lake . . . hates water . . .' Of course: clever toad. All witches avoid water like the plague and the stretch of lake lay to our left: I could see a glint of water in the direction Puddy had indicated. Gathering the others close once more, my stomach still contracting with pain, I crashed heedlessly through the bushes towards the stretch of water, tumbling at last down the steep bank to land us all splash! in the murky waters among the sear reeds and drowned twigs that littered its edge.

Not for nothing was this called the Dead Water, for nothing grew on or in it except the nastiest weeds. Even frogs, desperate for cool in the summer, eschewed its water, while in spring the shallowest puddle seemed preferable for their spawn. Long ago the lake had been fished-out and even restocking had failed, for the villagers said it was cursed by the drowned souls of a party of young men and women who had gone out on a raft for a dare on Beltane's Eve countless years ago and never returned. The raft had been found the following morning, caught in reeds at the edge, but of the dozen or so— the superstitious said thirteen—that had essayed the water there was no sign. Of course the villagers had gone out and dragged the depths with hastily made rope nets but these yielded nothing, and one intrepid fellow who had ventured the depths at the end of a line had burst to the surface with tales of huge snake-like leeches that had curled for him out of the watery dark and of a ring of dead bodies silently dancing among the tangled weeds of the deep, their white faces and open eyes full of the horrors of the drowned, and worms and bubbles rising from the open mouths that cried of devils and black magic. Certain it was now that no one would venture out on this black smoothness and I had seen none but the rash, unfearing wild pig ever drink from its waters when I had been out early for herbs.

Even now, stranded as we were among the shallows, me sitting in but two inches of water, Pisky bubbling up in his crock, which was bobbing up and down where I had dropped it, I had all the others clutched and clinging to my head and shoulders with beak, claw and damp feet rather than touch the waters.

'Pick me up, pick me up!' panicked Pisky.

'Help!' moaned Moglet.

'Let's up-an'-orf,' croaked Corby.

'Not healthy,' pondered Puddy.

All at once, of course.

I struggled to my feet, as much to escape their din as anything else, but then looked down with horror at the breeches I always wore, on our Mistress's instruction. I was damp from the waist down from sitting in the water and on the wet leather fat blue-grey worms crawled with open mouths, burrowing blindly for my naked skin. I struck out, brushing them back into the scummy water, only to feel them immediately fasten on my bare ankles. Stumbling to the bank I lay back against the sloping earth thrusting with panic at the evil things that still clung and sucked at my skin. Unexpectedly I was helped by Corby who fluttered from my shoulder and pecked at the slimy things with his beak, wiping them off into the sludge as a bird will clean his beak on a twig.

At last I was free and turned to struggle to the top of the bank when the pains struck us all again and we screeched and tumbled back towards the water. Desperately I clung to a gnarled tree root that jutted out above the water, my feet frantically scrabbling for a hold on the greasy earth, Pisky's bowl jammed under my chin, the others hanging on as best they could. Something made me look up and there a great bat-like shape blotted out the hazy light from a wisp-clouded harvest moon that rocked unsteadily through the trees, and with despair I realized that our Mistress had found us and was flying over our hiding place on Broom.

'She'll get us!' I screamed. 'We'll never escape!'

This time I knew She would at last kill us and then throw our bodies into the black waters of the lake, and I could not think at all, only feel as the cramps clutched at me again and my terrified friends clawed and clung till I could feel the trickle of blood from torn shoulder-skin. I felt a sudden rush of stinking air as our Mistress swooped down on us and the smell of singed cloth overwhelmed even the stench of scummy water: a burning fragment from somewhere had landed on my arm and there was a smoulder of cloth which I beat at frantically as the witch misjudged her landing and soared away to approach from an easier angle.

I heard Puddy trying to say something, urgently for him, agonizingly slow for the rest of us in those few moments when everything—pain, fear, drowning, burning, death—was rushing upon us like a great, irresistible storm wind that will snap and crack even the most pliant tree in its fury.

'Can't get us surrounded by water . . .' but even as I understood and acknowledged what he was saying I knew I could not wade out into that lake of desolation and stand, helpless, while my flesh was sucked away from my bones by the unseen horrors that lurked beneath.

'Island somewhere,' came Corby's hoarse voice, stirring into a sort of incredulous hope. 'If you could wade out, Thing . . . Think it's over there to the left someways . . .'

I do not remember scrambling up the bank, scurrying through the thin belt of trees that lined the shore, searching ever for a darker shape on the waters, ducking automatically from the swooping thing that held off only because of the branches that hid us from full view. I do remember at last seeing a dark lump that rose from the water some hundred yards out and recall too the fear and pain that accompanied my wild splashings through the shadows; I remember that at one stage the water sucked greedily at my waist, at another my foot turned on a treacherous stone and slime rushed headlong into my open mouth, but that at last my feet found dry ground and I staggered free of the clutching waters to fall to my knees, shedding cat, bird, toad and fish's crock, and lie prone, crying my exhaustion.

The islet on which we found ourselves was only a scratch of ground barely ten feet long and half that wide with a stunted tree and a prickly bush for company: I looked back and the bank seemed an immeasurable distance away. Had I really crossed that stretch of water? I shivered with wet and cold and beside me Corby ruffled and rattled his feathers and Moglet tried to wipe herself dry against my ankles, mercifully leech-free: I supposed my wild splashings and the speed of our progress had hindered the creatures' blind seekings. For the time being, too, we were witch-free, but a massy heap of clouds raced up on the increasing wind that rattled the branches of the stunted tree above me and whispered in the bush to my right, fluttering the ivy that clung to the ground round our feet. I bent and straightened Pisky's bowl which was dangerously tilted and heard him mutter and cough as he rushed around backwards: 'Horrid black stuff: chokes the lungs, black water does, not good for my gills. Oh, deary, deary me! If my great-grandfather could see me now . . .'

I put out my hand and stoked Moglet's damp fur. 'Are we all right now?' she asked anxiously, purring a little to reassure us both.

Corby and Pisky were conversing in low tones. 'Notice them trees?' I heard the bird mutter.

'And the ivy,' said Puddy. 'Should help.'

'Wouldn't be a bad idea to form a ring, though,' said Corby. 'Can you remember any of that stuff? You know . . .'

'A little.'

They turned to me.

'Best get into a circle and hold fast to each other: dip a finger in Pisky's bowl and touch his fin and toad here can do the same with a toe t'other side. Now, Thing dear, before it is too late . . .'

Hastily we arranged ourselves: me with Moglet and Pisky on either side, Corby and Puddy opposite. I did not question how or why for obviously these two knew something I did not.

'Now then, all close your eyes and empty your minds,' said Corby urgently. 'Let old Puddy and I do the thinking here, for this is what we knows. Go on, sharp about it! Listen to nothing save our words, our thoughts . . .'

'And don't let go,' murmured Puddy. 'Keep in touch . . .'

For a moment there was nothing as I knelt with closed eyes, listening to Corby muttering and Puddy coming in now and again with a single word, almost like the priest and congregation I had heard sometimes from outside the little church in the village. Then, as now, I did not understand what was being said, for it seemed to be in a language I had never heard, and yet in spite of this I felt a sort of strength flow back into my limbs and a string of hope seemed to circle between our points of contact; fingers, claws, paws and fins. I felt Pisky quieten under my touch and Moglet had ceased her trembling.

And then the pictures came into my mind.

A sunlit grove, whispering leaves, white berries, bearded faces with sad, dark eyes, a flashing knife and with all these an instinctive knowledge of great secrets, of ancient ways; between the mutterings something deeper and even more secret came from my left hand where Moglet's race-memory wandered back to an even earlier time where the dominant figure was female and the secrets were held only by women . . . On my right hand a golden sun, silk-embroidered cities, a great wall that wound like a snake; from somewhere else there was a rumble as the Sea-God stirred and cones of bright fire erupted on the hillsides bringing cliff and temple tumbling together; tall candles, a man kissing the cross-hilt of a sword—

'Hold fast, hold fast to that which is great, that which is good,' came the message between us. 'Keep your eyes closed, closed . . .'

Perhaps if I had not been reminded they were shut I should not have opened them just to see—

'She's coming again!' I screamed, jumping up and breaking the circle, and the others scattered as the great bat-like figure swooped down on us again, howling imprecations, only to veer at the last moment to avoid the tree, whose twisted branches defied a landing.

'A circle again, you dumb idiots!' yelled Corby, but the spell was broken and we were in disarray, all concentration gone, running hither and yon in the small space afforded us like rats terrier-struck in a pit. Again and again the figure dived down

37

on us and in the end we stopped trying to escape and cowered between the prickly bush and the stunted tree clutching at anything to stop ourselves being scooped up off the island, up, up into her clutches.

Up? Or down? For suddenly it felt as though the island had turned upside down and we now hung by fingertip and claw from the strands of ivy as flies on a ceiling; I had Pisky's bowl under my chest and so great was the illusion of being topsy-turvy that I remembered being amazed that the water from his crock did not pour all down my front.

But still She did not land, could not reach us, and I glanced up, or down, I was not sure which, and saw her hovering some twenty feet above, or below us, and I almost did not recognize her. She had grown incredibly old and ugly and was naked except for a few shreds and tatters that hung from her shoulders. And her belly—her belly was a huge, monstrous puffball of growth that rocked and swelled in front of her. Even as I watched in terrified fascination it seemed as though it were being struck like a great gong from within, a soundless blow that yet brought an answering scream from my Mistress.

'It is time!' she shrieked. 'I give birth to my son, my monster, who shall rule you all! But I need blood, blood for him to suck, blood to bring him alive, and I will have it!' and she raised her arms and chanted a spell I remembered: the fire-bringing one, only this time much stronger and more vindictive than I had heard it when she had used it once or twice to relight our fire when the wood was too damp to do anything but smoulder. As we gazed up at her we saw her body redden with reflected flame and I glanced down to see flickers and sparks among the fallen leaves at my feet. Springing up I stamped frantically but all the time the ground was growing hotter and the stones started to glow like the embers of a fire, even as a tongue of flame licked the trunk of the twisted tree and ran up into the branches like a squirrel. Tearing off my cloak I flapped despairingly at the flames, and beside me Puddy and Moglet were leaping up and down squealing at the pain from singed paws; Corby had fallen on his back, feathers browning, and poor Pisky's bowl was steaming as he gasped away his life on the surface.

Then something inside me snapped, and I behaved like a

mad thing, for the dreadful pains were twisting my guts again and I came outside myself with pain and stood like a creature of no substance and all substance and I was nothing and everything and had no power and all power. Stretching out my hands I gathered the flames into them and cooled them and rolled them into a living entity in my palms. Throwing back my head I stood as firm as a pillar of stone upon the ground beneath and opening my mouth I cursed the witch that hovered and swooped above us. Using no language and all language I cursed her into Hell and eternal fire, I cursed the monster she bore and wished it non-born; I cursed them living and dead and forbade earth, air or water to receive their bones. Then, gathering all my strength, I took the ball of fire that yet clung to my hands and flung it straight up into her face.

While I had been cursing her, she had dipped and wavered and I could see her shocked mouth and suddenly wary eyes. But as soon as the ball of fire left my hands she swerved away on Broom and then seemed to redouble her strength, as I collapsed like a pricked bubble on the stony ground, whimpering for the pain in my burnt hands. But at least the fire on the island was out, and the stones once more blessedly cool. The others clung to me and I felt Puddy spit into my burning palms and mutter something and at once they were soothed.

'Good try,' croaked Corby, 'but I'm afraid she's coming back . . .'

We all looked up at her then, waited for her to come down the inevitable last time, the time when we would have no strength, no reserves left. We were all brave now, I think, for there comes a time when death must be faced, and it is only the manner of the dying that matters. And as she rose to a greater height the better to gain momentum, then turned and bore down on us like a meteor, I felt strangely calm.

Like a meteor? With flames streaming out behind her? Even as I wondered, as I dared surmise, there was a sudden mew of excitement from Moglet, Pisky stopped going backwards and I do not think I heeded Corby's expletive or Puddy's awed croak. She had swerved her face and body from the ball of fire I had thrown but it had landed on the tail of Broom, where the bunched heather and twigs were already tinder-dry and needed only that final spark.

39

Down, down she came, either not knowing, or not caring in her madness that Broom was on fire, but then it added its scream to hers: 'Mistress, Mistress, I burn, I burn! Put me out, put me out!' And it wavered in its course, bucked like an unbroken horse and twisted off course so that she passed us by yet again, missing the island by a hand's-breadth and soaring back into the blackness above. By now her bearer was truly on fire and I saw her lips move, one hand to belly, the other beating at the flames behind her. She must have been reciting the Flame-Cooler spell, for I saw the fire falter, turn for a moment blue and green and then steady, but at the same moment there was a rip of lightning to the east and a crack of thunder that momentarily deafened us, and I saw that her travail was beginning.

Desperately she tried to control her bearer, to quench the flames, to catch us, to give birth at one and the same time, but she could not do it and Broom in its insensate agony bore her away from us to the centre of the lake, to try and quench its tailing flames in the dark waters. Just as desperately she screamed imprecations and beat it with her fist, raising it by sheer willpower. By now she was afire also and the tattered remnants of clothing flamed and sparked. Even from where we stood, mesmerized by the drama that had suddenly made us spectators instead of victims, we could smell the sickening stench of burning flesh. In spite of my fear, my misery, my hatred of the evil tyrant who had kept us thralls to her pleasure for so long, I could not help a tremendous surge of pity: if then it had been within my power to quench the flames, to end her misery, I think I would have done so.

But the Power was now Another's, a greater force than mine, with perhaps a greater pity also, for at that moment there came a great fork of lightning that blinded us with its light and for a moment illuminated the whole world in which we stood. The same fork split our Mistress from breastbone to groin and a great gout of night-blackened blood ribboned into the air, and out from the gash emptied a twisting, tumbling manikin with mortal face and body and the claws and wings of a bat. It mewled and screeched and clawed at the air like a falling cat and its mother, our Mistress, stretched and grabbed at the hideous creature with hungry arms and it turned and bit

40

her and scratched and sucked at the black blood that ran down her thighs and dripped, hissing, into the lake. It crawled up her legs and up to her breasts but, scorning the empty, flapping dugs, reached up for her throat and fastened there, sucking the last of the life-blood from scorched and blackened flesh. At last she realized just what she had spawned and beat at it with her fists: in vain, for it clung now like a lake-leech so that she, greasy hair now spitting and bubbling with the flames, her Broom and her manikin were one, sinking indivisible to destruction.

In a last effort she pointed Broom at the sky and they shot up like some huge, rocketing pheasant, but even as I thought they might escape another bolt of lightning struck them. For an instant time stood still, they hung in the air as though pinned to the night, and then—and then they plummeted slowly down, a dying, screeching, moaning, blackened bundle. And the waters of the lake rose to greet them, to eat them, to drown them, to exterminate them. There was a fearsome hiss as the burning mass hit the water which fountained into black fingers around them, fastened and drew them down, and then for a moment it seemed as though a ghostly ring of dancing figures ringed the yawning chasm that received them—

'Hang on lads,' warned Corby. 'And lasses. Here comes trouble . . .'

Huge waves, displaced by the falling bodies, were rearing and racing across the empty waters and instinctively I clung to the stunted tree, Corby and Moglet in the branches above me, Pisky's crock in my free hand, Pisky in my pocket. Then we were deluged with evil slime, weed and black water till I was sure we would drown; there was a moment's respite as the wall of liquid surged past us to beat against the banks and, frustrated, fall back so that we were subjected to the process in reverse. At last, choking and gasping, my mouth and eyes were free, but then came an immense pulling and we all clung for dear life as the waters rushed away from us to the centre of the lake, where it seemed a great whirlpool sucked all down into a vortex.

For a moment the last of the waters swirled about our feet, and then came a great rumble like thunder and I felt as though the soles of my feet had been struck a blow that drove them up into my hipbones, just like jumping off a roof in the dark, not knowing where the ground was. They stung with pain and instinctively I lifted them off the ground as a second jolt, slighter than the first, disturbed the island.

Then all was quiet.

We shook ourselves, moved all our legs, arms, wings, fins, joints and muscles to make sure they worked and felt hastily all over to make sure none of the leeches from the dark water were left behind. Just as we were reassured there came a great wind that thrashed the branches of the trees on the bank and buffeted us and tugged hair, fur and feathers the wrong way. On its heels came the rain: cold, hard, freezing us in a moment. But as we gasped and chattered with the chill the quality of the downpour changed and it was soft and warm. The rain came down like a torrent and we stood beneath a waterfall, and if we were wet before we were now drenched. But it was a cleansing, gentle rain, washing away all dirt, all grime, all fears and tears in its caress and even Moglet, who hated the wet, stood and steamed and licked and steamed again, and I emptied Pisky's crock three times, until the water felt like silk.

And then it stopped, as suddenly as it began, and the moon shone bright and sweet, a curved lantern high above us, and the stars pricked out one by one and, wet as we were, we collapsed where we stood and slept like dead things until dawn.

THE GATHERING:
THREE, FOUR, FIVE, SIX, SEVEN

The Escape

WE AWOKE to a beautiful morning, and a different world.

One by one we crept back to consciousness, stretched stiff joints, yawned, opened our eyes. And all, without exception, let out some exclamation of surprise: in fact my initial awakening was to an uncharacteristically unladylike screech from Moglet.

'Spiced mice! Marooned . . .'

Sitting up and surveying our position I was as inelegant as Corby: 'Cripes!', while Puddy was puffing and panting and Pisky, who could see nothing at all except the sky, was rushing around in circles bubbling 'Lemme see! Lemme see! Lemmelemmelemmesee . . .'

I lifted him up automatically, tilting his crock and murmuring soothing thought-sounds. Slowly I stood up and gazed at the scene around us. As I said before, it was a beautiful morning, the sun shining on the colouring of the leaves; the breeze, what there was of it, was from the south, birds sang their thin autumn songs and all in all the world seemed a promising place. The woods stood around us on the bank as though there had been no storm of the night before, no rain; the island was the same island, the stunted oak still holding its leaves, the prickly bush discovered as a holly with clusters of berries lightening to crimson, and the dark, secret ivy still clinging to the ground at our feet . . .

It was everything else that was different.

Before we had been surrounded on all sides by black, thick, scummy water, now the island on which we stood was still an island, but an island on dry land. We were about ten feet above the dried-up bed of a lake which had disappeared in the night.

The ground beneath our perch was hummocky, pebbly, undulating, bare, but it was not a lake, not a pond, not even a puddle: it was dry, dry as a bone. Wildly I turned about. The bank was the same distance away, the bare expanse on which our islet stood was lake-size, but there was no water, no leeches, no nothing! I gazed down at the lake-bed: no scum, no mud; I looked out over the bare expanse to the lake-middle: stones, sandy soil, bones—bones?—bleached and bare, a heap of rocks in the middle like a sunken cairn, but still no lake, no water . . .

Slowly I sat down again. 'What—What happened?'

There was a moment's silence, then Puddy delivered his opinion. 'Earthquake.'

I looked at Corby.

'The old lad may be right; summat happened, sure enough. Seems the land here rose and the lake drained away when old Mistress went to perdition.'

I remembered the thump to the soles of my feet, the roaring noise, the vortex.

Pisky bubbled: 'My great-great-great-grandmother told me of somesuch: when there is great evil the land and the sea conspire to destroy it. Earthquakes can happen undersea as well as on land and can swallow whole cities . . .'

Moglet said: 'And you called out a spell, Thing; you said neither earth nor air nor water could receive Her body . . .'

'But my feeble curses couldn't have made any difference! Besides, I didn't realize what I was saying at the time.'

'Doesn't really matter what did it,' said Corby thoughtfully. 'There was more'n one thing on our side. The oak, f'r instance: even has a sprig of mistletoe in the crook of that branch . . .'

'Holly and ivy,' said Moglet.

'What do you mean?' I asked. 'And where is the water?' But they did not answer. I persisted. 'What do you mean, holly and ivy and oak and mistletoe? What's that got to do with it?'

Puddy tried to explain. 'It's what one's used to: gods and suchlike. Forces. Good and evil.'

I remembered him chanting with Corby and turned to Moglet. 'Holly and ivy?'

'Older things in the world than we know, and sometimes they can be on your side. Sometimes . . .'

'She was a bad 'un, right enough,' said Corby. 'Bad through and through. And there was only one place for her.' He nodded to the sunken place in the middle of the once-lake. 'Down under there is fire like you never did see before, all running and boiling and bubbling like porridge, and that's where She belongs, her and her manikin. Down there all the bad things gets churned up and chewed-like, and then sometimes the old Earth gets indigestion, collywobbles, and burps or farts out the bad airs through them volcanoes and those hot mud-holes what travellers speak of.'

'Geysers,' said Puddy.

I looked at them with new respect: what a lot they knew! 'You mean She won't ever come back? Not ever?'

'Not never,' said Corby. 'Just bits and pieces, she is now. 'Sides, plughole is blocked with them rocks, see?'

'Then . . . Then we're—we're free?'

'As air—an' twice as hungry . . .'

'Then why . . .' I suddenly felt terribly lonely. 'Why does my stomach still hurt?'

We gazed at one another. Moglet tested her paw, and lifted it hastily. Corby stretched his wings: one side went the full distance, not the other.

'Still got heavy head,' said Puddy.

I shook Pisky's crock but could see the pearly pebble firmly fixed in his mouth. 'So we're not really free at all,' I said slowly. 'Her spell is still on us.'

'Seems so,' said Corby. 'Yet I would have thought—'

We were interrupted by a wail from Moglet. 'I'll never walk properly again! No mice, no birds . . .' and she spat at Corby.

'Now then, now then,' he said, backing away. 'You're not the only one, you know: Thing here has still got the cramps, and—'

'But not as badly,' I said thoughtfully. 'And at least we're free of her. There must be a way to break this last spell. Let me think . . .'

But it appeared I was not much good at this; besides, while the others were being quiet to let me concentrate they made a further discovery about themselves which was alien to me, who had spent at least part of my time out of doors when we

45

lived with the witch. The first I knew of this new element in our lives was when Moglet crawled up on my knee and hid her head away from the nice, fresh air in the crook of my arm. A minute or two later she was joined by Puddy, who at least apologized as he crept into a fold of my tattered cloak. Next Corby shuffled up close to me, on the pretence of looking for woodlice under a stone, and Pisky started to swim backwards again.

'All right,' I said. 'What is it?'

'Outside,' said Puddy after a considerable pause, which the others were unwilling, it seemed, to interrupt. 'It's big. Bit overwhelming.'

'Frightened of the open,' supplemented Moglet, sniffling a little. 'Not used to it, Thing dear—what happens when it gets dark?'

'Long time since I've been out in the wide-open spaces, as you might call 'em,' said Corby. 'Bit—well, different you know, if you've been used to a cage of sorts for as long as you can remember. There's rather a lot of it, too, if you follows my meaning: sky and trees and ground . . . Sun's a bit bright, too.'

'Know where you are if there's a still crock or bowl,' muttered Pisky. 'All this moving about and rocking back and forth and jiggling up and down and not a bit of weed to soften the light—'

'Well, you miserable lot!' I cried, jumping to my feet and scattering them like discarded toys. 'Here we all are, free from—from Her, and all you can do is grumble! As for all this talk of being afraid of the open air and not liking the sunshine and what happens when it gets dark and being jiggled back and forth—'

'Up and down,' said Pisky. 'Up and down for jiggles. Back and forth for rocking. I should know! Up and down gives you stomach-wobbles; back and forth makes you water-sick—'

'Oh shut up!' I was becoming exasperated, the more so because, at the moment, I could see no further than the next five minutes, knew they were looking to me for guidance and hadn't the faintest idea how to proceed. So I fell back on anger. 'We're free, *free*, don't you realize that? Surely that means something to you after all those years we spent shut up in that hellhole? All you wanted then was to be free and look at you

46

now! Whingeing and crying because you've got what you wanted, but it's going to take a little getting used to! The powers-that-be give me patience! Whatever did I do to be saddled with such a bunch of—of stupid animals!'

I had not meant to say that, and luckily for me they knew it, for even as the bright tears blurred my vision, making the trees on the bank dance up and down like unsteady puppets, I felt a rub of fur around my ankles and Pisky burped past his pebble.

'Don't blame you,' said Corby. 'Big responsibility, changing one's way of life.'

'Insecurity breeds uncertainty,' added Puddy.

'Oh, blast you all,' I said unsteadily. 'I love you all, you know that . . . Right! First thing to do is get off this island, then count up our assets and take a vote on what we do next. We'll go back to the hut and see if there is anything we can salvage, then we'll plan our next move. Any questions? No? Good.' And as we climbed down from the islet, with difficulty, I added: 'You're not alone in feeling a bit—afraid—of the open, but don't forget most people have managed it all their lives. It's just that we will take a little while to adjust to it, that's all.'

I hoped that I was right.

Whatever I had thought to find at our former home I do not know—some food perhaps, clothes, useful things like cooking pots—but my hopes were doomed to disappointment, for as we neared the clearing where we had lived it was obvious that either the villagers had been up all night or they had risen at dawn, for they were there before us. As we crept down the track that led up to the lake we could hear them shouting to one another and banging and clanking, and as we came nearer we slid behind the big bramble bush, Corby hopping off my shoulder, Puddy out of my pocket and Moglet from my arms and Pisky's crock set with its mouth to the scene.

Through the thorned branches I could see our former home, or what was left of it, and that was not much. The hut had been mostly wattle and daub, built on the foundations of an earlier home, basically stone, and the roof had been thatched. I had expected that the roof would have gone and probably much of the upper walls, but what I had not expected was the total destruction that met my eyes. The peasants, some twenty or so

47

of them, mostly men but I counted some women too, were tearing down what remained of the walls and scattering the stones about the clearing, stamping and chanting as they did so, words that, half-heard, appeared to relate to their relief at the disappearance of the witch. It was possible that they did not yet know of her death. What was certain was that they would ensure She would not return to her former home. I saw a large crock of precious salt standing ready: they were even ready to sow this on the ground which had held her, thus ensuring that no plant would grow there for the next ten years, to be infected with the evil she might have left behind.

'I wish I could hear what they are saying,' I muttered. 'Perhaps if we moved a little closer . . .'

'Not you!' said Corby sharply. 'We don't know that they aren't still on the lookout for you, and if they catch you—' He made expressive gurgles in his throat. 'Don't forget they will think you and She one and the same.'

'I'll go,' said Moglet. 'I can creep through the grass, and even if I don't understand human speech I can tell by the tone of voice whether they mean us harm.'

'Me too,' supplemented Puddy. 'Won't notice old toad. Perhaps we can hear them think, too.'

'Well, just be careful,' warned Corby. 'Toads and cats are known witch-familiars . . .'

They were back within a half hour or so and the tale they had to tell was disturbing. Apparently some of the villagers had seen our Mistress soaring over the lake and then struck by lightning but were not sure of her fate. The manikin had also been spotted, although a few people thought it might be me, and that I had fallen to earth somewhere and was in hiding. They were going to finish making the hut and its environs unlivable-in, the priest was coming to pronounce a blessing or curse or somesuch, and then they were going to look for me, just to make sure.

'Said they would burn you,' said Moglet. 'All up, in a bonfire.'

Frightened and bewildered, for I had never harmed any of the villagers that I knew of, I glanced round at the others. 'What shall I—we—do?'

'Time for a strategic withdrawal,' said Corby.

'What's that?'

'Beat a hasty retreat. Come on, where's a handy place to hide till they've cooled off a bit?'

We finally climbed to a convenient perch in the old oak tree that stood at the junction of the path from the lake to the remains of the hut, where it joined another that I used to use down to the village. From here we were hidden and could watch the comings and goings, and were an audience for the priest when he came, incense and all, to cleanse the witch's former abode from any lingering taint of evil. At noon he came back down the path, accompanied by most of the villagers, and I was just going to climb down after they passed for some nuts and berries at least, for we were all starving, when a shouting arose from the direction of the lake and a youngster dashed past down the road that led to the village and was stopped by two tardy peasants returning from the hut with the empty salt crock.

'Whoa there, lad,' said one of the men, neatly stopping the boy by dint of tripping him full-length. 'What be your hurry, now?'

'They've been up to the lake,' he gasped, winded. 'Found the bones of those drownded all that long time ago and ol' witch's burnt-out stick and no water left, none at all. I've to fetch the priest again and a cart for the bones so's they get decent burial . . .'

'Well, get along then,' muttered the other and aimed a kick as the lad staggered to his feet again and set off running. 'Come on, Matt: I've a mind to see all this for meself.'

And the two left the crock where it was and set off at a fast pace for the lake.

Again I was about to climb down and seek sustenance when Moglet growled 'Wait!' and a moment or two later it seemed the whole village streamed away below us in the direction of the lake; men and women, some still with tools or pots in hand; children and babes-in-arms, the latter carried by their siblings; the old and lame and fat on sticks and one in a litter. I even noted the village whore, dressing herself as she went, arguing with a sheepish fellow who was apparently unwilling to pay the full price for an obviously interrupted session. Bringing up the rear, jouncing and rattling on the uneven

49

track, came a large cart driven by the miller and filled with his wife and the priest, once again hung all about with crosses and baubles and beads and robes and candles.

We waited for a moment or two longer when they had passed, until we heard shouts and exclamations from the lakeside, then I jumped down and extricated the others, arranging them on my person like a verderer's gibbet, for that seemed the quickest way to travel.

'Where now?' I panted, for together they were no light weight.

Corby spoke in my ear, claws firm on my shoulder. 'Now, if'n they are looking for you, where's the last place they'd look?' And as I still did not understand he tweaked my hair. 'Come on, Thing, where's your brains? Where's the one place they ain't at, right now?'

'Ow! The village?'

'Right! Best foot forward now, and see if we can't make summat of this yet!'

Ten minutes later we stood in an empty village square. Doors and windows swung open, piglets rootled, a tethered dog barked, chickens pecked at the dirt, but of people there was no sign. I had never had time to stand and admire the buildings before, for my visits to the market had been short, sharp, fear-filled: in and out as quickly as possible before someone threw a stone, or worse. But our Mistress's money had been good, and I was always charged over the odds for even the scraps she had me buy. Money! Suddenly I remembered: the money she had given me the night before—was it only a few hours past? It seemed like a year!—was it still in my pocket? Frantically I felt about. Yes! I drew them out into my hand: three small gold pieces, three large silver ones, six copper coins.

'We're rich!' I shouted. 'Look, Corby, Moglet: I can buy stores to take with us . . .'

'Buy? Buy!' snorted Corby. 'Why buy? There's no one about, things are here to take—and do keep your voice down, Thing, there might just be someone still here!'

'But I can't just take things: that would be stealing, and then they really would be after us!'

'They're after us anyway, but all accounts, and you might as

50

well be hung for stealing as burnt for summat you ain't done! Come on, don't they owe us something for all the hard words you had and the shit they chucked after you? We'll only take what's necessary: it's for the sake of us all . . . Hurry, do!'

We needed food: a small sack of flour, a joint of fatty ham, a piece of cheese, half-a-pound of salt. All this went into a sack, together with a cooking pan, a large spoon and a couple of wooden dishes. I had my sharp knife, almost dagger-long, and flint and tinder, and I thought a length of fine rope and a small trowel would come in useful. Needle and thread were necessaries, filched from someone's workbasket. Anything else? Well, if I were to look tidily inconspicuous I would need a new cloak, preferably with a hood, my hose was a disgrace, and I had no shoes. I was tempted by yellow stockings and a red jacket, but in the end settled for brown wool hose, sensible short boots, and a splendid cloak that almost reached my ankles, with a deep hood, all in a mixture of dyed green, brown and black threads and thick as two pennies laid together. I think it belonged to the priest, for it lay just within the church porch. I also took a length of linen and a piece of leather, for I thought they might come in useful, too.

The only trouble with stealing was that you got used to it with alarming rapidity, and my greed nearly had us caught. Puddy had just found the most useful thing yet, a green glass bottle with a fat belly, a sensible corked top and threaded all about with a net of twine, ideal for carrying Pisky, and I entered the shop where he had found it. It was full of jars, boxes, containers, bottles, chests and other paraphernalia and I set down everything I had gathered just to admire and then covet an utterly useless bowl with decoration of interlacing gold snakes on its rim, when there was a squawk from Corby outside and Moglet came racing in, bad paw and all.

'Quick!' she mewed. 'Some of them are coming back! Oh, Thing dear, please hurry!'

For a moment I panicked, then common sense reasserted itself. 'How many?'

'Two—three. Old woman with stick, girl, young man.'

'That'll be Gammer Thatcher: she lives at the far end with her daughter and son-in-law. Bad-tempered old soul:

51

probably couldn't get to the lake fast enough to get a good view so pretended she was ill . . .'

I had a few moments to get myself ready. Rope round middle with knife; sack full on my right shoulder; Pisky transferred (only for a short while I hoped) to carrying-bottle—not without protest—and slung from my waist; Puddy in pocket, Corby on left shoulder, Moglet tucked in my jacket, new cloak over all.

'Ready?'

A muffled: 'Yes . . . S'pose so . . . Just don't jiggle up and down . . . Headache . . .' and I stuck my nose out of the doorway. All clear. Keeping to the sides of houses, scuttling behind the church, I soon left the village behind and found myself in unknown territory. Ahead was a track leading through fields of harvested grain, an orchard, a vegetable patch and ahead, low scrub melting into forest. A path led off to the left across the fields, another to the right, behind us the track back to the village.

'Which way?' It may sound stupid, but provisioning and unaccustomed freedom had taken up all my thoughts. Where and why were new.

'Away from the village,' suggested Corby sensibly.

'Under cover,' added Puddy.

A donkey, tethered on common ground to our right, trotted over as far as his tether would allow, and I more or less understood what he was trying to say.

'Want directions? Cut my rope, let me get at those thistles over yon, and I'll tell you which way is best.'

Three minutes later we left him chewing ecstatically, safe in the knowledge that to the left was marsh and, eventually, sea; to the right the track led back to the lake; but straight ahead if we walked about two miles, we came to a great ditch that marked the boundary between the lord of this demesne and the next, and beyond that was forest for days. Once beyond the boundary none from this place could pursue . . .

We took the middle road.

THE GATHERING:
THREE, FOUR, FIVE, SIX, SEVEN

The Fellowship of the Pebbles

CLIMBING UP into a tree is normally fairly easy, climbing down the same. Sitting in a tree and just relaxing is a fine way to enjoy oneself, while the world passes by beneath. Using the vantage-point of a tree to spy out one's surroundings, or as an emergency escape route is useful too, but I had never tried sleeping in one. All night . . .

In theory it is a very good idea if you are travelling light with no fixed idea where you will find yourself at nightfall, and are too small a party to risk wolf, boar or robber by staying on the ground, and there are no convenient caves, ricks or ruins to provide shelter. Just find a nice, comfortable-looking tree with a fork in the main branches for a sleeping-place and lowest support not too far from the ground, hoist your belongings up with a rope and follow. Settle your bits and pieces in a convenient niche or crook, lean back in comfort against the main trunk of the tree and spread your legs along a branch or even let them dangle. Wrap your cloak about you and wriggle comfortable; tuck your hands around your body to keep them warm, close your eyes, listen to the pleasant little rustles and chirps of the nightlife around you and—

'Want to get down,' said Moglet. 'Must . . . You know.'

'Oh dear . . . Can't you just do as Corby does? Over the edge?'

'Can't. It's . . . private. *You* wouldn't . . .'

'Maybe not, but I saw to all that before I came up here!'

Perhaps I should have said that all the necessary functions should be attended to before climbing the tree. So, now compose yourself for sleep, shut your eyes and—

Crash!!

'Bloody hell!'

Peering down from the branches: 'What on earth are you doing, Corby?'

'What the bleedin' hell do you think I'm doing? Fell off, din't I? Trying to get me balance on that rotten branch, weren't I? Cracked, din't it? Well, what you waiting for? Not an effing squirrel am I?'

For the third time compose yourself for sleep, listen to the pleasant night-sounds—

Screech!!!

I should also add that if there is the slightest chance that a screech-owl might startle you out of your wits, it is perhaps a wise precaution to attach yourself securely to the trunk so that you do not fall out of it yourself.

One last word on trees as sleeping-places: they look much more comfortable than they really are, and in some of them, especially the more bendy and wavy ones, the actual motion when there is a wind blowing can make toads and fish sick—if, of course, you are idiot enough to take them up there in the first place.

We stood three nights of this, and could have made little more than six leagues progress during the days, when I called a conference.

'Now, listen!' I said. 'We can't go on like this . . .' I was raggedy at the edges from lack of sleep and jumped and twitched at every sound, so had decided we would rest in the middle of the day and, leaving Corby as notional lookout, we had all settled under the shelter of a huge beech and slept for a couple of hours. Then I had lit a cautious fire—our first—and made thin pancakes to eat with a slice of the fatty ham. It tasted like the best food I had had for ages, and I had finished with a handful of late brambles and some just-ripe hazelnuts. Moglet had shared the ham and I had shovelled away at the earth under the nearest heap of leaves to provide a feast of insects and worms for Corby and Puddy, and had as usual coaxed a sliver round Pisky's pebble. We were fed, a little rested and warm and now, while daylight chased fears away, would be the best time to pool our ideas and decide where we were going, why and how. I knew animals found it difficult to concentrate, certainly on abstracts, for any length of time, so decided to keep it as simple as possible.

'We have been on the road—all right, Moglet, through the forest and in the trees—for nearly four days now; food is running short, we haven't had much sleep and we haven't made much progress, either. I reckon at this pace we might make a hundred miles by next new moon—if we survive that long. And we don't even know which way we're going, or why . . .' I glanced around at them, all attention, for the moment. 'Now, let's think about this. Firstly: what was the most important thing we did four days ago?'

'Escaped from Her,' suggested Moglet.

'Good! That was what was more important than anything else at the time. And we did it: we escaped! More by good luck and—' I glanced at Corby and Puddy, '—and a few charms than our own skill, perhaps. That was step number one. What was most important next?'

'Getting you—and us, probably—away from those nasty minded villagers, I reckon,' said Corby.

'Right again. So we've managed two important things: we've gained our freedom, and we've kept it—so far. But what is most important to us now?'

'Food,' said Corby.

'Water,' said Pisky.

'Shelter,' said Moglet.

'Safety,' said Puddy.

'All short-time daily goals, yes,' I said. 'But what about the longer term? Why are we all together like this? What are we aiming for? What's stopping us, for instance, just splitting up and going our separate ways and finding different homes or colonies or ponds or what?'

And it was the usually feather-brained Puddy who got it right, rushing around his bowl in great excitement, making wavelets splash against the sides in his desire to get it out.

'We want to get rid of the nasty pebbles so we can eat and stretch and fly and walk and not be bad-tempered with headaches all the time,' and he bumped his nose against the glass in the direction of Puddy. 'We aren't any of us really free till we do that. Not until I have a pond of golden wives, Puddy has a lady toad and plenty of stones to hide under, Corby can go off and swim through the air again, the cat has cream and a fire and can go hunting at nights and you, dear Thing, can walk upright and not have cramps in your belly . . . So, can I have some sand and a nice plant in my bowl now 'cos I'm clever and it takes a golden king-carp like me to tell you what you ought to know anyway, and I want the plant now and how about another slice of that centipede or midge or whatever it was—'

I clapped my hands then, both to stop and applaud him. 'What a clever king-carp! Yes, that is just what I meant. We are all here and belong together because we have a common aim: we want to get rid of these hurting, disfiguring pebbles! They have been with us ever since we can remember—and that's another thing: do any of you find you are recalling more about the time before?'

It was a regrettable digression for they all spent the next quarter hour telling me of brief flashes of memory they had experienced. I had had these too: I could remember now some time when I was without my burden; a pleasant villa in the country, a brown-faced nurse, music from a tinkling fountain—

'All right, all right!' I clapped my hands again. 'So, for all of us, part of our Mistress's curse is wearing off. But not these burdens,' and I touched my stomach, Corby's wing, Moglet's paw, Puddy's forehead and dipped my finger to Pisky's mouth. 'So this is a stronger spell, but one we must be rid of if we are to lead normal lives, as Pisky suggests.'

He stood on his tail and waved his fins but I interrupted quickly before he could remind us again about sand and plant.

'Now none of us can remember the stones being put in place, but that our Mistress set great store by them there is no doubt. There is another thing, too: She was so frightened lest they be discovered that she covered them all with a disguise of skin. Each of your pebbles, whether you can see them or not, is hidden under a covering like a blister: this is one of the things that makes me think they were stolen. What is more, I believe they were all stolen of a piece from the same person, for if you remember when we were apart from each other she would chastise us unmercifully, yet when you clustered under my cloak she would not dare touch us herself but would order Broom to beat me . . .'

'Brave Thing,' murmured Puddy.

'Saved us all,' said Moglet, and nuzzled against my hand.

'Nonsense,' I said gruffly. 'What I was trying to get at was that once the stones were together within us, near touching, they themselves gave us some sort of protection. A sort of power, if you like . . .'

'The Fellowship of the Pebbles?' suggested Corby caustically.

'Don't be silly! And yet . . . Yes, perhaps even that. This is why we must stay together for our own protection and seek the owner of these stones, for obviously they must be important to him. Or her. We must find this mysterious person and ask them to take the pebbles back. They will know how to remove them without hurting us.' I hoped I was right. 'But where do we look? That's our real problem.'

They were all silent for a minute or two.

'Can't be from nearby,' considered Puddy. 'She'd never risk nearby.'

'How do we know the owner won't kill us when he finds us, or we find him?' said Corby. 'May think we pinched the bloody things!'

'It's a possibility,' I admitted. 'But we shall just have to explain. After all, only an idiot would burden themselves with these things voluntarily, and might be even bigger idiots to return them. I think that whoever it is will be so glad to have them back that he will reward rather than punish.'

'Could be an ogre,' said Moglet nervously. 'Or another witch. Or a dragon . . .'

But at this Corby, Puddy and myself all jeered: there weren't any dragons. They were just a myth, a tale to frighten children.

'Now, concentrate: how do we go about looking for him, this pebble-owner?'

We were silent again for a while.

'Ask someone?' said Moglet.

'But who?' said Corby. 'Use your chump, feline. Most people wouldn't have any idea what we were talking about.'

'Magician might know the answer,' said Puddy. 'Or wise man. Or sage.'

'A good idea,' I said. 'But how does one go about finding one? And how would we know we were going in the right

57

direction? I don't even know whether there are any magicians or wise men any more, like Moglet's dragon—'

'My great-great-great-great-great-great-great-great-great-grandfather used to live in a lake where dragon-shadows floated over like kites at noonday,' said Pisky unexpectedly. 'All colours they were, like jewels, and they sang songs like cymbals and temple-gongs . . .'

'But that must have been a long, long time ago,' I said gently. 'For each generation of king-carp lives for a great many years. No, I think we must try and find the owner of these stones. Somehow we must decide on a direction and it must be the right one, then when we have done that we can worry about food and transport and the quickest way of getting there.

'Now, can any of you remember anything the Mistress ever said or hinted or implied that might give us some idea where these came from?'

We all thought. I could recall little except that She had always seemed nervous that the pebbles would be found; not by the villagers certainly, for she was always contemptuous of them, and there were only certain times when she would not let me, who carried one of the stones in my navel for any to discover, out of the hut on errands. In winter I had been glad not to go when the easterly wind howled across the icy meadows, or when the wind veered northerly and flakes of snow or sleet stung one's cheeks; but sometimes when those same winds brought long, hot days, settled weather and even the far distant smell of the seas over which it had travelled—

But Corby was there before me. 'There were times when she wouldn't let you out, Thing, even though we were down on provisions, times when it seemed she tested the wind to see if it blew too strong from one direction, or near it. Then she kept us all close, even in the hottest weather, when all within stank, as though she feared the scent would be carried downwind too far.'

'The east wind,' said Puddy, 'and the northeast. So, who looks for these pebbles lives to the west, or southwest. That is the way we must go.'

It was so simple, now we came to consider it! And the very next pond we came to Pisky was given his layer of sand, fresh water and a little green plant with two snails on it for company. He was so proud and happy that he was like a housewife in spring, moving that plant busily from one side of the bowl to the other, until Moglet remarked that perhaps we should fit wheels to it. The snails, too, though of somewhat limited intelligence, discovered something neither Pisky nor I had: the pebble would revolve in the fish's mouth and therefore, with some reminding, they would make a paste of whatever I offered Pisky, smear it on the pebble and revolve that segment into his mouth, which kept him going and was one less chore to worry about.

From then on, perhaps because we had a definite goal in view, however vast and faraway was the southwest, we made better progress and the weather held good for us. Now was the month of Leaf-Change, so we hastened as well as we could to beat the frosts of Leaf-Fall, splitting our sleeping into an hour or two at midday and pressing on well into dusk before seeking shelter and rising again at dawn. I had crept into a couple of villages we passed, usually at twilight when my appearance would cause less comment, for more flour, cheese and eggs, and supplemented this diet with berries, roots and nuts, and we were only hungry half the time.

Then with the new moon the weather changed and we ran into rain and wind, a roaring wind that swung crazily from south to northwest and back again, and we were chased from the shelter of barn by barking dogs, from warm rick by angry farmer. Corby was not too bad, Pisky of course couldn't care less and Puddy was more or less comfortable, but Moglet and I were thoroughly wet and miserable and shivered and growled and spat at ourselves and the others impartially. My cloak was reasonably weatherproof, but there came a time when it was so waterlogged and heavy that it would have been a pleasure to throw it away, and one night when it was too wet to light a fire and the flour and salt were damp and the cheese mouldy, I just threw myself on the ground scattering sack and animals anywhere, and sobbed my despair.

'Oh, I wish I were dead!'

THE GATHERING:
THREE, FOUR, FIVE, SIX, SEVEN

Mushroom-Eaters

'Now THEN, that's no way for youngsters with all their life afore them to be speaking! Just a little rain it is and isn't the earth glad, her being so thirsty after the suns of ripening? And the wind running free like a 'prentice let out early . . . And can't you smell the salt of the sea and the pines and the black rocks and the heather and curving downs that he brings with him?' The voice was high, light and ran on like a stream over small stones.

At the first words I had sprung to my feet, knife at the ready, and of course all my friends were now clustered under my cloak, hampering any footwork I might need. But as the voice went on and on soothingly, a hand holding a flickering lantern appeared from beneath the stranger's cloak, was held steady for a moment and then moved slowly up and down so we could see who was speaking.

A tall, tall man, seeming almost as tall as a tree in that flickering, smoky light, and as thin as a shadow seen sideways. Clothes all browns and greens, like the earth and the grass and the leaves, and then a merry red cap atop an untidy cluster of black curls, all twisted and gnarled like the potbound roots of a youngling tree. A face round and guileless as a child's, full red lips and rosy cheeks, but skin tanned and seamed like leather; a pair of snapping black eyes, by turns bright and shy.

The figure bowed and set down a covered basket.

'Thomas Herrilees Trundleweed at your service, Missy. Commonly known as Mushroom Tom, by'r leave. On account of my tasting 'em and treasuring 'em, and gathering 'em and selling 'em, too. Out in all weathers I am, best to find my little darlings and talk to 'em and tickle 'em awake and pluck 'em and eat 'em raw, or cooked in a little butter, or added to a stew, or even dried at a pinch . . . And whom may I have the honour of addressing?'

His flow of talk was having its soothing effect on me, and apparently on the others as well: Moglet's fur flattened again. 'Seems all right, Thing dear . . .' Corby rearranged his feathers. 'Hmmm . . . Harmless enough, I reckon; still, keep a hand to that knife.' Puddy snorted: 'Mushrooms!' while Pisky rushed round and round, dislodging the disgusted snails: 'My great-great-great-aunt on the paternal side told me of the efficacious properties of fungi . . .'

All this communication took but a moment, then I bowed in return.

'My name—my name is Thing, and these are my friends,' and I introduced them.

'Thing? A Thing is a thing is a Thing—and there's more to you than a name, I'll be bound, you and your friends . . . Still, a merry meeting, masters and mistresses all!' He hesitated a moment then smiled, showing strong, long teeth rather like a horse. 'None of my business why you are all out in the wet on a night like this, but Tom fancies company and has a pot bubbling and a fire burning just a little-ways ahead. Perhaps you travellers would do me the honour to share both, and perhaps a tale or two to brighten the evening?'

It would have been churlish to refuse, but anyway I had the feeling it would be all right, especially as Moglet needed no second invitation but was curling herself around his ankles, while Corby gave an approving 'Caw!' So we followed him down an almost invisible trail to the right to find a ruined cottage with half its roof sagging to make the inside like a cave, and the aroma of a stew, that smelt like pigeon and hare and onions and turnip and mushroom, hit me like a blow to my empty stomach. A fire burned brightly in the old fireplace and a trickle of smoke rose from the hole in the turved roof.

We crowded in and Tom let down a flap of hide to make us enclosed and cosy.

'There, now! That's something like, isn't it?' Without waiting for an answer he had my wet cloak hanging over a rail near the fire, stoked the fire with more peat and wood till it blazed high, tasted the stew, brought forward a bundle of heather for me to sit on and with a wave of his hand invited us all to sit round the fire. 'Now, who's hungry?'

Some half-hour later I leant back and licked my wooden platter clean. 'Mmmm . . . That was the best meal I've ever tasted. Thanks!'

'Best till next time as you're starving and cold! That's one of the best things about food: every much-needed time is the best. Like love . . .' He stared at the fire. 'All warm and cosy, now?'

I glanced round at the others: Puddy had earlier found some disgusting scuttling things in a corner and was nodding happily; Pisky burped round the remnants of the paste from the bread that had accompanied the meal; Corby was perched on a stack of logs, already half-asleep, and my little cat, her creamy black-barred stomach as tight as a barrel, was stretched out on the hearth, paws and eyes dream-twitching.

'Seems so,' I said. 'I don't know how to thank you. We—or I at least—had come to the end of my tether, I think. We all started out with such high hopes, but it's so slow, and winter's coming on and there is so far to go—' I shut my mouth with a snap, realizing I had said too much.

But Tom didn't seem to notice, stretching behind him for a flask. 'Perhaps you'll join me in a little nightcap? Very thing to settle the stomach, soothe the nerves, dissipate the ill-humours that a soaking may bring and avert the chills: you don't want to be sneezing and coughing and shivering tomorrow, now do you?'

It was the last that decided me. I didn't want to catch cold, and the liquid looked innocuous enough. I had heard of drugs and suchlike, but if I were to watch him drink some first . . . I accepted the little horn cup he offered, and pretended to sip.

He laughed. 'Nay, it's not poison, little Missy, and 'twill do you no harm. See, I'll drink some first,' and he swallowed half his cup. I took a cautious sip: it tasted of honey, sunshine and herbs and ran down my throat like hot soup: unlike hot soup the warmth seemed to spread into my stomach, chest and limbs till I felt warm to my toes. I took another sip: definitely more-ish.

'Nice,' I murmured.

He topped up my cup. 'Drink up, then: plenty more where

that came from.' Leaning forward he appeared to throw some dust onto the fire: immediately it flared up then died down again and now appeared to shimmer like silk, all colours, red, blue, green, purple . . . In its depths I saw great trees as high as hills, hills as tall as mountains, and mountains touching the clouds . . . Little faces peeped out of the corners, cheeky mischievous faces which thumbed their noses at me and giggled. A fiery snake coiled itself into a knot and interlaced itself with another. Great molten rivers ran, earth shifted, winds blew, seas came and went, sun and moon and stars ran together in a mad dance . . .

'And where did you say you were going?' said someone.

'To find the owner of the pebbles, somewhere in the southwest. But maybe first a wise man, a sage, to show us the right path . . .'

'And where do you come from? And why? And how?' The voice seemed to come from the fire and dreamily I answered it, dreamily I told the fire the whole story.

'There now,' said the fire. 'There now . . . Finish your drink and lie down by me and rest till morning. There's nothing to fear and you are safe and your friends are safe and travelling will wait till later . . .'

I felt the spring of dried heather and bracken beneath me, a cloak over me, heard the rain pattering harmless on the roof, had Moglet curled up against my chest and I was warm and full and safe and so, so tired . . .

'You told him everything!' accused Moglet. 'Every single thing!'

'All about the pebbles,' added Corby. 'And about the Mistress and Shape-Changing and her manikin.'

'And about trying to find someone to take this great lump out of my mouth so I can eat again properly: I've never heard so much talk since my great-great-aunt on the maternal side came back from—'

'And about losing our memories and not knowing where we came from,' added Puddy.

I had awoken some five minutes past. It was obviously well on into the morning, though no sun shone; it was not raining either, though the air was damp. Beside me the fire was damped down, a thin wisp of smoke curling up with its acrid, peaty smell. Swung over the fire was a small pot, contents simmering, and on a rack above my small sacks of flour and salt were drying.

'Did I?' I couldn't remember. I only knew that I felt rested as I had not in years, warm and comfortable, and extraordinarily well-disposed to the world in general.

'It was that drink that done it,' said Corby. 'Loosened your tongue something frightful!'

'My paternal grandfather's cousin twice removed—no, thrice times—told me sometimes men fell into the waters and drowned because of strong liquor,' added Pisky, unhelpfully I thought, seeing there was nothing but his bowl for me to fall into.

I took refuge in indignation. 'Well you lot didn't try and stop me! You were all flat out and snoring like pigs, as I remember . . . And, after all, what harm did it do?'

'Why, none at all, none at all,' came a voice from the doorway. 'Old Tom's got more than one secret tucked away in his noddle, and no one the wiser.' And he came in, smelling of falling leaves and earth, in his hands a flat basket of mushrooms. 'Mind you, there's not all of it I understood: 'tis a long time since you've used proper speech, aren't it, my flower?'

At his last words something flashed into my mind and was gone again, as swift as a blink. 'Proper speech?' I said. 'And why did you call me your flower?'

'Manner of speaking,' he said easily, and bent over the pot to stir it. 'As to speechifying: well, I understand a lot of what the birds and the trees and the creatures says, being as I've lived here and abouts many, many years, but though I reckon you can understand me well enough, some of your words come out like a man with the runs, all anyhow and in a hurry. Now then, 'tis breaking-fast time.' And he held out his hand for my bowl. Thick gruel, nutty and sharp, with honey on mine, but none on Moglet's. Corby had a strip of dried meat, Puddy found something to his satisfaction in the hearth, and a small gobbet of the same, squashed, satisfied both Pisky and the snails. I had a second helping.

When we were all satisfied, Tom squatted down on his heels

and tickled Moglet under her chin. 'Like to come a-mushrooming, then? We've some six hours of daylight, and—'

'We really should get on,' I interrupted, getting to my feet. 'Thank you all the same.'

'—of those perhaps two, two and a half will be fine,' he went on, as though I had not spoken. ' 'Twill rain heavy again tonight, but clear by midnight and wind'll veer southeast for a day or two's fine weather. So, there's no point in you a-setting off till the morrow, to get wet again. 'Sides, then I can put you on the road to another night's shelter and a lift partways, if'n I can get my baskets full. So, how do you say you help a man out for an hour or so?'

I learnt a lot in those two hours, about both mushrooms and fungi. I learnt to recognize the poisonous ones, especially the most dangerous of all, Death-Cap, deadly even to touch; I learnt that the prettiest—Red-Cap, Yellow-Belly, Blue-Legs, Blood-Hose and Magpie, the latter little white stars on black—were harmless but tasted foul, but that some that looked disgusting, like the tattered Horn of Plenty, the wavy-wild Chanterelle and the Oyster, the dull Cob and the Green-Nut, can all be cooked or eaten raw. Tom also gathered some he would not show me—'Later, Flower, later'—and with Corby's keen eyes and Puddy's ground-level view we had two baskets full before it started to spit with rain. We must have covered at least four or five miles, but had circled and were within easy distance of the ruined cottage, so did not get too wet. Moglet and Pisky, left behind at their own request, had obviously been idling away the day in sleep for they were both lively and hungry when we returned; I pointed Moglet to a rather large and hairy spider with short legs—the sort that go plop! when they drop off a shelf—and told her to cull it for Puddy and Pisky, but she pretended she couldn't see it: I think she was frightened of spiders. Tom set me to making oatcakes and getting a good blaze going, then fished around outside for a crock containing fat. He produced a large pan and some slices of smoked ham from a flank hung in the rafters and fried these up with a handful or two of mushrooms, including the raggedy Chanterelle we had picked and before long the insidious good smells were making us drool.

I fetched a jug of water from a stream some two hundred

yards away and we feasted like kings, forcing me to say with a grin: 'You were right: every much-needed time is best! I shall know how to find those mushrooms again and they will help our diet on—on the way . . .'

'Mind you, most of those we saw today you'll only see in woods: a tree-mixture, with some oak and some birch thrown in, is best.'

'Well, I suppose we shall find plenty of woods: it's safer travel that way, rather than trying the roads . . .' I hesitated: I still couldn't remember, but the others had said—'I believe I told you all about us last night?'

He chuckled. 'A goodly tale, and one to keep old Tom a-thinking on cold, dark nights!'

'It wasn't just a tale, it was true, all of it! At least, so the others say,' I amended. 'I don't really remember what I said . . .'

'Didn't say as how it wasn't true, just said it was the kind of tale to keep a man awake at night and wondering . . . You did say as you were a-looking for the party as those—pebbles, as you call 'em—belong to, and thinks your way might lie southwestish: well, I think as you are travelling in the right direction. As for finding a wise man or a magician to help you on your ways—well, there's plenty of magic still left in this old world and your direction is as good as any, especially as I heard tell a while back that a venerable sage lived near the sea thataways . . . But that, as I said, was a while ago, when the land was full of battle and surmise, and the beacons flared from down to hill—Why, what's the matter, Flower?'

'Beacons,' I murmured, feeling strangely uncomfortable. 'I seem to recall something about beacons . . .'

'Memory is a thing that can play strange tricks: it seems yours is buried deep and will only be dug up piece by piece. Don't try too hard, 'twill all come in good time.'

I was silent for a while, staring into the fire: ordinary pictures now. 'How can we ever thank you?' I said at last. 'Not only have you housed and fed us, but taken us at our word and kept our confidence . . .'

'And who else would there be to tell, youngling? 'Sides, Tom's always kept his own counsel since—Never mind . . . You've all been good company, and worth your keep, for Tom gets lonely, sometimes.'

'Do you live here all the time?'

'Here? Why, bless me, no! Tom has homes all over the place: he has another ruined cot like this, an abandoned charcoal burner's place, a hollow tree six feet across, a cavelet, even the corner of a derelict cell that once held an eremite—my home is everywhere and nowhere! Meadowland, ditch and hedgerow; pine forest, oak wood; heath, fen and bog, wherever my little darlings grow! And they may be found in the most unexpected places, too: halfway up a tree, under a turd, in among the ashes of last week's campfire . . . And they all have their uses, wet or dry, oh yes!'

And for a moment he looked sly and crafty and I did not like him so much—but then, like sun in and out of cloud, he was his normal, jolly self again.

'And does he live off his mushrooms, you ask yourselves, and the answer is yes: he gathers them and he eats them and he markets them, too. Tom's patch is a hundred miles all ways, give a league or two, and stretches north to where the hills begin and south to the great river; west to the farmlands and east—why, east as far as here, and lucky you are to find him this late, for winter comes and he should be working south now, to fetch up a moon or two hence in a snug little nest he knows.'

'It sounds an interesting life,' I ventured. 'But don't you ever get . . . well, lonely?'

For a moment his face darkened, shadowed, then again he laughed. 'No, for I see those I sell to when I have a need for company—and there, my friends, is where you can help me out. I have three baskets of mushrooms here, including those dried, which I would be obliged if you would deliver on your way tomorrow. Then I can stay here a further two-three days and look for some old Tough-Trunks: haven't seen any round here for a couple of years but they makes excellent eating, and if I try a couple of the larger clearings there might be a few left. They likes a bit of air and sun, see, but the shelter of the trees to run to if'n they wants. Left more'n a day or two 'twill be too late, for they're coming to the end of their season. Then, if I'm lucky, I can travel the way you go and pick up goods in pay to see me on my way. The folk I'll send you to will travel the next day to sell in the town, for mushrooms is best fresh, and so they'll carry you in comfort a mile or ten nearer your goal . . . How long is't since you laughed, Flower?'

It seemed such an odd question, coming after all that talk of mushrooms, that I gaped.

'Laughed?'

'Aye, laughed. Rolled around on your belly and held your ribs till they ached, and howled with merriment and joy? Laughed till tears ran from your eyes and your ears hurt?'

I could still only gape at him: I didn't know what he meant. The only laughter I had seen was the wild cackling of our Mistress when something pleased her, and sometimes I had seen young men and girls from the village laughing in the fields at harvest, as they chased each other in and out the stooks of corn, teasing with chaff, dried milkweed or poppy-heads . . . I didn't know what it was to laugh.

I stretched my mouth as I had seen them do and gave an experimental 'Ho-ho-ho, Ha-ha-ha' as I remembered the sound, but it didn't seem quite right and certainly felt very silly. It had an unexpected effect on Tom, too, for it sent him off into paroxysms of giggles that sounded strange coming from a grown man.

'I don't believe you know how!' he accused, and giggled again.

'Can't remember,' I said crossly. 'What does it matter, anyway? I'm not missing anything.'

'Don't be too sure about that, then! All folks feels better after a good laugh: almost as good as a—Never mind: you're too young. Like to try some of Tom's magic?'

'You can do magic?' I gasped.

'Oh, not your old spells and suchlike, only the magic what's in my little friends here,' and he opened his pouch and took out some more mushrooms, a large red one with white spots on it and some tiny brown ones with a little knob on top. 'This one here, the big fellow, is what they call the Magic Mushroom. Why there are folks overseas who worship this one like a god on account of it gives them pleasant dreams if they take it in moderation, and kills their enemies for them taken in larger amounts: I reckon enough of 'em died finding the right doses . . . I ain't going to give you none of him 'cos you has to think of size and weight and age and tolerance to make the dose right for dreams and wrong for t'other, but these little fellows—Fairies Tits when they're fresh and Mouse-Dugs dried—these fellows I can measure out for you and give you nothing more'n a good laugh or two. Not that they ain't bad when taken too much, but I'll only give you a tickle.

'Well? You looks doubtful: then I'll take 'em too, like the drink last night, but I'll take twice as much . . .'

In the end he persuaded me, not so much from his words as from a mutter from Puddy: 'Seen 'em before: not poison in small quantities. No more than the number of my toes, mind . . .'

And that is exactly the number he gave me, lightly cooked in the fat remaining in the pan-juices: fourteen tiny little mushrooms. I tasted one: nothing special. I waited till he had eaten half his—double my quantity—before I started on the rest.

Then I waited for the laugh. Nothing.

He read my mind. 'Oh, you has to linger awhile for them to work . . .'

'How did you come to know so much about mushrooms?' I asked curiously, while I waited.

That darkening of his face again. He seemed to hesitate, then shovelled the rest of his mushrooms into his mouth and drank the pan juices. When he looked at me he was smiling.

'A tale for a tale, then? 'Tain't much, when all's said and done, not really . . .

'Well, see, once Tom loved a fair lady and they lived in a fine house in a town many miles from here. Now Tom had a good living then and they were both happy, this beautiful lady and he, and their happiness was crowned when she told him there was a child on the way. And as is the way with ladies in that condition she came to have strange tastes, wanting things out of season and difficult to come by. But Tom, he kept her satisfied, going miles out of his way for strawberries in April and brambles in June. Then came a time, and she was near her lying-in, when of all things she wanted mushrooms, some of those wood mushrooms that grow best near pines. And Tom knew where he had seen some, near to a clump of fir trees, so off he went and picked them and rushed back and tossed them

69

in a pan and carried them in to her on a silver platter, and she cried with joy when she saw them and kissed her Tom and turned to scoop them to her mouth . . .'

He stopped, and I knew, oh I knew, what was to come next and tried to stop him, but he shook his head.

'Better out than in, Flower . . .

'I should have known that smell: smelt of sleep, smelt of death.' Now there was no third-person Tom, it was himself . . . 'They was Destroying-Angel, all white in their purity, all black in their intent, and my lady died in agony and the child with her. After that I was a little mad, I think, for they shut me away . . .

'But I had time to think, there in the darkness of soul, and when they finally let me out and I found the business sold and all moneys gone, I didn't care: it was the mushrooms that had taken from me all I held dear and by my own ignorance and I swore to spend the rest of my life learning about the little devils until I was always one jump ahead and could fair say I had beaten them at their own game. And so I have.

'So, old Tom's a mushroom expert, you might say . . .'

'I'm sorry,' I said.

'No need to be, no need. 'Tis time past, and if there is one thing I did learn then it was to look to time present . . .

'And, talking of the present: how do you feel?'

Now he came to mention it, I was beginning to feel different, as if my stomach had a pleasant little fire chuckling away all warm inside it. The fire light seemed stronger too, making all colours brighter, but a little fuzzy round the edges.

Nice . . .

Then it happened. Tom got up to throw more wood on the fire, slipped, and for a moment, trying to regain his balance, stood on one leg like a heron, lanky and ungainly, arms flapping like wings, and such a comical look of surprise on his face that I felt a little tickle of amusement jerking my tummy, then another and another, till I was like a pot waiting to boil, bottom all covered with bubbles. I couldn't help it: I came to the boil, slowly but surely. Snorts, spasms, gasps all accompanied these completely new feelings till, with a painfulness that only those who laugh out loud but seldom could appreciate, merriment rose to the surface and, once there, wouldn't stop, and I was boiling away like a pot of forgotten water, salted by the tears of laughter that coursed down my cheeks. At first I thought I was dying, for I could not laugh and breathe and cry at the same time and got the hiccoughs, but in the end everything sorted itself out, except that by that time my ribs ached and so did the bones at the back of my ears.

The trouble was that once started, I couldn't stop: Moglet's studied aversion and turned back and Corby's offended stare only set me off worse than ever.

Tom poked me in the ribs: he too was laughing fit to burst, his arms hugging his ribs, knees up to his chin. 'Tell—tell me: why—why do you wear that terribly tatty little flap of—of leather? Oh, dear me, what with a fringe of hair like a taggley pony and that flap of hide there's nothing but eyes like post-holes to be seen—oh, dear me!—all across your face.'

I giggled helplessly. ' 'Cos—'cos I look like a fright without! I've worn it ever since—ever since I could remember! Our Mistress made me, so I didn't frighten the villagers to death! Got a face like a—like a cross between a pig and a snake without it . . . Oh, dear: how do you stop laughing? It hurts . . .' And I doubled up.

'How—how do you know what—what you look like, then?'

'Mistress showed me—in a mirror of polished metal . . . Ha! Ha! Ha! You should have seen me! Oh, dear, I shall die if I don't stop this . . . Said I was too ugly to go abroad without a mask, so I made—tee-hee!—this. Ho! Ho! And if any ask— He! He!—I say I am marked bad with the 'pox!'

'You don't mind looking like that, then?'

'Can't, can I? Always have, s'pose . . . Oh, mercy, mercy! Stop making me laugh!'

'What with that mask and walking around doubled up with that—stone—in your stomach, you look—you look much like a hobgoblin!'

'A hob—hobgoblin? Oh dear, yes, I must do! How—how hilarious! What a fright! Enough to scare the children, and the old folk from the chimney-corner . . . He-he-he . . .'

And thus was changed in my mind the hidden hurt of the day when our Mistress had found me trying to gaze at my reflection in a pail of water—just to see whether my fingers lied when they felt a straightish little nose, a wideish mouth and

71

long lashes—and, muttering a few words, had shown me what a horror I really was, in that polished mirror of hers: jutting brow, little snake-like eyes downturned at the corners, a crooked nose, squashed like a pig's, uneven, jagged teeth, and a drooling, loose mouth. The whole face, from brow down, was covered in skin-blemishes: blue scars, pocks and a web of red like a spider's which had spread up from the red pebble in my navel like the plague . . . After that I had begged a piece of soft leather from her and hung it on a thong threaded through the top over my nose and across the rest of my face.

And she had laughed even more when she had seen it.

But now it was I who was laughing, and far harder than she had ever done.

After that I fell suddenly asleep, exhausted by the strange thing called laughter, but the others told me in the morning that even in my dreams I had been giggling happily, though when I awoke I could not recall a single thing.

THE GATHERING:
ONE, THREE, FOUR, FIVE, SIX, SEVEN

The White Horse

THE LAST sight we had of that extraordinary man, Thomas Herrilees Trundleweed, was of him bowing us exaggeratedly away, and then striking his head on a branch some seven feet up as he straightened, and being showered thus with last night's raindrops. I had smothered a giggle against the back of my hand, remembering the release of the night before, but he was, by then, too far away to have heard anyway. I was still not sure whether I really liked him, in spite of his kindnesses, for he was too mercurial and fey to understand completely, but I had to admit we had been very well treated and were now better off with a route to follow for the next few miles, full stomachs, dry clothes, fur and feathers, the promise of a lift partways, a grounding in the art of mushrooming—and in the case of the latter, a further present.

That morning Tom had handed me a small package of the dried Mouse-Dugs, as he called them, enough for two adult dosings.

'Though I doubt if you'll find any other that hasn't laughed for seven years . . .' But when I had queried the specific number seven he had just winked and tapped the side of his nose. 'It's a number, just like any other, ain't it? 'Sides, old Tom listens to the trees and the birds, don't forget.' And that was all I could get out of him, try as I would.

We made fair progress, although the village we were aiming for was a good ten miles away, and arrived soon after noon. Tom's contacts were an elderly couple, quiet and reserved, but ready enough with food and lodging once we had explained who we were; they said that it would be a waste of time to set out for the market till the following morning as it would take at least three hours at their donkey's sedate pace. So I had to curb my natural impatience to get on, and spent the afternoon learning to weave simple baskets and carriers, which was their trade. I grew quite proficient after an hour or so, and by the time the light faded and rushes were lit I had managed a creditable back-carrier, which they gave to me, pointing out that my sack was almost threadbare. The broad top of the carrier meant that there was somewhere for Moglet to perch, so that only one shoulder—Corby's—would be sore, and this I padded with a scrap of leather.

We suppered from fresh bread, goat's milk and cheese, and they parted with some eggs and a loaf for our journey, taking but one copper coin, so we bedded down in the lean-to shed at the side of the cottage with light hearts soon after eating, warned of an early start. They woke us before light as they had stock to feed and the little cart to load with their weavings and the mushrooms and me, and we eventually set off an hour before daybreak, to arrive at the market as early as possible. We slipped away before they came to the town proper, for though neither of them had made any comment about my friends, the woman especially had cast curious glances at my mask, and I judged it better not to risk us with the more open townsfolk.

So, considerably heartened, we set off again on our way south and west. Before long the broad road on which we found ourselves became too well populated, and we took to the byways and woods again, only using the main thoroughfare very early or very late and in this fashion, lucky with our nightly lodgings—ruined hut, upturned wagon, barn and, once, church porch—we made another fifty miles or so.

Then our luck changed. The road we were following took in another and turned to run due southeast/northwest for many miles, and though we followed the left hand for many miles it soon became evident that we were bearing ever more easterly, and when I assisted Corby with his keener eyes to the top of the tallest tree around he came fluttering to earth with the news that there was no change in direction 'as far as a crow can see'. I was disheartened, for that meant either a detour to find another road, or crossing the present one and plunging into

74

forest that looked far less hospitable than the one we had so recently left. A detour was too risky, so for the next day or two it was scratched arms and legs from briars, whipped head and shoulders from tangled branches and snappy twigs and a rapidly dwindling store of food.

One thing I learnt: staying in one place and going round and about with an expert gathering mushrooms was one thing; gathering them without one on the march was another. You only saw them if they were right in front of you, or at least in eye-reach, and then one had to stop, dislodge Corby, wake up Moglet in the carrying-basket, set down Pisky, where he moaned that he couldn't see, and, if you were lucky, get away without disturbing Puddy in the side-pocket. Then, when you had examined the mushrooms they might turn out to be the wrong sort, or if they were the right kind there weren't enough of them to justify cooking or, more often, they were a species I had not come across before.

We were down to our last handful of flour and a rind of cheese when we came to a small village. Here, in the forest, were signs of cultivation: trees had been lopped and felled for building and fuel and the scrub thinned down in the direction of a navigable river, unluckily flowing the wrong way for us, otherwise I might have risked trying to hire a boat, but here the only transport available seemed to be large working rafts, and I did not have the strength to pole one of those against the current. Leaving the others on a knoll overlooking the river I slipped down to the village and paid the usual stranger's over-price for bread, cheese, apples and a hand of salt pork. This reduced our savings to two silver and two gold coins: these latter I was wary of changing, for the last time I had been short-changed and almost openly accused of being a thief, for obviously no one who looked as I did could possibly come by gold honestly.

I was anxious to rejoin the others as soon as I could because for the last few days, even as the trees had thinned and broadened into great stands of leaf-dropping beech and oak and the going had become easier, I had had the uneasy feeling that we were being followed. Not that there had been anything to see, merely a fleeting impression of something white through the trees to the left, the right; the half-heard sound of a footfall, muffled by leaves, ahead, behind; a soft breathing in the night-hours; a feeling of loneliness, of an empty heart . . . None of the others had seen anything, although they too were uneasy.

However, today the sun was shining full on the knoll, they were safe and sound, and we ate till we were comfortable. Stomach full I felt decidedly soporific: after all, if we had an hour or so's rest now, safe out of sight of the village, it would mean less time tonight in a possibly uncomfortable sleeping-place.

Unbuttoning my jacket to the pleasant rays of the sun, I laid aside my mask and stretched out, pillowing my head on my cloak.

'We'll stay here for a while,' I told the others. 'Moglet: you can keep half an eye open, can't you?' For I could see that Corby and Puddy fancied some leaf-turning.

Closing my eyes I slipped effortlessly into dreamless sleep.

'Pig, pigs, pig-person! Wake up, Thing—' Moglet's urgent mew in my right ear and I was struggling to open my eyes, to make some sense of what was happening. There was a rootling, grunting, scrunching noise, a strong, not unpleasant piggy smell and then Corby's raucous croak: 'Geroff! That's mine, you big bastard! Find your own, you great vat of lard—' and then the sound of a stone striking the earth and a yelp from the crow. I leapt to my feet, the sun in my eyes, and squinted at a herd of swine grunting their way slowly along the fringes of the forest, and standing about six feet away the swineherd, another stone ready to follow the first.

Snatching up my mask with one hand and fumbling with the fastenings of my jacket with the other, I cursed Moglet for not waking me sooner.

'Fell asleep . . . wind in the wrong direction . . .' she whispered.

'Well-now-then,' said the swineherd. 'What-have-we-here?' Each word was slow, measured, calculating. He was a dirty-looking man, short and squat but powerful. He smelt of pig and frowsty nights of drink and even as I watched he took a flask from his pocket and offered it to me. I shook my head but he took a draught and replaced the stopper but not the flask. Instead he eyed me up and down and smiled. Not a nice smile:

his mouth was too fat and he looked to have twice as many teeth as he should, yellow, sharp teeth with little pits in them. His skin, too, was pitted and the pits black; his nose was upturned, the nostrils sprouting black hairs like his ears, and his eyes were too small.

I backed away a step or two and Moglet backed with me, her fur anxious. Out of the corner of my eye I could see Corby hopping up and down, luckily undamaged, and the movement of grass as Puddy crawled closer.

'Keep back,' I thought-ordered them. 'I don't like the look of this fellow . . .'

'You'd like him even less if you'd had a ruddy great rock up your arse,' was Corby's succinct reply. 'And we're not abandoning you in a dangerous situation,' he added. 'Fellow like that means business. Where's your knife?'

'Words first,' said Puddy. 'Action second if necessary. You've never used that knife in anger . . .' No. It was the one I used for vegetables, peeling and slicing. But it was very sharp.

The swineherd had moved forward as I moved back, and now he was the same distance away as before. 'No-harm-meant,' he said ingratiatingly, and stretched out his free hand to my still half-covered chest. 'Pretty-little-bubs-them. Shame-to-hide-them. Like-to-touch-them-I-would . . .'

I backed away again, looking away past him to where I had left our belongings, with Pisky's bowl in the shade of the wicker carrier. I received his anxiety and sent back a re-assurance, but inside I was panicking. I did not know what this man intended: did he mean to kill us for our paltry belongings? He could not know I had our remaining coins hidden away in a pouch in my breeches. Perhaps if I offered them to him he would let us go . . . Frantically I dug down and his eyes followed my hand, his tongue passing slowly over his lips.

'Getting-them-off-for-me-then?' the voice was suggestive, nasty.

I held out the coins. 'That's all I have. Please take them and leave us alone . . .'

His eyes lit up and he snatched the coins away from me and bit them. 'Good-good . . ' He took another pull from the flask, pulling the cork with his teeth and spitting it to the grass. 'Why-don't-you-speak-proper? Why-the-mask? And-what-you-got-over-there?' and he gestured in the direction of our belongings.

He wasn't going to leave us in peace, he wanted everything. 'Take it all,' I said despairingly. 'Except my little fish. Then please let us alone . . .'

He put down the flask and placed the coins atop, where they winked in the sunshine. 'Don't-hear-you-right-girl. Ain't-answered-my-questions. Let's-see-what-else-you-got-in-there—' and he made a grab for me but I jumped back, and this time my knife leapt to my hand, glinting to match the coins.

'Let us alone, or I'll—I'll kill you!'

He couldn't reach me but unfortunately Moglet had not moved fast enough and he grabbed her and held her high by the scruff of the neck, his other hand flashing to his own knife. He made as if to strike her and I screamed, a scream that was echoed by a strangled wail from Moglet.

'Help me, Thing dear, help me!'

'No, no!' I yelled. 'Anything you want, anything!'

Apparently this time he understood, for he lowered my kitten, but his knife was still at the ready.

'Don't-want-me-to-harm-your-pet? All-right-put-your-knife-down-over-there-and-I'll-let-it-go. That's-right . . .' For a moment longer he held her, then opened his hand and she dropped, choking and gasping, to crawl back to my side. I bent to stroke her, but a moment later a hand was at my throat and I was forced backwards to the ground and his other hand tore at my belt. 'Get-'em-down, get-'em-down,' he muttered and pulled my trews past my knees. In hideous shame I tried to cover my red-pebbled belly with my hands and roll over, but he slapped my face till my head rang. 'Lie-still-curse-you-or-it'll-be-the-worse-for-you—'

At that moment he broke off with a yell for all at once he was attacked by the spitting fury of Puddy, whose venom shot up into his face, the claws of an enraged Moglet, scratching blood from his hands, and the beak of an angry Corby, who tore at his rear.

'Run, Thing, run!' they yelled, but with a fist the swineherd punched Moglet from him, with a foot he kicked Puddy away and his knife flashed within an inch of Corby. I knew it was no use and called on them to stop.

'Go away, go away, my dear ones: you cannot help me now. Go into the forest where he cannot find you, and drag Pisky's bowl with you. I'll be all right, only please, please go!' But still they hesitated, crying and cursing, till I used the words of command. 'Go, and do not disobey. I command you by all that holds the Earth, the Waters, the Sky in their accustomed places; the Now, the Then, the Hereafter . . .'

I heard them leave me, and the desolation of the abandoned tied my stomach in knots, spilt the tears from my eyes and cut at my heart as keen as any knife. The sun went behind cloud and the figure standing over me assumed the proportions of a giant. Why doesn't he kill me, I thought, and get it over with? And I sent a hope-call for my dear ones, to be left to fend for themselves. Let them be brave and resourceful, I prayed, let them find their own peace . . .

The swineherd unbuttoned his trousers. Staring upwards, all at once I realized what he intended: he meant to use me as Broom used to punish our Mistress, for the great thing that poked out from his groin was smooth-knobbed, and ridged and gnarled along its length like Broom, and it throbbed and pulsed and swelled like Broom, and like Broom it had a great bush of furze at its base the colour of dead heather, and it waved and nodded and beckoned just like Broom and any moment now it was going to thrust into my stomach where the pebble hurt and bring forth great gouts of blood and pain, and I began to whimper and cry.

'Oh, do not hurt me! Do not hurt me—I cannot stand more pain! Please, please!' I did not want to writhe and curse and bleed as she had done—

The sun came out from behind the clouds, there was a thudding noise on the turf, a wild neighing, and all at once the swineherd was gone, clear over the top of the knoll, and soft horse-breath was sweet on my face.

'Come up, youngling, come up! He is gone and you are safe, for the moment. Gather your things quickly, for he will be back . . .'

I stared up in bewilderment at the tattered, ragged-maned horse that stood over me.

'Gather your things quickly, before he returns,' he repeated. 'The others are safe: I will take you to them. Come!'

* * *

That night we had a fire, and ate at our leisure, and slept in the open. No looking for a tree to climb up, a hole to crawl into; that night we slept at peace for the first time since we had left on our great adventure. It is difficult to explain just why we all felt this sense of security—and we all felt it, not just me—except that the finding of the white horse, or rather his finding of us, was at the root of it all. Not then nor after did we ever question his unerring sense of direction, his knowledge, his warm benignity: we just accepted them, and him as something special.

Not that he was a splendid white stallion of some eighteen hands, like the great chargers I seemed to recall from some other time, some other place; he was small, perhaps a little larger than pony-size, with cloven hooves and tatty feathers, a long tail and mane, curly and tangled, and large, soft, brown eyes. It was probably those eyes that set the seal on it: they seemed brown most of the time, but in sunlight they were blue-green, in shade brown-green and they beamed—there is no other word for it. Reassurance, comfort and a strange other-worldliness shone from those eyes, and yet they were not happy . . .

He promised us nothing that first day, except that he would take us to a place of safety: he had carried us all smoothly and swiftly through the forest, stopping as twilight fell in a particularly pleasant glade to let us down. After gazing at us reassuringly for a moment or two he went to lie down a little distance away, leaving us, as I said, feeling so calm and confident that I had lighted a fire without further thought, and we slept in the open that night all wrapped under my cloak, for the nights were chill—all that is except Corby, who preferred to roost off the ground.

In the morning the white horse was still there, quietly cropping the sweet grass that still lingered in the hollows. He seemed shy of approaching us, so I went across with one of the small russets I had bought the day before.

'Please have one: they are nice and juicy.'

Lipping the apple gently from my palm, he scrunched it with evident enjoyment. 'Thank you.'

'Talking of thanks, I quite forgot to offer mine—and ours—for the rescue and the ride and—and everything.'

'I had been near you for some days: I thought sometimes you realized I was near.'

'I thought someone, or something, was following us, but I wasn't sure. And if you hadn't, I don't know what would have happened to us. That—that man, with his—his—' I still wasn't sure what it had been.

'I followed you because you seemed a small and vulnerable party to be making your way in such a determined manner, and I was curious. Besides, you are a maiden, and even in my present state I have not forgotten my duties.'

'Duties?'

'To defend all maidens and the pure and unsullied from Evil, in whatever form that may come . . .' The answer was confident as if it came from a much bigger animal, but my eyes must have mirrored my astonishment, for the white horse blew softly in my ear. 'Things are not always what they seem,' he said. 'I was not always the wretched thing you see me now . . . No more of that. Now tell me, youngling—'

'My name is Thing,' I interrupted. 'And may I know just whom I have the honour of addressing?' I knew that was the correct way to ask someone's name because I had overheard two gentlemen meeting on the road one day, and they had addressed one another in just that way. I had crept away and practised it.

'You may, but not just now. Give me a name of your own: whatever you would call a white horse.'

I thought of all the things that were white: clouds, linen, daisies, dough (sometimes); swan-feathers, chalk, marble, eggwhite; snow—Snow. 'Would you mind if we called you "Snowy"?'

'I would not mind being called Snowy at all,' he said gravely. 'I do not think I should have liked "Doughy" or "Eggwhitey" as much . . .' He had been reading my mind! That was another thing: all of us could understand him perfectly, but none of us considered this strange, although we had been used to our own methods of conversation for so long. And he seemed to sharpen our understanding of all the other creatures we met along the way, as if he were a catalyst through which all

81

tongues became one. What surprises me now is that we accepted it without question at the time, but perhaps that was all part of his magic, too.

'And now,' he said. 'Would you like to trust me with your purpose in journeying so far and so poorly attended? I can see you have a tale to tell—but perhaps you would prefer it if we talked as we went? I am afraid I am not strong enough to carry you far in one go, but if you can manage to walk a league, say, and then travel on my back for the same distance, we could probably manage double your usual journeying.'

'You go our way, then?' I said, delighted.

'For want of a better, my road lies with yours for a while, yes,' replied the gentle creature.

It was a day of sun and shadow, wind and the falling of leaves. As we went I told our new companion our story, right from the beginning. He questioned me closely about our Mistress, then sighed. 'You are sure She is indeed dead?'

I was sure, and he sighed again. 'Then that is that: no hope that it may be changed.' He seemed to make up his mind. 'Then, if you will have me, I shall be with you till your journey's end.

'You wanted to find a magician, a wise man: I heard tell of a great sorcerer who lived once in the arm of the west. I had supposed him dead or fled, but you have such faith that it is possible he is still there. If he is, I think I know the way.

'Come, my friends: the sooner we are there the better. I have an idea the hour-glass has been turned for the last time . . .'

The Rusty Knight

IT HAD been a beautiful morning. For some days now we had been following the upstream course of a big river, which the white horse, Snowy, said was called the Tamesis. It was fordable, but he said the going was better on this side and we could make another seven leagues or so before crossing and striking more southward. We had woken that morning to the loud, sweet song of a little wren, and everything touched with frost fingers. It was near the end of the month of Leaf-Fall and soon we should be in the Moon of Mists, but the morning was sparkling and still and clear. We had spent the night cosily enough in an abandoned charcoal-burner's hut, but the sharpness of the morning turned my nose pink and snapped at my cheeks, or so Corby said. 'You look just like a ripe apple, m'dear,' which was a generous compliment to my maskless face, for I now only wore this disguise if there was a chance of meeting other folk on the way. Not that this was a frequent occurrence, for we left the road if we heard steps on the way, and hid till they were past.

Snowy had made no comment on my disfigured face, for which I was grateful: he just seemed to accept it as the others had. I always considered this a peculiarly delicate gesture on their part, until I overheard Moglet one day remark to Corby: 'I don't know why Thing bothers with that silly piece of leather: she looks all right to me', to which the gracious bird replied: 'She could be as beautiful as Heaven or ugly as Hell, as the saying goes, and it would be all the same to me: humans all look alike, don't they? I can't tell one from t'other 'cept by their height and the length of their beaks, and hers is nothing to

83

beat the drum for. Now mine, mine you would call a patrician beak . . .'

So much for vanity.

The road swung away from the river for a while and lay between high banks where beards of traveller's joy draped the bushes and blackbirds feasted from the last brambles and watched the haws ripen. We had climbed a little and now stood on an escarpment. To the left, down by the river, a few houses hugged its curves, smoke rising straight and thin into a pale sky. Below us in a clearing was a winter barn full of hay; the southering sun shone on gleaming pebbles on its roof, and only when I saw their restless shift and heard the bubbling chatter carried up to us on the still air did I realize they were those tardy travellers, house martins, adorning like pearls the rough surcoat of the barn roof. Beside the barn someone had planted a line of fruit trees and these, for rapture of the morning, had shed their last leaves to lie, discarded red petticoats, around their feet, and stretched bare silver limbs to embrace the shafted sunlight. Beneath our feet, as we trod the rutted road, fallen leaves leapt away like frogs from our intrusion, and somewhere amidst the smells of cold stone, damp earth and the sweet sweat-smell of Snowy, was the evocative scent of burning apple logs—

'Listen!' It was Moglet, large pointed ears flickering back and forth.

We stopped and at first I could hear nothing, but as I watched the others their reactions told me what was afoot long before the faint sounds reached my ears. It was a stealth of ambush, a fight-back, a battle, and as we hurried towards the sound, half-afraid, half-curious, I found my heart beating with a rare excitement as if something special was about to happen. We rounded a corner, the road dropped away in a steep decline and there beneath us where the road banked high, river on one side, forest the other, a lone man in rusty chain mail was trying to fight off three sneak-thieves with his fists and a broken sword.

Even as we watched he was beaten to his knees then rose again, staggering, with scarce enough breath to call for help, and the next moment returned to the attack, in the name of one St Patrick. He was a bonny fighter, but I could see he had no

84

chance at all, and would be lucky to escape with a broken skull and the loss of his pack.

I turned impulsively to Snowy. 'We must help him! We can't just stand by and let him be killed!'

'Are you sure you want to be involved? We could lie low till they have done . . .'

Somehow I knew this was no cowardice on his part, more a test of me, the biggest coward I knew. But—

'Of course we must help him! We must draw them off, distract them—'

'I can imitate a horn,' said Corby, hopping up and down.

'Hear me shriek!' said Moglet.

'Poison in their eyes,' muttered Puddy.

'You can borrow my water,' bubbled Pisky. 'But only borrow, mind . . .'

'Right,' said Snowy. 'I shall gallop round through the trees and try to sound like a troop of horses, dropping you off, crow, to make your horn-calls on the other side of the road, with cat doing her screeches. Toad, you shall be left nearer to aim your poison, and the maid here shall hide in the trees with the fish and bang against a pan and shout 'A rescue! A rescue!' in as deep a voice as she can. Ready?'

We had no time to think. Up on Snowy's back, then away like the wind down through the trees and into action. It was wildly improbable, highly dangerous, wholly exhilarating— and it worked. A perfect cacophony of horn and trumpets sounded from the river side of the road, accompanied by ear-splitting screeches. A cavalcade of horsemen thundered through the woods; one attacker was half-blinded by an evil jet of poison that shot from the bushes at his feet and my clattering sounded like at least three men in armour blundering through the trees. In a moment the three attackers were flying for their lives down the road away from us, leaving a huddled figure heaped in the ditch, pack still intact by its side. We approached warily from our various concealments, one eye on the dust of the attackers' retreat, the other on the victim. The only one making any noise was Pisky, furious at not being allowed to help in the attack, sulking vociferously at the bottom of his bowl.

The knight lay on his face in the muddy ditch.

'He's awfully still,' I said doubtfully.

Puddy hopped closer. 'He's breathing, though.'

'All bloody,' said Moglet. 'Not nice . . .'

'I've seen worse get up and walk,' said Corby. 'But not much.'

Pisky decided to ignore the whole thing.

'Well,' said Snowy, 'we should get him away from here in case they come back; we should be safer under cover. If you will pull him on to my back and walk beside to keep him steady we can make a mile or two to an abandoned anchorite's cell I know of in the forest. Can you manage his pack as well?'

Somehow we did manage, though we were all exhausted when at last we laid him on the floor of the cell, a gloomy place that smelt of old bones and cat-piss. I placed the knight's head on his pack, but carefully because the back of his head was sticky with blood, and covered him with my cloak. He moaned a little and moved his legs, so we knew they weren't broken; I flexed his arms: they were whole too, though his knuckles were broken and bruised with the fighting. He seemed to be whole in body, no holes or gashes, but I fancied from the bruising and his ragged breathing that a couple of ribs might be broken, but I dared not completely remove his rusty chain-mail coat to confirm this. His head seemed worst hurt: it bled freely from a gash on his forehead, he had a black eye and a bloody nose, but these would heal; I was more worried about the injury at the back: a lump was already forming, though the blood oozed more slowly now.

I sat up from my examination. 'Can we light a fire? He's very cold . . .'

'We're safe enough here,' said Snowy.

Corby rattled off for some twigs for kindling, I found some larger pieces of branch and soon we had a fire blazing away in the corner. I remembered the so far unused piece of linen I had taken from our village, what seemed so long ago, and knew at last how to make my peace with Pisky as well. With dampened cloth, carefully dipped in his bowl, I wiped away the worst of the blood from the knight's head and bound up his wound as best I could; he moaned a little and grimaced but still remained unconscious, and I looked up anxiously at Snowy.

'Will he be all right?'

86

'Lift his head a little and give him half a cup of water from Pisky's bowl. Wait: put the cup on the ground and I watched as he bent his head and covered it with his mane. I wondered for a moment whether he was checking for weed or snails, but when he nodded to me to take up the cup the liquid within was warm and cloudy and smelt of herbs. 'Now, give him a drink.'

I put the cup to his lips. 'Drink, Sir Knight: you are in safe hands.'

Obediently he swallowed the liquid and, as I held his head on my arm, a pair of autumn-brown eyes opened and gazed into mine. Too late I remembered I was maskless.

But he was whispering something. 'Thank you, beautiful one . . .' His eyes closed and he was unconscious again, but he had looked at me, he had spoken, he would get better . . . He must, for at that look, those words, something in my middle had started galloping round like a colt in spring, ungainly and clumsy and untamed, and I knew I could not let him die, even if common sense told me that it was not me he had seen but some lady of dream.

'He'll do for the moment,' said Snowy. 'There's a spring down in the trees a small walk away. Make your suppers and put on some broth for when he wakens. I'll fetch herbs, and I think you'll find a flask of wine in his pack: put a cupful in the broth.'

We kept watch all night, in turns, lest he should need us, and I put his broken sword in his right hand in case he woke and thought it lost. Dawn came in frost again and a chill wind, and I built up the fire and tucked my cloak more closely about him—though my teeth were chattering with cold and I could well have done with it myself. The broth I had prepared tasted strong and stimulating and I had a cupful myself and soon felt warmed through.

The sun spear-slanted among the trees as it rose and a shaft touched the Rusty Knight's face. His eyelids fluttered, he frowned, moved a little, and hastily I put away my dreams and donned my mask. The others crowded round: he opened his eyes once more, this time in puzzlement, put his hand to his head, shut his eyes again, groaned, winced, lay still. After a moment his eyes re-opened and this time he spoke, too.

'Wha—What happened? Where am I?'

I explained as best I could, introducing the others, lifting his head, offering the broth, but I was nervous and the words got tangled up and didn't sound right, so I tried again and that was worse.

The Rusty Knight raised himself on one elbow and opened his mouth again.

'By all that's holy! Would you credit it? I am attacked, I am wounded, I am rescued—and by what? A broken-down nag, a tatty black bird, a scraggy cat, a frog, something-in-a-bowl and—and a hobgoblin who talks scribble!'

Peter and Paul

BUT BY midday his breathing was worse and he had lapsed into unconsciousness again, muttering and moaning in delirium.

Snowy looked grave. 'It would seem there is infection in the chest: I can do nothing about that, but if it is untreated he may succumb. Dangerous as it may be to move him, I think we should try.'

'But where?' I cried, hearing the tiredness and tension in my voice. 'There's just forest for miles!'

'Not quite: two leagues to the north there is a hump of folding hills where two brothers from an order of monks tend sheep from late autumn to lambing; they are experienced with animals of all kinds and would at least know what was best for the knight, of that I am sure. Come, we will have to start now, otherwise it will be night before we reach them.'

It took over five hours, for Snowy could not carry his burden for long and had to rest as did I, burdened as I was with the others. Each time we had to move the poor knight he seemed worse, and I was in a right old state by the time we heard the distant bleating of sheep and emerged from the twilight of the forest to smoothly sweeping downs and the Evening Star pricked clear into the deepening blue of a frosty sky. The shieling was built of stones and mud and lay low to the ground, surrounded by wattle-fenced enclosures filled with restless sheep, just driven in for the night by a monk in brown habit and a couple of shaggy, point-nosed dogs. To the left was a barn, full of hay and housing a two-wheeled cart and a donkey, whose braying blotted out the baa-ing of sheep, calling of monk and barking of dogs.

We approached warily, my hands palm outwards to show we came in peace, and Snowy whispered a word of advice. 'Play dumb, youngling: once they see he is injured you may leave the rest to them.'

I took his words literally, and when the monk came running, a tall, thin figure with robe kilted up thin shanks to knobbly knees, I mouthed distress and pointed to our burden. Luckily he understood immediately.

'Tut-tut, whatever have we here? A poor wounded fellow and an assortment of animals . . . Deary, deary me! May the Good Lord preserve us!' and he crossed himself. 'This person needs attention, yes indeed . . . An accident, perhaps?' He had a thin, high, fluting voice and his eyes were kind.

I mimed sword-play, an attack.

'Ah, yes; I see. How unfortunate: travelling has become so fraught these days . . . Well, well, well! Never mind, we must get him to shelter and comfortable as soon as possible. Brother Paul!' He had a surprisingly loud hail.

'Coming, Brother Peter!' and a fat, squat monk came running out of the shieling, his robe, even hitched as it was through his belt, trailing a little on the ground behind. 'What is it, what is it?' His voice was as deep as the other's was high. 'May His Holy Angels defend us! A wounded man, with servant and—and pets? Brother Peter, the place for him is inside, with a robe to cover, a posset to soothe and a fresh bandage for that head . . .' And, fussing and fretting, he led the way over to the barn. 'Now then, now then: baggage and animals to remain here with Brother Donkey, and servant and master to the house . . .'

I thought-transmitted delay to the others, a later visit with food, but they were already abandoning themselves to sleep. Snowy was lying down, Corby had shuffled to the beam above the door, Moglet was curled up in the hay, weather eye open for the dogs, and Puddy, eyes shut, was sheltering under a convenient crock. I put a somnolent Pisky beside him, drawing hay round them both.

'I'll be back . . .'

I doubt if they heard for all had been made to walk, crawl and hop further than usual during the day. My eyes were closing too, as I followed the monks to their home. I looked round for the dogs, but they were obviously well-trained and were already kennelled, but unchained, ready, I supposed, to patrol the sheep pens against thief or even wolf, though the latter usually left their hunting so far south till winter really bit.

The room I was drawn into, in the wake of the monks and their burden of wounded man, was long and low, heat well-trapped in the rafters. To my right was a huge fire and simmering pot, a drying rack of herbs suspended from the ceiling; two stools, a table and hooks for cloaks and tools. Facing me were two pallets, straw-stuffed palliasses on a wood and rope frame; to my left sacks and bales of provisions, more tools and a barrel of apples. On shelves were arranged jars of ointment and pots of unguent and packets of dried leaves and there was also room around and about for shepherd's crooks, a large wooden tub, two leather buckets and a besom. My nose wrinkled as it was assailed by the assorted odours of plain stew, baking bread, leather, hay, sheep, dog, tallow, herbs, strong medicaments and rather smelly monks, and my eyes stung with tiredness.

Peter and Paul laid my knight carefully on one of the pallets and covered him with a woollen blanket, twittering and muttering to each other as they did so; then the taller one indicated the other pallet.

'Rest there, traveller, while we attend to your master and prepare supper.'

I had meant to stay awake, to watch that they were careful of my knight, to return with food to the others, but as soon as my head touched the pillow, rustling with lavender, rosemary and thyme, I was asleep.

In the morning I woke guiltily, aware that I had overslept, vaguely remembering that I had woken briefly to drink a bowl of thick broth, then had fallen asleep again almost immediately. Aware, too, that I had neglected my friends in the barn shamefully, for I had not returned as promised.

Sunlight streamed in dusty bars through the open doorway beyond my bed, and the fat monk was sweeping out the dust into the yard, making the sunlight dance with motes that climbed and fell, twisted and turned like tiny peasants celebrating a miniature feast day. There was music too, for somewhere I heard the soft clucking of hens and the monk was humming through his nose, a little bass tune that repeated itself, then paused and was repeated in a higher key. It was soothing and yet somehow disturbing, as though it perhaps required a respect that lying lazing on a bed was not according it, so I jumped up. The broom fell with a clatter—a perfectly ordinary broom used for sweeping and nothing else, I was glad to see—and the little monk came fussing up, inquiring whether I had slept well and pouring me a mug of goat's milk and handing me a heel of bread.

Miming my thanks, I took these over to see the knight. It seemed he slept, though his breathing was ragged and he frowned a little. They had stripped him down to his shirt, and the discarded spotty mail lay to one side; his face had been cleaned up, to re-dress the head wound, and though now much of his head was covered with the bandage, over his brow a few springy curls escaped, russet as beech leaves, and looking curiously soft. Wondering a little, for lambs' coats look soft as down and are wiry instead, I stretched out a hand and lifted a strand, where it curled round my fingers like a living thing; soft, yes, but with a strength and hold I had not anticipated. It gave me a curious delight to touch, and next I laid a finger on one frowning brow and traced the curve to its outer edge. The skin beneath was burning hot, and under his high cheekbones the flesh was drawn in, hollowed, and a dark red stubble shadowed his chin.

I drew back as the monk approached, to take the empty mug from my hand.

'It is a pity you are dumb, poor creature, else could you tell us this knight's pedigree and destination. Brother Peter and I are most worried about his condition, indeed we are, and fear that he needs better care than we can provide in our humble quarters.' He fussed round the patient, laying a hand on his forehead, shaking his own head, drawing the coverlets higher. 'Not good, not good at all. We are used to sheep of course, sheep in a fever we can deal with, but this man needs Brother Infirmarar.

'Now, there is water to wash yourself; we prefer those who relieve themselves to go to the corner of the yard, where we have a trench. Waste products attract flies; flies lay maggots; maggots pester sheep. Simple enough if one uses logic . . .'

I washed my hands, wiped my mouth and escaped from his chatter to the yard. From thence, affecting an unconcern I did not feel, I sauntered over to the barn. The sheep were back in the fields, the pens were empty, save for one limping ewe, and there was no sign of Brother Peter or the dogs. I rounded the corner to the open front of the barn.

'Good morning,' I said heartily. 'Ready for some breakfast?'

'What happened to supper?' said Corby.

They let me suffer and apologize for fully two minutes before Snowy took pity and explained that 'the thin one' had been over with a handful of oats for horse and donkey and some scraps for Moglet.

'And two eggs,' said Corby, 'for me. Broken eggs, and not of the freshest. Still, they were better than nothing.' And he glared at me.

'Then this morning,' said Moglet, 'I had goat's milk. And more scraps.'

I lifted the straw from Puddy and Pisky. The latter was languidly waving his tail and Puddy had a moth's wing sticking from the corner of his mouth.

'I see you two are all right,' I said.

'Fair,' said Puddy. 'Fair.'

'Likewise,' bubbled Pisky. 'A nice little sliver of moth . . . But you left me where I couldn't see, couldn't see, and you know how important it is to me to have a good view. A fish hasn't much choice, you know, shut up like a genie in a bottle—'

'A what?'

But he didn't reply, and went on grumbling till I explained that the straw was to keep his water temperate.

'And how is the knight?' asked Snowy. 'Any better?'

I described his condition as best I could.

'I feared as much. I have seen that gasp of the breath in man before, and it can be grave.'

'I just wish there were something I could do: I feel so helpless . . .'

'We could do,' corrected Snowy, gently. 'We are all in this together, for the present, anyway.'

'Yes,' I said. 'Yes, of course.' I must stop thinking of him as my knight, because he wasn't and never would be. And what would I, ugly, deformed Thing, want with a knight? And if I had one, what would I do with him? Tie him down to a bed or something forever, fasten his legs and arms down tight, just so I could get that strangely exciting feeling curling his hair around my grubby little fingers? The idea was ridiculous, and yet lying there he had seemed so vulnerable, so nice, so—

'Someone coming,' warned Moglet.

I peered round the corner of the barn: Brother Peter was striding down the nearest field, his gown flapping vigorously against his thin shanks, the two sheepdogs slinking at his heels.

He saw me and waved. 'How is our patient, the gallant knight? Such a well-set-up young man! Such strong shoulders, and a fine pair of . . . And his hair: my dear, such an unusual colour . . . Ah well.'

I shook my head, remembering in time I was supposed to be dumb.

'No better? I feared not. And, much as I—as we—would like to keep him longer, I think it best if we take him up to the Priory.'

I manifested alarm.

'Much better for him, much better. He will have a comfortable bed in the infirmary, where they have salves and ointments and infusions and draughts which will go a long way towards reducing the fever and healing his head.

'Come, now, we shall go and consult with Brother Paul: we always decide things together.'

My—our—knight was worse, I could see that. The two monks consulted in a corner, a high mutter, a deep rumble, bobbing their heads up and down like ducks' tails, but at last they came to agreement.

'He must be taken to the Priory,' said Brother Paul.

'So pack up his belongings,' said Brother Peter. 'We shall harness Brother Donkey to the cart, and perhaps you might ride your white nag—strange animal that: never seen hooves like that on a horse before—or perhaps you may prefer to walk: he does not look overly strong.'

'It is not far,' added Brother Paul. 'You will be there before nightfall.'

94

'Brother Paul will stay behind with the sheep,' explained Brother Peter. 'Sheep must be brought down before dark. Foxes; wolves; thieves after a nice piece of mutton, for all it is a hanging offence . . .'

'May the Lord forgive them.' Brother Paul cast his eyes upwards. 'And may we remember that He shared His last hours with such . . .'

'Amen, amen,' intoned Brother Peter.

They were like two turtledoves, bowing and cooing to one another.

The two-wheeled cart was harnessed to the protesting donkey and a bed of bracken prepared. The two monks carried out the poor knight, bandaged head bobbing, and laid him carefully down, padding him round with blankets to stop him from rolling. I added Pisky's bowl, Moglet and Corby to the load, keeping Puddy in my pocket, and balanced Snowy on on side with our wicker carrier, the other the knight's pack, covering all with the knight's mail, now rustier than ever, for I thought it better if I tried to walk.

The day was fair enough, but a rising wind from the west scattered leaves about our feet and blew Moglet's fur the wrong way, and I was anxious lest it rain before we reached our destination. The way was uphill at the beginning and I found it hard going, but Brother Peter strode ahead, seeming almost to pull the cart himself plus the donkey, for the latter was mutinous at first, only cooperating when we reached flatter countryside and Brother Peter remembered the slices of raw turnip Brother Paul had put in his pocket, which was fed to the happier animal at appropriate intervals. The sky darkened early, and as we passed through the first of two small villages, large drops of rain plopped on my cloak. For a hopeful moment I thought we might stop and shelter but Brother Peter strode on, only stopping to cover the knight (who looked the worse for his jolting and bumping) with his cloak, under which crept Moglet and Corby as well.

Then it started to pour down in earnest: my cloak offered me some protection, but the poor monk was soaked in minutes and his sandals squelched and his robe dripped, and so did the end of his beaky nose. I pulled the end of the cloak over the knight's face, for he was getting rustier than ever, and I could see a stain of dark blood on his bandages. The donkey now stepped up his pace without bribery and we staggered and stumbled and rattled over tracks that were rapidly becoming impassable. At last, at long last, I saw through the drifting curtain of rain a lantern, a dim, twinkling light suspended over a pair of high, closed wooden gates. Away to either side stretched stone walls: Brother Peter lifted his staff and beat at the gates, the while hailing in his loud voice.

There was a shuffling, another voice raised in query, a drawing of bolts, a swinging back of one of the gates, and suddenly we were in a courtyard full of scurrying welcome . . .

Illuminations

'COME ALONG now,' said a not unkindly voice, as Brother
Matthew came into the stable carrying a large binding strap.
'You and your animals will be eating us out of priory and
refectory soon: how about taking your nag out to eat fresh
grass instead of our precious hay, and bringing back some
kindling in this strap to set against your keep?'

Brother Matthew was one of the younger brethren, lay
brothers they were called, who were mainly concerned with
the physical work of the Priory of St Augustine. Shared with
Brother Mark it was his concern to care for the stock and the
provision of wood for the fires. They kept two heavy draught
horses, five cows, three goats and a billy, two pigs for fattening
and one for farrowing, and about three dozen hens, some
of which, the poor layers, would be eaten during the winter.
These two monks also kept the stables and courtyard clean,
and the harness and tack oiled and mended, and this all
between their numerous calls to prayer, signalled by the little
bell in the chapel. I had been told that all the brothers,
whatever their tasks, and all visitors, which included me, were
expected to attend prayers three times a day—morning, noon
and night, and the ordained monks those in between as well.

His request wasn't unreasonable and I got to my feet,
yawning and shivering a little in the cold morning air that
was rushing, unnecessarily fast, through the open door and
dissipating the nice fug we had built up during the night. We
were in a stable along the western side of the courtyard, a small
one obviously for donkeys or ponies, for the stalls were not big
enough for the larger horses. The mangers contained loose

hay, more bales of it were stacked in a corner, and there was a comfortable layer of straw on the floor which I had not had to muck out, for I had asked Snowy and Moglet to please use the midden corner in the courtyard, and had persuaded Corby to turn his tail over one particular spot, which he usually remembered. If Puddy did anything I didn't find it, for he was eating less now and sleeping more, it being near winter-sleep for him, and of course the snails took care of Pisky.

I think it rather surprised Brother Mark the first time I escorted Snowy and Moglet over to evacuate themselves and empty out my bucket and wash it out, for he called Brother Matthew and they came over afterwards and asked me how I trained my animals. Of course I did not answer but merely shrugged my shoulders, for Brother Peter before he had returned to Brother Paul had told them all that I was dumb, as he truly believed of course.

Even had I not been the knight's servant, I believe they would still have treated me with kindness, for they believed, I think, that in strangers and the lost and afflicted they received their own God, who by all accounts was stern but kind. Sometimes, in the words they used in prayer, I thought I caught an echo of something I should remember, but was never quite sure. One thing I did find special was the chanting of the monks: a sort of extension of the humming of Brother Paul at the shieling, it had its own sort of magic. Sometimes in the night I would wake and hear them and the sound always made me comfortable and secure; when I was in the chapel, what with the dancing of the tallow dips and the question/answer of the chants, it made me feel as if I always wanted to be good and kind, and I usually managed to find something special for the others as a consequence: a bigger share of my supper for Moglet, some oats filched from the big horses for Snowy.

The knight was housed in the Infirmary, on the opposite side of the courtyard from the gateway, and one floor up. When we had arrived I had been allowed to carry up his pack and mail and see him safely bestowed on a raised pallet, and water and clean linen brought, before I was firmly shooed away to where I belonged: in the stable with the animals. I was allowed upstairs once daily to see my master, and I could see he was profiting from their care, for after a couple of anxious days when his bedside was always attended by a couple of the brothers praying, his fever abated slowly and—although the brothers had kept him largely unaware of what went on around him, aided I suspect by Brother Infirmarar's poppy-juice—he was nevertheless much better. On my brief visits, more to do me good than my master, I suspect, I was supposed to contribute to his recovery: at first I had not known what was expected of me and just watched as Brother Infirmarar sank to his knees by the unconscious man's bed, folded his hands, bowed his head and began to mutter in a foreign language. It was only after he had put out an impatient hand to tug me down beside him that I realized that I, too, must bow my head, fold my hands and pray. This last wasn't so difficult after all, for as I was supposed to be dumb I didn't have to say anything.

Once the knight was safely in the monks' care, why didn't we leave and continue our journey? One reason, I suppose, was that the brothers believed me his servant, the animals his pets. That would not have stopped us slipping away unnoticed while they were all in chapel, of course, but there was another, stronger reason why we did not leave him: it just never occurred to us that he was not part of the team. We would wait till he was better and go on together. It may not have been in any of their minds, of course, but they never said anything and I never asked: perhaps it was only that I was being selfish . . .

I think the monks all became a little wary of me, because of the way I could apparently manage my friends without words of command, and I even caught Brother Mark crossing himself one morning surreptitiously after I had forgotten to bring back the water bucket and asked Snowy to bring it back on his return. Because of this, perhaps, they tended to leave us alone, and this started me thinking of my curious position within our group, and the difficulties this posed in the world of man. I could communicate with my friends and some of the lesser beasts—the pigs and the donkey in our village, migrating birds—but though I understood human language I could only answer in what the knight had rightly called 'scribble', on that awful day when he had called me a hobgoblin. And I didn't know how to correct this. I knew the words, understood the inflections, appreciated the intonations, but still my words came out like accidentally spilling a bag of dried peas: all over the place. To get any further—and especially to be able to explain things to the knight, I realized guiltily—I should need to practise words properly: everyone wasn't as clever as Mushroom Tom, who had lived so long away from people that the language of nature was more real to him.

One afternoon when, having collected a large bundle of wood in the morning and helped with mucking-out the other stables, I was free and bored and playing a game of tag in the courtyard with Moglet, who was bored too, I heard my name—or rather what the monks called me: 'Boy!'—called from an upstairs window. That was another thing: the monks accepted my hunched back, my mask, my silence, but I would not have been allowed within the Priory if they had known I was female—or perhaps they guessed but were pretending not to know. After all, if I wished to relieve myself I had to squat, not having one of the useful pipes that men were equipped with, that allowed them to stand and spray all over the place for this most necessary of functions, and I couldn't be sure no one had seen me. I remember, when first I had noted this distinct advantage that males had, I felt envious; then I had thought perhaps it was more of a disadvantage, for one had to find somewhere to put it, to tuck it away, and I had finally come to the conclusion that being a female was probably tidier.

'Hist! Boy . . .' The voice came again, louder this time, and I looked up towards the library, which was on the upper floor to the left. The shutters were open at the end nearest the gateway and a youth leant out, his sandy hair catching the last gleams of the misty sun.

I nearly said 'Hello!' back again because he had a nice, cheerful face, but I waved instead and Moglet came to wipe her dusty fur clean on my ankles.

'Doing anything special?' asked Cheerful Face.

I shook my head and picked up Moglet, wary of an extra chore.

He glanced around, saw the courtyard was empty but for us two. 'Hang on a minute: I've a favour to ask.' The head disappeared, but a moment later it reappeared, attached to a small wiry body clad in the usual brown, rope-girdled sack, at the bottom of a small stairway set in the wall at the corner of the courtyard. 'Come up for a moment, if you can spare the time—please, that is?' It was the honest smile as well as the words that made me decide: I put Moglet down, but the young Brother held out his hand. 'Please bring your little cat: I like them.'

'It's all right,' said Moglet. 'He means it. He looks as if he has a comfortable lap. And perhaps milk . . .'

I followed the boy up the stairs, Moglet trotting just ahead of me.

She was disappointed about the milk, but there was a sliver of cheese. The room in which we found ourselves was obviously an annexe to the library proper, for an archway filled by a curtain separated it from the dusty main room, and here was a cheerful brazier burning, two candles, a large sloping desk, a table and two stools. On the table were quills, inks, brushes and tiny pots of different coloured liquids, tightly stoppered. On the desk was a partly written manuscript.

The boy followed my gaze. 'That's Brother John's work: he has an ague at the moment so I'm on my own. I'm his apprentice and I have to finish the script on that page, but apart from the gilding I'm not yet allowed to make the illustrations. I'm to practise on these scraps of vellum— see?—and while I'm pretty good on leaves and flowers, I've had very little practice on animals. That's why I'd like to borrow your little cat—such splendid colours she is, all the bars and stripes and splotches of autumn woods—that is, if you could persuade her to sit still for a little while? I hear you're very good with animals,' and he smiled ingenuously. 'If you could manage to come two or three times—just before dusk is the best time, they leave me alone then—I could get some good sketches done. Please?'

I spoke to Moglet, who was agreeable so long as there was a tit-bit and she could pose near the fire.

'She says yes,' I translated. 'For a piece of cheese or somesuch and a share of the fire for each sitting,' and it was only when I saw the boy's eyes round with shock that I realized I had broken my vow of silence.

'They told me you were dumb,' he said after a moment,

101

fiddling with a brush, but as he didn't rush away to tell on me or shout for help, I made up my mind to trust him and, speaking very slowly, carefully, weighing each word, I explained.

'I-am-not-dumb. I-have-been-with-my-friends-so-long-I-find-it . . . it . . .' I wavered.

'Difficult,' he supplied.

'Dif-fi-cult-to-speak-man-talk.' I stopped.

But he had understood. 'You know the words: it's just practice, I suspect. You're not deaf, are you?' I shook my head. 'Good. And you can understand what I say?' I nodded. 'Fine! Tell you what: I'll draw little cat—what's her name? Such a pretty little thing . . .'

She bridled visibly, and the tip of her tail vibrated. 'Nice man . . .'

'Moglet,' I said.

'Moglet it is, then,' and he bent to tickle her just behind her ears. 'And if you can tell her what I would like her to do: stand, sit, lie down—you know—at the same time as I'm drawing her, I'll teach you to talk properly. How's that?'

I turned a somersault (easy with my humped back) and then had a sudden thought. 'Keep-it-a-secret?'

'Of course! Half the fun!'

As it turned out, the fact that it took almost a month for our Rusty Knight to be anywhere near ready to continue the journey was a blessing in disguise, for in those four weeks Brother Jude-the-Less as he was called grew amazingly proficient at drawing cats, birds, toads and fish and my hands and feet (he was delicate enough not to ask me to remove my mask once I had explained) and I—I found I could speak human-talk. Not all at once, not every time, but day by day it grew easier to express myself so that others could understand. I suppose the most difficult was the radical switch from thought-pictures to word-symbols to describe the same thing. Apart from the more primitive sounds that normally expressed fear, pain, hate or desire, my animal friends usually presented most of their thoughts in visual gradations of fur, feathers, scales and so forth, in size and texture of touch, position of limbs and tail, attitude, flicker of eyes and movement of whiskers, ears or mouth. Apart from that, when it was less a

102

matter of immediate communication than of thought, they sent vibrations in the form of pictures into one's mind, and I had become adept at receiving messages from their various eye levels, even through the distortion that Pisky's waterbound existence gave him.

At first I thought the human way of expressing oneself a clumsy and longwinded one, especially as people didn't always say what they really meant, but gradually I became used to it. I still sometimes got the order of words wrong, or missed out the, to me, unessential ones, but soon I found I could carry on a reasonable conversation with Brother Jude (the Less). We were undisturbed at our lessons because I would only creep back and forth by way of the side stair when the coast was clear, and at that time the monks were sitting down to break their daily fast before the first of the three evening prayer sessions. Brother Jude, being a lay brother, had a meal in the middle of the day and a snack in the evening.

I still performed my daily tasks of taking Snowy out to graze—although fresh grass was getting more difficult to find—fetching water, helping clean out the stables and sweep the courtyard, and I paid my daily visit to the Rusty Knight. By now the fever was gone, the gash on his forehead had healed and he was all cleaned up and presentable. They had bandaged his ribs as well and these, together with his ragged breathing, appeared to be mending. He was often awake now when I went to visit him, but there was a blank look in his eyes as though he were still dreaming and he obviously didn't recognize me, nor could he yet answer coherently the questions Brother Infirmarar or his assistant put to him.

But one day I had to face reality.

That day he was awake when I paid my visit, and not only awake but sensible and he recognized me.

'Sit down,' he said. 'There, on that stool. No, bring it nearer. I don't want the whole world to hear our conversation.'

We were chaperoned, but only by old Brother Timothy, who was deaf as a blue-eyed cat and spent most of his days nodding away happily in a corner. Reluctantly I turned back to my inquisitor. Now that he was better and cleaned up and tidy I saw him properly for the first time, and I am afraid I ignored his first few words because I was listening to the lilt of them rather than the meaning.

'. . . remember it all. The monks have told me how I was brought here, but why did you give them the impression you were my servant?'

'I didn't: they just assumed it. They think I am dumb.' Between the words I was studying his face. His hair curled as I remembered it, the colour almost that dull red of hedgerow hips.

'How could you possibly be dumb, when I remember that torrent of words with which you and—and your animals overwhelmed me? I do recall some animals?'

'Yes. They are my friends. We are travelling together.' He has a broad, high brow, I thought, and his dark eyebrows are straight when he frowns and a lovely curve when he doesn't—

'And where do you travel?'

'To find the answers to our problems . . .' He is very pale still, and his cheeks hollow beneath the bones. He has a very firm chin—

Brother Timothy stirred from his stool and put a fresh piece of peat on the brazier, nodding and smiling over at us.

The knight lowered his voice. 'Speak softly, now . . . What problems have you?'

'You see me: you called me hobgoblin, remember?' He had a firm mouth, too, under that curling moustache, but it looked as though it would curve upwards and transform his face if he smiled. 'The others are deformed too. We seek release from this bondage.'

'But surely if you are deformed there is no cure?'

'Not deformed by nature, by a spell.' His eyes were brown like peaty water, yet clear and sparkling too.

'A spell! Then—' The curtain at the end of the Infirmary opened and another of the brothers entered, bearing a steaming bowl. 'Quiet, now. I'll ask for you tomorrow, earlier maybe. Now, go!' I turned away but his hand shot out and caught my wrist. 'Do you really talk with your animals, as the monks say? And what is your name?'

I nodded. 'We do talk, and—and the only name I know is "Thing" . . .'

Suddenly he grinned: it made him look five years younger. 'Perhaps you aren't so daft after all . . .'

I reported back to the others.

'We can go, then, now he's better?' said Corby.

'We could, I suppose,' I said slowly. 'But I had hoped . . .'

'That he would join us,' said Snowy softly. 'I think—I think we should give him the choice. You would be better with an escort, my little wandering ones. You will do well enough here for the time being . . .'

This left me wondering how long the white horse would remain with us if the knight joined us. We still had no firm destination, but that we were on the right path towards the owner of the pebbles I had no doubt. Since the witch's death our pains and cramps had been better, and once we had headed in the general direction of the southwest they had eased even more. Pisky was able to eat a little more, Corby's crippled wing stretched farther, Moglet's paw was less tender, Puddy complained less of headaches and I was standing at least an inch more upright, with only a stab now and again, as if I were pulling at stitched leather.

Out of, perhaps, a general feeling of optimism and inner gratefulness for the knight's recovery, I offered to comb out the tangles in Snowy's tail and mane. He was looking much sleeker and fatter since we came to the Priory, and he seemed calmer and less sad, so I thought it would be nice if he had to leave us sometime that he should do it looking tidy as well. When I offered he seemed to be surprised, and glanced round at his tail as if expecting it to be immaculate, then shook his head ruefully.

'You are reminding me that I have neglected myself . . . If you please, youngling; I would deem it a favour.' He tended to talk like that, rather formally, but I supposed he had probably lived among courtly people at one time. A teasing thought about talking and speech touched my mind for a moment but was gone before I could identify it, so I started on Snowy's tail: burrs, tangles, mud, nasty bits and all. It took the rest of the evening, but by yawning-time it was sleek, curled and oiled like even the best horses in our village had been—though they had been beribboned as well—for the feasts of Beltane or Lugnosa.

'I'll do the rest tomorrow,' I promised, as I blew out the lantern and settled to sleep, my head on his comforting flank, Moglet on my lap, Corby on his beam, Puddy and Pisky tucked up in their hay. My last thought was of the morrow, and seeing my—our—knight again . . .

But when I finally reached the Infirmary it was to disappointment. The knight was propped up in bed, but the Prior was there on a courtesy visit with his chaplain, and I was only allowed to join dumbly in the prayers before being dismissed. I did try to creep back later but Brother Matthew caught me and set me to replaiting and lashing some frayed rope-ends, which was a boring task that took till supper, which I always collected from the kitchen after six o'clock prayers. That evening, I remember, it was cold salt pork and black bread and, for once, a mug of ale, which I found sour but warming. Because of the pork, fatty from fingers, I had to go and rinse my hands at the well before starting on Snowy's mane with my rather battered comb. I made him lie down and leant against his warm flank, pulling all the mane over to my side. It had incredibly long, soft, silky hair and as I gradually worked from withers to ears it began to shine like a rippling curtain. I only had to cut out a couple of the really tangled bits, and he began to look beautiful.

'You should take more care,' I said, as I reached his ears. 'It was a shame to get it all tangled like that. Now, just your forelock—What's that?' For as I lifted the hair from his forehead my hand touched a knobbled lump in the centre and he started violently away, rising to his knees and giving a little whinny of pain. I patted his neck. 'Poor old fellow! Did someone give you a bad knock, then? I'll be gentle, I promise . . .' But he pulled his head away. 'Come on,' I urged. 'It won't hurt, I swear, and you look so—so beautiful now, almost like a faery horse—'

Snowy rose to his feet, and all at once he seemed to grow twice as large, and his hide shone like silver in the flickering lamplight.

'Oh wise young maid, wise for all your tattered clothes and crouched back—you have discovered what all others could not see . . .' He tossed back his forelock and stamped dainty cloven hooves on the straw. 'See, maid; see, O wandering ones! See, and marvel, for this is probably the only time you will witness such again!'

I stared at the jagged coil of gold on his forehead, curled like a shell and rising perhaps an inch from the bone.

'Trotters and swill!' I breathed, my reverence in direct contrast to the words. 'A unicorn!'

At these words the others, hitherto in disarray because of our jumping up and down, crept closer and gazed up at Snowy.

'A unicorn!' breathed Moglet. 'Magic!'

'Should have known,' muttered Corby. 'Evening, Your Gracefulness . . .'

'A unicorn without a horn,' mused Puddy. 'Unusual . . . Cloven hooves: obvious when you think about it.'

'Want-to-see, want-to-look; can't see a thing down here. Want-to-see, want-to-look!' So I lifted Pisky's bowl to a level with Snowy's head. 'Hmm . . . My grandfather's cousin mentioned unicorns, but I don't see much more than a white horse here . . .'

'And that is all I am now,' said Snowy quietly. 'My precious horn is gone by the sorcery of a witch—your Mistress, little maid. You tell me she is dead and so there is no hope for me but to travel back to my once-kin and try to end my days, my now mortal days, in peace.'

'But how?' I asked. 'Why? And can't you grow another?'

'The how and the why I will tell you another time, perhaps. Suffice it for now to tell you that the spell is unbreakable, as far as I know. Once, a drop of dragon's blood, freely given, could reverse the spell, but there are no dragons any more that I know of. I had hoped . . .' He hesitated.

'Yes?' I encouraged.

'I thought maybe a wise man, a magician, could find a solution. There was one such, The Ancient, who lived the way we travel. But he must be dead a hundred years since . . . Then, when I heard your story, knew you had been cursed by the same witch, I had thought that some way we were bound together, might even find the answers—'

'Yes!' I almost shouted. 'I am sure now there is someone, something that can help us all. Maybe not the immediate answer right away, but at least an indication of our next move . . . Don't give up on us, Snowy dear: we need you!

Er . . . Should we call you something more formal now?'

'Snowy will do,' and his voice was gentle. 'My secret name is not for you, I'm afraid.'

'Well, Snowy then: where do your kin live?'

'The last I heard, they too were in the southwest, in the forests of the Old Land.'

'A double reason for coming our way! Please . . .'

For a moment the unicorn-without-a-horn laid his cheek against mine.

'You are very convincing, little maid. Very well: I will stay with you all for as long as you need me . . .'

I realized afterwards that I should have been quicker to recognize our unicorn for something special, even if not for what he was, for of course there had been that question of words and language that had been nagging me. I had become so used to only communicating with my friends, and they with me, that we had all forgotten that talk across different species was unusual; of course most birds could speak with one another, gull, owl or sparrow, but they did not communicate, except in the most superficial way, with felines, reptiles and fish and the same applied to the others, and of course humans were special: it took a long time to work out what they meant, even if you were one yourself.

We five had almost evolved our own language and were so self-orientated that it had never occurred to us to question how easy it had been to understand, and be understood by, the white horse. Of course, coming across him in a moment of crisis had meant less formality, but now that we had been formally introduced, as it were, I understood why we had always felt so safe with him and why his manners and way of speaking sometimes sounded so old-fashioned: magic ones couldn't be expected to talk slang like we did.

Once again I was looking forward to my meeting with the knight, for there was now lots to tell him, but once again I was disappointed. For the second time it was other visitors, dumb attendance, lots of prayer, but on the next day we had the Infirmary to ourselves and he once more indicated that I should bring a stool close in case someone came in unexpectedly.

'Now,' he said purposefully. He was propped up against high pillows, had on a clean linen shift open at the neck, and a little bulge-ended cross rested on a chain around his throat. 'Now . . .' he began again, perhaps unnerved by my intent gaze. His skin was still pale but now there was a faint tinge of colour under the high cheekbones and his moustache was jauntier, the ends not drooping towards the corners of his mouth as it had before. No bandages now marred his head and a shaft of sun lit his russet curls.

'What are you staring at?' He glared at me.

'You,' I said. 'Very gratifying. Rather like picking up a stone and finding it an egg. Are you feeling better?' I had been practising my words, and they were coming out beautifully, though perhaps not exactly as planned: sometimes the thoughts better unsaid were coming out with the politenesses.

He had the sort of face that could scowl or smile, harden or become tender as if the expression had never been used before—

'I want an explanation,' he said and folded his arms. 'Begin.'

'Where?'

'At the beginning of course, er . . . Thingummyjig.'

I had a new name: I was delighted, and did not attempt to enlighten him.

'Right,' I said. 'Once upon a time there were five of us living with a witch . . .' It took some time to tell it properly, but when I finished he was staring at me as if he could not believe his ears.

'Take off that mask, Thingumabob,' he commanded.

I wriggled: another name! 'No,' I said.

'Oh—please, then?'

'No,' I said again, and explained why.

He gazed at me broodingly. 'Shame,' he said at last. 'Shame . . .'

'I don't mind,' I said, which wasn't exactly the truth. 'But I think I would rather have known all along that I was ugly than have been surprised into it. Disconcerting, it was.' That was a good word, and I said it again to make sure it came out right a second time, and then explained to him how Brother Jude (the Less) had been teaching me to speak properly. He was impressed, I could tell, because he stroked his moustache and under his hand I saw his lips twitch a little.

109

'And where do you go now?'

'To find the owner of the pebbles, of course: this is mine, see?' and I pulled up my jerkin.

'Put it away,' he said hurriedly, and went quite red. 'You shouldn't—never mind.'

'You mean it's a secret?'

'Very. Don't do that again.'

'But I just wanted to show—'

'All right! Enough . . . Just don't go—displaying—it like that again. Understand?'

I didn't, but I nodded wisely. 'Are you coming with us, then?'

'With you . . . ?' He was plainly at a loss.

'Well, we came together, so we'd better leave the same way, I suppose, or the monks will think it rather funny.'

'Oh. Yes. Of course.'

'But I didn't mean just the leaving bit, I meant about coming with us to find a magician first. It's obvious you are also under some spell or other too, with that rusty armour and broken sword—'

'Nonsense!' he shouted. Really shouted, so that I fell off the stool in surprise and ended up on the floor. He glared at me again. 'Nothing of the sort!'

The curtains at the end of the Infirmary parted and Brother Infirmarar came rushing in. 'You called, Brother Knight, you called? You are worse? Dearie, dearie me: too much excitement, I fear. Your servant must return to the stables, but before that we shall pray together, and then I will bleed you . . .'

I reported back despondently to the others, but Snowy comforted me.

'You did your best. Don't forget that we shall be leaving together and he may well change his mind once we are on the road . . .'

And so it was that, some five days later in the Moon of Frost, we seven were assembled at the gates of the Priory. Snowy was loaded with our gear and the knight's, the animals all in or on my wicker carrier. The knight and I were on foot. The Brothers came to wish us 'God-speed', and Brother Jude (the Less) even

110

gave me an affectionate hug, at which Brothers Matthew and Mark looked suitably scandalized. We were provisioned for three days and I saw the knight hand over a suitable 'donation' to the Head Prior, for of course they would not charge for their charity to us. The size of the gift occasioned much bowing of heads, folding of hands and the beginning of what looked like another prayer session, but we didn't wait for the end because I nudged Snowy and we moved away, the knight following.

'Looks like snow,' said Corby, and ruffled his feathers against the cold.

gave me an affectionate hug, at which Brother Matthew and
Mark looked suitably scandalised. We were promised, for
three days and I saw the knight hand over a suitable donation
to the Head Prior, for of course they would not share bed or
head, though I knew that for the asking ... I think I nodded like
another prayer-session, but we didn't wait for the end because I
nodded snow, and ...

THE GATHERING: ONE, TWO, THREE, FOUR, FIVE, SIX, SEVEN

Crossroads

WE HAD our first confrontation that very evening.

We had walked due south from the Priory, because Snowy
said there was a reasonable road some couple of leagues away
that was heading in the right direction. At first the knight
strode ahead, scornful of our slow pace, but after the third stop
he made for us I could see he was still not as strong as he
thought. He leant against a tree, ostensibly being very patient
and forbearing of our tardiness, but I could see the beads of
sweat on his forehead. Somehow I knew that his pride was a
very big thing in him, and if necessary I should have to pretend
sometimes to give him an excuse to indulge his weakness—

Another knight in another time, a woman feigning fatigue to
hide his convalescent wound, an uncomprehending child who
could run forever—

I shook my head, and the vision faded.

'I'm sorry we're so slow,' I said. 'But poor old Snowy is
laden down and I've got much shorter legs than you. It was
kind of you to wait.'

He shrugged. 'Doesn't matter. But the days grow shorter:
perhaps we should look for a night's shelter soon.'

I snatched at his suggestion. 'Snowy says there is a ruined
church some half-league away: most of the walls are standing
and Puddy says it will be fine.'

He scowled. 'Which is Puddy, for God's sake? A toad! He
says, the horse says ... Never mind. Lead on then, but it had
better be there!' and he gave Snowy a gentle slap on the rump. I
hoped he didn't mind: I had forgotten to tell the knight he was
magic.

The church had three walls left, but only a scrap of roofing, in the corner nearest where a desecrated altar still stood. The knight stood in the ruined nave and stared upwards to where a trefoil window, framed in still-green ivy, showed us the last of a reddening sun.

'Vandals,' he muttered. 'Barbarians.'

Again my mind gave a sudden jump: soldiers in armour; horses, spears, swords; long hair, beards, distant shouting; a hiding place—Gone.

'What is there to eat?' demanded the knight, but did not wait for an answer, lifting his pack and my baggage from Snowy's back. 'How about a fire, Thingummy, while I make this fellow more comfortable . . .' and I crept to the roofed corner and Corby brought me sticks. The knight rubbed Snowy down with a wisp or two of dried grasses, then gave him a handful of oats from the provisions sack. 'There you are, old lad: there's still grass between the stones, and a dew-pond over there . . .'

We ate; cold lamb, rye bread and cheese, and shared a flagon of ale. The empty jar would be useful for water, in case we were away from a supply, so I packed it with our things: the knight had a proper one in his pack, but just in case he decided—But I would not think about things like that.

The fire burned brightly and we had no need of the lantern the Brothers had so thoughtfully provided.

'This is cosy,' I said, throwing the rest of the crumbs to Corby and taking Moglet on my lap, where she continued to clean lamb-fat from her whiskers. 'Find something to eat, Puddy?'

His throat moved up and down towards the roof of his mouth, which was a toad's way of toothless chewing. 'Would you believe gnats? It's sheltered here: fine tomorrow, too.'

I translated the last bit to the knight, and added that Snowy had said we were free from danger for the time being.

'I don't believe all that falderal about speaking with animals,' said the knight, crossly. 'None of you said a word just then: nobody even moved. I think you are just making it all up.'

Patiently I explained about thought-messages, about the niceties of body-communication, but obviously my words were not enough.

113

'Prove it! Make them do things . . .'

'They're not performing animals!'

'I never said they were!' He was getting crosser by the minute: then he sighed and shook his head. 'Sorry, Thingummybob—You must have some other name than that?'

I looked at the fire, and shrugged. 'I've known no other, ever since I can remember.' I didn't want to add that it was just 'Thing', because I rather liked the way he added bits like 'ummy' and 'ummybob' at the end: it made it more personal between him and me. And nice.

There was a nudge on my chest. 'If he wants some sort of proof,' sighed Moglet plaintively, 'I don't mind chasing my tail, or something like that . . .'

'Count me in,' said Corby and Puddy and Pisky, one after the other, for I had been thinking to them what the knight had been saying, even while we were talking, and that hadn't been easy.

'All right, Sir Knight,' I said. 'My friends have volunteered to prove that we do communicate. First, here's Pisky. You remember I told you about the pebbles we were burdened with? Well, his is in his mouth so he can't eat properly. See?' And I held up his bowl.

The knight peered closely. 'Won't it come out? No, you did say you'd tried. Poor fish: he won't get much bigger if he doesn't eat. Still, he's a handsome fellow, though, and with a bit more weight to him would be a real beauty. Very imposing fins . . .'

'Shall I ask him to wave them for you? First one, then the other and then his tail?' I took his silence for answer and relayed my request to Pisky, who performed his trick slowly and gracefully, ending with two extra large bubbles. 'Thanks,' I said. 'Now, Puddy dear, forward. I shall ask him to turn around three times and then croak,' I added to the knight. Puddy rather ponderously executed this, and I tickled him under his chin. 'Puddy's pebble gives him headaches,' I added. 'It's in his forehead, as you can see. But we have all felt somewhat better since we started out on our quest. Now, Moglet: her pebble is in her paw—show him, darling—and she

114

can't put much weight on it, but I will ask her to walk backwards three steps and then sit down. Will that do?' I glanced at the knight: his eyebrows were up somewhere near his hairline.

'My turn,' said Corby, as Moglet returned to my lap. 'I'll do the mating-dance if you like.'

'Corby's pebble is in his wing,' I explained, as the crow creaked his way through his ritual, ending with a couple of beak-scrapes on the knight's right boot. 'That's his burden: he can't fly any more.'

By now our audience was goggling. 'All right,' he said slowly. 'I believe you have some hold over these creatures. But how do I know this isn't just something you've taught them, that they wouldn't do the same each time?'

I sighed: he really was a sceptic. 'Well, then,' I said. 'How about you deciding what you want Snowy to do—if you don't mind, dear one? He's a unicorn, by the way, so he understands all speech, even yours. So, just ask him yourself what you want him to do.'

'Unicorns, punycorns,' said the knight. 'Oh well, where's the harm? Here, horse: go over to the west window and find me that piece of wood that's lying underneath and bring it over here for the fire . . .' He obviously thought the whole thing was a joke, but his expression when Snowy laid the wood at his feet was a study. 'All right,' he said at last. 'If you're a unicorn, where's your horn?'

Snowy tossed his head, exposing the golden stump.

'Don't touch it, please,' I warned. 'It still hurts him . . .'

Then the knight did a strange thing: he got to his feet and bowed to the white horse. Taking his broken sword from his pack, he offered it to Snowy, hilt first. 'May my sword, broken or whole, never harm thee or thy kind, O Wondrous One. I offer you my friendship, my respect, my trust . . .'

Snowy bowed his head in return. 'Peace, friend,' he said. 'If I could mend your sword, Knight, I would, but the spell under which you lie is stronger than I, no longer a unicorn, can break.'

I started to translate to the knight, but saw he had understood the gist of Snowy's message.

'What spell?' I asked him.

He frowned and shook his head. (I wished he wouldn't frown so much: he would soon grow two little lines between his eyes if he went on like that.)

'No spell. Misfortune, perhaps. Nothing else . . . Time for bed.'

But that night, and for a while afterwards, he talked in his sleep. During the next few days we made fair progress, thanks to clear days and cloudy nights, which made the weather unseasonably warm. Our Rusty Knight had obviously taken to heart our burdened plight, for he no longer strode ahead but suited his pace to ours and we made at least three leagues a day. He had money, a purse of silver coins, so we were never without food and several times sheltered in villages at night instead of the open. At those times I persuaded him I was happier in the stables with my friends, and everyone accepted me without question as his servant.

In this fashion we made fifty miles or so and it was near The Turn of the Year when we had another confrontation. Somehow, during all those miles together I had persuaded myself that we would continue to travel together, all seven of us, until we found someone to show us how to get rid of our burdens and spells, so I was utterly unprepared when we came to the crossroads.

The road we had been following had been well used, judging by the ruts, wheel-tracks and potholes, but on this particular day we came to another, much larger, going straight as a die north-south, and here the knight stopped.

'Well,' he said. 'It was fun while it lasted, but this is where we part company.'

For a moment I did not understand. 'Part company?' but even as I said the words I realized what he meant, and I felt as if someone had kicked me in the stomach and then pulled out the stuffing.

'Yes. Part company. Our ways lie in different directions henceforward.' He tugged at his moustache. 'I never said I would go all the way with you. Besides, I think your expedition is a waste of time. You're obviously hoping some miracle-man, like the fabled Arthur's Merlin, is sitting waiting for you, just longing to wave his magic wand and solve all your troubles.' He snorted. 'Me, I have more commonplace ideals. I'm going south to the nearest port to cross back to the Frankish lands, where I can easily find work as a mercenary. A few spots of rust on my mail mean nothing: I can afford more armour anytime I choose, and as for swords—'

'A few spots of rust!' I exploded, raging against his departure. 'A few spots! Why, you are covered with it from shoulder to thigh like—like a beech-hedge! And any other armour you buy will be covered the same way in five minutes flat! You can't just get rid of a witch's curse by—by snapping your fingers—' I stopped.

'And how,' he said, his voice nasty, and the scowl more ferocious than ever, 'just how do you know about curses and spells and things? And your answer had better be good, or shall I believe you are in league with the Powers of Darkness yourself!'

I backed away. 'You talked in your sleep . . .'

He flushed angrily. 'And who says you should eavesdrop on a man in his most private moments? Besides, 'twas but dream, no foundation in fact—'

'We all heard you,' I interrupted. 'No help for it. You were shouting. All about a witch and a spurning, and the curses she laid upon you because of it. The rusty armour and the bit about asking the hand in marriage of the ugliest creature in the land. And how it was your father's sword, and—'

'I've heard enough!' he shouted, very red in the face now. 'It's all a pack of lies, the lot of it, and I won't stay to listen to a word more on the subject. Goodbye!' And he snatched his pack from Snowy's back and flung it over his shoulder, before setting off at a determined pace southwards, towards where the smoke of a fair-sized village showed on the horizon.

I ran after him down the road, not thinking, just not wanting to lose him, hoppity-skip-jump down the rutted way till I fell flat on my face, out of breath and crying. With the last of my strength I yelled out: 'And after we saved your life! And learnt to love you . . .' That last bit hadn't meant to come out at all, and I lay where I was and the rebellious tears seeped through my mask and dripped onto the road, where they dried in an instant on the hard-baked clay.

A moment later there was a snuffle and Snowy nudged my

shoulder. 'Don't worry, dear one: I am sure he will think better of it . . .'

'He won't!' I howled. 'He's a pig, and an ungrateful wretch into the bargain!'

Moglet sat on my back and teased at my hair with her claws, but gently. 'Come on, Thing dear, we love you . . .'

'And will go on with you whatever happens,' added Corby.

'Of course. Goes without saying,' said Puddy, from the now lopsided basket on Snowy's back.

'My great-great cousin twice removed said constancy was greatly to be admired,' declared Pisky. 'Don't make salt-drops, Thing dear: my very constitution shrinks from the thought of salt-drops . . . And can you come and straighten me up? I don't want to lose my snails.'

I laughed through my tears. 'Dear friends,' I said, 'you are idiots, and I love you! Who cares about Rusty Knights, anyway?' And we camped just across the road and I made an extra effort to give them a very special midday meal, even scrabbling under leaves to find insects Puddy could share with Pisky and letting Moglet and Corby have one of the pig's feet we had bought the day before. I drank the last of the goat's milk and even doled out a little fresh cheese to the others. By now it was darkening, and I gave Snowy an apple.

'Shall we move on a bit?'

He scrunched contentedly. 'We can camp for the night right here. The night will be fine and we can build a fire without fear of passers-by: the road is empty of strangers.'

I did not really care for the thought of a night in so exposed a position, even with the lattice-shelter of bare trees, but he had never been wrong, so I moved a bit further into the woods and soon had a fine blaze crackling up through the trees and spread my cloak among the fallen leaves, ready to dig a shallow pit if it grew too cold.

Perhaps because I was a little lonely, in spite of the nearness of my friends, perhaps because, although safe, I felt far from home, wherever that was, perhaps just because, I took off my mask and sang a small song, a lonely sort of song that came into my head from nowhere and ran down to my lips and tongue. I sat gazing into the fire, seeing ruined castles, great pits of flame, towering mountains and endless forest, and I sang the song of the traveller far from home. It had no words, just a rising and falling tune that could have rocked a babe to sleep, but in my mind's eye I was in a green and pleasant land; rolling meadows, gentle hills, smoke rising from a little cottage set in the angle between sea and down. In that home there were children, a woman waiting for—

I broke off suddenly as my tune was echoed by a voice from the road. Springing to my feet, my hand snatched at my dagger, but Snowy murmured 'Steady, now!' and through the trees came the Rusty Knight.

Over his shoulder, besides his pack, was slung a sack of provisions, and these he slung to the ground, before remarking: 'Trying to set the forest on fire? I could see your blaze for miles . . . Well, now: how are we all? Had something to eat? If not, I've got—'

'You've come back?' I interrupted, scarce believing, still poised dagger in hand.

'Well . . . Had a think about it, after I left you. Thought of what my mother might have said if she had known I was leaving you parcel of sillies to go forward on your own; thought about my duties as a knight to protect those weaker than myself; thought about my Christian conscience, too. Came to the conclusion I might as well see you to wherever you're going, before I set off on my own travels again. So, here I am again, for the time being at least—Whatever's the matter, Thingy?'

For I had leapt across the fire to embrace him in my enthusiasm, remembered in mid-leap I was still carrying my dagger but not wearing my mask, leapt straight back again to rectify both errors, and then jumped to his side once more, only to find that the idea of hugging him was ridiculous, so just stood there, feeling foolish.

'Welcome back,' I said inadequately. 'I say: how did you know my song?'

'Your song? I first heard that sung in some court or other abroad oh, years ago. It's a Frankish tune; I was going to ask you where you knew it from . . . I've forgotten most of the words, but it is something about a lady waiting in vain for her lover to come back from the wars. I remember the air, though: very pretty.'

119

I couldn't tell him how I knew it, because I didn't know, but there were more important things to think about than a sad tune that teased at memory. He was back, he was coming with us, and the others shuffled closer, Moglet even going so far as to twine round his ankles. He bent to stroke her.

'They all say they're glad to see you back,' I said. I didn't interpret exactly: would he have been as happy with Corby's 'Well, I suppose he's better than nothing: at least he has silver for food', and Puddy's: 'Tell him not to shout all the time: gives me a headache'?

'Have you eaten, Rust—er, Sir Knight?' I asked.

He glanced at me quizzically. 'If we are to become fellow-adventurers 'tis as well for you to know my name, and where I come from . . .'

His name was Connor Cieran O'Connell of Hirland, and he was the younger son of a chief. When his father died, as was the custom, his lands and belongings had been divided equally among his kinsmen, and to Connor's lot had fallen a bag of gold and his father's sword, so, landless, he had set off to seek his fortune. He had travelled a great deal and had earned his knighthood in the Frankish lands, for some 'trifling service' as he put it, to a Duke. Earlier this year he had travelled back to his homeland, found his brother dead, his mother remarried and an unwelcoming cousin the new chief. So he had decided to make his way back to the Duke's court and seek employment in the endless wars that part of the world produced.

'A man's life,' he said, and scowled at me. 'Still, there may have been something in what you were saying about swords and rust and—and spells and things. I'll tell you someday. But for the present we won't mention it again. Right?'

I nodded. 'Don't worry,' I said. 'I know it will turn out all right; I feel it in my heart, Sir Connor.'

He smiled then, and his smile was all I had known it would be.

'I wish I had your faith, little Thingummy, though I think it depends more on hope than experience. And never mind the "Sir": call me Conn.'

'Yes—Conn,' I said shyly.

He glanced around at us all, his eyes sparkling, and pushed up the edges of his moustache with his finger. 'A crippled cat, a creaky crow, a torpid toad, a miserable minnow, an unhorned unicorn and you and me, Thingy: did you ever see a more unlikely combination for high adventure? 'Twould make the angels themselves laugh fit to weep . . .

'Come, my friends: supper and bed, before I change my mind and regret the very day you rescued me!'

But he was smiling again . . .

THE GATHERING

The Turning-point

IT MAY have been the sunlight that awoke him, low enough now at midday on the shortest day to shine momentarily on the neglected heap of pebbles; it may have been his dreams, too intolerable to be longer endured, concerned as they were with happier times, the search for his treasure—whatever it was, the dragon jerked in his sleep, coughed like one strangling, and opened his eyes to stare out over the snow-shrouded hills beyond his cave. He blinked once, twice, the narrow slits of pupil narrowing still further, then their gaze shifted to the piled stones before him, and a great sigh moved the scaly flanks that hung, mere skin upon bone now, behind the sharpened shoulders.

The sun prismed an icicle that hung from the mouth of the cave, and a single drip of water plopped onto the rock beneath. The dragon considered this for a moment, then his forked tongue flickered out of his mouth and he hissed. It took a long time for him to uncoil stiff joints and rise, and the sunlight had shifted away from the mouth of the cave by the time he reached it. Stretching up, his yellow fangs snapped off the icicle at its base and then scrunched the ice between his teeth, swallowing the pieces before they melted so that they rattled and chinked on their way down to his stomach.

He burped uneasily, then suddenly sniffed the air like a surprised hound that scents hare when he least expects it. For a moment his whole body tensed, straining after the elusive hint of something alien, then his brow wrinkled and he shook his head as if to clear it. Again he sniffed the clean, cold air, but the trail had gone stale, cold.

He went back and lay down again, this time not even glancing at his pebbles, but now his sleep was lighter, uneasier, and once or twice he rumbled and frowned and raised his head, as though the thing he thought he might have sensed had left the faintest trace of itself behind, to tease at the edge of consciousness with the merest shadow of hope . . .

Ki-ya the buzzard moved cramped pinions, one eye on the weather outside, the other warily watching the now sleeping dragon. He had sought shelter two days since during the blizzard, and had perched on the pinnacle of rock just inside the cave-mouth, stomach empty, one tail feather damaged. Now that feather, groomed, smoothed, oiled, would carry him on a favourable wind, but he would have to take care. A week ago he had strayed from his home territory, a bold yearling male, and the great southwesterly had caught him foraging on the edge of the moor. A more experienced bird would have sought shelter but he had thought, with his young defiance, that he was strong enough to ride out the storm, to slip the winds under his wings and rise above the worst of it, but the elements had decided to teach him a lesson and had lifted him high, high on a thermal, then tipped him sideways across the mouth of the Great Western River and flung him helter-skelter to the teeth of the Black Hills, where he had spun crazily from one down-draught to an up and vice-versa, until the wind had veered in a night, and dawn had found him disorientated and dispossessed on the ledge of the dragon's lair.

At first, with the northering wind fetching a blizzard, he had not noticed that the inner side of the cave was occupied, and when he had it seemed the heap of bones and scales was merely that. Now it was different: nest-tales had included Dragons, Fire-drakes and Wyrmes, but this was his first encounter with one. He was not even sure this was a dragon: parent tales had described him as such, but with fire in his belly and flying, higher and faster than even his own kin. But this thing looked near dead and its fires were out: still, a good enough tale to carry to The Ancient, if he were not off on his travels again. Fair exchange for a decent dinner . . . His stomach contracted and he spread his wings.

* * *

Five or so days later, living by rick and midden, tolerably full but defeated from straight flight by adverse winds, he followed a trail of footprints through the new snow some quarter mile below. The trail wound over the downs for half-a-league, going in his direction, and lazily he let it lead him, switching off the nagging pull and ignoring the pre-set markers for a while, till he saw the footprints halt in a huddle of creatures a mile or so from a village. Coasting down, for now he could feel a favourable veer in the wind was imminent and see the build-up of high, scattered cloud to the west, which would mean a good six hours' clear flight, he alighted silently in a tall pine some fifty yards from the party. Two humans, a unicorn if his guess was right, but in a sorry, hornless state, a crow, a . . . cat? something that looked amphibian in a basket and a bowl with a tiddler in it. The smaller human was holding the bowl and breathing on it to melt the thin coating of ice.

The crow glanced up. 'Greetings, brother!' He had a crippled wing.

'Greetings: may the wind lift your wings and smooth your passing, your eyes never grow dim, nor your beak or talons less sharp.' It was the standard predator's greeting. 'Whither away?'

'Southwest, to seek a sorcerer they say still lives there.'

'All of you?'

'All of us.'

'A quest?'

'Something of the sort . . .'

'Travel well, brother: I shall be there before you,' and he coasted up until he felt the familiar tickle of wind slide round to hug his body and then he spread the fingers of his wings to grasp at the air, joying in the buoyancy, the waves that met and passed him, the crests that he rode as easily as a gull on the estuary.

He screamed his name: 'Ki-ya! Ki-ya!' that all should know him. Here was another tit-bit of news: he should reach the old man in a couple of days. He screamed again.

But *they* would have a longer journey . . .

THE GATHERING

Hedged by Magic

IT WAS a long, hard journey and a long, hard winter.

At the turning of the year I had thought we were over the worst of it, but with the lightening of the days came a darkening of the weather. The Moon of Snows lived up to her name and by Inbolc, or Candlemas as Conn called it—a much prettier name—we were still up to our ears in the white stuff. Well, nearly. Well, Moglet was, and in the drifts Snowy was in to his belly. Twice we were forced to make long detours, once for unseasonable floods, and for two weeks we were holed up in one village, snow to the lintels. Conn's money ran low and mine was finished and by the Moon of Waters we were cold, hungry, tattered and snappy with each other. Puddy and Pisky fared better than the rest of us because they went into half-hibernation, stirring only on warm days and requiring little or nothing to eat. Corby and Moglet were reasonably sheltered and not unfed but Conn, Snowy and I fared worse. Conn, despite his long legs, found the going hard and his mail, which he wore all the time now to lighten Snowy's load, heavy and cumbersome, and he still did not have my belief in journey's end and the magician to lessen his burdens. Snowy, for all he was a unicorn, albeit no longer magic, could still feel hunger, cold, the weight of his burdens, and the frost struck cruelly at the poor, tender stump of his horn. And I? I felt I was colder, tireder, hungrier than all of them put together, and even the binding of my feet with rags, the wrapping of sacking around my shoulders and chest and Conn's purchase of a squirrel-fur hood did little to keep out the shivers that chattered my teeth and rattled my bones.

We almost quarrelled and parted company more than once, but now it was Snowy that kept us together. As the weather gradually changed for the better he declared he could smell spring on the softer winds from the south, and broke into a trot now and again, snuffling the breeze and discovering the new, tender mosses and thin slivers of fresh grass revealed by the thaw to persuade us. We crossed the downs and came to the high moors, and the last, bitter fling of a winter whose reign was nearly over. Below us to our left lay a grey-green expanse that Conn said was the sea, but all we were concerned with was struggling through bog, slough, bitter thicket and twisted, stunted wood. One night we spent crouched in the lee of some towered stones on the flank of the moor and even Snowy stamped his hooves and looked uneasy, and I dreamt of our Mistress and woke screaming till Conn clapped one hand over my mouth and with the other stroked my back until I calmed.

Then, suddenly, things changed.

We came off the moor after five days, slipping and sliding down a steep combe to a valley, and it was as if the Moon of Birth had arrived three weeks early and spent her first few days all out, day and night, to persuade us our sense of timing was all a-kilter and surprise us with her husbandry. On either side of the narrow track that led deep between bank and wood, bracken was uncoiling in shy green crooks, grass spiked in surprised clumps, colts-foot shocked with their bright heads, furred bramble leaves were gently unfolding and everywhere birds sang. Rounding a corner to where a stream chattered across stony hollows a willow was already greeny-yellowing with slim leaves, bending to the water to admire its reflection, and downs-pastured lambs ran wag-tailed to their dams with dirty knees and black faces as they heard us approach. Somewhere high above us a lark strove mightily with the heavens, and other birds darted busily across our path, twigs, dead leaves, sheep's wool and dried grass in their beaks, nest-building leaving them too busy to do anything but ignore our passing. A balmy breeze from the south kissed us in greeting and Corby shook up all his feathers.

'Not bad,' he said. 'Not bad at all. Feel like a dip in that puddle over there. Too much grease on your feathers and you can't fluff 'em up at night . . .'

'Think I'll try a walk,' said Moglet. 'Sun's warm. And a drink from the stream.'

Puddy emerged, looking rather saggy and crinkled. 'May we stop? Definitely need some water . . .'

Pisky swam to the top of his bowl. 'I fancy a little dip, and perhaps a change of water. My grandmother always said . . .'

Conn and I watched them, and I kept an eye on Pisky in case the stream ran too strong, and re-filled his bowl with fresh water and set it in the sunshine to warm.

'D'you know,' said Conn, stretching upwards till his fingertips burnt red in the sunlight, 'I think they've the right idea. Mind if I wander off downstream and have a dip? The winter's sweat is sticky on my body like scum,' and he ambled off down the road, whistling an experimental happiness.

I turned to Snowy. 'A good idea: I could do with a wash. How about you, dear one?'

'If you could set down the packs for a while . . .' I unloaded him and he pranced like a yearling to the nearest patch of grass and rolled, his tummy pink and his hooves tucked up close to his body. I wandered down till I found a pool then undressed, hesitating for a delightful moment of anticipation before gasping into the water. It was freezing and exhilarating and glorious; putting on my old clothes while I was still damp was rather nasty, but I heard Conn returning and dared not shame him with my ugly nakedness.

He came striding down the road, jerkin and mail over his arm, his hair curled tight, dark red with the water, and it gleaming in drops on his shoulders and running to the darker hairs on his chest, and a smile on his face as he saw me. I felt a jolt in my insides like someone had kicked me, but without the pain and yet with it—

'Fish for dinner, Thingy dear!' and he held aloft two silver trout. 'And I'd never have caught them but that the wash of my dive into the water threw them up onto the bank, and they surrendered without a fight . . . I had not realized how long your hair was; right down your back it is and black as Corby's wing,' and he flicked the damp fringe on my forehead as he passed and I was absurdly pleased, almost as though he had told me I had turned pretty overnight, and I watched the muscles on his back and shoulders as he broke up some dead

127

branches for our fire, and longed to touch their hard knots . . . Then laughed at my foolishness and went to gather up the others, fussing over them more than usual, stroking and holding them.

The fish were delicious and fed all of us, one way and another, although in truth they were but one man's dinner, but I made oatcakes to go with them for Conn and myself, and we had the snow-fed waters of the stream to wash them down. That night we found an old barn and slept warm and dry in the last of the winter hay and woke early, for though none of us said so, I think we all felt that the end of our search was near. And as we walked that day it seemed that spring walked with us, or ran a little ahead and turned and beckoned so that we had no need to ask the way, and all our aches and pains were smoothed away and we paced as if in a dream . . .

And so we came to the barrier.

'We can't get through there,' said Conn, scratching his head. 'Not without an axe or two,' for our way was blocked by a tangle of briars and thorns well above man-height. 'We shall have to go round,' and indeed the track we had been following branched off to the left and right as though there had never been a way through, though the barrier seemed to stretch as far as the eye could see without a break.

'But that's the way,' I said, pointing ahead, as sure as eggs, though I could not have explained why.

'It can't be,' said Conn. 'You must be wrong. There's nothing behind there, there can't be . . .'

'There is,' I insisted. 'I'm sure of it. Come on,' and without thinking I walked forward straight into—and through—the thorny mass, just as if it hadn't been there. Snowy followed by my side, the others on his back, but when we found ourselves on the other side and I turned to look for Conn, I found he had not followed us.

'Bother!' I said. 'Conn?' Faintly, very faintly, I heard him call back, as though he were on the other side of a house, for the thorn hedge had closed behind us as though there had never been a way through. 'I shall have to go back for him,' I said, and started forward, but this time I merely scratched my hands and arms, for the thorns would not give way. I shook the branches frantically, but try as I would they did not shift, and all the time I could hear Conn calling, calling . . . Bursting into tears I tore and pulled at the thicket till I was covered in scratches, but it was no good.

Rushing over to Snowy I clasped him round the neck. 'Help me, dear one, help me!'

He breathed gently down my neck. 'There is no way back, only forward. He can come to you, but you cannot return to him. You will have to use your mind, make him believe he can walk through, just as we did . . . Concentrate: call him to you.'

'Call him?' But even as I questioned I knew what to do. Kneeling down I heeled my palms over my eyes till all was blackness and dug my fingers into my ears till all was silence and thought hard of Conn, conjuring him up in my mind from feet to crown of head and then walking towards him in my mind, back through the hedge, till I stood again by his side and held out my hand.

'Come,' I said. 'Come with me. Don't be afraid . . .'

But he looked at me as though I were someone different.

'I cannot go through there: it is solid. Must be five or six feet thick.'

'It's not there,' I said. 'Not there. It's an illusion . . . Close your eyes, take my hand, and believe!'

And I took his hand and led him through the way I had come.

'What on earth—Are you all right, Thingy?'

I opened my eyes and they hurt with sunlight and I took my fingers from my ears and they rang, and there was Conn coming across the grass towards us. I stumbled to my feet and hobbled towards him.

'I'm fine . . . You all right?'

'Think so . . . Extraordinary thing: one moment I thought I'd lost you all, and then there was this gap—What is this place?'

We were standing in a glade, full of sun and sound and smell. To our left was the hedge we had come through, but already it seemed some distance away, and between it and us there were trees, some blossoming, some in full leaf, others with the tints of autumn and bearing scarlet and yellow fruit. Before us a meadow, full of daisies and buttercups and clover and blue, white and yellow butterflies. Beyond that was what I thought might be the sea, now sparkling and blue, with little white lines dancing towards the shore. To the right were more trees, a wood of conifer, all greens from black to yellow. Squirrels ran up and down the trunks and along the branches, nuts in their mouths, and tall ferns rustled as deer came out from the shadows and sniffed the air and gazed at us, their furred ears swinging back and forth, their tails wagging. Behind us a little spring gushed out of the rock and ran away, disappearing into a shallow pool. And by the spring was a cave, and at the mouth of the cave lines of strata where martlet and martin bubbled and chattered. And I could hear the sea and the trees and the birds and the bees and the wind in the grass and smell pine and ripe apples and clover and—

And on a rock-seat in front of the cave, apparently asleep, sat the largest owl I had ever seen.

'It's an illusion,' I said, but I wasn't quite sure.

'Not all of it,' said Conn, plucking and scrunching a rosy apple from a nearby tree.

Snowy was cropping the short, sweet grass and, reassured, I lifted down Puddy, who made for the stones by the pond; next I put Moglet down, and she was off batting at butterflies in a blink, but never quite catching them. I carried Pisky over to the pond and submerged his crock. 'There,' I said. 'I think it's all right . . .' Corby had not waited: turning over a pile of leaves he had found some grubs, or what looked like grubs.

'Have an apple,' said Conn, already on his second, but I shook my head. At my feet the runners of a strawberry were thick with tiny pointed, scarlet fruit which burst in my mouth in an explosion of delight.

But things were just not right: they looked as they should, felt as they should, tasted and sounded as they should, but where in the world would you find a place that held all seasons as one? The promise of spring blossom, the warmth of summer sunshine, the fulfilment of autumn's apples, the consolation of winter's conifers . . . But it didn't feel bad, not as though it were an enchantment to thrall us into evil: there must be an explanation.

I looked around me again for some sort of clue to these contradictions. My friends seemed to find nothing strange in the situation: they were peaceful and happy enough for the

130

moment. I supposed I was meant to be too, but somehow I felt annoyed with whatever-it-was for presuming I could be so easily lulled into compliant acceptance of the situation. For something to do I picked and ate another strawberry, appreciating its tart sweetness, the gritting of pips in my mouth. One got stuck between my teeth, and I nudged it loose with my tongue; if anything were designed to convince one that life was normal a pip between one's teeth was the thing . . .

I felt a tickly feeling between my shoulder blades and whirled round: the owl was shutting his eyes again.

'All right,' I said. 'Explain!'

But the bird remained silent, eyes firmly shut, feathers fluffed, just as we had first seen him. I was sure now that I was right so I marched up to where he was sitting in the bright sunshine on that throne-like chair, and addressed him again. 'I know you're foxing,' I told him. 'Tawnys don't sit out like that in the sunshine at midday. And all the rest of this,' I waved my hand, 'is just too perfect. So, bird, tell me what all this is about or I'll—I'll break your blasted neck!'

There was a little silence. The others left off eating or playing and came up behind me, Pisky swimming up the stream to where the spring gushed out, Corby wiping his feathers with his beak, Puddy damp, Moglet with pollen on her flanks, Conn with an applecore in his hand, Snowy smelling of new grass.

The owl opened one eye. 'Just try it, that's all: just try it!'

He closed the eye again. He had spoken so Conn and I could understand, man-speech, but even as I registered this I realized he had also answered so the others could understand as well, the different sounds and attitudes echoing one behind the other with the fraction of a second between so that only I, and most probably Snowy, would know this was some kind of magic. I shook my head: only one way to deal with this. I did the same thing, talked so they could all understand, but whereas the owl had talked to each in their individual speech, I just used human speech and the special language my friends used. It was still like trying to do five things at once.

'I will, don't think I won't! We haven't travelled all this way to find a magician, a wise man, just to be put off by apples and strawberries and—and things! Now then, I know this is the right place, so please tell us where we may find your master?'

The owl opened his eyes again, and now they were full open, considering. 'What business have you with The Ancient?'

'That's ours to say, to him. Tell your master we are here!' I sounded bold, but inside I was shaking. For the last few minutes—hours?—since we had arrived, ever since we had come across the thorny hedge in fact, I had seemed to assume charge, and now I realized how that was entirely against my nature; with Conn and Snowy so much better qualified than I, the strain began to tell. So I repeated what I had just said, but my voice was uncertain, to my ears anyway. 'Tell him we're here . . .'

The owl shifted on his perch. 'You're too late.'

'Too late?'

'Too-hoo late. By about two-hoo hundred years . . .'

'What do you mean?' But even as I spoke I could feel the frustration, the despair of having walked so many, many miles for nothing, and my stomach contracted as it used to when we were with the witch, and it seemed the others were similarly affected, for I heard a curse from Corby, a wail from Moglet and sympathetic noises from the others, echoing my distress.

'Do you mean, by all the saints, that we've come all this way for nothing?' began Conn angrily, and it was only Snowy who said nothing, his large, dark eyes switching from me to the owl and back again. Somehow this gave me confidence, and I looked hard at the fluffy bird again. There was something cloudy, undefined about the area behind him, something not quite right . . .

'You say your master died—er, two hundred years ago? Can you prove this?' I spoke carefully, politely.

'Why, of course! Come this way,' and he waved an inviting wing.

Conn had learnt enough about my friends by now to go back for Pisky's bowl without being asked, and we all followed the owl as he flew into the cave. Inside it was light, dry and airy, about twenty feet long by ten or twelve wide; torches burned quietly in sconces and there was no need for the owl to indicate a recess in the right-hand corner, for we could not have missed it.

Behind a kind of crystal curtain hung a suit of clothes,

enclosing a skeleton. The clothes were ornate, jewel-encrusted, richly embroidered; the skeleton was—a skeleton, with a few wisps of greying hair still adhering to the skull. Though there can have been no wind behind that curtain, yet the whole thing swayed, very gently, back and forth.

The owl waved his wing again. 'There you see the mortal remains of my dearly beloved master, trapped into a living death by a treacherous maiden,' he intoned. 'Here he wasted away, imprisoned by the webs you see fastening his legs and arms, enchanted by the power of a woman's wiles. For weeks he endured, railing against his fate, but at last he succumbed . . .' The owl wiped his eye, visibly affected. 'With his last breath he forgave the errant maid who enslaved him, and now his remains are a reminder to mortal man that even the greatest may not be proof against female pulchritude and greed . . .'

It might have been a servant showing unexpected guests around a castle in the owner's absence, and I didn't believe a word of it. Conn, on our travels, had sometimes beguiled us with folk tales and legends, and among the latter I remembered various episodes in the life of one Artorius, a Romano-Saxon king of Wessex and his magician friend Myrddin of Cymri—but even Conn sometimes mixed these tales with others about an Arthur Pendragon of the Old Lands and a shaman of Scotia called Merlon—and although all these tales bore some similarity and indeed did have a treacherous maiden in them, sometimes it was the king who fell foul of her and other times the magician, so this hotch-potch of the owl's was obviously meant to beguile the superstitious into connecting a very-present enchantment with something that happened, or might have happened, two hundred years ago, and was obviously intended to deter us from further inquiries, pack ourselves up and go away.

But I had no intention of going away; here we were and here we stayed until we got some of the right answers, at least. I would have to be careful, though, and play it just right.

'Thank you, O Guardian of the late-lamented One,' I said, bowing to the owl. 'May we now go back outside? I find this sad atmosphere somewhat oppressive, and I am sure my companions do also,' and I rushed back into the open, hoping

133

for a glimpse of that shadowy something I thought I had detected behind the owl. Nothing. Still . . .

'What the hell are you doing?' queried Conn, but I turned my back to the cave and gave him a big wink.

'Trust me . . .' I turned to the owl, back once more on his perch on the stone. 'May I question you a little further before we gather up our belongings and take our leave of this fair place?'

'But of course,' said the owl, fluffing up his feathers and mollified, no doubt, by my obsequious tone. 'Pray proceed.'

'Your master (rest his soul) has been dead—or in this state in which we found him—for two hundred years, you said?'

'Alas yes, almost to the day. And many the pilgrims, like yourselves, who have passed this way to marvel and to mourn . . .'

'Alack-a-day,' I said, and bowed my head. 'It is the world's loss . . . Men say he could have been the greatest sorcerer and magician since the world began—'

'The greatest,' asserted the owl, nodding his head wisely. 'Indubitably.'

'Yet I question this,' I said. 'Tell me—'

'Question it?' said the owl in a different voice. I looked again: yes, I was not mistaken. There was a sort of greyish, wavery background to the bird.

'Yes,' I hurried on, for I was almost sure now: 'for I have heard of other such who gave counsel and comfort to the great ones of the land who were accounted less great than this Ancient One we came to seek, and then lived their allotted span and passed away amid scenes of universal grief: they did not succumb to mortal wiles, they—'

'My master was greater far than these—these minor tricksters you speak of,' said the owl, and he was definitely becoming more ruffled. 'My master is—was—the greatest sorcerer the world has ever seen! Master of the Art of Illusion, Traveller in Time, Licentiate of Language, Far-Seer . . . Why, he was a man so great that the kings of the world came to him on bended knee asking him to solve their problems, work out their battle strategy, choose their companions, and would not rest until he had seen them and given them the benefit of his experience. It's not my fault if they didn't listen . . .'

I pretended not to hear this last. 'Yet he succumbed to a bronze-coin's-worth of tawdry female,' I said warmly. 'Just like any other male. No magician worth his salt would even admit to—'

'Do you dare to question The Ancient?'

'Oh, I don't question his mortality, his frailty: I do question, yes, whether he ever was the great magician he claimed to be!'

'Not claimed to be: is! Er . . . was.'

'No! For no magician as great as that could possibly behave as vulnerably as you say; no sorcerer with his reputation could be so reduced by a mere woman—' I moved closer. 'And no Master of Illusion worth anything could resist the temptation to try and con ordinary people into believing he was dead and gone, if only because he was too lazy to—'

'Lazy!' came an indignant voice. 'I've never been accused of being lazy all my life! And I am the greatest!'

'Then stop mucking about, Ancient or whatever you call yourself,' I said.

'Right! You've asked for it,' he said, and materialized behind the owl.

The Ancient

'YOU'VE asked for it!' repeated The Ancient crossly, swatting at the owl, who fluttered onto his shoulder and shut its eyes again. 'I'm not used to visitors, don't want visitors! Anyway, you've come too soon—stop digging your claws in, Hoowi!—and I'm not ready . . .' and he went on grumbling and grousing to himself, a seamed old man with nut-brown wrinkles, bright blue eyes, long white hair and a longer tri- forked beard dyed yellow, red and blue. He wore a lopsided paper crown that kept slipping to one side, a mothy green velvet cloak edged with tarnished gold braid, and what looked like a rather lived-in yellow-woolly night robe. His feet were shoved in scuffed purple slippers; his fingernails looked chewed, although what teeth he had were decidedly rocky. His voice was high, nasal and singsong; not lilting like Conn's. His nose was rather large and definitely hooked; his ears stuck out, and behind the one that wasn't saving the paper crown was a quill pen; round his neck hung a rope of blue glass beads.

'Done weighing me up?' he snapped, but I fancied the snap was as harmless as an old dog threatening flies.

I bowed: time for politeness and diplomacy. I had tried him very hard and he had let me, but I thought that so far he was merely amusing himself, pretending wrath merely to see me crumple at his feet in awe. My bow extended so far I could almost bump my forehead with my knees, for this man was an unknown quantity.

'Dear Sir,' I began. 'Am I correct in supposing that we have reached journey's end? That I am, in fact, addressing The

Ancient, a magician and sorcerer without parallel, whose reputation reaches far across the land?'

'That's not what you said two minutes ago . . .'

'Ah, but then you were playing games with us. I may have seemed presumptuous, but I assure you it was the presumption of desperation. We have come so far, and it has been such a hard journey, and we are so—so in need of your help . . .' My voice quavered: I couldn't help it.

'Indeed, sir, the little lassie speaks only the truth.' Conn's hand was on my shoulder. 'She can be a mite sharp-tongued perhaps, but this Thingummy has had one hell of a life and you have only to look at her to know she is really as guileless as a newborn lamb. She—'

'I know, I know,' said The Ancient. 'You all are. Lambs to the slaughter, all of you; except perhaps the White One, and even he has been foolish enough to forget the rules of faery and lose his heart along with his horn . . . Never mind, never mind. Come, all of you: you are all welcome. We shall eat, and then we shall talk.' He looked at me. 'Here you, Flora who brought the Fauna,' and he wheezed at some joke only he could understand, although I felt a sudden jolt of recognition I could not account for. 'Go back into the cave. On a shelf you will find oatcakes, butter, honey and a flagon of mead, a crock of goat's milk and some cheese . . .'

They were there as he said, and of course the silly skeleton had gone, as had the crystal curtain. Moglet had milk and cheese, Corby oatcakes and cheese, Puddy appeared to be devouring fireflies, though there were always as many again, but for Pisky there was something special: the old man scooped him up in his bowl, and sprinkled something into the water.

'Here, Emperor of the fishes: my de-luxe mixture.'

This kept Pisky quiet for at least ten minutes, then I saw him glance down at his flanks, flirting his tail, standing on his head: 'Emperor of the fishes, he called me. Did you ever! Emperor . . .'

At last I leant back, wiping my sticky mouth on the back of my hand: I was full. Any more and I should be uncomfortable. I looked round at the others. Snowy was lying down, legs tucked under. Puddy had his eyes shut, which meant he was still chewing; he burped. Pisky was still. Corby groomed his uninjured wing, oiling it evenly with his beak. Moglet was licking her stomach, with long, even strokes that left sticky runnels on it. Conn was lying full-length on the grass, chin in hand, his rusty armour a discarded heap in the shadows. It was a still, warm night, with just the faintest breath of a mint-smelling breeze to touch our faces, ruffle my hair. Somewhere a bird still sang, sweet and low, and fireflies danced among the trees. Perfect.

'Now then,' said The Ancient. 'We shall talk . . .'

I do not remember what tongue we spoke; I know we all understood. One by one we told The Ancient who we were, how we met and why we were travelling together. It was thus I learnt more fully of Conn's encounter with our Mistress and a little of what it had meant to Snowy, and less and less did it seem that our meetings were chance.

'So, you are bound together, all of you, by the unfortunate wiles of a powerful witch,' mused The Ancient. His throne-like rock seat gave him an advantage, for sitting on it he was taller than any of us standing up, even Conn. 'And so she is dead . . . I find it hard to believe she is gone, for she was an adversary worthy of even such as I, but she moved away to the east many, many years ago, so long that I have forgotten her name. Strange, for once I could recall her with ease . . . You are sure she is dead?'

We reassured him.

'One of the best Shape-Changers ever, too: I remember once . . . No matter.' He stroked his beard. 'Not at her best recently, I gather. However, good as she was, I fancy I could give her a run for her money. Watch this!'

And as we gazed his edges grew blurred, then he disappeared completely, leaving in his place a white rabbit washing its whiskers. Then it wasn't a rabbit but a hedgepig. Then a rather foolish-looking sheep. Then just a head, looking rather like Tom Trundleweed. Then a brightly spinning ball. Then nothing. Then The Ancient again.

He beamed at us. 'How's that for Shape-Changing, then?'

Conn applauded, clapping his hands, but I frowned. 'That's not Shape-Changing!'

'Then what is it, clever-sticks?' and he frowned, too.

'Illusion. Like your hedge. And a lot more here, I shouldn't be surprised.'

'You're a fine one to talk of illusion!' He had half-risen from his seat, and Conn put a hand on my arm.

'Now then, Thingummy dear,' he muttered. 'You may be right and all that, but the laws of hospitality—'

I began to apologize, but The Ancient cut me short. 'She's right, you know, right in her own way. Comes of spending her formative years with that old bitch of a witch What's-her-name . . . No, no apologies. I'm not a true Shape-Changer, but I am an Illusionist and, though I say it myself, the best!' He failed to look modest. 'One can't do everything, and I concentrated on what I did best. Worth remembering that: forget what you want to do, find something you do better than anyone else, even if it's only turd-throwing, and become undisputed champion: better a champion shit-shoveller than a forty-second-rate turnip-carver . . . Where was I? Ah yes. Time-Traveller, too, and Master of Languages and the Crystal Ball. Not very good at the last: lost the old ball . . . Some are good at one thing, some at another. Never fancied the Resurrectionists, for example; there is always a price to pay for immortality, and sometimes it is far harder to render than the common coin of mortal clay. And who knows what one might have to bear? Watching those one has loved pass into decay and die; perhaps seeing all one believes in, had fought for, pass into disrepute . . .

'The enchanted may mourn, but they may not weep: that relief is the only compensation for mortal grief. My friend, the White One, knows that, do you not?' And he nodded at Snowy, who bowed his head until I could see the maimed stump where his horn had been.

Without thinking I rose and went to his side and knelt down and kissed him. 'Never mind, dear one, The Ancient will help you find a new horn—you will, won't you?' I asked anxiously. 'We've come all this way . . . Forgive my rudeness and help them. Please?'

'Depends on what you want, doesn't it? I can't work miracles!'

'Sure and we don't ask for the impossible, your Sagacity,' said Conn earnestly, rising to his feet. 'All we seek is your wisdom. As you said, it seems we are all enchanted by the same witch, and I, for one, will not believe that her spells cannot be broken.'

'Broken, perhaps not: bent a little is what we seek. Never go at magic straight on, you'll only bruise your hopes. Sneak round the edges if you can. It's like Roman law: or,' looking at Conn, 'killing a boar, if you like. Get round to the flank.' He blew his nose on an orange scarf he pulled from his cloak. 'Now then, my White One, let's begin with you: what do you wish for? You know, of course, that it would take far stronger powers than mine to undo the ill to your enchanted prince? Only a life, freely given, may release him, and then only to a Between-World . . . So, if it is possible, you would wish your horn to be restored?'

Snowy bowed his head, and I thought I could see the gleam of a tear in his eye. 'Yes, then if—if all else fails, I shall still have the right to rejoin my brethren in the west, and live out the rest of my life with them.'

'Then I do have some hope for you; small hope, 'tis true, but one grain of salt on an egg is better than none at all. The witch's curse was powerful enough, but there was more concentration on the boy than on you, and I am fairly sure, from what you said, that she cut off the closing words that stifle all hope.

'Your horn, my friend, may be restored by one thing and one thing alone: a fresh drop of dragon's blood, freely given!'

'But that is not fair!' burst out Conn, coming over to Snowy's side. 'There are no dragons! They all died out—oh, hundreds of years ago! You're just saying something to comfort the poor old thing that can't possibly come true, and that's the cruellest kind of hope—'

'Wait!!' thundered The Ancient, and for a moment, behind the doddery old man who rose unsteadily from his seat, I caught a glimpse of another, a tall stern-faced warrior wearing purple and blue and carrying a wand in his right hand . . . Then the vision faded, but it was my turn to catch at Conn's arm, anxious not to offend.

'Yes, wait, my dear . . .'

'For, if I mistake me not, all your problems resolve around the same end,' said the old man, slowly resuming his seat,

140

as if there had been no interruption. 'Tell me now, Connor O'Connell, as you seem to like the sound of your own voice. What is your heart's desire?'

'My desire? Why sure and that's plain enough to see. My sword, my father's sword, is snapped in two and needs to be made whole; my armour is rusted past polishing and I want i once more bright!'

'And then?'

'Then? Oh, I see. Well, then I would go off to Frankish lands or Germanica and hire myself out as a mercenary, or maybe even seek adventure farther abroad. There is money to be made in service, you know, and perhaps more as free-sword.'

'No settling-down, then?' The Ancient stroked his beard, the yellow bit on the right.

'Me? Not likely! There's all life to be lived out there. No, worthy Sir, I'm just not the settling-down kind!'

'Pity, pity,' said The Ancient, 'for part of the lifting of the witch's curse depended on your asking the hand in marriage of the ugliest female in the land, as I recall—and that part cannot be altered, not in essence, anyway.'

Conn went bright red. 'As to that—if I ever find this female, then 'tis to be hoped that for her sake she is rich; if she is, then might I ask for her hand, for then she'll be so grateful she'll give me her dowry, and I'll kiss her goodbye. And if she's not rich—why then she won't get asked. And any that question my right to travel this world in tarnished mail, then my sword—if I can get it reforged—will teach them a lesson they won't forget in a hurry!' He looked very fierce and pushed up the tips of his moustache, then spoilt the whole effect by apologizing to Moglet for nearly treading on her tail.

'You also wished your sword whole again: that curse cannot be lifted save by the same magic the White One seeks. In your case that sword, which bears magic runes not seen by mortal eye, can only be welded together by flame from dragon's tongue, again freely given.'

Conn started up in protest, no doubt once again to point out that dragons were extinct, but The Ancient waved him to silence, and I felt a sudden surge of excitement, as if there was more to come.

He turned to me. 'And you: do you believe in dragons?'

'I believe in them, yes of course, because everyone knows they existed once. My—the witch sometimes used powdered dragon-bones in her spells: the one to make different coloured flames, I think . . .'

The Ancient positively beamed. 'Well, then?'

'But Sir . . .'

'Yes?'

'I must confess to believing, like Conn, that they—they . . .'

'Well?' He scowled.

'Well, that they—are extinct.'

'Like witches and unicorns, I suppose. And magicians,' he added maliciously.

'Well, no . . .' I trailed off.

'You see? Never take things like that for granted, youngster. You, of all people, with your upbringing, should know better! I daresay if you told the folk in—oh, say Sarum or Silchester of your life with the witch, they would pelt you with refuse for lying.' He leant forward. 'Now, leaving aside the question of dragon/no dragon for the moment, why have you come on this quest? What is your desire?'

'To get rid of my pebble,' I said, on surer ground. 'And so have the others,' and I nodded at Corby, Puddy, Pisky and Moglet. 'You see we all want to be whole and unencumbered and free of pain again. I want to be able to walk upright, Corby wants to fly, Puddy wants to be rid of his headaches, Pisky needs to eat properly and little Moglet wants to run fast enough to catch mice. And to do this we must find the person or thing who rightfully owns these pebbles and give them back; the witch stuck them fast but I expect the rightful owner might have a way to extract them. Oh, and we'd like our memories back, too,' I added.

'Don't want much, do you?' but he was smiling. 'Right: Let's have a look at these famous pebbles . . .'

One by one we showed him our encumbrances, and he himself picked up Pisky's bowl. Then, when he had inspected them all, he did a very strange thing.

He laughed.

He laughed till the rheumy tears ran down his cheeks, leaving rather dirty runnels; he laughed till he wheezed and coughed and, speechless, pointed to his back and Conn kindly went and gave him a couple of good thumps between his shoulder blades to stop him choking. At last he sat up, wiped his eyes on the orange scarf, blew his nose again, and took a swig from Pisky's bowl.

'Oh dear, oh dear,' he said at last, still chuckling. 'Oh dearie, dearie me . . .'

We looked at one another, feeling like idiots, and it was Corby who voiced our feelings. 'What we done, then? Must be mighty foolish to make the Man o' Wisdom laugh as if we were the village idiot who saw his face reflected in the pond, thought it were the moon, an' tried to pluck it out to stop it from drowning—'

'No, no, my friend!' said The Ancient, trying to compose his features. 'I'm not laughing at you: I'm laughing with you, and for you, for I think I have solved the mystery!'

We all began talking at once, but he raised his hand for silence.

'I'm going to tell you all a story,' he said. 'So settle down and listen . . .'

Dragon-Quest

SO IT was that the warm night closed around us like a cloak as we heard the tale of a young dragon sent out on his Master-Quest. We heard of the gold he collected, of the brilliant jewels he snatched, stole, retrieved, found; we heard how the last search, for his personal pearl, had led him to this land, and how he had stored his treasure high in a cave in the Black Mountains, and one night had left it unguarded to pay one last visit to the villagers nearby who had feasted him regularly during his years of search. How in that last feasting a black shadow, a greedy, grasping thing, crept to his cave and stole his hoard, fleeing into the forests of the night where he could not find her. And how the dragon could not return to his homeland without the jewels, and lay a-dying from grief and frustration in that same cave.

How the thief fled far, far away, as far as the winds would take her; how she had to hide the jewels, possession of which, given the correct spells and formulae, would give her a mastery of magic greater than any ever known. How she had not hidden them from the dragon by burying them deep, lest they be dug up; neither had she thrown them into the deeps, lest they be trawled to surface; nor had she hung them from a tree, lest they fall: rather had she fastened them safe into living creatures snatched at random from the highways and byways, as they came to hand. A netted crow, a toad pulled from under a stone, a kitten taken from its doorstep, a fish scooped from a rich man's pond, a child taken under promise of protection—

'It's us!' I shouted, bobbing up and down like some crazy creature. 'It's us!'

'It's-us-is-us-is-us,' bubbled Pisky. 'Which have I got? What am I? Tell me quick!'

'My headache is a jewel?' pondered Puddy.

'Cripes!' squawked Corby, peering under his wing. 'Bleeding 'ell! A sapphire for a splint . . .'

'Don't want it,' mewed Moglet. 'Take it away, Thing dear! Don't want a diamond . . .'

'I don't particularly want a ruby navel either, my pet,' I said, after a quick peek to confirm, picking her up and cuddling her. 'But at least we now know what they are. And just think how costly that paw of yours is now!'

Pisky was trying to squint at the bulge in his mouth. 'What-is-it, what-colour, which-one? Quick! Quick!'

The Ancient took pity on him. 'A moon-pearl, precious one. The dragon's special stone . . .'

'I-knew-it-I-knew-it!'

Puddy had got his by a process of elimination. 'An emerald? Hmmm . . . could be worse, I suppose. Green *is* my favourite colour . . .'

'Ruby, emerald, sapphire, diamond, pearl,' I said, musing. 'Is that why we used to—still do—hurt? The spell she put on us to keep them hidden?'

'Yes,' said The Ancient. 'But the spell worked against her in the end. At first, individually, she could keep you in thrall but later, collectively, and without realizing it, you formed a bond between yourselves that was enforced by the holding of the jewels: if you like, the dragon's power was transformed into a shield against harm, as long as you kept together, and neither the witch, nor anyone else, could really hurt you. Especially if you kept in physical contact with each other.'

I nodded. I could remember when she had had to set Broom to beating us because she dared not do so herself; those times when we huddled together under my cloak.

'And so she never really benefited from the jewels,' said the old man. 'You never gave her the chance: by the time her knowledge was sufficient to use them you lot had adopted them for yourselves. If you hadn't that last experiment would have worked, and powers that should lie hidden would have walked the Earth . . .'

I shivered: I could still remember with loathing that night on the island when our world had nearly come to an end . . .

Conn had remained silent until now. 'But—does that mean that there really is a dragon still alive? That somewhere, in those Black Mountains you spoke of, he is waiting for Thingy and her friends to return his jewels?'

'I think he has given up all hope,' said The Ancient, 'but yes, he is still there.' He glanced round at us all. 'He is the only one who can rid you of your burdens, his jewels; he is the only one to mend your sword, Connor O'Connell, and grow your new horn, White One, with a blast of fire and a drop of blood. He is *your* only hope, my wandering ones . . .'

'I knew we all belonged together,' I said. 'I knew it!'

We talked far into the night—at least the others did, for all too soon the excitement, the warm night, my full stomach, the earlier travelling and, most of all, the knowledge that our quest had not been in vain, that there really was hope for us all, however far away, induced in me the most complete and utter weariness, and my eyes kept closing in spite of themselves. In the end I fashioned my cloak into a pillow and lay down, an equally soporific Moglet tucked up to my chest. As we dropped off to sleep Conn was questioning the magician on Time-and-Space Travelling, and I heard him ask what the other side of the moon looked like.

'Very disappointing . . .'

And so I fell asleep to dream I travelled in a silver tube with windows open to the stars to where the moon grinned away like a yellow cheese; and then I spun round to her backside to find—

'But supposing you could,' said Puddy. 'Just how much would colour weigh?'

I drifted off again to find myself trying to scrape colours from a leaf, a stone, a jewel and weigh the differences in little pots and pans on my fingers . . . But before I knew where I was I had taken all colour from everything, and the whole world was white, white as snow; but white is a colour too, and I had to catch each snowflake and take away the white, and wash the white from every fleece of every sheep in the world, but Snowy was the only white thing that wouldn't play and ran off into

146

the forest, but I could still see him for now everything else was without colour, clear as glass, transparent as crystal; and The Ancient was an icicle, and then he melted and dripped all over me—

'Come on children,' he said. 'It's starting to rain. You'll be better off inside.'

And Conn picked me and Moglet up in one sleepy heap and carried us into the cave and plonked us down on a heap of bracken and heather, covered with some soft, silky material, and we snuggled down and I could smell thyme and rosemary. Someone covered me with my cloak, tucked it round snug, and then someone else was singing, a wordless song that ran and turned and curled back on itself like the golden ring Conn wore on his finger . . . And then I felt him lie down beside me, and his hand stroked my hair, and the trees and the rocks began to sing too, and the wind and the waters, a song so heart-catching and sad and beautiful that my eyes were full of tears, and yet I was smiling—

'Liebestod,' said The Ancient, at least I think that is what he said. 'But for you it will be Liebeslied . . .'

I didn't understand the words but I did understand my feelings, and I snuggled up to Conn's breathing, sleeping body and my heart sang with the music.

After breakfast the next morning—a helping of what looked like gruel but tasted of butter and nuts and honey and raspberries and milk—the magician led us outside into a morning sparkling with raindrops and clean as river-washed linen, but strangely the grass was dry when we seated ourselves in a semicircle in front of his throne. Hoowi, the owl, was again perched on his shoulder, eyes shut, and he took up Pisky's bowl into his lap. Although the birds sang, their songs were courtesy-muted, for The Ancient's voice was softer this morning as though he were tired, and indeed his first words confirmed this.

'I have been awake most of the night, my friends, pondering your problems. That is why I have convened this meeting. We agreed yesterday that you had all been called together for a special mission, a quest to find the dragon. You need him, but he also needs you.' He paused, and glanced at each one of us in

147

turn. 'But perhaps last night you thought this would be easy. Find the Black Mountains, seek out the dragon's lair, return the jewels, ask for a drop of blood and a blast of fire and Hey Presto! your problems are all solved.

'But it is not as easy as that, my friends. Of your actual meeting with the dragon, if indeed you reach him, I will say nothing, for that is still in the realms of conjecture. What I can say is this: in order to reach the dragon you have a long and terrible journey ahead of you, one that will tax you all to the utmost, and may even find one or other of you tempted to give up, to leave the others and return; if that happens then you are all doomed, for I must impress upon you that as the seven you are now you have a chance, but even were there one less your chances of survival would be halved. There is no easy way to your dragon, understand that before you start. I can give you a map, signs to follow, but these will only be indications, at best. What perils and dangers you may meet upon the way I cannot tell you: all I know is that the success of your venture depends upon you staying together, and that you must all agree to go, or none.

'I can see by your expressions that you have no real idea of what I mean when I say "perils and dangers": believe me, your imaginations cannot encompass the terrors you might have to face—'

'But if we do stay together?' I interrupted.

'Then you have a better chance: that is all I can say. It is up to you.' He was serious, and for the first time I felt a qualm, a hesitation, and glancing at my friends I saw mirrored the same doubts.

'And if we don't go at all—if we decide to go back to—to wherever we came from?' I persisted.

'Then you will be crippled, all of you, in one way or another, for the rest of your lives.'

'Then there is no choice,' said Conn. 'And so the sooner we all set off the better,' and he half-rose to his feet.

'Wait!' thundered the magician, and Conn subsided, flushing. 'That's better. I have not finished.'

'Sit down, shurrup, be a good boy and listen to granpa,' muttered Corby sarcastically, but The Ancient affected not to hear.

148

'There is another thing,' said he. 'If you succeed in your quest and find the dragon, and if he takes back the jewels, and if he yields a drop of blood and a blast of fire, if, I say . . . then what happens afterwards?'

The question was rhetorical, but Moglet did not understand this.

'I can catch mice again,' she said brightly, happily.

But he was gentle with her. 'Yes, kitten, you will be able to catch mice, and grow up properly to have kittens of your own—but at what cost? You may not realize it but your life, and the life of the others, has been in suspension while you have worn the jewels, but once you lose your diamond then time will catch up with you. You will be subject to your other eight lives and no longer immune, as you others have been also, to the diseases of mortality.

'Also, don't forget, your lives have been so closely woven together that you talk a language of your own making, you work together, live, eat, sleep, think together. Once the spell is broken you, cat, will want to catch birds, eat fish and kill toads; you, crow, will kill toads too, and try for kittens and fish; toad here will be frightened of you all, save the fish; and the fish will have none but enemies among you.

'And do not think that you either, Thing-as-they-call-you, will be immune from this; you may not have their killer instinct but, like them, you will forget how to talk their language and will gradually grow away from them, until even you cross your fingers when a toad crosses your path, shoo away crows and net fish for supper—'

'You are wrong!' I said, almost crying. 'I shall always want them, and never hurt them! We shall always be together!'

'But will they want you,' asked The Ancient quietly, 'once they have their freedom and identity returned to them? If not, why is it that only dog, horse, cattle, goat and sheep have been domesticated and even these revert to the wild, given the chance? Do you not think that there must be some reason why humans and wild animals dwell apart? Is it perhaps that they value their freedom, their individuality, more than man's circumscribed domesticity? Is it not that they prefer the hazards of the wild, and only live with man when they are caught, then tamed and chained by food and warmth?'

'I shall never desert Thing!' declared Moglet stoutly. 'I shan't care whether she has food and fire or not, my place is with her!'

'Of course . . . Indubitably . . . What would I do without her . . .' came from the others, and I turned to the magician.

'You see? They don't believe we shall change!'

'Not now,' said The Ancient heavily. 'Not now. But there will come a time . . . So, you are all determined to go?'

'Just a moment,' said Conn. 'You have told Thingmajig and her friends just what might be in store for them if we find the dragon: what of me and Snowy here? What unexpected changes in personality have you in store for us?' He was angry, sarcastic.

'You,' said the Ancient, 'you and my friend here, the White One, might just do the impossible: impossible, that is, for such a dedicated knight as yourself . . .'

'And what's that?'

'You might change your minds . . .'

'About what, pray?' And I saw Snowy shake his head.

'What Life is all about . . .'

'Never!'

'Never is a long time . . . Ah me, I'm getting old: another clitch.'

'What's a clitch?' I asked, trying not to let the thought of losing Conn and Snowy at the end of it all, if ever we got to the beginning, upset me too much.

'A clitch?' He sniggered. 'It's like "It always rains before it pours" or "Every cloud has a silver lining"—you know, the sort of hackneyed phrase everyone says over and over again until it becomes boring and predictable and—and a clitch. Cliché,' he amended.

Although I had heard neither phrase before, I tried to look wise. 'Comme: "Toujours la politesse", ou "chacun à son goût",' I suggested, then was shocked when I realized I didn't know where the words had come from, let alone what they meant.

'Exactly,' he said, glancing at me sharply from under thatchy brows. 'Exactement, p'tite . . . Couldn't have put it better myself . . .'

Conn looked as if he was going to say something, but didn't.

'Well,' said The Ancient. 'It's midday: supposing we meet again at supper, and you can tell me what you have all decided. Think about it carefully, mind, and don't forget what I told you.' But he sighed: it must have been clear to him even then that none of us believed his dire predictions.

We all spent the intervening hours characteristically, I suppose.

Snowy disappeared into the wood and every now and again I saw his shadow flickering among the trees. Conn went to a little knoll, got out his broken sword and, holding it up before him hilt uppermost, prayed with his eyes open, face to the sky. Pisky spent the time rearranging his bowl to his liking, pulling the weed this way and that, nudging the poor snails all over the place. Corby went into a corner by himself, walking about in circles and muttering. Puddy found another corner and sat quiet, looking as though his head were aching. Moglet chased a butterfly or two, then washed herself from ears to toe and tail, then went and sharpened the claws on her good paw. And I? I, I regret to say, did none of these useful, constructive things. Instead, I crept closer till I could see Conn's profile, then lay back in the long grass and watched the clouds pass, then rolled over on my stomach to regard the busy ants scurrying to and fro. I listened to the ascending lark, smelt the cowslips, stroked Moglet and ate wild raspberries. And fell asleep and dreamt of nothing—

Conn shook my shoulder. 'Suppertime, Thingumabob . . . Made up your mind?'

We all had, as I found out when we rejoined the others. We were determined to set out on this perilous venture, keep together and risk whatever came.

The Ancient heard us out, Conn the spokesman.

'Then all I can do, my friends, is to prepare you for your journey as best I can—and wish you luck. You'll need it . . .'

I was dreaming, a long, slow, wordless, placeless dream, and there were people I knew but could not know, and then someone was pulling me away and I was rushing faster and faster until the wind howled in my ears with the speed of my passing, and I was being pulled upwards to a hole in the ceiling, and then I bumped my head and fell back with a thud and—

'Wake up, child!' said The Ancient. 'The others are almost ready, and you'll want a bite to eat before you set off.'

I stumbled out into a mist that curled round my feet like an attenuated cat. Everything looked unreal, almost as though I were still dreaming, or had missed out on a day somewhere. I rubbed my eyes and Conn was busy loading up Snowy and the others were waiting, more or less patiently, for their turn. A hand appeared at my elbow: a hunk of bread with a slice of cheese tucked inside. A mug of goat's milk followed and I munched and drank, then moved forward to help the others.

Besides the meagre provisions we had brought with us there were flour and salt, apples, cheese and a large jar of honey, and the water-bottle was fresh-filled from the spring. Poor Snowy looked very laden, so I took Moglet in my arms and Puddy in my pocket and, to my surprise, Conn put Corby on his shoulder and strung Pisky's bowl round his waist.

Catching my look, he grinned. 'We'll swap later! Besides, as we eat the provisions the old horse—sorry, unicorn—will find his burden that much lighter.'

The Ancient was in his best today: a purple robe sewn with silver stars and his beard in three shades of blue, although his conical hat with a crescent moon on its tip was crooked and threatened to slip over his ears, protruding though they were. In his hand was a roll of soft leather.

'Your map,' he announced. He unfolded it and we stared at squiggles, arrows, letters: it didn't look like a map at all.

I pointed to some humps and bumps. 'What are those?'

'What do they look like?' snapped the magician. 'Hills, mountains, that's what!'

'And the squiggles?'

'Rivers, streams . . .'

'The dotty places?' At least the forests were shown by recognizable trees.

'Waste land: moors, heaths, bogs . . .'

'The straightish lines?'

'Roads. Such as they are. Roman mostly: the straight ones are, anyway. Probably a bit out of date . . .'

Conn put his finger on the middle of the map, on a thing that looked like a cross between a star and a spider. 'What's this?'

'A compass: north, south, east, west—'

'I've seen something like that before,' said Conn. 'Only they didn't call it a compass: a magic needle, I think. I was hitching a trip cross-channel on a Skandia galley—and damned uncomfortable it was too, full of great sweaty fellows splashing everyone with their oars—and they had this little sliver of metal suspended in a stone bowl of oil. They reckoned they could find their way in dark, fog, storm because the thin end of the metal pointed always north, whichever way they turned. The captain said he had it from a trader from the east, in exchange for a bale of furs. Swore he had the best of the bargain, too.'

'There you are, then!'

'But we've no piece of metal,' I said. 'And if we are to go in any special direction . . . And what's that, round the edge?' I looked closer. 'That says "ENE", or something: I've never heard of that word . . .'

'It's initials,' said The Ancient impatiently. 'East-north-east: those letters are your direction-finders. And you *have* got a magic needle, of sorts: the White One knows one way from t'other, and come to that so does the raggedy bird.'

'Roughly,' said Corby, looking slightly offended at the adjective. 'As the crow flies, of course . . .'

'There are some tiny circles marked as well,' said Conn, peering closely. 'There is one on its own, and there's three together, and four—'

'Those are your markers,' and the old man looked at each of us in turn. 'And you have to go their way. One, then two, then three and and so on up to seven. They are all standing stones, some higgledy-piggledy, some straight, some in circles. You go by the directions I have marked in the margin: there is the letter one, and a direction. Follow that and you come to the first stone, then letter number two and its direction et cetera.'

'Sounds simple enough,' said Conn, but he was frowning.

'It is simple: just follow your noses. And the directions, of course,' he added hastily. 'Now: are you all ready?'

'Thank you,' I said, 'from all of us. For the hospitality and the help and the food and—and everything.'

He pinched my cheek, not hard, but I could feel it through

my mask just the same. 'Think nothing of it, Flower: it has been vastly amusing, so far. I was out of practice . . .'

I didn't quite understand what he meant. 'Shall we see you again?'

'Very likely, if you follow the instructions and remember what I said about staying together. Don't look so gloomy: you will have your sunny days too, you know . . . Now, see that wood over there? Well that's a good enough marker for your first direction, east by south. That's your way. Goodbye, and good luck . . .'

The mist had thinned, and so had his voice: it sounded now like an echo.

We had all been straining our eyes to the wood, answered 'Goodbye', and then turned to wave, but he had gone. So had the glade, the cave, the stream. We were standing on the highest point of a bleak moor in the burning-off of a summer mist that rolled away from our feet as rapidly as Brother Jude-the-Less's manuscripts rolled up across the table if they weren't weighted down. Nearby was what might once have been a ring of stones, but there was nothing else recognizable for miles: even the wood was a half-day's walk. It was as if something had picked us up from somewhere and dumped us down again nowhere.

'Well, I'll be . . . blest!' said Conn, scratching his head. 'However did he manage that?'

But nobody had an answer. There was the illusion-bit, which I thought might help, but even I was uneasy about this. If I explored it too deep I should have to explain how it was we seemed to have only been with the magician a couple of days, reaching him in early spring, while now we were standing in countryside that was—

'High summer,' said Moglet. 'How nice. Didn't know we'd been there so long . . .'

There: where was there? What about all the anachronisms of season? The strange sleep that had fallen so easily on us all, a blanket of time-consuming dream so that one woke unsure whether one still slept? I should have pinched myself, but didn't, I don't know why.

We all felt the same, I could see that, but no one wanted to talk about it: a bit like suspecting there might be a wasp in the preserve, but hoping it will fly out of the window before you have to disturb it.

It was Snowy who pulled us together. 'The wood is indeed east by south, and that is our first direction, is it not? Come, my friends, this quest is for all, and better to start at once than to question too much. We are together, that is what matters. Friend Corby, do you confirm the direction?'

Corby shuffled on Conn's shoulder. 'As the crow flies, unicorn, as the crow flies. Not that crows allus fly straight, mind . . .'

THE BINDING: UNICORN

The Castle of Fair Delights

AND SO we went south by east and past the wood, and on to a different mark as we passed through it. The going was easy, the foods of the wayside plentiful, and both Conn and I found we had more money than we thought in our pockets, so it was easy to keep us all provisioned. It was almost dream-like, that progression, from the high heathlands to the downs, the plain to the valleys: everywhere they were bringing in the first cutting of hay, and the air was full of the sun-warmed smell of the drying grasses, the honey-heavy perfume of may, the bruise of wild garlic. Lambs, colts, calves, kids were younglings now, no longer babes, and the birds were feeding their second brood; sweet cicely pollen-powdered my knees, keck-parsley my hips, angelica my shoulders; corn-poppies, Demeter's bane, bled at my feet and elder laced my hair, and all day and every day the sun walked with us. There may have been days when it was cold or cloudy or it rained, but in truth I do not remember.

It was, therefore, something of a shock to all of us when we were brought abruptly back to the realization of our quest by finding the first standing stone. Bare, ragged as a sore tooth, twice man-height, it stood alone on the crest of a little hill and pointed with afternoon's shadow finger to the valley beneath, a valley ringed by forest and bearing in its midst a fair castle, towered and beflagged. The building lay in greensward; at the front a wide driveway led to the massive doors of the courtyard and at the back was what looked like a jousting-yard. From the four corners of the main building where little wooden towers rose like siege-toys, fluttered pennants, banners, flags in stripes of yellow and gold, seeming to beckon us down to this place that might have been painted onto the landscape one moment since, a scene from some legendary tale. Indeed I blinked twice, to make sure it was really there, and it was only on the second blink that I saw something I had missed before: the crescent-shaped lake that lay to the left of the castle. Even at this distance it was dark and deep and still, a black scar on the green.

'Ah!' exclaimed Conn. 'And isn't that a sight to gladden the heart? There we shall surely find a warm welcome and hospitality of the finest if I'm not mistaken, Thingummy. And as the finger of the stone points that way and the direction on the map says the same . . . Well, then?'

I frowned. For no reason I felt shivery.

'If it's so fair . . .' said Puddy.

'And we're supposed to face great danger?' supplemented Moglet.

'What the hell's wrong with it?' added Corby. 'Must be something we can't see from here.'

'My great-great-great-grandfather was fond of remarking that the prettiest flies often hid the sharpest barb,' contributed Pisky, helpfully.

'Oh, come on now! You're just a bunch of confirmed pessimists!' exploded Conn. 'You see something nice and welcoming and all you want to do is run away from it, just because it *is* pleasant! That old magician did say that the sun would sometimes shine on our endeavours, didn't he? Well it is, and down there is a castle as fair as any I've seen, and I'm longing to sit at a table bearing venison pasties and beef and oyster pies and drink a decent Frankish burgundy. And when I've eaten and drunk I should like to be shown to a chamber containing a man-sized bed laid with real linen sheets and pull a bear-pelt over my toes—not lie out under the stars itching with hay-ticks and walked over by hedgepigs! Down there is civilization and that's where I'm going, and you can come or not, as you please!' He tugged at Snowy's bridle. 'Well?'

'It is as The Ancient said,' he replied cryptically. 'This is the way we must go.'

'Told you,' exulted Conn. 'Now, are you others coming or not?'

He knew we would, if only because we remembered what the old magician had said about the importance of keeping together, and indeed, as we descended the gentle path that led to the fringe of woods surrounding the castle, we all began to wonder—us pessimists, that is—what foundation, if any, our fears were grounded upon, for the day was fair and the sun indeed shone, and little fluffy clouds deliberately either missed it or else hid it for a moment only, just to remind us how beautiful it beamed uncovered; bees fed on deep trumpets of creaming honeysuckle, grasshoppers made a raspy music and above us larks climbed to their pinnacle of song—

Then we descended to the wood.

The trees closed in, the sun was a sullen greenish glow; there were no flowers for the bees, no grass for the grasshoppers and no bird sang. Silence, and only our footsteps on the loamy track that led, straight and true, through the heart of the trees. I felt as though I were in a bowl of silence, as confining as Pisky's crock; drowning, oppressed unbearably by the lack of sound. Conn had stopped whistling the merry tune he had had on his lips a moment since and even the echoes had fled without memory. We all trod softly, as if some terrible thing lurked asleep in the shadows, only waiting a snapped twig to waken to attack.

It was Moglet who voiced our fears: 'Why no birds? Where are all the creatures who should be here? Are they all frightened of something?'

I could not have answered, but luckily there was no need for at that moment a half-dozen men-at-arms appeared on the path before us, clad in blue and yellow, spears at the slope, and at their head a knight, mounted on a black palfrey. He was elderly, moustached and bearded, and his hand was held up and open in the universal gesture of greeting.

'Peace, friends,' he called, and we halted. At that moment I had Corby on my shoulder, Moglet in my arms, Puddy in my pocket, head out, and Pisky's bowl dangling from my elbow, and I could feel their united suspicion as they turned to the stranger.

Conn and I confirmed his gesture of greeting, and he dismounted, waving back the men-at-arms to stand easy.

'Greetings: name's Egerton de Ruys. Glad to welcome you,

Sir Knight,' and he strode forward to clasp arms with Conn. He had a nasal, pinched sort of voice and clipped his words off short; one eye socket was empty: a retired knight, if I was not mistaken. 'You and y'r servant very welcome, by'r Lady! Saw you from the west tower, don't y'know, and m'niece, the Lady Adiora, sent me to beg you to take advantage of our hospitality in the Castle of Fair Delights and sojourn awhile. Be glad of y'r company.'

'Well, and that's gracious enough,' said Conn. 'Hear that, you disbelievers?' But seeing that he was apparently talking to a broken-down pony, a hunched servant carrying a scrawny crow, a frightened kitten and a small fish, he pinched his lips together and stroked his moustache, trying to look nonchalant. It was evident that the time spent in our exclusive company had made him forget that, to anyone else, talking to animals and a mere servant like that would be considered eccentric, to say the least.

'Sir Egerton: your servant,' he said formally, and introduced himself. 'My—my servant and I would be glad to accept your hospitality . . .' and he turned and scowled at us, as if daring us to contradict.

So we came through that last fringe of wood, silent still save for the jingling of harness on Sir Egerton's horse, the plod-plod of the men-at-arms and the thudding of my heart.

The track broadened as we left the trees, and as we approached it I was better able to admire the grandeur of the castle. The bottom storey-and-a-half was built of stone, perhaps fifty or so years ago and, I guessed, founded on an earlier structure, Roman perhaps. The upper storey-and-a-half was completed in wood, as were the four towers, the whole gilded and pierced and painted in blue and gold and decorated with carved and sculpted figures of knights, ladies and mythical beasts with three heads or a dozen feet, and there were many little narrow windows, like surprised eyes. A bit draughty in winter, I thought. However, it was difficult to remember snow and ice on so pleasant a day, though paradoxically it certainly seemed cooler down here in the valley. Once more for no reason I shivered, and glanced sideways at the lake: it should have sparkled with sunshine and glinted in the breeze that cracked and snapped the pennons and flags atop the towers, but instead it lay dark and still, dead, and I felt the others shift and press closer as we passed through the heavy wooden gates into the courtyard. This was paved with white cobbles, and to left and right were stables and sheds, and servants in a scurry: one boy's task, I noticed, seemed to be solely that of picking up any stray leaf, straw, or other piece of rubbish that might mar the otherwise pristine approach. I hoped Snowy wouldn't disgrace us by relieving himself, because that would obviously have meant shovels, buckets and mops almost before he had finished.

The stable to which we were assigned was, again, almost too clean and, apart from two palfreys, clear of horses. Sir Egerton indicated the end stall, away from the other mounts.

'Can put your—er, nag, here, don't y'know. The other creatures—er, pets?'

'Er . . . yes,' said Conn, his swift glance at us coloured by his suddenly luxurious surroundings to the extent that we obviously appeared to him suddenly exactly as we were: dirty and disreputable. 'And my—my servant, er—Thing-ummy . . .'

'Well,' said Sir Egerton, rubbing at the white whiskers on his chin. 'Can see you have problems, yes indeed. Never can remember their names meself! Like to leave the animals here, and you and your er, servant can be housed within? M'niece don't care much for cats, or birds come to that, and that fish don't look big enough for eating.'

I was frowning dreadfully at Conn, but he affected not to notice. 'Why, of course, of course! Just leave the—the animals comfortable, Thingy, and follow me.'

Making sure there was fresh fodder and water for Snowy and stowing the others in the manger, I wiped my grubby hands ineffectively on my jacket. 'I'll be back,' I said shortly. 'Just spy out the land.'

'Don't like this place,' wailed Moglet.

'Neither do I,' said Corby. 'Summat wrong some-wheres . . .'

Puddy hunched up. 'Don't be long.'

Pisky was at the very bottom of his bowl and said nothing.

I turned to Snowy. 'Keep an eye on them, dear one.'

He shook his head. 'I agree with the crow. Listen hard when

160

you are in that place, watch closely. All is too fair, too clean. And guard the Rusty One: we don't want to lose him.'

'Lose him?'

'Are you coming?' said Conn, poking his head round the door. 'For goodness sake! Leave those animals alone for a moment, can't you?'

So, it was just 'animals' they were, was it? For a moment I almost hated him.

But only for a moment, for as soon as we entered the castle proper I was traitor too to my friends, and had eyes and thought only for the delights that surrounded us. We entered from the courtyard through a pillared portico raised, surprisingly, only a couple of feet from the white cobbles, unlike most castles in which the ground floor was used for stores and the main floor was reached by outside steps: this place was obviously not built for siege.

There were no windows in the great hall in which we found ourselves, but large oil lamps hung from the high ceiling in chains and a cheerful fire burned in a huge fireplace opposite the doors: another innovation, for most hearths were still in the centre. The walls were hung with fine fabrics and tapestries, and a long table stretched the length of the room, with the usual dais at the end for the gentry. The floor, again unusually, was not covered with rushes but laid bare a very fine and detailed mosaic of a hunting scene. It must have predated the present building by a couple of centuries at least and some pieces were missing, others trod pale of colour, but at one end a very convincing stag fled its pursuers, antlers laid back across its shoulders, one terrified eye glancing back at the pursuing hounds, while at the other end a huntsman wound his horn and another notched his bow.

'Ah, my weary travellers, you are welcome!' Down a marble staircase behind the pictured hunters floated a vision. Even to my inexperienced eyes she was a very lovely lady, clad in a clinging robe of blue, fair hair bound and twisted in bands of gold, slippers of the same colour on her feet. Her gown had a long train that whispered over the patterned floor as she moved towards us, hands outstretched to Conn, no eyes for me, and on her fingers and slim wrists more bands of gold. A Golden Lady with hair to match, and eyes as blue as her gown.

161

And now Sir Egerton was introducing them but to my eyes they needed none such, for her hands were in Conn's and his eyes locked to hers as if they would never let go. She was near as tall as he and slim as a wand, and as she talked and smiled and nodded her little pointed teeth shone and her pink tongue flickered over her lips and they had no eyes for any but each other.

I suddenly felt very small and mean and hunched and dirty and would have given anything not to have seen these two together, to be back with the others, outside, free . . . And even as I thought this I felt the ground beneath my feet groan and move and cry so that I almost stumbled, but even as I looked around, terrified, I saw that no one else had noticed anything out of the way. There it was again! A voiceless moaning, a wordless fear, an empty desolation that beat at the soles of my feet until I felt as though the whole floor moved, and in the flicker and sway of the oil-lamps the stag looked more terrified than ever; his eye shut and opened, his muzzle dripped foam and the hounds bayed their blood-lust—

I dropped to the ground, staggering at the shift in the floor, my eyes shut, my hands over my ears to stop that awful sound—

But Conn was shaking me. 'Whatever's the matter, Thingy? Are you all right? Then for heaven's sake stand up and behave yourself! Whatever will the Lady Adiora think of you? Come now . . .' and he raised me and pushed me in the direction of the lady, but I would not look at her, and hung my head and shuffled my feet.

'But how clever of you, my dear Sir Connor!' she exclaimed, and I detected a slight lisp. 'How amusing: a hunchie! Does it do tricks? Tumble? And it wears a mask—it must be perfectly hideous! *Do* let me see . . .' and she stretched out her hand, but with a curiously protective gesture Conn drew me against him.

'No creature for laughter or amusement, my Lady,' he said quietly. 'Merely a poor unfortunate that cannot help either the shape or the looks the dear Lord saw fit to burden it with. And it is under my protection, as are the other creatures I travel with—'

But immediately she was all smiles, all contrition for her

162

thoughtlessness, as she came to lay her hand on his arm.

She also trod on my foot, quite hard.

'But of course, Sir Connor! I did not mean to make fun of your servant or your playthings. 'Tis just that I, too, have an interest in finding—employment—for like unfortunates. You will see them tonight . . . And now, if you will follow me?' She gathered the train of her gown. 'I declare! It is so good to see a fresh face! Sometimes I feel I shall *die* with boredom in this out-of-the-way prison . . .'

And she took his hand, as naturally as if they had known each other years, and led him towards the stairway and the first floor, me trailing miserably and awkwardly behind.

The room we were to share was octagon-shaped, in one of the towers overlooking the back of the castle. This part was built of wood, in the Moorish pattern, Conn told me, and the tall, leather-curtained windows looked out over the enclosed courtyard behind, curiously bare of ornamentation except for tubs of bay and myrtle, and with an open end enclosed by tall, pointed stakes of wood, with a gateway set in, firmly latched and bolted. Around the two sides were pavilions, set some ten feet from the ground, but there was no indication what it was used for: on closer acquaintance it was far too small for jousting or tourney. As I stared down at its emptiness, again I felt that desolation that I had experienced below, though all seemed fair on the surface.

'Did you ever see such a bed!' exulted Conn, and I turned back from the window to see him stretched out full length on a massive couch set on a platform, hung around with curtains and spread with clean linen and plump cushions and a great coverlet of wolf-skins. 'Here's luxury, then!'

'Just what you wanted,' I said. 'Except it's wolf and not bear.'

'One's as warm as the other, and there's only one thing wanting to make it perfect,' and he winked at the ceiling, but did not elaborate. 'Tell you what, Thingumajig: I reckon we've cat-fallen on our feet here, and no mistake! My nose tells me dinner's on the way, and did you see Milady? Have you ever seen anyone more beautiful?'

'No,' I said truthfully, for though our Mistress had been

163

more lovely still in some of her Shape-Changes, that had been magic and not painted prettiness like the Lady Adiora. 'Conn . . .'

'Mmmm?'

'Did you notice anything—odd—downstairs? I mean a sort of feeling, a strangeness in the air, a sort of—well, unhappiness?'

'Not a thing, Thingy, not a thing!' He leant up on his elbow. 'Was that why you came over all unnecessary?'

I nodded. 'I just—felt something. Queer. Nasty . . .'

He leant back again, obviously bored with my imaginings. 'Well, there's nothing nasty here, I assure you. Just good living, a beautiful lady, and—'

'And' was a servant, attired in the castle blue and yellow, scratching at the door with a flagon of wine and a Roman glass, green and fragile. One glass.

Conn filled and raised it. 'Here's to adventure, Thingy: may all quests be as promising! Oh, look here, the servant must not have been told you were with me . . . A sip from mine: come now, no need to sulk!'

I wasn't sulking, far from it, but I suppose it must have looked that way. Obediently I sipped from the other side of the goblet: it was sweet and heady. I watched Conn help himself to another glass.

'You haven't eaten yet.'

'No hurry, no hurry!'

But by the time other servants brought hot water and cloths and filled the tub in the corner, I had practically to undress him. A lot of water went on the floor while he splashed and sang, a mournful ditty of great emotion and little tune, and I had to help him into the clean linen, hose and embroidered surcoat that the Lady Adiora had thoughtfully provided, both to please her eye and put him more firmly in her debt, I had no doubt.

He spoilt the whole effect by falling asleep, fully clothed, on top of the bed, waking up crumpled and cross when a great dinner-gong sounded below some half-hour later. I had taken advantage of his unconsciousness to use the cooling water for a bath myself, and felt immensely better and enormously hungry when he woke, and trotted down to the hall quite happily at his heels, telling myself that my earlier unease was merely engendered by fatigue, an empty stomach and an overactive imagination.

This time there was noise enough to drown any half-imagined sounds from beneath my feet and food enough to ease the stomach-cramps—which strangely enough had re-occurred quite sharply since we came to the castle—and entertainment to feast the eye as well. Though I was seated well below the salt I had a good view of Conn and the Lady Adiora. She had him on her right hand, Sir Egerton on her left, and I could see they were all enjoying themselves. The food was excellent—there was even the venison Conn had craved—and I stuffed myself on pig and truffles and roast duck till I had no room left for the other dozen or so dishes. So I relaxed, pleasantly full of rich food, and listened to the conversation on either side.

My companions were inferior servants of the other gentlemen who attended the feast—there were no ladies save our hostess—and, although they ignored me except for a nod of courtesy and a look of disdain at my shabby wear, they chattered quite freely amongst themselves, and once I had done pigging I listened more carefully. What I heard disturbed me. There were six knights in attendance on the top table, four of whom were staying at the castle, the other two neighbours. They were all well attired, handsome, and of an age or younger than Conn, but once I realized what their servants were saying I observed them more closely.

The conversation I overheard went something like this:

Servant One: 'Yours doesn't look too chuffed . . .'

Servant Two: 'Yours neither. (Belch) 'What do you expect? Stranger appears and knocks their noses together!'

Servant One: 'Yours had had it anyway. Six weeks . . .'

Servant Two: 'So what? Yours took longer, but look at his eyes! Doubt if he'll carry those saddle-bags round much longer.'

Servant Three, from across the table, picking at his teeth: 'What gets me is how she does it! Cool as the lake and twice as deep.'

Servant Two: 'Cool? By'r Lady, she's no more cool than this stew! Randiest whore I ever seen.'

165

Servant Three: 'Anyway, this one's no better than his stamina, and by the looks of him he's travelled hard already—'

Servant One: 'Nothing to the road he has to ride!'

The others sniggered, then one of them glanced at me and winked his companions to silence, and after that I turned to their masters with more awareness. I saw pinched faces under the handsome exteriors: hollow eyes, nervous fingers crumbling unregarded bread, sidelong glances; tongues licking lips, but not of gravy; a hand too ready to stray to knife or dagger; damp palms, pallor, greed—and all directed to where Conn sat, blissfully ignorant, picking at a capon with idle fingers, his gaze always toward the sparkling Adiora, looking more beautiful than ever in a midnight-blue dress sewn with silver thread, her hair unbound save for a silver fillet round her brow. In spite of the look of bemused happiness on Conn's face, and the sight of his moustache once more elevated in eagerness, I felt uneasy: it seemed the lady's interest had antagonized just about everyone except Sir Egerton, who was dozing happily.

All at once I wanted to be back on the quest again together, in spite of my present ease and comfort; I wanted the sweet horsey smell of Snowy's flank to snuggle up to; I wanted Corby's caustic comments, Puddy's good sense, Moglet's soft fur, even Pisky's endless reminiscences, tangled as a nest of grass snakes . . . I wanted Conn back with us, dusty, irritable sometimes, gentle always—

Oh heavens! Hours ago I had promised to go back and report to the others, and by now they must be starving! Pretending I was still hungry I helped myself to a plate of the beef and oyster stew, then slipped away from the table unnoticed and found my way back to the stables. I expected the usual wails and moans about hunger and promises not kept, but they were remarkably quiet. It appeared Puddy had caught a couple of fat bluebottles and had shared shreds with Pisky, so it was only Moglet and Corby for stew. I thought of telling them about Conn's infatuation, about the strange sounds I thought I had heard, but decided it would be foolish: everything would probably be different in the morning, and after all we should be on our way again in a day or so. In the meanwhile, I was missing the promised entertainment at the feast, so after ten restless moments I announced I was going back inside.

Then in their eyes, all five pairs of them, I saw the knowledge of my neglect and guilt lent an angry and spiteful spark to my tongue.

'No reason why I shouldn't go and enjoy myself once in a while! Everyone but me seems to have fun, gets to eat at a table like the gentry, sometimes joins in pleasant conversation, exchanges gossip, has a change of company every now and again! Everyone but me, it seems, finds themselves among their own kind! And what have I got? The promise of a smelly stable and a load of helpless animals!' And, thoroughly frightened at my reaction, guilty at my outburst and lonely as hell without either my friends or Conn, I went back to the feast, to be faced by a thoroughly distasteful entertainment I would have done well to miss.

This consisted of 'performances', if you could call them that, by dwarves, manikins, cripples and deformed animals. I found it very easy to imagine myself and the others in their place, and it seemed worse when I saw Conn, his flushed face and sparkling eyes telling only too well their story of too much food and wine, applaud and laugh as heartily as the rest at some poor creature with but one eye in the centre of its forehead and no arms, doing a wretchedly inept tumbling act which ended with it falling into the hearth and setting up a bewildered howl as its hair caught fire. I felt even sicker when they put an emaciated dog with only three legs into a sack with a giant rat: I did not wait for the outcome but ran out to the coolness of the courtyard and was sick on their nice, clean cobbles.

After that I was too ashamed to return either to the others or the feast, so crept away to the shadows of a side-stair and up to our chamber, and there lay down by the fire and sniffled myself to sleep.

I must have slept heavily, for when I awoke the bed in the shadows was already occupied. Still feeling slightly sick and with a nasty taste in my mouth, I blinked sleepily at the fire, which someone had replenished for it was now leaping and dancing like those wretched creatures downstairs, throwing shadows crooked enough to give one the frights. And it was not only the flames that made the shadows caper on the wall, for somehow there was a different shadow-play from the bed. The firelight shone ruddily on Conn's red hair, his eyes, shining bright, and over his thin, white body. But not only Conn: the Lady Adiora hung over him, and her hands and legs and teeth were busy on him, holding, twisting, biting, clutching, pulling, tearing until I heard him groan as if in pain and jumped to my feet despite my thumping head and scuttled over to the bedside.

'Stop it!' I cried shrilly to the lady, who was clad only in her golden hair. 'You're hurting him!' And I drew my dagger, prepared to drive her away by force, for he now lay gasping as in a fever, with her sitting across his loins and raking his chest with her pointed fingernails till the blood darkened his skin like sloe-juice on a pigeon's breast. But he only gazed at me with unseeing eyes and groaned the more and she leant across and struck me on the cheek.

'Don't you dare interfere, you dirty little hunchie! You're— you're no better than those others in the dungeons: you should never have been allowed inside! Now, get out! Out, I say, or it will be the worse for you!' And she spat at me so hard that the gobbet stuck to my mask and I had to wipe it away with the back of my hand.

Slowly I sheathed my dagger and looked again at Conn, whose eyes and hands were on the lady's breasts.

'Er . . . it doesn't understand, my beautiful.' He turned for a moment to give me an apologetic smile. 'Do as she says, there's a good, er . . . Thingummy.'

'And don't come back!' she hissed.

'But—but she's hurting you!' I faltered, but at that they both gave such a snigger that I started back, and then suddenly knew what they were doing.

I understood all at once about our Mistress and her Shape-Changes and the sticky head of Broom; about the swineherd who had threatened me with that great thing sticking out in front; all about what it meant to be a female; most of all what the parts of Conn's body were for, and hers—and mine, and it was as if someone had flung me naked from the warm into a bank of snow, so that I gasped with shock and disbelief and ran to the curtained doorway and fought my way through the thick folds and stumbled tear-blinded down the steep stairs, my shadow running hunched before me from the flaming cressets in the wall, until I fell down the last few steps to lie, stunned, on the patterned marble mosaic of the empty hall.

It was the cold that brought me to: I suppose I must have lain there no more than a few minutes, yet in that time it seemed everything had changed. The oil lamps still guttered in their chains, the dampened fire still stuttered and lisped in the fireplace, but the air was filled with an echo like a great gong and the mosaic beneath me sweated with fear. I managed to raise myself to my hands and knees, and from where I crouched I could see the glazed eye of the great stag, running away from me, hear the beat of his terrified heart, the thud of his hooves, the harsh rasp of his breathing and wiped a fleck of bloodstained foam from my hand. And then I was running with him, crashing heedless through the undergrowth, careless of stinging bramble and whipping branch, and the ground sprang away from beneath my feet and the knot of fear in my stomach grew into a physical pain that made me cry out, but still the pursuers came on and at last I turned to face them and an arrow hissed through the singing air and thudded into my breast and I was bleeding, dying, dead—

'Come back, come away, dear one!' All at once I heard my friends calling me, and with a great effort I dragged myself back to reality, staggered to my feet and hunched my way to the great oaken doors that led to the courtyard, struggled with bolts and latches strangely heavy and stiff, flung myself through the gap that offered and stumbled down the shallow steps and across the cobbled yard to the safety of the stable, where Snowy took my arms around his neck, Moglet caressed my ankles, Corby brushed his sound wing across my face, Puddy hummed gently and Pisky sang me a bubbly song.

'I'm sorry, so sorry!' I sobbed. 'And so afraid!'

'We know,' whispered Snowy, 'but you are safe now . . .' and he let me cry out my tears and remorse and wipe my eyes on his silky mane. When I was comforted enough they asked me what had happened, and first I told them about Conn and the lady and then of the fear and sorrow that I had experienced in the hall.

They listened attentively, but it was Corby who summed up our problem, in his own inimitable way.

'So he's temporarily not one of us,' he said slowly. 'And there's something nasty under the floorboards . . .'

THE BINDING: UNICORN

The Terror under the Floor

AFTER A good night's sleep we went over it all again, and I had
to endure once more my memories of Conn and the lady, but
my friends instinctively made it easy for me, and once again it
was Corby's good sense that made it bearable.

'Time you grew up anyway, Thing dear, and my guess is that
it was only a thing of the flesh and nothing to worry about in
the long run. Sometimes with humans, I understand, it is a bit
like eating: wasn't it the Rusty Knight himself that said he was
tired of plain fare and craved venison? Fair enough, but a diet
of venison day and night will make you liverish, and before
long you're back to bread and cheese and ale, the stuff that
keeps you going most of your life.

'So, let it be: he'll return to plain fare soon enough . . .'

After I was reconciled to all this—superficially at least—
there was still the wonderment of realizing where men and
women fitted into each other like mortice and tenon, their
bodies tongued and grooved and dovetailed like fair furniture.
But I had not thought that this coupling could be a thing of
such violence, of cries and tearings, of hurt and passion. Still,
it was interesting, just the same, and I thought about it at
intervals for quite some time. The only sure thing in all this
cogitating was that a body such as mine, all humps and
crookedness, would need a very fine carpenter indeed to marry
the parts to another.

Of the strange noises in the hall, the feelings of terror and
despair, Snowy at least was positive something should be
done. The trouble was, we did not know whether there was
anything actually underneath the floor, as I suspected, though

171

when I went back later and stamped, quietly, I reported back that there seemed to be an echo of sorts beneath my feet.

'Sounds like a cellar,' said Puddy. 'Or a dungeon.'

Something tickled at the back of my mind: hadn't the Lady Adiora said something about a dungeon? But my thoughts were going back farther than that.

'The castle seems to have been built on the foundations of a large Roman villa,' I said slowly. 'And if I remember—if I recall—someone must have told me that those old villas had great storerooms underneath, and lots of pipes and channels for a hot-water warming system; sometimes these cellars extended even beyond the foundations of the house itself if there wasn't a ready supply of water adjacent—'

'The lake!' said Corby. 'But they don't use it now: go a half-mile for fresh water from a river through on the other side of the woods. Heard one of the nags grumbling 'bout doing the journey three times a day or more when there's company.'

'Water in that lake looks dead,' said Puddy. 'Can't have been alive for years.'

'We must take a look,' said Snowy. 'All that you have said, Thing, makes me believe that there is something gravely amiss here. A larger amount of fodder than is necessary for the beasts here is collected daily, and some of it carried outside the castle walls. As far as I remember there are no outer stables, nor any cattle grazing . . . I think, friends, it is time we took some exercise.'

So it was that I rode out of the stable, Moglet and Puddy inside my jacket, Pisky's bowl slung round my waist and Corby wobbling on my shoulder, to ask the soldiers on duty that the main gate be opened.

We were greeted by a shout of laughter. 'Call that thing a horse?' guffawed one of the gate-guards. 'And as for that tatty bird . . . Any more in the travelling circus?'

I frowned most dreadfully, and I could hear Corby grinding his beak, but Snowy behaved just like the clown they believed him: stumbled a little, flicked his ears back and forth, swished his tail and gave me some good advice in the midst of all this as well.

'Go easy, Thing dear: every human likes to laugh, and the more they despise us the more ready they will be to disregard

172

us as a threat to whatever they are hiding. Play as silly as me, there's a good girl. And, wise crow, fall off your perch and try and look ridiculous, if you can . . .'

So we found ourselves outside the gate, with a good deal of chaffing on the guard's part, and a secret rage in my breast. I turned Snowy's head eagerly towards the side of the castle nearest the lake, but quite unexpectedly he stopped suddenly and lowered his head and I slid gracefully down his neck to land on the turf in a heap. I got to my feet, spilling cats and toads and fish all over the place.

'What on earth did you do that for?' I demanded furiously, but even as I asked I heard the sound of laughter carried from the gateway, and turned to see them all still watching us.

'That was the reason,' said Snowy. 'So, today we shall not go near the lake, but shall rather ride innocently through the forest for a while. Get up again, Thing: I promise none of this will be wasted.'

So that day we rode the perimeter of the castle, but some hundred yards hidden in the forest. We found neither bird nor beast to disturb its stillness, but we did find another exit. We had originally approached the castle from the east, joining the woodland ride that approached it from the south; but running near north there was another ride that ended on a knoll looking over a swift-running river, which was obviously where the household water was collected each day. Beyond this was a wooden bridge, a small village on the other bank, and thick forest. We followed the ride back towards the castle, and found that we emerged some quarter mile from the strange enclosed space at the back of the building, and even as we watched from the shelter of the trees we could see that the pavilions inside were being enlarged and painted, and at one time someone opened the bolted wooden gates and we could see the gravel within being meticulously raked into formal patterns and the tubs of shrubs being moved to the sides.

Snowy sighed, and I could feel him shiver beneath me. 'I think we are almost too late: tomorrow and the day after it will rain, and then I think they will leave it till the full moon . . . We have five days. Tomorrow we shall have to risk going by the lake. It is too soon, I fear, but it is a risk we shall have to take if we are to free them.'

'Them?' I echoed, but he only shook his head, and carried us swiftly back through the rest of the semicircle of forest.

The next morning we were out again, but this time attracted far less attention from the guards, as Snowy had predicted. Again as he had promised the sky was overcast and a little warning wind rattled the flags on their poles, then died away.

I had attended supper again the previous night in the great hall, and had had to face once again the sight of Conn, utterly besotted, eyes only for the Lady Adiora. Upstairs there had been castle servants who shouldered me out of the way when the bathing-water was produced, and there were others to air his new clothes—russet and green, fine wool and silk—and make up the bed, so I was largely redundant as far as I could see. We had only exchanged a couple of words, when he had fallen over me in his hurry to bathe and change and then, as I had apologized for being in the way, he had looked at me with an air of puzzlement as if he did not recognize me, and had merely asked, after a moment, if my room were comfortable. I had said yes, of course I had, for it was obvious that he had forgotten about the rest of us, or at least put us to the back of his mind for the time being. So I had not reminded him I had been banished to the stables, had not told him our fear of what the dungeons held, and most of all had not let him know how I hated the Lady Adiora for stealing him away and despised him for letting her. In all this, of course, I was forgetting Corby's wise words, but solecisms and banalities, however true they may be to the objective eye, are no use at all to one who is subjectively green with jealousy all over like an unripe apple, even if that one has absolutely no right to be . . .

So, as I said, we went out that next morning to spy out the land on the lakeward side of the castle. I dismounted on the other side of a clump of sear and withered reeds and tipped Puddy and Pisky into the waters to see what life there was, if any, and Moglet was detailed to work her way around the the edge, keeping as far as possible out of sight. Corby was set as lookout and Snowy was to crop aimlessly towards the castle and an interesting-looking dark, gullied gateway set in the castle wall. I was the distraction: if I thought anyone was watching I behaved like the village idiot, capering around and turning somersaults and picking daisies for a chain.

We agreed a sun-time, which I reckoned would be near enough an hour, and it must have been near midday when we met again, casually enough, behind the clump of reeds. Pisky and Puddy were last at the rendezvous and I had to haul them both out of the water, gasping and distressed, all too ready to blurt out their joint discoveries.

'It's all dark and lifeless and choking and black with slime and mud and there are no fish—'

'Water's stagnant, been like that a long time. Once connected to the castle. Long pipe, blocked up with mud. Tried to get down it but failed.'

'Pipe is all choked up with clay and dead bones and gravel—'

'Could be cleared. Water level is above pipe-mouth.'

'—and nasty, smelly, stinking water. A hand beneath the water and you can't see a fin in front of you. No water-bugs, no snails, no red bottom-worms even, no nothing . . .'

'There's something like a sluice gate above that pipe,' said Moglet unexpectedly. 'I've seen something like that before: the wood is sound, but it looks as though it hasn't been used for many years, and would need a good greasing before it would shift. The rest of the lakeside is barren, and there is very little cover.'

'The Romans' water system worked something like that,' I said, still wondering how I knew. 'Water from an outside source ran through pipes that were heated in cavities under the house. A—a hypocaust . . .'

'Well,' said Snowy. 'I've been cropping grass till I'm swollen-bellied, but I still can't see a way into the dungeons, or whatever they are, to find what I know is there. There is nothing but that barred gate to see.'

'That pipe runs right beneath the grass and through that gate,' said Corby. 'The grass is a different colour. Dug years ago, but you can always tell.'

'But the water can't get through,' I objected. 'Moglet and Puddy and Pisky said so. It can't have anything to do with floods or things drowning—'

' 'Ware strangers!' hissed Corby, and we all ducked down behind the reeds except Snowy, who was too big.

From the front of the castle came half-a-dozen or so stable-hands carrying sacks and fodder and as we watched they moved, bowed with the weights, to the dark gateway in the wall. One man took out a large key and unlocked it and they passed inside—and out from that unlocked gate flowed such a miasma of fear and despair that it crawled as palpable as a fog to where we lay hidden, and such overwhelming sorrow struck my heart that I beat my hands against invisible bars and sobbed out my prisonment.

'Shut up, Thing!' warned Corby. 'They're coming out again.'

And as we watched the stable-servants emerged with baskets of ordure and cast them into the cesspit beyond the lake and rapidly infilled with fresh earth, but as they did so Moglet and Snowy sniffed the wind.

'Deer, boar . . .'

'Hare, coney?'

'Bear? Wild pony, certainly.'

'Badger . . .'

'We must get in there somehow,' said Snowy urgently. 'My nose tells me that there are dozens of animals in there, and we still don't know why!'

The idea seemed ridiculous to me. Why keep animals imprisoned underground? If one wanted meat one either grazed cattle or hunted, that was part of life. Why keep them fed and watered underground, when it was so much cheaper to let them roam free? Deer and boar were plentiful, at least outside this forest, and so were the smaller game. Everywhere else but here: was that the answer? Was that why they stored them? But what of the absence of any kind of life: no birds, no hedgepigs, no mice, no rats? And the overwhelming fear that overlaid all? But why, *why*? There must be a simple explanation . . . A feast and a fair, that was it! They had some deer, boar and hare for the feast, ready for easy slaughter when the time was ripe. And the others were for the usual tainted entertainment this place seemed to afford. The smell of badger that Moglet had detected in the droppings must mean that one corner of that enclosed space they had been tidying and gravelling yesterday would be reserved for baiting, and the bear must be a tame one, trained for dancing. The wild ponies?

176

Those I supposed would be for the lady's horsebreakers to show off their arts. If the general standards of entertainment in this place were anything to go by, this was an improvement: better than the stupid torturing pleasure they usually seemed to take with strange, twisted things like me . . .

'No,' said Snowy, who had obviously been reading my thoughts. 'No, there are too many, dear child, and their fear has infected all the land around. It is more than mere sport or entertainment.'

'Then what?'

'I am not sure. Not yet . . . But one of us must get in there to find out.'

It started to rain, quite heavily. One of the men carrying over more hay looked up and saw us.

'Hey you: Crookback! Yes, you . . . Bring that nag of yours over here and make him useful, otherwise we'll all get soaked.'

I would have refused, but Snowy spoke urgently. 'This is just the chance we have been waiting for! Take me over . . .'

'You're not a beast of burden at the beck of anyone!'

'Don't argue, for once. Just do as I say.'

So I left the others sheltering as best they could and led Snowy over. 'You want to borrow the pony?' I asked, sounding, and looking too, I suppose, like a halfwit.

The stable-hand grabbed Snowy's bridle and thwacked his rump. 'C'mon, you bag-of-bones!'

I watched him load up, noted Snowy's meek head hanging down, saw him led down a slight incline to the mouth of a tunnel that revealed itself now I was nearer to the barred gate, then made my way back to the others.

Puddy and Pisky were fine, revelling in the warm summer rain, which was coming down faster now, but Moglet made a wild leap at me, burrowing under my jacket and proceeding to soak us both, and Corby, nothing loath, tried to huddle under my cloak. We made our way back to the castle, more or less together, and I stowed away the others, for I could not know how long Snowy would be. Then, as luck would have it, I ran straight into Conn and the Lady Adiora.

We had obviously missed their riding out, for they were now returning wet with rain, Conn mounted on a beautiful strawberry-roan, apparisoned with red velvet, both now dark with rain. I rushed over to clutch at his bridle but he looked down at me as though I were a stranger, all the while listening to the lady's prattle.

'. . . but because of the weather we had better postpone it. My weathermen say it should clear up by New Moon, so probably four days hence. You will have to practise your archery, meanwhile—What is that dirty creature doing?' In a different voice. I was frantically pulling at Conn's bridle to try to gain his attention. 'Send it away! That part of your life is gone, my love, but if you still have a fondness for the creature I will find it work in the kitchens . . .'

Conn pulled away from me. 'Not now, not now,' he said. 'Later, Thingy, later . . .'

I spat on the ground as they passed, but the angry tears were not far from my eyes, and when I went into the castle that night I was denied the table and pushed towards the kitchens, where a greasy scullion grabbed me and made me turn one of the spits while he dipped his fingers in the gravy and lay back at his ease, and every time I tried to escape he pulled me back by my ear, cackling with laughter at my discomfort.

I was worried, for Snowy had not returned by the time I went over to the castle, and each minute dragged interminably. When I finally escaped the rain had stopped and the summer stars were shining faintly, and low clouds obscured the moon. I had only had beans and bread for supper and water to wash them down, but managed to salvage a beef-rib bone from under the nose of a great hound and, dusted down, it would be more than adequate for Corby and Moglet. I hoped Puddy had managed to find one of his unmentionables during the day, and Pisky could have a sliver of the beef.

But when I reached the stable all this planning was forgotten, for there was Snowy, head drooping, flanks heaving, trembling as though in an icy blast. The bone went flying as I rushed forward, and I will give the others their due, that bone was not touched until we had heard Snowy's story.

At first I thought his distress was due to ill-treatment and abuse, and I ran my hands over his hide, his joints and tendons, looked to see he had water and fodder, but all was as it should be. And then, though he had volunteered nothing, I realized that the aura of near-palpable suffering that emanated from him was an exhaustion of the spirit that has had to suffer mental ill-treatment as real as if it had been beaten or starved, and I put my arms around his neck and leant my head against his jaw.

'Tell me—tell us—dear one, what has happened, what you saw that was so dreadful . . .' And as he told us it was as if we were there and could see through his eyes, hear through his ears, smell it and taste it and feel it.

As he had approached the open gate in the wall a great stench of animal came from it, and out of the dark, yawning mouth of the tunnel a belch of fear, raw and undigested, that had made him stop in his tracks, and the men had used a whip to urge him on, jesting that he could smell the wolves and was afraid he would be turned into their dinner.

And wolves there were, penned next to the great dusty bear and her yearling cub: three grey, slinking animals, eyes slitted sharp as their teeth. And next to the wolves two large badgers, almost as big as the half-dozen wild boar, both these pig-like animals full still of rage and lust for killing, wasting their strength on futile rushes against the bars as the men approached, the badgers' claws rattling impotently against the metal, the boars' tusks ringing as they clashed with their prison. And opposite these fierce creatures were the grass-eaters, the proud stag with his three terrified hinds, the wild ponies, mountain goats, hares, coneys—and their keepers rattled the bars and taunted them as they threw them their food, gave them their water, telling them how their days, hours, minutes were numbered.

'Four days from tomorrow you've got, my fine creatures, and then you'll be so much skin for the buzzards! Midsummer Night will be perpetual night for you all! And not from each other, oh no! 'Twill be the fine lords and ladies as will lead the massacre, and them getting points each for the ones they kill. Not so many for the bears, 'cos they're a bigger target, though more difficult to finish off, but big points for the hares, 'cos they're smaller and move faster. Roast venison all round from you, my fine fellow and your dames; only ones we can't eat are the pesky wolves and rancid badgers, but they'll do for bait for the next lot of meat-eaters. Ah yes, roll on the Midsummer-Night massacre!'

And so, Snowy told us, big-eyed with wonder and horror, he had had to calm all those beasts, tell them what they needed and hoped for.

'And what was that?' I asked, knowing what the answer would be even as I asked the question.

'Why, that we would rescue them all, of course,' he said.

THE BINDING: UNICORN

Midsummer Madness

AND, LOOKING at the faith shining from those strange brown-grey-green eyes I almost believed we could, even as I asked the hopeless: 'But—how?'

So he told us.

In essence the plan was to open the exit gates beyond the slaughter-yard and guide the animals away from the castle to the ride leading through the woods to the bridge across the river that marked the boundary between this petty tenure and another. The plan entailed opening well oiled gates, the control of panic among the animals and slowest ones to go first, and also a distraction at the castle end to divert those attending the Madness. Snowy promised to organize the animals and keep them from panic, if the rest of us could ensure the opening of the gates and the distraction.

'There,' he said. 'How about it?'

We all agreed enthusiastically, caught in the euphoria of the moment, but it was the common-sensical Puddy who brought us back to reality.

'A good idea,' he said, with his sometimes maddening slowness, 'but what would distract the lords and ladies enough not to send their servants chasing the beasts? And how would we escape afterwards? And what of the Rusty Knight? Remember, The Ancient insisted that we had all to keep together, and this is only the first of our trials. By all accounts he has eschewed his loyalties already.'

Conn! Oh, dear Gods, I had forgotten him already!

No, I had not forgotten, that was not the right way to think of it. He was in my thoughts day and night, and I was made both fiercely jealous and desperately miserable by his defection to the beautiful Adiora, but he had assumed the proportion of a dream, not to be confused with the day-to-day realities of eating and drinking, sleep, discoveries, plans for the escape of the animals. I cursed myself for my forgetfulness of his place in the general scheme of things as I gazed blankly at the others.

'Thing-dear will think of something,' said Snowy comfortably, and such was the assurance in his voice that at that moment I truly believed I would, and put the problem temporarily from my mind.

But there was still the question of a distraction, and it was Corby who suggested fire. 'Top half of this place is all wood, and would make a merry blaze . . .' and so I volunteered the next day to scout around on the upper floors and try to find a convenient corner to set combustible material. For the escape afterwards Snowy promised that we would not be left behind. Pisky asked why the animals couldn't be let out now, please, but Snowy confirmed that there were guards on duty day and night around the castle, and escape before massacre-day would be impossible.

We settled down for the night, curiosity allayed by Snowy's story and a definite plan of action to follow, but perhaps because of this the stimulation of thought made us restless, bog-eyed sleepers when at last dawn broke on another grey, dripping day.

The stable-servants 'borrowed' Snowy again, and I asked him specifically to look out for and question the prisoned animals as to the whereabouts of a particular item I thought might be in the dungeons; Conn and the lady went out riding again, accompanied only by two discreet grooms, and I shut my mind to reclaiming him for the time being. By dint of dodging servants on occasion and behaving as if I belonged on others, I managed to gain access to the upper floors of the castle. The first floor consisted of bedchamber after bedchamber, a magnificent solar and a small library, but the next floor with its jutting towers was more hopeful. Those rooms facing to the front of the castle were all occupied, but of the others overlooking the back Conn was in one and the last was full of empty chests, discarded pallets, hangings in need of repair and tattered tapestries: these were all dry, and would give off a good smoulder-smoke if lit.

All this reconnoitring took time, and I still had not had a chance to speak to Conn alone by the time the rest of us gathered in the stable after supper. I had managed a bowl of scraps for the others, having been relegated to the kitchens again, and also a useful pocketful of fat strips, ideal for starting a fire. I had also checked the gates out of the slaughter-yard: these had been opened again today, and while I noted the ease with which the bolts slid back, I also saw that it took two men to swing them open, largely because the ground sloped slightly upwards at this point. A careful removal of accumulated stones and debris was all that was needed, and I saw how I could play an idiot and build mudpies at this point, and also lay out a couple of arrow-pointers the way the animals were to go.

Snowy was able to confirm what I had suspected, that a pipe, now blocked with debris, led into the upper part of the dungeon and thence into a disused cistern, cracked and perforated.

'That must be the pipe that leads to the lake,' I said eagerly. 'Which animal is nearest?'

'Luckily for us it is the badgers; their cage holds both pipe and cistern. I have asked them to clear away what rubble they can and pile it under the pipe. Some of the smaller coneys are going to squeeze through their bars to help. Now it's up to you lot at the lake end. Have you spied out the escape route?'

'Tomorrow,' I promised.

The next day was the penultimate one before the intended killings, and there was a lot to do. The most important thing, of course, was to investigate the escape route, but my idea about the underground pipe, which had started merely as a secondary diversion, now assumed greater importance in my mind, for if it succeeded it would mean no more 'games' like these could be played at the castle ever again: fire from above, water from below . . .

But I was thinking ahead too fast: back to the first priority. That morning I begged a ride on one of the water-carts, Corby paying for our passage by playing counting tricks with stones, to my dictation: Pisky, Puddy and Moglet I kept hidden under my cloak. As soon as the cart stopped at the river and they started to fill the water-skins I excused myself, saying I would walk back. There was a wooden bridge across the river and I strolled across, to be accosted by a sleepy bridge-keeper on the other side, who demanded a copper coin before I could proceed to the village, five huts and a tavern.

'Lord Ric's demesne,' yawned the bridge-keeper. 'Naught to look at for miles. Forest clear through for five leagues at least, then the Hall. Looks of you, you wouldn't want to try it without a mount.'

'Where does the river come from?' I ventured.

'Gawd knows! Somewheres to the west. Now, you coming or going?'

'Going,' I said, and went.

So far, so good. A bridge guarded by one man, a forest north for miles, a river flowing east/west: the animals had a good chance if they got this far; it was to be hoped that there were meadows or clearings for the coneys and hares farther up the riverbank.

Now for the sluice in the lake. Luckily I got a lift back with a later water-cart because the pebble in my stomach was pulling again—no, not a pebble, the dragon's ruby: I kept forgetting. It was midday when we reached the scummy waterside, and I asked Pisky to swim down as far as he could to determine the construction of the sluice, and Puddy to hop down the pipe to see how far in it was blocked; I set Corby to find likely pieces of wood in case we had to lever up the sluice, and sat back on the bank for five minutes' rest, Moglet on my lap.

After a moment or two she became restless. 'Why can't I do something?' she demanded. 'Everyone else is being important . . .'

'I was just coming to that,' I said carefully. 'I couldn't manage without you, Moglet dear. We need a sentinel, a watcher, and I can't be in two places at once.' I was improvising rapidly, my thoughts in careful man-speech so she wouldn't understand. 'You were just what I had in mind; would you go behind that clump of dried grasses, keep an eye on the comings and goings at the castle, and watch the tunnel-gate as well?'

184

Pisky reported back, choking, that the nether end of the sluice was deep in mud, but that the mechanism seemed simple enough; the only bar to raising it seemed to be a block of iron placed crossways across the wheel that had to be turned north/south to engage a number of teeth that governed the height. Puddy said that, as far as he could judge, the tunnel, apart from silt, was clear up to within a foot of the walls of the castle: the echo of his splashes changed in quality with the weight of the walls above him. We called it a day after I had leant over as far as I dared to try turning the wheel, and had fallen in. The wheel needed greasing and I needed a bath.

That night I told an exhausted Snowy what we had found out. He nodded.

'The badgers have worked hard all day, and they say there is only a foot or so more of debris to move; they reckon they are right under the castle walls now. But the last bit will be the hardest: there are rocks and hard-packed earth in there.'

'How deep is the water in the pipe?' I asked Puddy.

'Inches only. The silt piled up at the lakeward end is what holds the water back. Once the pipe is clear it will run straight down to the dungeon, provided the digging beasts get it clear. Pressure of water will take all before it—the last six inches, anyway.'

I instructed Snowy to have the badgers excavate through as far as they dared, leaving an airway of about three inches at the top; the pipe's diameter was at least two feet, but we didn't want anyone excavating so far that they leaked the plot. On the other hand, if I could wind up the sluicegate just a little, at least we would know if our plan might work.

'Is it level, or does it slope down towards the castle—the pipe, I mean?' I asked Puddy.

'Slopes down. Only gradually. Exit is some foot or two lower than the lake end.'

'Bother!' I said, thinking rapidly. 'That means someone will have to come back for us, Snowy dear, after you have led the others out. Can you find someone else to lead them down to the river?'

'I am the only one who speaks all their languages. Perhaps I could send back a couple of the ponies . . .' he hesitated. 'Is all this necessary, my dear?'

185

'Yes,' I said. 'Very necessary. The majority of the animals may well escape this time, but what about the next ones? And the next? We want to make certain, don't we, that it never happens again, and if we flood the dungeons it will take them a long time—a very long time—to dredge it out again. Perhaps never, as the lake is on a higher level than the castle. Then maybe they will give up this sort of thing forever. I hope so . . . Send us back whatever help you can, for there will be all five of us—'

'And what about the Rusty Knight?' asked Snowy.

What indeed about the Rusty Knight? About Conn, the red-haired wanderer who had captured my heart . . . I had not seen him, except fleetingly, since the night we arrived. And when I had tried to speak to him it would seem he had forgotten all about us, for his eyes were only for the Lady Adiora in all her seductive beauty. For a moment or two I felt sorry for myself, lying sleepless on the straw in the stable, while he—while he luxuriated in silks and linen, but then the straw pricked at my spine and with that discomfort came the realization that I hadn't done much, hadn't done anything in fact, to wrest him from his diversion. I had crept away like a whipped slave on the lady's bidding and had sobbed from the hurt his careless-ness of me had engendered, but had I gone back upstairs and tried to win him back to us next morning? No. Had I fought for what I wanted, even though it might be impossible? No. Had I reasoned with him, bribed him, suborned him, warned him? No. Had I reminded him of the quest we were bound upon, of The Ancient's words, of the dragon? No. Had I rebelled, fought, poisoned, stabbed? No . . .

In fact I was a coward, that was the truth, as soft as Moglet who now lay across my chest, sides gently heaving, needing the reassurance of my body for her tentative purr. But then Moglet had me, and I had—? Them, of course, Snowy, Corby, Puddy, Pisky and my little cat. We were interdependent. Independent, too, by very virtue of our differences. But Conn? He and I should have been closer, for we were humans; but then he was a man, and men were different, it seemed. They had all sorts of privileges and greeds and lusts of their own, which they were allowed to indulge quite freely, it seemed, but didn't they too have such fundamental qualities as loyalty, for instance? Couldn't he, even for the short time the quest might take, leave his pleasures for another time?

I realized, of course, that he did not see the Lady Adiora quite as we did. To him she was a lovely body, a luxury, a dream to be indulged. To us she was a shallow, heartless quean who exploited the fears and vulnerabilities of helpless animals for her own pleasures and satiation, much as she was using Conn—

I sat up suddenly, disturbing a protesting Moglet. Of course! Just as she had to have this midsummer madness of a massacre to satiate her lust for cruelty, so also did she have to have this succession of men to satisfy her other lusts; not only Conn, but also those other knights with pale faces and jealous eyes who had stared at him on that first night. And Conn would become a cast-off, just like the rest of them, so soon as a fresh male appeared! Now I understood the mutterings of the servants, the angry looks of the desiccated knights. She was the spider, they the flies, to be seduced and devoured, sucked dry and discarded as and when she pleased.

And poor Conn believed she was the love of his life, true and tender and everlasting! But how could I possibly disillusion him, show him he was only one of many? And how, most important of all, persuade him to leave her the day after tomorrow? How make him understand what she was, his impermanence in her life? Make him realize about the massacre, her part in it? I didn't know, I just didn't know. And there was so little time . . .

There was less time than I had bargained for. That next morning there was more hustle and bustle than usual and I caught at a servant's sleeve.

'What goes on?'

'Her Ladyship's weathermen have been at it again, that's what! They say all's changing, and that if we leave the entertainment till tomorrow 'twill be wet. So, 'tis tonight, an hour after sundown, and there's lights and tapers and rushes to set—don't bother me, I've enough to do!'

I rushed back to Snowy. 'It's today, tonight, at twilight! We'll never be ready!'

'The animals must be told,' worried Snowy. 'And if it is to be tonight they won't bother feeding them. I wondered why I had not been sent for . . .'

'But you must get in there, they won't know what to expect! If we ever manage it . . . There's Corby to stake out, the sluice to make operable, and—oh Gods! Conn . . .' And I ran my fingers through my tangled hair in desperation.

'Stop panicking,' said Snowy gently. 'All will be done. Just tell me when you expect everything to be ready . . .'

Hastily revising practically everything I set approximate times, my mind racing ahead with gates to clear, dried rushes and fat to add to fuel, Conn . . . oh dear! And the problem of everyone being prepared to escape.

'Just be ready at the end of the lake nearest where all will be moving,' said Snowy. 'Someone will pick you up. It may not be me, but you will be rescued, I promise. Now, your only real problem is to persuade the Rusty One to cooperate.'

'But you—how will you get in to tell the other animals?'

'That is the easiest part! Go over now and tell the head-groom—that sharp-faced fellow in the striped yellow breeches—that your master has donated me to the entertain-ment. Go on: do as I say!'

'But—but that means . . .'

'That I shall be there to lead them to freedom, yes. Go, child: do as you are told. It's our only chance.'

I wanted to say no, no! We can escape, we can leave the other animals to their fate, we seven can get away, but knew it would be no use, knew that our unicorn would never agree. To him those lost, frightened animals down there in the dark were just as important as we were and that was right, I knew, but the miserable cowardly bit of me would not admit it. I knew that those prisoners were just as important to the world as the king in his castle, the knights in their armour, the maidens in their towers, and I wished there was something, someone, who would look kindly on our enterprise just for the sake of all the lost and frightened and persecuted ones who could not help themselves. Conn prayed regularly: perhaps I should too. I shut my eyes and tried to think of a force, a power, a stream of goodness, pity, love.

'Please, please help us!' I prayed. 'Help us to free those

animals, help us to ensure it doesn't happen again. Help me to help poor Conn, help me to take care of them all; keep us together and safe . . .'

I should have liked to record that I felt an enormous force sweep through me in answer, making me feel ten feet tall, full of courage and capable of dealing with anything, but I regret to say that all I felt was Moglet's claws in my right ankle.

'Breakfast?'

After that I was too busy to think of anything, except the searing compunction I felt as they led Snowy away.

They had laughed at my offer at first. 'What, that decrepit old bag o' bones?' they had jeered. 'Don't you know we don't take jades? Down there we have the pick of the fields and forests—what, an old hack like that?' Then: 'But perhaps, being white and so slow an' all, he'd be an easier target for some of the less-practised ladies . . . All right, then, we'll take him.'

And then, before I had time to think how desperately easily all this could go wrong, it was off to the kitchens to steal oil, tallow and fat-scraps, and racing upstairs to secrete it behind the other materials for Corby's fire. And back down again for some dried rushes . . . Then over to the lake. The waters had risen with the rain of the last couple of days and I had to grope for the lever that worked the sluice: it would still not budge further, but I had brought some tallow to grease it later. Then over to the wooden gates, and a frantic clearing of any dirt and stones that might impede their easy opening: no one took much notice. They were too busy with last-minute raking of the gravel, the fixing of tallow-dips, the hanging of silks and flags to the pavilions. Then I left the others in the stable while I attempted the task I had secretly been putting off till the last moment, the most difficult one of all . . .

Halfway up the steep, twisting stairs to Conn's room I hesitated. It was well into the morning: suppose he was due to go riding with Lady Adiora? Suppose he was with her now? Or perhaps with the other knights and newly arrived guests in the solar? Perhaps with Sir Egerton in the library? I realized I was trying to put more obstacles in my own way, and that maybe I could put it off till later: it was no use, procrastination would just make it worse. I should have to search until I found him and hope it would not be too long.

But I need not have worried. Pushing aside the curtain to his room, still not sure what to say, how to persuade him to leave with us, I found him stretched out on the bed, still apparently in the blue-and-silver garb he had worn to last night's banquet and certainly with the day before's stubble on his chin, and a stale, perfumed air about him. He lay flat on his back, his arms folded on his breast, his toes pointed down for all the world like a knight laid out for his burying. If it hadn't been for the frown and the open eyes I might well have believed him dead.

Going over to the bed I laid my hand hesitantly on his arm, still not sure of what I was going to say. 'Conn? Are you all right?'

He didn't move, not even his eyes: it was as if he were in a trance. Then—'Thingy?'

'Yes.'

'Haven't seen you for days—weeks.' Slowly his eyes swivelled round to meet mine. 'Yes, I'm all right. I think . . . Where have you been?'

I forebore to remind him how I had been thrown out. 'Oh—around. You know . . .'

'Mmmm. What's been happening?'

'Nothing much. What about you?'

'The same.' He sighed. 'Er . . . I've been thinking . . .'

'Yes?'

'I had almost forgotten, in this—this Castle of Delights, that we were supposed to be on a quest. Came to me last night. Wasn't sleeping. You know . . .'

I nodded. 'I know. Restless . . .' Keep up the pretence, especially as I knew how awkward he felt by the staccato sentences, just as he had been when he first met us, before he had become used to us and spoke with that lovely, running lilt I remembered so well.

Then, to my horror, my utter embarrassment, my downfall, he suddenly started to cry. Not noisy sobs, his head in his hands, but the slow, hopeless, unable-to-stop kind of tears that trickled from the corner of his eyes and ran down to his ears, leaving little snail-tracks glistening in the space between.

'Conn! Oh Conn, don't! My dear, don't cry!' and I reached

190

forward, quite without thinking, and held his hands, my heart bursting. 'What is it? Who has hurt you?'

He released one hand, but only to wipe away the emotion, then sniffed, blew his nose on the linen sheet, and drew me down to sit on the edge of the bed beside him. Propping himself on one elbow he regarded me steadily. 'Thingummy, I've been a fool!'

I agreed wholeheartedly, but inside. 'No,' I said. 'Of course you haven't! Whatever makes you think such a silly thing?'

'Don't deny it, you know I have!' Luckily he went straight on without expecting any more protests, because I am sure a second time around he might have noticed my insincerity. 'I've been a complete idiot! I fancied myself a youth again and tried to behave like one, when I should have remembered I am nearly thir—'

I put my hand over his mouth. 'Age doesn't matter,' I told him firmly. 'Just how you feel . . . Er, were you talking of the Lady Adiora?' I knew he was, but guessed it would be easier for him if I pretended I hadn't noticed his infatuation. I was right, for immediately he loosed a torrent of words, conveying his hopeless adoration, her surprising reciprocation, his forgetfulness of aught else—and then came the interesting bit. I think he had temporarily forgotten that I, the deformed, ugly little Thing, with potentially no knowledge of Life with a capital L, would, or should, be unable to understand what he was saying.

'—and I thought it was only because it was the first time for ages, you know, when one gets too keyed up and can't perform. Like drinking too much wine, when the intent is there but you can't raise a thing. But she seemed to be satisfied enough when I found myself in a permanent state of arousal, but getting nowhere. I tried, dear God! how I tried, but I just couldn't come off! It was all right for her, me with a permanent hard-on, but I got nothing from it except frustration and a sore prick . . .'

I understood enough now to anticipate his next remark.

'Then I remembered that old witch, cursing me in the forest, all that long time ago. She said—'

'That your desires would remain unfulfilled until you asked the ugliest woman in the world to marry you!'

He sat straight up on the bed and glared at me, his brow a thick, uncompromising and unbroken line across his forehead. 'How the hell—!'

'You talked in your sleep. When you were sick after that ambush. And you told The Ancient too, remember?'

He subsided, but not for long. 'Well, I'm damn well not going to ask any female to marry me, ugly or no! Sod that for a game . . . No, if I'm to get no satisfaction, I'll put the temptations out of the way from now onwards. Pity, never fancied celibacy. Still, could shave my head and become a monk, I suppose . . .' The grim lines were smoothing themselves out from his face.

'The Ancient said that some spells could be broken if one sneaked up on them, took them by surprise, went in by the side entrance,' I reminded him, though how this would apply in his case I could not imagine. 'He also said that if we completed this quest and returned the dragon's jewels our troubles would be solved. Remember?' Not *exactly* how he had put it, but still . . .

'Just what I was thinking first thing this morning,' he said, more cheerfully. 'I reckon we should be going back to the road in a day or two—'

'No!' I cried. 'A day or two will be too late—' and for the next quarter hour, half hour, I tried to explain to him what was happening, what we had planned to do.

It was no use: he utterly refused to believe me.

'But that would be like—like the Slaughter of the Innocents! No hunter would trap animals like that and wipe them all out without a chance of escape. It's—it's just not done, that sort of thing!'

'But it will be done, just like that, unless we carry out our plan!'

'Rubbish, Thingumajig! Now you're letting your imagination run away with you—'

'Come with me!' and I half-pulled, half-dragged him from the bed. The lancet windows overlooked the yard at the back. 'See? They have everything ready!'

'But for what? Lady Adiora said there was to be an outdoor entertainment, that was all . . .'

'Then why all those bows and spears stacked over there?

192

And the carts outside the walls, waiting to carry off the dead animals? And the sand and sawdust in those leather buckets to cover up the blood, lest the ladies feel squeamish?

'Conn, wake up! *Believe* me . . .'

He still shook his head, but there were frown lines between his eyes. 'No, you must be wrong . . .'

I could feel the tears of anger and frustration seeping through my mask. 'Well, if you don't believe it, hard luck, that's all! We'll manage without you: you can stay with your—your precious Adiora and—and—and *never* "come-off", as far as I'm concerned!' and I turned and stumbled away towards the door. His bundle of clothes, the ones he had travelled in, were in a heap in the corner: we still had his mail in the stable. I glanced back. He was staring down from the window and his fingers were tapping restlessly on the sill. Gathering up the bundle of clothes I fled downstairs. Perhaps he would come. Perhaps . . .

The others were restless for action after being cooped up, and I hastily packed up all our gear and humped it and them over to the lakeside, then went back to beg some scraps for a meal, coming away with some bread and cheese, a ham-bone destined originally for the stockpot and a half-empty jar of honey. That would have to do, but I remembered to fill the water-bottle from one of the river-water buckets.

It may seem strange that no one grabbed me by the scruff of the neck and asked what the hell I was doing and where I was going, but everyone was, thankfully, far too busy preparing for the evening's festivities. In the kitchens the spits were turning with fowl and game and pork, bread and pies filled the ovens and the tables were already laden with sweetmeats and glazed confections, but I was too busy and apprehensive to feel hungry. Guests were still arriving, and already the wineskins were being broached, and more decorations were being carried through to the hall.

I crept back to the others, wondering what poor Snowy was feeling at this moment, far beneath us in the darkness. They could not help but hear some of the preparation and, perhaps because of this, my stomach began to stretch and pull in sympathy with the trapped ones. I would not have had our unicorn's courage, I knew that.

The others had sensibly hidden in the reeds with our gear, and we ate frugally, not knowing when food would come our way again, so I saved a little of everything and packed it with the rest. Then I stripped off, for as much as I hated the idea I knew I should have to climb down into that scummy water and clear away all the debris I could from round the sluicegate.

The water was cold as death and smelt of rotting corpses, and I was gagging as I came up for a breath of fresh air.

'It's impossible! I can't shift it!'

'Let me take a look,' said Puddy, diving neatly into the stinking water. He came up filthy, and looking grave. 'Gives me a worse headache than ever, down there,' he said. 'There's a great pile of silt on both sides of the gate. Goes down two or three feet at least. Have to be scooped away.'

'What with?' I said despairingly, for looking round there was nothing to scoop with, no container of any sort except Pisky's bowl—

'No!' said the little fish. 'Not never! Not my bowl . . .'

I was not even conscious of having transmitted the thought, but quickly reassured him. 'No, no, my pet, not your bowl. I'll—I'll just have to dig it away with my hands and throw it up on the bank.'

'There's the cooking-pot,' said Corby slowly, 'or, better still: this!' and he stalked over to Conn's pack and tapped sharply on the hidden shape of his conical helmet. I drew it out, rust-spotted and dented—it couldn't look worse. A little mud . . .

For two hours I struggled with the slimy muck that squelched between my toes, choked my nostrils and layered my body with its evil-smelling slime, and I was hot, dirty and exhausted when Puddy finally took another dive to see if it was clear. His report was optimistic.

'You've shifted all that was blocking it. Now try the lever—gently, mind. We don't want the water through yet.'

I put my weight on the lever: nothing. I tried, again and again, and at last, to my gratification, felt the whole thing stir, quiver under my hand, and shift all of an inch to the next ratchet. Puddy went down again.

'It's moving. Jaws are locked and the wheel engaged with the teeth. Don't move it any more for a moment,' and he disappeared again. Five minutes later he reappeared gasping for breath. 'Water's trickling down the pipe. Three inches of debris only holding it back at the other end. Badgers did a good job. Can hear the animals.'

'And Snowy?' I cried. 'Is he all right?'

'Sorry. Forgot. Get my breath back and—'

'Oh, no! I can't let you go back!'

'My fault for not checking.' And back he went, and this time he was so much longer that my nails were digging into my palms by the time his head emerged plop! from the water and he swam, very tired, to the bank.

I stroked his back and his belly and used some of the water from Pisky's bowl, eagerly offered, to wipe his eyes and mouth, then puffed a little of my air into his lungs. 'Are you all right? You're a very brave toad . . .'

He perked up a little, but his skin was still pale and bloodless. I snapped my hand fast round a passing damselfly and stuffed it in his mouth. His throat worked up and down, an absurd wing sticking out of the corner of his jaw, but at last he swallowed, breathed more easily, and squatted down comfortably.

'I went right through, down the tunnel, over the barrier and into the dungeon. Snowy sensed I was coming and was there to meet me. Place stinks: haven't cleaned it out this morning, of course, but neither have they fed or watered them and they are all hungry and thirsty and it is stifling hot. But Snowy has kept them in stout heart, and he shines like a light in the darkness—'

'A light?' I questioned, momentarily distracted.

'Why, yes: the silver light, like star-glow, that shines from him all the time. You must have noticed it?'

But I hadn't. The others had, of course, and it was strangely humbling to remember that I was merely a human being, and because of that missed so many things these animals took for granted, like a unicorn's light . . .

'I fear, though,' added Puddy, 'that his light grows dimmer, for he is near exhausted, I think. He says be sure to wait by the north side of the lake. Oh, and try your best to persuade the Rusty One. I think that was all,' and he shut his eyes and went promptly to sleep, after the most sustained bout of communication I had ever heard him make, albeit the words had taken an agonizing ten minutes to emerge. It felt that long, anyway.

A horn sounded from the battlements behind us; it was about the sixth hour after noon, and a warning that the banquet was about to begin. I hid Moglet, Puddy and Pisky in the reeds as best I could and piled our belongings nearby where they would be readily accessible. Tucking Corby under my arm I scuttled back to the castle and was only just in time, for the gates were being shut as the last of the guests, a straggler knight, clattered into the courtyard.

I was pushed roughly out of the way for all the stables, including the one we had used, were full, and ostlers and grooms had no time for someone underfoot. So I made my way past them and into the Great Hall, where the noise and bustle were, if possible, worse. Creeping round the wall I went to the kitchens, and my only problem there was not to be grabbed to hold, baste, cut, drain, chop, pour, slice or wipe anything as the whole place was full of the reek of burning fat, people's feet and elbows, temperamental shouts and greasy tiles, but no one noticed as I slid past and made for a little-used staircase that wound up to the unused tower. Luckily the torches were already burning in their sconces, and there was one near enough to the room we had chosen for it to be easy enough for Corby to climb onto the stool I dragged out for him and pull it from its fastenings when the time came. I hid him behind a pile of heaped hangings, gave him a hug and my blessing.

'And mind, as soon as you see me wave . . .' The tall window gave an excellent view of the yard and the double gates. 'Are you sure you will be all right coming down?'

He eyed the drop. 'Nothing ventured, nothing gained,' he said gloomily. 'Just you take care, Thing dear: we couldn't manage without you.'

Just for a moment I had a sickening realization of how inadequate I was; of how easily things could still go wrong; of how we seven were so separate, that should be together; how futile this venture really was—but luckily it was only a momentary pang, however sharp, for there was still so much to do, and doubts such as these had no place with action.

I went to see if Conn was in his room, but he had gone down with the others to the banquet. It was lucky, though, that I had checked his room for there, lying beside the bed, was his broken sword, so that meant a journey back to the lakeside, over the wall by the pigsties, where the others greeted me: nervous, on edge, and definitely scratchy. I reassured them, feeling far from confident myself, then made my way back to the castle, having to knock at the postern for admittance and receiving a cuff for bringing the porter out while he was relaxing with ale and a pie.

I aimed at the banquet, where the air made my eyes smart with its smoke of candles, tallow, fat and incense. Conn was at the top table but he was only picking at his food, and the Lady Adiora was fully engaged with a young knight on her left whom I had not seen before, though I noticed she kept a proprietary hand on Conn's wrist the while. Taking advantage of shadows and the distracting screech of pipes and the patter of drums from a troupe of musicians in the centre of the hall, I sidled up to the table nearest the main doors and scrabbled on hands and knees up on to the platform of the top table. Luckily distraction was provided by a juggler, in competition with the music, tossing brightly coloured wooden balls in the air, who lost his rhythm and his footing when he tripped over one of the bone-gnawing hounds.

I crept up to Conn's side in the ensuing merriment and plucked at his sleeve.

'What the devil—Oh, it's you, Thingy.'

'Yes it's me,' I said, unnecessarily. 'We're all ready. Don't forget: Snowy is going to lead the animals out and across to the river. The rest of us will wait for you at the north end of the lake. I've got all your gear. Oh, and don't worry if the castle catches fire: it's all part of the plan,' and I didn't give him time to question, but slid back the way I had come.

Now for the real business of the evening. Climbing out over the castle walls again, I made my way to the gates at the far end of the slaughter-yard. It was still light, although there were dark clouds massing to the west and the sun was glimmering through them like a lantern through strips of cloth, yellow light flashing intermittently. The air was heavy and close, and it was not only fear that made me sweat as I crawled round to my position. The bolts in the gates appeared well oiled, the gates themselves were free of obstruction, but I had not bargained for the two-wheeled carts that were already drawn up at one side, for the carcases I supposed.

There were three drivers, playing five-stones in the lee of one of the carts, and I had to retreat swiftly in case they saw me. This was an added and unforeseen danger: would they stride forward and stop me opening the gates? I crouched behind the near wall, biting my nails, thinking furiously, but the more I thought the more my mind chased itself in circles, like a wasp in a jar. And as I thought, conjectured, despaired, the answer came from another source. A serving-man poked his head over the wall and waved his hand at the men cheerfully.

'There's ale at the side-gate. Cook's in a good mood. But you've to save a couple of hares and the smallest of the hinds—on the side, you understand. His cousin's brother will pick 'em up later . . .' And he tapped his nose and winked.

The drivers understood well enough; with a glance at each other they hobbled their horses and almost ran in the direction of the side-gate, one remarking to the other: 'Well enough: there's coneys and to spare, so they said, and the wife fancies a badger-skin mantle. Pity they don't hold these do's more'n twice a year . . .'

Creeping forwards I went over to the carts: the grazing horses glanced at me incuriously and went on with their feeding, and I had not their language so could not explain that I wished them to pursue a policy of non-cooperation: instead, with my knife I cut through the leather strips that hobbled them and prayed that they would gallop their carts to the four winds once the animals were running.

And even as I moved back to the shelter of the gate, and the advantage of a knot-hole in the wood that afforded me all but a minimal viewpoint of what was going on, the fine lords and ladies came out from their feasting and took their places in the bright pavilions. The sky was more overcast than ever to the west and great clouds, castled and battlemented now, reared high and threatening, yet seeming not to move at all, and over everything was a sickly, greenish light, lurid and yet speaking of dark to come. The air was breathless and tasted of wet iron.

The audience, the murderers, were dressed in gay colours, the ladies in blues, yellows and reds, with fillets set with rough-cut stones on their brows; the gentlemen sported browns, purples and greens and all voices were high and shrill, light and laughing, and the liveliest and most beautiful of them all was the Lady Adiora. One could almost believe she had eaten magic mushroom to see her, all laughter and glinting teeth and tossing hair and swaying body. By her side, as she led him to the most resplendent pavilion, Conn looked dull and heavy and uneasy, and I could tell he had eaten little and drunk less for once, his eyes the only alive things about him, darting anxious glances from side to side.

I watched him carefully, for on him, on his reactions to what was about to happen, depended all our perilous venture. If he understood, soon enough, how depraved the Lady Adiora and her guests were, then he might be able to escape with us and the Seven would be together again; if, on the other hand he could not see how wrong it was to herd some fifty or sixty animals into an enclosure from which they could not possibly escape and proceed to make a sport of their slaughter, then he was lost to us indeed, as we were to him. No quest, no return of the jewels to the dragon . . .

A trumpet sounded. A herald, clad in the castle's colours of blue and yellow, advanced to the centre of the courtyard, and the knights and ladies settled themselves to listen with a great shushing of skirts and creak of leather, jangling of ornaments and clashing of ceremonial mail.

'My Lady Adiora, Sir Egerton, brave knights, fair ladies, esquires, gentlemen and franklins: this night will see the culmination of our pleasures, an entertainment especially designed by our hostess to determine the best archer amongst her guests. Shortly there will be released below you in the yard various ferocious beasts and creatures of the wild' (affected screams from the ladies) 'some large and some small. The Lady wishes me to emphasize that in no way are you in any danger from these animals, ladies, for the pavilions have been placed too high for even the tallest to reach.

'You will each receive a bow and arrows—' the servants were distributing these as he spoke '—and each set of six arrows is notched or fletched in a different manner so as to be readily identifiable. After the—er, destruction of the game, scores will be added up for each hit. The highest number will win this jewelled casket, donated by the Lady Adiora. If several arrows hit the same animal, then that blow which would be deemed most fatal will be the winner.

'May the best marksman win!' and the herald stepped back and out of the way as four servants went to the wooden doors that led down to the dungeons, ready to fling them open on command.

This then was it. I glanced at Conn, and saw him expostulating with his hostess, his bow lax in his hand, and she ignoring him for the young knight I had seen earlier; but I could wait no longer. I was not aware of even breathing as I raised my hand clear and glanced up at the northwest tower; I had to strain my eyes for the night was now drawing in fast and my gaze had become accustomed to the glare of torchlight in the yard, but I managed to make out Corby perched on the lintel of the narrow window, and saw him flap his wing in answer to my gesture and disappear inside.

Then Lady Adiora must have given some signal, for at that moment, with a grinding of bolts and a creaking of hinges as cages were opened, the prisoning doors to the dungeons were thrown wide and I, like the rest of the audience, peered down into the blackness beyond, nose wrinkling against the stench. Already my hand was reaching for the bolts on the outside gates when something moved back there in the darkness, and two dozen arrows were notched to two dozen bows as we all waited for the prey to pour out, defenceless, into the brightly lighted arena—

But what did emerge was not at all what any of us had expected.

THE BINDING: UNICORN

The Running

OUT OF the darkness trotted a dainty white horse, trim and neat, mane curled, tail flowing, and on its back was a hare, an ordinary brown hare.

Fingers relaxed on bowstrings, arrows drooped and were unnotched and a buzz of speculation ran round the audience. The white pony, in whom I scarcely recognized a transformed Snowy, knelt on one knee and bowed, his companion nodding on his back, paws stretched forward to prevent him sliding over the withers. Then Snowy executed a few light dancing steps, first to the left, then to the right, so that he zigzagged across the yard and in doing so approached the pavilion where the Lady Adiora was sitting, a bemused expression on her face. I distinctly saw him say something to Conn, who backed away with an unreadable expression on his face, then he was approaching the gate where I was hidden.

'All well, Thing dear? This nonsense will go on for a minute or two longer, but when I kick my heels against the gates, open them as fast as you can—' and he was gone, trotting like a white fire around and around the yard, faster and faster, now and again bucking and kicking up his heels, whilst the hare, descended from his back, was punching the air in the centre, turning somersaults, leaping in the air and twisting like a falls-riding salmon and now the audience were applauding and the bows and arrows were being laid aside, one by one. And now Snowy went faster still, until the wind of his passing streamed and extinguished the torchlight, and he seemed like a continuous incandescent circle. The hare bounded higher and higher and if one closed one's eyes the images spread right over

201

the darkness and were still there when they opened again. All at once they stopped and with an almighty kick Snowy opened one of the gates, neighed shrilly, and called forward the other animals waiting at the entrance to the yard. Immediately I pulled back on the other gate and even as I did so a brown flood poured across the gravel. Coneys and hares, two badgers, a bear and her cub poured out of the gate and raced towards the woods and the river, led by the hare who had performed with Snowy.

The surprise lasted long enough among the audience for me to glance up at the northwestern tower in time to see a black, spiralling, flapping shape launch itself down the side of the building, bounce off the roof beneath and catapult out of sight to the ground. From the window it had left curled a lazy puff of smoke . . . Dear, good Corby! I hoped he had landed safely, then stopped thinking as the horses with the carrion carts at last took off across the gateway. I had to somersault out of the way and then was narrowly missed by a squealing of swine who rushed out at the same time, eyes red, teeth fearsome under curled lips. In their midst ran Snowy, and as he passed me he called: 'The lake, the lake!' and I suddenly realized just what I should be doing. I risked one last, despairing look for Conn, but he seemed to have disappeared in a melee of shouting knights, screaming ladies, floundering servants and the tossing antlers of a great stag. One or two of the guests had drawn their bows and I heard a sudden cry as an animal was hit. Another arrow thudded into the open gate at my side, a couple of servants ran over to try and close the gates, a snarling wolf leapt and I fled.

Scuttling along as fast as I could I reached the lakeside to see a lick of flame and then another reflected from its black surface. I looked up at the tower: smoke was now thick and oily, fed well by the rancid fat I had poured over the rubbish earlier. A freshening wind from the west pushed the tongues of flame towards the roof between the northwest and northeast turrets. A cry of 'Fire!', and I ran back towards the castle to the point where I had seen Corby fall. I found a still, black shape on the grass. Sobbing with fear I reached forward and gathered him into my arms, feeling with a sudden stab of relief the strong heart beating warm and fast beneath the draggled feathers.

He opened one eye. 'Hullo, Thing: sorry to be a nuisance, but I still feel a bit groggy. Knocked myself out, I did, when I tried a glide—forgot all about the blasted old wing, didn't I? Sorry and all that . . .' and his eye closed. It opened again. 'How's it going, then?'

I ran back to the lakeside, to find the others huddled expectantly beside the baggage, laid Corby on Conn's pack, with strict instructions to the others to look after him, then went round to the sluicegate. Grabbing the lever I heaved with all my strength: nothing. I heaved again, crying out with the pain in my stomach as the muscles of lifting fought with the cramps from the red stone, that contracted as the others expanded. At last there was movement beneath: a grudging, slurring sound, and the lever moved a little and I heard the rush of water seeking its lower level in the pipe. Eagerly, in spite of the pain, I strained at the lever again and with a crack! the handle broke off in my hand and I tumbled back onto the bank, the loose wooden lever sailing over my head to land on the grass behind me.

I crawled back to the sluice; the water was still running, but even as I listened I could hear the suck of mud and stones against the gate. Despairingly I shook the wooden structure, but the water had slowed to a trickle now, and there was the sound of running footsteps behind me. I turned to see three or four of the castle servants making for the near side of the lake, leather buckets in their hands.

There was only one thing for it: I dived into the stinking water, my hands scrabbling at the stones that choked the partially opened sluice. Lungs bursting I tugged and pulled upward at the gate, but it wouldn't shift. I rose to the surface gasping and blowing, to be greeted by a hand on the scruff of my neck hauling me out onto the bank to lie in a half-drowned heap.

'Out of the way, stupid child! This is man's work,' said Conn, and he dived into the water just as the servants with the buckets arrived.

I was in a panic, and instead of realizing that three or four buckets of slopped-out water could not possibly halt the fire that was now almost enveloping the whole of the wooden upper structure of the castle I lost all reason, and flung myself at the servants, knocking the bucket out of one's hand and doubling another over with a butt to the stomach, then ran back to look anxiously at the turmoil of water that swirled where Conn had disappeared.

His head emerged, black with mud, his eyes like eggwhites in a dirty frying pan, his mouth opening briefly. 'Bloody thing's well and truly stuck—' then he disappeared again. I felt a hand on my shoulder and turned to see one of the servants, dagger upraised, but even as I ducked beneath his arm a grey shape snapped at his heels. He swung with his knife and kicked out at the same time and the cubling wolf yelped as his shoulder was laid open and spun and collapsed as the boot caught his head. Instantly I straddled his inert body and snatched up Conn's broken sword, which lay where he must have dropped it.

'Don't dare touch him!'

The servant circled warily, dagger glinting in the lurid light that heralded storm; he feinted but I stood still, the hilt of Conn's sword to my stomach, both my hands to it, the jagged end of it about two feet from my body. Two of the other servants came running to his aid, the other went back to the castle presumably for more support, but help for me was at hand. Two other wolves, full adults, a dog and a bitch, hackles raised, had come to look for their cub and now snarled at my side. The young cubling struggled to his feet, shaking his head, obviously not too badly hurt. Even so, we were outmatched, for each of the servants was armed. I do not know how it would have ended but there was a sudden tremendous flash of lightning, a crack of thunder and then a roar that shook the ground as the sluicegate at last opened fully and a torrent of water plunged down the pipe towards the dungeons.

That was not all: a figure, back-lit by another flash of blue sheet-lightning, appeared to leap from the disappearing waters, as black in itself as the clouds now racing in from the west, its mouth and eyes white gashes in the dark, and it howled like a devil from hell. What it actually said was: 'Thank Christ that's over! I thought I would choke . . .', but it came out like: 'Worra-worra-worra!' To a man the servants flung down their weapons and fled convinced, I am sure, that some black demon had drunk the lake dry and, appetite unslaked, had now risen to devour them. Watching them run I laughed weakly and collapsed, shouting: 'We've done it! We've done it! Oh bravo, Conn!'

'Bravo, maybe,' said my Rusty Knight, looking more like a tall, thin hobgoblin than a warrior, 'but how the hell do we get out of here? And what in the name of goodness are you doing with a wolf in your arms?'

For I was soothing the young cub, afraid he was concussed still, and the two adults were anxiously nuzzling and licking his injured shoulder. But even as Conn spoke, the answer to his first question came in the form of two mountain ponies, who galloped up, manes tossing nervously at sight of the wolves. They patently offered themselves as mounts, though we had not their language: out of the corner of my eye I saw a further detachment of men appear beneath the castle walls, this time armed with swords and staves. With them was a knight, fighting to control a panic-stricken horse that screeched with fear as burning sparks from the building floated down on its quarters, singeing its tail.

'Up!' said Conn briefly, tossing me onto the back of the first pony and handing me a frightened Moglet, (inside-jacket-at-once), a pocketed Puddy and Pisky's bowl. Corby was recovered enough to ride on my shoulder and Conn snatched his sword from my hand and mounted the other curvetting pony, the packs set before him. 'Right: go!' he shouted and dug his heels into his mount, which careered off in the direction of the wood, mine following, the wolves bringing up the rear, the youngster recovered enough to run, albeit with a limp.

We fled across the field to the white blur that was Snowy, guarding, encouraging and shepherding at the entrance to the ride in the woods that led to the river and safety. I glanced quickly back at the castle: all the upper part was well ablaze by now, and, as I watched, one of the towers, the southeastern, swayed and collapsed into the cobbled courtyard behind. The slaughter-yard was still full of people milling around, and even now the stragglers among the animals were making their slow way to safety: a couple of bewildered coneys, a disorientated boar, a hind heavy with young, the last glancing anxiously behind her to where her stag, horns flailing, hooves striking out, was discouraging those few who essayed to follow the escaping animals, though few among the former audience could still believe that this flight and fire and flood was part of a planned entertainment.

My heart lurched for the stag when I saw his reason for lingering: an older hind lay twitching in her death throes, an arrow in her throat. I slipped from my pony's back and ran over to Snowy, indicating the stag. 'Call him in, dear one! She is dead, his lady, but he has another in calf to care for and this one.' I nodded at a younger hind who trembled indecisively just inside the wood.

Snowy nodded. 'Just wait for the coneys—they are smaller, but just as precious,' and a moment later he called out shrilly. Reluctantly the great stag, a twelve-pointer red, still angry and sad at the death of one of his wives, joined the other hind and the one in calf, snapping at two arrows sticking in his shoulder as if they were of no more consequence than buzzing flies. I slipped over and pulled them out as gently as I could.

'Come,' said Snowy, 'to the river. There is nothing left for us here . . .'

We were lucky that no humans followed until daybreak, for some of the animals, good for short runs, were paw-weary and fur-dulled by the time they reached the river. The swine had passed their lower brethren and crossed the bridge first, without a word of thanks; most of the hares, too, were over by the time we stragglers reached it. The five or six houses in the village on the other side were all barred tight shut—I should think the vision of all those animals charging across must have been too much for them. Even the bridge-keeper was missing.

The she-bear had waited with her cub to thank Snowy: she, too, had arrows in her hide but nothing serious for her coat was thick, and we removed the barbs before the animals slipped into the river, noses making arrowheads in the flowing water as they swam quietly upstream to a place they called Malbryn, bare hills to the northwest. The ponies who had carried Conn and me clattered across the bridge, all wild again; the shuffling badgers, tireder I should think than the rest of us put together, rattled their claws, snuffled and shuffled off bandy-legged into the undergrowth, and the great stag—so like the mosaic on the floor of the Great Hall we had left—bowed his head to us and led off his two surviving hinds.

It was the poor bewildered coneys who needed most help, and in the end we had to go back and find the last ones, weary and disorientated. I also ended up carrying one little doe in my arms across the bridge, but luckily on the other side we found a wise old buck who had come to investigate the commotion, and agreed to lead the survivors to a warren some two miles away, by easy stages.

As I watched them leave us it was sad to think that these animals, united in purpose so short a while ago, were reverting again to hunters and hunted, without more than a breath's pause. A cold nose touched my hand and I started back as three great grey shapes fawned at my feet, pushed at the back of my knees, nudged my thighs.

'They give you thanks for the cub,' said Snowy. 'They wish me to say that they and theirs are yours to command until the debt is paid.'

'Ask them—ask them then not to hunt those who were their companions,' I said, thinking of the tired coneys. I glanced down doubtfully at the pointed muzzles, the swelling cheeks, the slanting yellow eyes, and smelt the breath of meat-eater that curled up through the sharp teeth and the grinning, foam-flecked jaws. 'That will repay, and more.'

'They promise,' said Snowy. 'But they will travel a couple of leagues before they kill anyway, to lose the trail.'

'Call it quits, then,' I said, and knelt to embrace each of them. This time the words came plain to me.

'There is still a debt to pay,' said the bitch softly. 'One day, when your need is great, one will come . . .' and they melted into the trees like shadows.

Dawn was breaking. I looked at Conn. 'You're *filthy*!'

'Seen yourself?'

'The river is clean and flows quiet on this side,' said Snowy. 'Go wash, children.'

As I luxuriated in the clear, sharply cool water, washing the ooze and slime of the lake, the sweat of flight and the smuts of burning from my aching body, conscious of Conn, a shadow to my left, doing the same, I glanced up and saw a buzzard wheeling lazily against a sky the colour of daisy-petal tips.

'Ki-ya, ki-ya, ki-ya,' he called.

Snowy on the bank above neighed once in answer. 'He says the castle is in ruins: they are coming to seek for succour this side . . . Sir Rusty Knight, if you push quite hard on the bridge-piling to your left—'

The piling collapsed, its weakness no doubt exacerbated by the unusual amount of traffic it had had during the night, and the whole structure slid gracefully into the river, to drift away down the current even as the thud of hooves announced the arrival of the advance-guard from the castle. There were shouts, curses; Conn leant over to pull me from the water. Hurriedly I donned clothes and mask, grateful to realize that he had been too busy bridge-pushing to see I had been barefaced.

We set off along the riverbank towards the rising sun, but I don't remember much of the next half-hour or so; I was so tired that I could not even feel elation when Conn swung me up in his arms to carry me after I had stumbled and fallen for the second or third time.

Later, as he laid me down in the shelter of trees to sleep, my head on a mossy bank, and had assured me that, yes, the others were all right, I heard something that sounded strange after all those terrible days at the castle. Momentarily I forgot all about how tired I was and sat up, clutching at his arm.

'Listen, Conn, oh listen! All the birds in the world are singing!'

THE BINDING: TOAD

The Trees that Walked

AND AFTER that all the birds in the world did indeed sing for us day and night, for a while at least. Although we found the stones we sought quite soon and followed the line of the second one, it was many recuperating days later before we happened on the next test. Meanwhile, I found we all seemed to be drifting into a dream-like state, not noticing the world about us. Towns and villages, feuds and dissensions, forests and rivers, all drifted past like a vision, and the most detached of all was myself, who probably should have been the most impressionable after my long years incarcerated with the witch. But now only our quest seemed real, the rest grey and apart . . .

When our next adventure came it was over almost before we realized, in a flash of fire: like paying one's penny in advance for the entertainment and then finding the performance over before one had had a chance to lay one's cloak upon the ground to appreciate the entertainment.

Only this was not entertaining . . .

The country we travelled turned upwards, and before long we were in the high down where wind twisted our clothes and pulled our hair and puffed from behind boulders and blew up our trews. Grey rock stuck up through ling and bracken like knees and elbows through tattered clothes and birds slid sideways in the wind. Villages were few and far between and the people startled and shy at our approach; not because they saw in us any threat, I think, it was just that visitors were rare.

Perhaps because of this the hospitality was greater when they granted it. One night, a week or so after we had escaped from the castle, we had been regarded at first with suspicion followed by tolerance, then given pallets and marrowbones, hare-stew, goat's milk cheese and bread, and were invited to sit round the host's fire for music with pipe and tabor. No one at any time thought it strange of us to be travelling with an assortment of animals, and all expected a story, a song, a tune to pay the way rather than the few coins we had to offer. That night Conn told a tale, I sang a lullaby I remembered from somewhere, Corby picked out a chosen stone or two and everyone was cosy and warm when one of the host's friends— for we were an entertainment in ourselves, and the whole village expected to be invited to meet us, that was clear—asked our destination.

But when we pointed north and east he crossed himself.

'Not the way of the Tree-People?'

'Tree-People?' questioned Conn.

'Yes. Those that walk the forests and devour travellers . . .'

'Walk the forests. . . ?'

'We never goes that way now. Time was there was safe passage through the heathland to the northeast. Time was trade came through the hills. But then *they* came . . .'

'Come, now, Tod,' said our host uneasily. 'That's talk, no more. None here's seen them—'

'Ever travellers come from that way?' said Tod. 'No. Ever travellers go that way and come back to tell? No. Ever anyone from round here go that way? No . . .'

I took a nervous sip of my mead. 'But we are bound that way . . .'

'Then more fool you,' said Tod. 'More fool you . . .' Around that fire others seemed to agree, for there were shaking heads, spittings into the embers, a furtive crossing of hands, pointing of two fingers, sighings, groans . . .

'Oh come now,' said Conn. 'What solid proof have you? Travellers do not return the same way if they quest as we do; visitors do not come that way for probably there is an easier route. And if you listen to old wives' tales here no wonder none of you ventures further!'

I looked at him with admiration. Since our time at the castle he seemed in some subtle way to have grown into his years. No more did he think of this as some careless expedition to be endured, now he was as dedicated as the rest of us; no longer

210

was he just my dearest Rusty Knight, he was a thinking, caring man. But not once had I referred to the things he had confessed to me at the castle, nor had I ever mentioned the faithless Lady Adiora, much as my bitter tongue had wished it. For I knew, deep down in that submerged part of me that was totally female, that a man sets great store by his pride and that only a nagging wife or a fool would remind him of his fall from sense, and then be lucky not to have a slammed door and empty chair to remind them of their folly.

And I was neither wife nor nag—but would have wished for the choice.

The men round the fire stirred uneasily, glanced everywhere but at each other, then a short, stout man spoke up.

'We've been up there. Found a skellington. Flesh cleaned clear off . . .'

'Up where?' asked Conn sharply.

The man shrugged. 'Anywheres. Near the trees. Doesn't matter: they can walk. Come out of the night . . .'

I shivered. 'What come?'

'Knobby peoples. Root peoples. Tree peoples . . . Folks say as they *are* trees. Eating trees . . .'

'*Eating* trees?' I tried to keep the panic from my voice.

Conn put his hand on my arm, and his brown eyes were warm and kind.

'Folktales, Thingummy, folktales. Part of the night and the entertainment. Worry not, little one: they shan't touch you. Trust Conn . . .'

Oh, how I loved him! How that careless touch tingled my whole body, far stronger in that moment than the cramps that bound my stomach. Through the eyes and touch of imagination for one breathless instant I allowed myself the indulgence of my mouth touching his under the soft moustache, and flesh met flesh in a stab of loving—

'Doesn't sound all faery-tale to me,' said Corby, considering.

'Don't want to go!' said Moglet, stirring uneasily on my lap.

'No smoke without fire,' said Puddy gloomily from my pocket.

'My great-great-grandfather once said that some trees ate a village,' offered Pisky, helpfully.

211

'Oh, shut up!' I said crossly, annoyed with myself for relaying both the conversation and my fears to them. 'That's the way we have to go, so that's that! No, Pisky, not another word, or I'll—I'll move your snails!' This was a dire threat indeed, as Pisky felt threatened if any but he rearranged his bowl, which he did whenever he was bored. I felt mean as soon as I had said it, because in spite of the brave words I knew I was the most cowardly of them all.

No one in the room had understood our exchange of course, except possibly Conn, but the villagers looked tolerantly enough on someone who shook and twitched, breathed heavily, blinked, grunted and sniffed all of a sudden for no apparent reason. I saw one of them lean over and poke Conn in the ribs.

'That lad of yourn. . . ?' and he tapped his forehead. 'Never mind: that sort's usually good with horses. Rubbed that old nag of yours down a treat earlier . . .'

Conn winked at me and rubbed the back of his hand over his mouth to hide the smile-twitch.

Two days later we had climbed even higher, into an area of twisting tracks, moorland turning purple and bracken browning; of startled flocks of plump brown birds who broke cover almost from beneath our feet; of keen winds that hissed through the dried grasses; of solitary trees leaning away from the blast; of hunting creatures that slipped sly and secret from our path; of the water tumbling icy from no source we could see; no people, no habitations, no woods . . .

Of that I think we were most glad, although no one was idiot enough to refer to the talk in the village. That would have been inviting Fate, or the gods, or whatever. No woods, that is, until the third day, when the land broke into deep combes where the north-flowing streams had bedded into the rock. Then there were trees: spindly rowans clinging for their lives to cracked rocks with only a pocketful of earth to offer; pines twisted beyond recognition, oaks leaf-shredded, ivy twisted and gnarled, ash already almost keyless in the Moon of Plenty . . .

We breathed easier. Nothing had come to threaten us, nothing had answered the description the villagers had given us of knobbly Tree-People, of devouring trees, and that night we camped in a convenient hollow, a riverlet to our left, heath and a few scattered pines on its banks, a small copse to our right. It had been wet all day, with that fine, penetrating rain that looks like mist and is as good as a bath you don't want. We lit no fire, for luckily the night was suddenly warm and we had oatcakes, cheese, a bottle of wine and honey. After our meal we drowsed in the hollow, unwilling to unpack and settle for the night and too lazy to move for the moment, while the few summer stars pricked into the deepening sky, a curlew called on its homeward flight and directly above us a buzzard swung his dreaming circles. He must have a wonderful view, I thought dozily. Miles and miles, from the village we had left to the edge of the uplands further north, and who knew what from side to side, and all the while he could even see a mouse bend the grasses, a hare's ear prick the bracken, a beetle on a rock, a fish in the stream . . .

Suddenly he called: high, weird, lonely, a warning perhaps: 'Ki-ya, ki-ya, ki-ya . . .' and I saw Snowy fling up his dreaming head and warnings buzzed in my ears.

I sat up. Nothing had happened, nothing had changed. The others still lay where they were and Conn was chewing a blade of grass, his eyes closed. Dusk had crept down like an interloper to the bank of the stream, stretching towards the rocks, trying for entry. The trees to our right seemed to have moved in with the darkening to be nearer company, and the trees to our left *had their feet in the water and were already starting to cross*—

I could not put my fears into words. Instead, as I glanced behind me at the oaks, the ash, the ivy, then before me at the pines, the birch, the rowan—the hair on my head stirred.

'C—C—Conn,' I whispered shakily. 'S—S—Snowy . . . The trees. Oh, look at the trees . . . !'

Instantly all were awake and Snowy neighed once, shrilly, and started to circle us as fast as he could. It was no use; now I could actually see the trees moving, hear the rustle and squeak of leaf and branch, feel the earth tear beneath the protesting roots. Snowy's circle grew smaller as I rose to my feet, Conn at my side, and gathered the others into my arms. Now we could see gnarled roots stretch forth their questing feet, branches reach and curl, leaves glint and flash like eyes.

I was turned to stone. I could not move, could not speak, only whimper, seeing with despair the futile stump of Conn's sword waving and jabbing at the threat.

'Help us, dear Lord, help us . . .' It was my voice, but the words came from nowhere.

Then came another voice.

'Fire, Thing, fire! That is what they fear!'

With an astonishment quite separate from my terror I recognized the voice of Puddy, no longer slow and ponderous but sharp and decisive. Fire? Of course. Fire eats wood. With stiff fingers I fumbled for flint and tinder, but fear and a damp day would not produce even the tiniest spark. More urgently I chipped and struck: desperate, the tears ran down my cheeks and I prayed again and again: 'Please, *help* us!'

The strong voice came again. 'There is more than one kind of fire. Remember the words, remember what *She* used to say! Fire to set them back, to drive them away—the words, Thing, the words!'

I put my hands on Puddy and through my fingers I recalled the right spell as he put it on my tongue. The words, sharp and harsh, poured forth and instantly we were ringed by blue flame that licked and spat like a grass-fire. Immediately, or so it seemed, the crowding trees drew back and I saw clearly the evil, knotted, earthy brown faces, the squat bodies, the bulbous eyes, the yellow teeth, the pale tongues like the underside of slugs—

I seized a rotted branch and dipped it in the fire and ran with my torch at the nearest tree: there was a sigh, a hiss, a tearing sound and the ring melted, the trees dissolved into the night and we were alone once more—

Without another word we picked up our belongings and fled.

THE BINDING: CAT

Under the Mountain

ONCE MORE we were in the lowlands, in pleasant undulating countryside and heading due north. By unspoken consent the ordeal of the walking trees was forgotten, but once, in a quiet moment, I spoke of it to Conn.

'Did we see—what we thought we saw? Did those trees walk? Did they have grinning mouths and fingers like twigs? Or . . .'

'Or,' said Conn. 'Most probably. If we hadn't all been frightened out of our wits we would have seen an old army trick, I reckon.'

'Trick?'

'Mmmm. I saw something like it once in Scotia, and again in the Low Lands—only then they used reeds.' I wriggled impatiently and he ruffled my hair. 'Patience, child! When I saw it in Scotia it was an ambush, sort of. There were these savage highlanders sitting round their campfires—oh, perhaps a hundred, two hundred—and the besieging force was less than half that, and their only advantage lay in surprise. So they cut down a rowan or two and some gorse bushes—have you ever tried to cut into a gorse bush in the daylight, let alone when it's pitch black? Bloody prickles everywhere . . . As I was saying, they had some dozen fellows move these, bit by bit, nearer to the enemy, and the others lined up behind in the shadows. They were into the camp before the defenders realized they were there.'

'And the reeds?'

'Same idea, only this time the reeds were protection as well. A thick wall of reeds, green ones, the sort that arrows bounce off . . . There were more of them that time, so the odds were even. We lost. And ran.'

'You were with the attackers the first time?' I said, remembering what he had said about gorse-prickles.

'And the defenders the second. I reckon that's what the Tree-People do. An outlaw band with perhaps an old campaigner like me among them, preying on unsuspecting travellers. Probably been watching us for days.'

'You're not old,' I said absently, trying to reconcile what I thought I had seen with what Conn had just said. But his reaction to my remark was entirely unexpected. His thin, warm, pale-freckled hand closed over my grubby paws.

'That's nice: no, I suppose I'm not really, not by actual years. It's just that time sometimes seems to be slipping by . . .' He released my hands with a sigh.

I looked at him compassionately. So my Rusty Knight was afraid of growing old. Men took a lot of understanding, I thought. One part of them is grown-up, brave, lustful, full of confidence, and the other, as I had also seen at the castle, is still little boy, needing encouragement and reassurance.

'You should try being me,' I said, as cheerfully as I could. 'I don't even know how old I am . . .'

'And ugly to boot,' he said softly. 'Never mind, Thingummybob, I love you . . .' He patted my head as kindly and absent-mindedly as a lord would pat one of his hounds. And he couldn't, even now, get my name right! If it was my name . . . I was glad, then, for the mask, for it hid and soaked up the stupid tears of frustration and disappointment his well-meant words engendered. But what right, I told myself furiously, did I have to be either? I had made the mistake of falling in love, and cripples should never make the error of doing that, especially if they are also ugly. If I had known how it would hurt, this love, then I should never have indulged in it.

And yet I didn't want to let it go, to deny it, for it made me alive in a way I had never known. I tingled from top to toe. I felt beautiful inside, as beautiful as the Lady Adiora. Love made me aware of Conn's frustrations and anxieties, made me willing to sacrifice all I was, anything I had, for his wellbeing. And, in an obscure way, it made me understand and love my animal friends even more.

216

I sensed now why Pisky talked like an ever-running stream, knew why Moglet was near as great a coward as I was myself, acknowledged the slowness of Puddy—except for the other night—and understood Corby's coarse carelessness. I was also starting to comprehend—but the fringes only, because he was magic—what our beloved Snowy had loved and lost, and how his love was different, somehow stronger than life itself. And as I realized this, a great calm and peace stole over me.

It rained, and it rained and it rained. Non-stop. For three nights and three days, and it was just our luck that we were between villages and had to seek shelter every night where we could. The first night it was in a deserted barn by a crumbling cottage, the second in the open and the third—

'A cave!' called Corby. 'Just past the three stones—are those the ones we're looking for?'

For the last five miles or so we had encountered gently rising ground, and had begun to hear our own footsteps beneath us, each step with the faint echo of a drum. Snowy lowered each hoof with increasing suspicion.

'Underground caves,' he said. 'Deep ones, at that. With all this water about we shall have to be careful.'

So when Corby hopped into the cave ahead of us, giving a hollow and thankful caw! as he arrived, Snowy was the only one to hesitate, but he could do little but follow when we all rushed in to celebrate our shelter. My flint and tinder was dry enough from the oiled pouch I now carried it in, and I soon had a lusty fire going where the floor fell steeply from the entrance towards a large passageway we had had no chance yet of exploring. The cave had obviously been used before. There were two piles of kindling, some logs and peat in a dry corner, although it was clear that the usage was not recent, for boulders had rolled down from the cave entrance, partially blocking the passageway, and the store of wood was almost rotted through.

It all made a fine blaze, however, and I soon had our last strips of pork fat spitting from skewers above, curling and browning with a smell that made my mouth water. I still carried cheese and some rather stale oatcakes and had picked wild raspberries earlier, so we made a fine supper and afterwards lay lazily around the fire, listening to the rain outside, while the smoke rose up in a wavering pillar and flattened itself against the roof of the cave.

'Funny,' I said. 'D'you think the bats don't like our smoke?'

'What bats?' said Conn lazily.

I sat up. 'Well, the cave is a bit smelly, isn't it—'

'But dry—'

'But dry. And there are fresh bat-droppings around and bat-ledges up there, but no bats. And they wouldn't be flying in this weather. Perhaps they've gone off down the passage . . .'

'No bats,' repeated Moglet, from my lap. 'No bats; no rats, no bats but a cat . . .'

Of course Pisky took that up. 'No bats, but a cat; no dish, but a fish with a wish . . .'

'A crow that can't go, and so full of woe . . .'

'A toad with a node, who bears a load on the road—'

'Quiet!' said Snowy sharply. I thought for an instant that he was annoyed with the game, that he didn't want one of them to come to the bit of the 'unicorn with no horn'—I had already thought of rhyming 'Knight' with 'blight'—but as we stopped I could hear it too.

A queer, rumbly, shifting sound. A runnel of water slithered past my toe, and then another. I looked up at the mouth of the cave, some three or four feet higher than the place where we sat, and more muddy water was pouring over the lip. The sounds of movement intensified; small stones clattered over into the cave—but they were falling from *above*! I scrambled to my feet with Conn, even as a shape flitted past my ears, then another and another, flittering and piping, wide mouths agape on needle teeth, ears like open leather purses. I couldn't tell what they were trying to communicate, although the shrill sounds overrode the dull rumble that seemed all around us, but Snowy understood well enough. With a wild call he had us all gathering up our belongings in a scrambling haste. One moment Conn was loaded with everything, then I was, then Snowy and Moglet and Corby and Puddy and Pisky were passed from one to other of us like a first lesson in juggling but eventually—and this took but one bat-sweep round the cave—Conn had the baggage balanced on Snowy, Corby on one wrist and Pisky's bowl dangling from the other, and I had

218

Moglet inside my jacket and Puddy in my pocket.

The bats' cries grew more urgent and the rumbling louder: I felt the floor shift and sway under my feet and clutched at Snowy's mane.

'What do we do? Where do we go?'

'The bats will show us. Take a brand from the fire—nay, better two, one to light from the other, and some kindling. But hurry, dear one, there is little time!'

I snatched a glowing branch, whereupon it snapped and sparked about my feet. I drew a deep breath; we were together, don't panic, nothing can harm us if we're together . . . I picked up a convenient bundle of kindling and thrust it into my jacket, where a protesting Moglet fought with the twigs. Selecting carefully I picked out a large gnarled branch and then another. Thrusting the tip of the first into the fire I soon had the tip ablaze and swung it round the cave: the bats were sweeping and squeaking round a jut of rock to the left. Ahead of us was the unexplored passage we had noticed earlier and Conn was scrambling towards that.

'No!' called Snowy. 'Not that way, Rusty Knight: it's a dead end, they say!'

'But—'

There was a louder roar than before and by the light of my improvised torch we swung round to face the entrance of the cave. It was collapsing before our eyes. Where before there had been a clear, jagged outline with the fall of rain hanging like a curtain behind a stone arch, now the outlines were blurring before our eyes. The arch was changing shape, becoming rounder, lowering, cracking and the rain-curtain became a fall of stones that blotted out the last dim shapes we had seen before. But that was not all: the curtain now started to slide towards us, faster and faster, as if some wind had bellowsed out behind an arras.

'Follow the bats: it's our only chance!' cried Snowy.

I thrust my burning branch into Conn's hand, grabbed his belt and he jinked behind the rock: so there was another passage. The bats flew ahead into the cold darkness and I followed Conn's first hesitating steps. I turned my head for Snowy but even as he followed I saw the river of slurry engulf our fire with a despairing hiss, and then all was black except

219

for the flickering torch. The floor of the passage was painfully sharp with stones as we hobbled along. Of a sudden Conn's belt was jerked from my grasp. The torch went out and I could hear nothing but the great roar of stones behind, felt a great, stuffy blast of air buffet my ears and screamed as I fell helplessly into darkness—

THE BINDING: CAT

Stalagmites and Stalactites

IT WAS cold. I was lying on bare rock, there was no light, my head hurt. The end of the world? Not quite. A raspy tongue was scraping my chin under the mask with anxious zeal. There was a terrible cursing in my right ear.

'Caw! Blind me—why can't someone strike a light? Black as a raven's armpit in here . . .'

But there was light, of a sort. A dim white shape stood where I thought my legs should be, if only I could think and see straight.

Snowy bent his head and snuffed gently. 'All right, Thing dear? You will have a headache for a while—you bumped your head. But we're safe, for the time being . . .'

'No worse than *my* headache,' said a muffled voice from my pocket, and I felt Puddy squeeze himself out. 'How goes it, fish?'

'Well,' said some extremely angry little bubbles. 'I'm not broken, but a *lot* of water has slopped out, thanks to *nobody in particular*, and one of my snails is missing.'

'Here's your snail,' said Corby soothingly, 'and a couple of nice new round pebbles.' I heard three little plops. 'And a—oh, no: it's a bone . . . Sorry.'

'What sort of bone?' I sat up incautiously, to be rewarded with a pain that beat like a drum behind my eyes.

'Only a little 'un. Rat, mouse; bat perhaps . . .'

There was a shuffling behind me and Conn's groping hand closed on my shoulder. 'Sorry about that, Thingy dear: there was a drop at the end of the passage. No bones broken?'

'I don't think so,' I said crossly. 'Where—where are we?'

Snowy shifted his hooves. 'Under the mountain . . . Have you your flint and tinder safe?'

I felt in my pocket. 'Yes, but—'

'What happened to the torch you carried?'

I groped. 'Here . . .'

'Right. You have kindling somewhere about you, too; I saw you pick it up. Let's have some light, shall we?'

Given something to do, I felt better, and even more so when Snowy bent his head and touched the stub of his horn to my head. I heard his soft moan even as my pain lessened, and I reached forward to push him aside.

'Don't, oh don't! I can bear it. Don't hurt yourself . . .'

'We are one, child, all of us. All pain is to be shared, all troubles; all endeavour, all joys . . .' I felt an immense comfort, as though my mother had kissed me better, my nurse taken me on her lap, my father laid his hand upon my head. It was another of those elusive flashes of what I could not even call memory, and gone as swift as kingfisher-flash.

I lit the kindling—birch-bark, moss, twigs—and took from their friendliness a branch-tip of fire. As it flared I stood up, all aches and pains miraculously gone, and held it out to Conn.

'Hold it high—let's see where we are . . . Oh, oh!' I gasped in awe as Conn held up the torch. It flared and dipped and crackled and shone its flickering light upon towers, castles, trees, mountains, cliffs, frozen waterfalls, avalanches—all shimmering like ice and moon-glow. 'What—what are they? So beautiful . . .'

'Stone castles,' said Corby admiringly. 'Cliffs; snow-slides . . . Caw . . .'

'Stalactites and stalagmites,' said Conn, and he whistled through his teeth. 'Magnificent! I've seen the like in Frankish lands, but nothing so grand . . .'

As we stood there, admiring, I heard a faint tinkling sound as first one great icicle and then another dripped into the silence. Moglet wrapped herself round my ankles.

'Too big,' she said. I knew what she meant, and some of her unconscious, unspoken fear formed my next words.

'Which is—is the way out?' and even as I spoke the torch in Conn's hand flared and sputtered and I realized how little fuel we had left.

Then came Snowy's comfort. 'There are several openings on the other side of the cavern. To save fuel we shall go without light, travelling around the perimeter and exploring each passageway as we come to it.

'I shall go first as, to some extent, I can see in the dark. Thing dear can come next, holding to my tail—but try not to pull it—and the knight shall bring up the rear. We shall not travel too fast, and if I come across any obstacles I shall try and warn you in plenty of time. Toad and cat with Thing, crow and fish with the knight . . . It will take some time, but we have that to spare. Now, get ready, and remember to bring what wood we have left and any kindling. Easy does it!'

I don't know about the others but I kept my eyes closed, pretending to myself that it was only a game and that if I opened them there would be light. Puddy was quiet in my pocket, but I could feel Moglet trembling against my chest. Snowy's tail was soft and silky and comforting to hold and Conn's hand warm on my shoulder. It seemed we stumbled, tripped, wandered for hours; sometimes we climbed over rocks, sometimes squeezed round or ducked under; sometimes there was open space and nothing tangible save the last step and the next. If we paused for even an instant, the silence clawed back into our consciousness as palpable as the ever-present dark. But there was always the tinkle-drip of water, sometimes nearby, sometimes seeming miles away, by its very randomness making the black silence all the more terrifying—the drip of melting snow in an immense and deserted forest, the crack of ice on a hollow lake, a child crying in a deserted house—

By now my mouth was dry, my brain in a vacuum, my senses like little sea-anemone tentacles, scared of touch or bruise. Some of the passages Snowy didn't even both with, as if he knew at once they were dead ends; others we traversed for a hundred steps or so until they narrowed impossibly. I lost count: was this the fifth or twenty-fifth way we had gone? And all the while an uncooked lump as big as a cottage loaf, doughy and indigestible, was rising, ever so slowly, from my stomach to my throat, so that when the squeaking began all my tensions, all my fears, erupted in a small shrill scream.

'Quiet, child!' said Snowy sternly. The perspiration ran

through my fingers into his tail and Conn's fingers gripped my shoulder so fiercely in answer to my terror that I could not help but cry out again. 'Quiet: the bats are back!'

The bats! I had forgotten them, although it was they who had led us the right way after the deluge of water, mud and stones had destroyed our first refuge. I felt a sudden rush of air as myriad wings brushed my mask, stirred my hair, and a language I did not understand touched the high pitches of my hearing. Apparently Conn noticed nothing, neither did Puddy or Pisky, but Corby put his head on one side to listen and Moglet poked her head from under my jacket.

'What do they say?' I asked.

'That the way out is three openings to the right: we were nearly there,' said Snowy comfortingly. 'Best foot forward!'

We squeezed into a narrower passage than most we had tried, but even I beneath closed lids could feel the gradual difference in the quality of the light, and risked ungluing gummy lids. We found ourselves now in a smaller cave than the last. There was light but no magic castles of rock, no everlasting dripping. Ahead was a rift or chasm, and beyond it the cave mouth and the setting sun sending bars of rose-colour across the floor. We had been entombed for nearly twenty-four hours. No wonder I was suddenly ravenous!

Over the chasm stretched a natural bridge of stone, wide enough for two to cross abreast. I started towards it eagerly, only to be halted by a buffet of bat-wings and a hundred shrill voices, and Conn's voice, harsh and incredulous.

'Look! Sweet Jesus, Mary and Joseph! Look to the right, Thing!' He had got my name right at last but I did not heed it.

Across the chasm, stretched from side to side in eight equally spaced strands, was an enormous web. Even as we watched, a spider, as thick in body as a Lugnosa moon and as black and hairy as the Devil himself, legs jointed and hooked like some grotesque toy, ran across to the centre of the web and halted, multifaceted eyes glaring and mouth moving like the jaws of a wolf. I did not need Snowy's words to know we were beyond hope.

'The bats say that she stops all who would cross: see the corpses parcelled among the strands? They have tried to break through but fall helpless to the glue on the web. There is no way out for any of us, none, unless we can bring the spider to destruction . . .'

THE BINDING: CAT

Web of Despair

IT WAS Conn's fighting Hirlandish temper that brought me to my senses. With a cry of rage he had charged the web, only to be repulsed by a twang! of impenetrable strands, a sticky front and a menacing clatter of joints from the spider. Conn collapsed on the ground by my side, such a comical look of frustrated fury on his face that I forgot my worries and patted his shoulder.

'You all right?'

'All right! All right? I'll kill the bastard, sure and I will! Just let me take my sword to its evil body and I'll—' but then he stopped and of course remembered that his weapon was in pieces. 'Ah, wouldn't you believe it then! Just when I needed it . . .' He put his hands to his head and tugged at the unruly curls. All of a sudden he had shed ten years and was again an edgy, temperamental lad, the brogue tripping from his tongue like a slashed wineskin. 'Ah, 'tis terrible, terrible! How in the world can we get past that—that black bag of air?' He sprang to his feet and began to pace the ten feet or so of rock in front of the chasm. 'See, the bugger has stuck its net to the rock; there, there and there,' and he pointed to thick suckers that anchored the strands. 'And two at this side, one the other and two at the top—eight together, by the saints!'

Between the thick strands glistening with an evil, tarry glue that clung to whatever touched, were finer strands that glowed with a greyish light of their own. These were pearled with sticky droplets and clogged with pitiful little bat-parcels, some still feebly struggling in the last rays of the setting sun that slanted through the seemingly unattainable mouth of the cave.

Freedom! So near, so frustratingly near! Were we, too, to end like those bats, waiting to be sucked to the bone, then discarded into the torrent of water we could hear echoing in the chasm far below the web? Or would we choose rather to drown in those depths, so far beneath the open sky, the woods, the fields we were used to? Or would we huddle here, cowards all, and slowly starve to death?

'Time for supper,' said Snowy. 'What have you got in the pack, Thing dear?'

Not much: half a flagon of water, some ends of ham, rinds of cheese, honey. We ate what we could, bunched close together and shivering now, for the sun had gone down. Conn doubled his cloak to sit upon, for the rock struck chill, and Snowy lay down behind us so that my cloak would do as a coverall. Beyond us and the web the cave mouth was pricked with stars and a near-full moon swung into view, her pale light too high to penetrate the gloom of the cave. A couple of desperately hungry bats dared the web; one pulled back at the last moment, the other, with a high-pitched scream, became entangled and a moment later a pair of pincer-like jaws fastened on the poor, furry body. Poisoned venom quickly did its work and the stunned bat was rolled and twisted into an obscene shroud. The dry rustling and shaking of the web ceased, and the only sign of the terror that lurked there was a hooked claw that crossed the rising moon, a bar sinister on the gold.

I leant back against Snowy. 'What can we do? How . . .'

'We must think,' he said. 'Consider, assess. There must be a way . . . But now sleep, my friends, sleep. Often in dreams the answer comes. Sleep . . .'

And cold, still hungry, I dozed off, the comfort of a strangely silent Conn's shoulder my pillow.

'I'm thinking,' said Moglet.

After breaking our fast—a bad joke, this, on what we had left—Moglet had washed her face and perched on an outcrop of rock some discreet ten yards from the web. With inscrutable eyes she had watched the loathsome spider take two bat-parcels and suck them dry, then spit the bones to the torrent below. She had watched the giant insect wipe its jaws with a rattle of forelegs and, satiated, settle back in the middle of the web, to watch us.

The rest of us, excluding Snowy who said nothing, had spent some two hours in fruitless argument and discussion, first one and then the other putting forward wild schemes that could come to nothing. The only idea that had seemed remotely feasible, that of Pisky's to dare the torrent below, had been dashed by one quick look, a wary eye on the spider the while. If we managed to miss the ledges and projections on the way down and avoided being dashed to pieces on the rocks that reared up like fangs, we should surely perish in the swirling black waters that disappeared into a gaping hole in the rock to heaven knew where.

Twice Conn had tried to get near the bridge of stone that spanned the chasm and twice had been threatened by an immediately alert spider who had run down the web to meet him, jaws clashing. It even pursued him on to the rock floor of the cave the second time, to be driven back by some stones I flung in desperation. After this we were exhausted, and it was only then I had noticed and questioned the non-participating Moglet.

A careless retort sprang to my lips on her reply, engendered perhaps by frustration, but Snowy blew softly down the back of my neck before I could say anything.

'It is perhaps her turn,' he murmured softly, which I did not understand. 'Gather close, all of you, and send your thoughts to her aid. Close your eyes and empty your minds of all except that which will help her thoughts. Concentrate on cunning, wisdom, energy and, above all, freedom. Now, my dears, now . . .'

So we did. Huddled together, hungry, thirsty, cold and in despair, we nevertheless freed our minds and sent them over to where Moglet sat, a little receiving statue.

At last she stirred. She had been sitting bolt upright, large ears forward, eyes apparently unblinking. But now she performed a long, slow stretch, arching her rump in the air, tail a relaxed loop, front legs stretched out, claws a-scrape against the rock, ears back, head sloped down between her front paws, jaws almost at right angles in an exaggerated yawn. The ritual done, she sidled over to us.

'Well?' I asked, aware that the sun outside was at its zenith, aware of time trickling away like water through carelessly cupped hands.

'Stones,' said Moglet. 'Lots of them. A big pile. As heavy as you can throw . . .' And, exasperating animal as she could sometimes be, she folded her front pads underneath her and promptly went to sleep.

Stones it was then, gathered in the half-gloom by Conn and myself, pecked from ledges by Corby, hoofed from their hiding places by Snowy, until there must have been two hundred of them of all shapes and sizes.

Moglet opened her eyes and considered. 'That should be enough . . . Now then, Sir Rusty Knight, I want you to cut two strips from your cloak, about half a man-hand thick and a hand-and-a-half wide—'

'From my good leather cloak? You must be joking!' expostulated Conn.

'Do as she says,' said Snowy quietly.

Surprised into compliance, Conn did as he was told and laid the tanned strips by the stones. 'Now what?'

'Now,' said my kitten, thoughtfully flexing her paws, 'now I shall have to ask our white friend here to do some interpreting to the bats: don't speak their squeak myself, but I gather he does . . .'

Quickly she explained what she wanted, and while we were still exchanging glances wondering whether it would work, the bats had swarmed down and picked up, four to each strip, the pieces of leather. For a minute or two they practised flying in formation, a thing they were obviously not used to, the strips falling from their grasp twice, luckily onto the rocks close by. Then they were ready, hovering above us with strange clicks and twitters.

'Right!' said Moglet. 'Thing dear and Conn, will you please throw stones as hard as you can at the web in the bottom right-hand corner, there where the web has been darned; the small strands, not the thick ones. As soon as you have made a hole, start to make another, still at the bottom, but this time on the left-hand side.' She turned to Snowy. 'Tell the bats to go as soon as I say "Ready!"'

Conn and I started flinging the stones: his aim was much

better than mine. Some of the missiles went through the fine meshes, clattering across to the cave mouth. Many of mine dropped soundlessly into the water-filled chasm, but before long we had a sizable hole in the right side of the web. As soon as the first stone struck, the spider was down to investigate, throwing out fast streamers to try and plug the holes we made. The stones themselves seemed to have little effect on it, bouncing off the tough carapace like pebbles off armour, but its anger at our attempted destruction of its trap was plain to see, for, even while knitting up the severed strands, it chattered and snapped its jaws.

I heard Moglet's 'Ready!' to Snowy and would have stopped to watch the bats but for his hissed warning.

'Keep going: do not let your eyes stray!'

By now each stone was getting heavier and heavier, and as we switched to the left side of the web, Conn was throwing at least three to my one; in the end I was chucking them underarm, scarce able to see their direction for the sweat that ran down inside my mask and threatened to blind me. I thought I could do no more, but suddenly there was a loud twang! from above and the whole web dropped about six feet. With the speed of light the spider turned and ran up one of the central struts towards the roof. At last I could look up to see what the bats had been doing. The leather flaps had been wrapped round two of the central struts and, thus protected from the gluey stickiness, the bats had been able to bite completely through one strand so that the web hung now only from seven supports instead of eight. The other four bats had not fared so well: the second top main strut had not parted, and even as they tried to escape, one poor bat was caught in snapping jaws. No refinements this time: the spider crunched it with one bite and then spat it out to spiral down, back broken, into the torrent below.

Then the great insect went back to the repair of its web. Spreading itself on the surface of the rock above the break, it clung safe with the four back legs while holding the severed end in its front claws, dribbling some foul oozing mess on it and then drawing up the longer end to meet the shorter and binding all together with some kind of thread it teased from its belly.

'Now,' said Moglet, her eyes green with concentration. 'Take your sharp little knife, Thing dear, and a piece of leather to protect you from the stickiness, and saw through the left-hand bottom strut. You, Sir Conn, do the same for the upper right-hand one: you are the only one tall enough to reach, and your broken sword has a nice sawy edge. Don't worry: the spider cannot be in three places at once and I'll ask Snowy to get the bats to tackle the bottom strut on the right at the same time. That will account for four more struts; one is already through and the other nearly, I think. That leaves two, the extreme left one near the bridge and the one nearest us in the middle. Sir Conn, before you start please make a loop round that one—yes, more leather, please—and attach it by our rope in Thing's pack to Snowy. He may not be able to free it, but at least the shaking will give the creature pause.' I marvelled at my incisive, logical, quick-thinking kitten; never would I have believed her capable of five minutes' sustained thought, let alone the drive and determination she had shown thus far. She gave a quick lick to each front paw. 'I shall give each warning if the spider changes direction: off you go!'

An hour later we were totally exhausted, and the spider must have been too. The bats had gnawed through one more strand, Conn had cut through another and so had I, but all Snowy's weight had not shifted the bottom one. We had lost two more bats, but now the web was looking decidedly the worse for wear. Great holes marred it where the stones had gone through and the insect had only managed temporary repairs. Now, not counting the first strut the bats had failed to sever, four had been cut through and temporarily repaired, but did not look as though they would bear any weight until the tarry substance that anchored them had had time to set. And time was something none of us had to spare.

Moglet still burned with energy. Her eyes were huge in the early twilight, for the sun had sulked behind cloud since midday. None of us had had time to think of food but I would have given almost anything for a drink, and looking round at the others I knew they felt the same. For two pins I would have drunk Pisky dry and watched enviously as Moglet lapped a quick half-inch, with permission of course.

'Thirsty work,' she remarked, fastidiously pawing the top

231

clear of weed and snails. 'Now: one last go! Conn, take the last right-hand strand and bats the left. Thing dear, sharpen that knife of yours once more, for the strand in the middle here is the strongest—'

The right-hand strand parted. Conn ran to my side and together we sawed away at the middle one. The last left-hand strand suddenly snapped loose from the wall above the bridge and the bats screeched above our heads as the maddened spider came rushing down towards us. The bats suddenly flew in a cluster at her eyes so that she could not see, and at last with a strange thrumming noise our strand broke. The others, the mended ones, sucked stickily away from their supports and now the whole web hung suspended by one single line.

The black creature retreated to the middle of her ruined web, hairy legs waving, jaws snapping, eyes darting from side to side judging which repair to make next. Then, crouching back, it gathered its legs to spring—

'A torch, Thing, a torch!' called Snowy urgently.

With a speed I had not thought my tired body possessed I grabbed what kindling we had left, bound it with the cord from Conn's cloak to a piece of wood and struck tinder and flint. In a moment I had a blazing torch that illuminated the whole cave even as the spider leapt from the web to the rock before me. Waving the torch I advanced.

'Back, back you thing of darkness and deceit! Back, I say—' and I flung the fiery brand straight at its eyes.

With a screaming hiss it leapt back for the web, which rocked crazily at the impact. There was a crack! like a whiplash and the last strand parted. For an instant web and spider seemed to hang suspended, then with a rush both fell down into the chasm. The torch followed, and as we rushed forward for a moment it lit up the shattered body of the monstrous creature—arms and legs broken and askew, all smothered by the broken web. Then the foaming waters closed over it and spun it away into the endless rivers below the mountain . . .

THE BINDING: CROW

The Great White Worm

OUTSIDE, IN the clean, cool evening air, it was raining again. But now none of us would have exchanged the downpour for the deceptive shelter of those accursed caves. As for me, I opened my mouth and let the blessed water bounce off my tongue; I even sucked the ends of my hair for the precious drops. In spite of being drenched Moglet stood stiff-legged and tail-high as if she had just routed a pack of marauding toms from the backyard, revelling in our admiration and affection. As for the bats, they swarmed away in a great cloud, despite the rain, only to return in twos and threes to drop small fragments of food. I didn't fancy the idea myself but Corby, Pisky, Puddy and Moglet were delighted. It was the bats' way of saying thank you.

After a while common sense reasserted itself; I was pretty wet but Conn was in a worse plight. His cloak now, with all the pieces hacked from it and the cord missing, was more like a tatty head-cape, and he was drenched and shivering.

'Skin is supposed to be watertight,' he grumbled, 'but I'll swear this water is leaking through to my bones . . . There's a village of sorts down in the valley: I can see smoke. Shall we?'

Above our heads the last escort of bats swooped in farewell, and somewhere a buzzard called its lonely: 'Ki-ya, ki-ya, ki-ya . . .'

An hour later I was dozy with heat, more-or-less dry and had a stomach full of a thick, meaty stew. The last piece of bread still firmly clasped to my chest, I fell asleep on the rushes.

We found the four stones the very next day, on the edge of the uplands north of the village, and consulted The Ancient's map.

'North from here, due north,' said Conn. 'That should be easy enough. Even I know north. Well, that's three adventures past us and we're still all in one piece. Allonz, mez enfants! Four to go . . .'

'What's that?' I asked. The words sounded familiar.

'What? Oh, allonz et cetera? The Frankish words for let's get going,' he said condescendingly.

But I knew, even as he spoke I had heard them before—somewhere. Another of those tantalizing glimpses of another life.

'Don't you mean: "En avant, mez braves?" ' I suggested, and was rewarded by a startled look from those brown eyes, but he said nothing further.

The moors and forests through which our way led were bare, for the most part, of human life, but the cooler, crisp air did not deter an abundance of wild life. Hares, foxes, stoats, weasels; badger, deer, squirrel, marten; eagle, merlin, finch, tit; and the purple heath and heather, crisp, curling bracken and colourful butterflies, dingy moths and laden bees. Here I found, in the endless quest for berries and roots, two plants I had never come across before; one, with sticky-pad leaves, trapped small insects much as Puddy did with his tongue, and the other, looking deceptively like a large violet, had fleshy leaves which performed much the same function. Pisky declared the brownish water we replenished him with as 'a nice change'; Moglet managed, even with her damaged paw, to find voles and mice. At times voles in particular were almost too easy to catch, running away from us like a brown wave in the long grasses. Indeed Moglet became rather blasé about her new-found prowess, and shared her meals with Corby, so they both grew sleeker and better groomed. Snowy, too, enjoyed the change in diet. Now I only had to provide for Conn and myself and we relied mainly on what I could cull, for we had no bows, arrows or spears for hunting, and did not stay long enough in any one place to set snares.

We made good progress, only having to detour once when a stagnant bog barred our way, a question mark to safety with its green slime lying quiet on ominously inviting open stretches, midges dancing their one-day life above. The main impediment to any enjoyment was the rain that seemed to fall more plentifully on these bleak uplands, so perhaps it was with a sense of relief that we found the ground sloping away beneath our feet and that one day the rising sun showed us cliffs and the sea.

Again that nagging sense of a thing known and should-be-remembered tugged at my mind. The salty smell, the crash and roar of the waves, the endless shift of great waters, all these I had seen before, somewhere, sometime. Only the steep, black, boulder-shod cliffs were different; the ones I thought I remembered were—white? Cream? Gentler, with sandy beaches, not these pebble- and rock-encumbered stretches. A summer house by the sea, collected shells, sea-bright pebbles that faded without the lap of water, the grit of sand between teeth and toes, the salt-harsh cry of gulls—

The great gulls wheeled and broke before us, screamed a welcome, and for two days they accompanied us as we traversed the edge of those dark and frowning cliffs, unable to find a way down. On the third day we came to a small river, which afforded access to the beach below. It flowed gently between restraining banks to a large bay, some three miles across at the widest part but narrowing at its mouth to about fifty feet, enclosed by sharply rising cliffs. Here the sea frothed and seethed, eager to burst its bottleneck as the tide receded. The beach around the wishbone-shaped bay was broken with tumbled rocks and boulders but inland the terrain was smooth and low, until it rose behind to the moors we had left. In that fair and gentle valley lay a prosperous-looking village, more a small town, with houses on either side of the river and boats drawn up tidily on the shelving banks.

For a while as we descended to the beach, I became aware of a curious shifting movement among the rocks, and thought I could hear a strange mixture of sounds: keening, grunting, shuffling, splashing. The smell was less indistinct: a fishy, animal smell, but it was Corby's keen eyes, perched as he was on Conn's shoulder, that recognized all this for what it was.

'Caw! People of the Sea—ruddy millions of 'em!'

Almost at the same moment came Conn's voice. 'Seals! A great colony of seals! But rather late, I should have thought . . .'

Even as we adjusted to the sight, a boy of ten or twelve, clad in rough homespun and barelegged, rose from behind a clump of gorse to our right and stood regarding us wide-eyed.

'Hullo,' said Conn.

The boy's eyes opened wider than ever, as if he thought us incapable of ordinary speech. 'Be you they travellers what are spoke of and expected?' It came out in a rush and in an accent strange to me and hard to follow. 'If you be, then I bids you welcome, masters both, and ask that you follow me to't chief's house,' and he set off forthwith down a narrow track leading to the village, with many a scared, backward look. I almost expected him to cross his fingers against the Evil Eye.

We looked at one another.

'We are travellers,' said Conn. 'But as to being expected— Or spoken of, come to that—'

'Strange tales travel with the wind,' said Snowy. 'And, like smoke, they change shape in passing.'

'Well,' I said, 'we can only find out if they mean us by going down and asking.'

' "What am I?" as the worm said to the blackbird,' contributed Corby, gloomily. 'Oh, well, don't say as I didn't warn you . . .'

So we followed the boy, who kept pausing for us to catch up, as if afraid of losing us, but at the same time he kept his distance, as if afraid of what we might do if we came too close. We passed several huts and the people there also regarded us with a kind of wary fascination. The town was well laid out, with straight streets swept clear of rubbish, animals tethered or penned and folk decently dressed. Most of the people were tall and slim, many with fair hair, the men moustached and bearded, some with tattoos on their arms and fingers. As we walked I glanced over my shoulder: we were being followed. Men, women, children, all had put aside what they were doing and were pacing behind us. At another time this might have seemed menacing, but in spite of the numbers I was aware most of all of curiosity, and almost began to wonder whether we had all grown two heads, though the others looked normal enough to me.

After what seemed a very long walk, we reached a bluff overlooking the river and what I supposed to be the chief's house. It was a long, low building, the wooden supports curiously carved with serpentine figures picked out in red and blue, the shapes outlined with rows of white shells. We reached the entrance, preceded by a couple of townspeople obviously come to forewarn of our presence; no leather-hinged door, no curtained flap awaited us, instead two painted panels that fitted into well-grooved wood top and bottom and now slid apart to reveal a dark, smoky interior. I thought it a very good idea for a door and was busy examining the mechanics when someone nudged me forward and I found myself inside, adjusting my eyes to the gloom.

Wooden pillars down each side supported a steeply pitched thatched roof; behind these were stacked trestles and stools. In a central stone fireplace, raised some three feet from the ground, smouldered a peat fire, smoke wisping up through a square exit in the thatch. At the far end were curtained recesses, no doubt for sleeping and stores. Light was provided by stands holding small basins of strong-smelling oil with wicks floating inside, although iron sconces were set in the pillars should stronger illumination be needed.

Beside the fire stood a taller man than the rest, with white hair that curled to his shoulders, wearing blue woollen trews and a fine cloak to match, fastened by a cord drawn through ornamented bronze rings; on his right side hung a short, bright sword and his arms were braceleted above the elbow by golden snakes. By his side stood a tall, dark lady with plaited grey hair and the same strong features as her husband, and behind them lurked three tall boys and a girl, by the mark of their features their children.

'Welcome, travellers all,' said the chief. He, too, used that strangely accented speech—they clipped the hard sounds short and drew out the soft ones—but he spoke, majestic and slow, so that it was easier to understand him than the boy earlier. 'We have much to talk of, you and I. My name is Ragnar. My wife, Gunnhilde, and I welcome you to our house and our town of Skarrbrae. You must rest yourselves and eat. When the sun is low we shall speak again.'

He clapped his hands and hot water and towels were brought. Conn and I retired to separate recesses, where I luxuriated in a clean body once again. When we emerged, stools and a wooden trestle were set in front of us with great wooden bowls of some fishy broth, strips of dried fish and a coarse bread. There were also bowls of goat's milk and a refreshing herbal brew, in which I thought I detected camomile and feverfew. Snowy and the others were not neglected either, and while I wondered at why (to them) a pony was allowed within doors, a great pile of hay was set in front of him; Corby was given fish-guts, Moglet the same with goat's milk, and I crumbled a paste of bread into Pisky's bowl. Puddy stayed quiet in my pocket after a snorted: 'Fish!' I wasn't worried, as insects had been plentiful during our journey.

Stuffed full, we were led to a pile of rushes on which were spread fur rugs, and, perhaps because of the food, or the gloom, or simply because we were dry and warm and welcome, we all dozed off for a couple of hours. When I awoke, torches were being lit in the sconces along the pillars and Puddy was sitting three inches away from my nose, a wing and a leg of some large insect sticking out of the corner of his mouth. His throat moved up and down decisively. As I watched the bits disappeared, and he burped.

'Disgusting!' I said.

'Each to his own,' said Puddy. 'Anyway, I didn't think you would like it marching down the back of your neck . . .' and he crawled back into my pocket, where I could feel him hiccoughing quietly.

'Serves you right,' I said.

Corby came up and looked me in the eye—one of his to both mine. 'Does one crap inside or out?'

I rose to my feet. 'Those who wish to crap,' I said carefully, 'crap, to use your expression, outside.' I looked down at my pocket. 'And those who crap in my pockets, or sick-up because they're too greedy, get their mouths fastened together for a week!'

'Want to . . . the other,' said Moglet. So did I, so we all went outside for five minutes.

When we returned, Ragnar and his wife were waiting for us and invited us to join them round the replenished fire. Everyone else had disappeared, and I judged the serious part of the business was about to start.

Ragnar nodded at us. 'You may wonder,' he began, 'why it

238

is that you are looked-for: but perhaps you know?'

I glanced at Conn, who shook his head. 'No, we do not know how it is that you expected us,' he said slowly, choosing his words carefully. 'We are on a journey that means much to us but, I should have thought, little to others. Yet are we grateful for your welcome and hospitality, and if our appearance in your part of the country means that my friends and I can help you in any way, then I think I speak for us all when I say we will do our best.' He glanced round at us all, receiving our agreement. 'But may I ask why you need us particularly and how you knew that we should come—if, indeed, it is us you expected?' He sounded doubtful.

Gunnhilde took up some embroidery. 'It is a combination of a need and a legend. The need I shall come to later, but I assure you it is very real.' Her husband nodded gravely. 'First, the legend. Our people have lived here for many generations. They say that folk from the northern lands were wrecked on this coast during a great storm; the survivors scrambled ashore and settled among the fisherfolk who already lived here, in a village much smaller than you see it now. The marriage of different peoples and variant skills brought both peace and prosperity to this part of the country; we had the sea for fishing, our friends who visited us every year—'

I looked at Snowy: the seals? He nodded.

'—sweet water from the river, good earth for crops and the uplands and forests for hunting and timber. For many years we prospered—I speak of a time before I was born, you understand—but a wise man, a shaman as we call them, who once lived and died here warned of a time when the sea should boil, the fish flee and our friends come no more to visit us. Then, it was a tale for children but even so his words were remembered, for who knows what the gods have in store? My mother's mother told me of the prophecies when I was a child and I remembered. But unlike some prophecy it was not all doom: there was a promise of deliverance also.' She glanced at her husband. 'You tell them, for you know the words as well as I.'

'Indeed I do, for it was a tale to fright children into the dark imaginings of the night. We learnt it as it was told, in verse, so that no meaning should be lost by later mis-telling or exaggeration. It goes thus,' and he straightened his back and delivered the lines in a deep, sonorous voice. I didn't think much of them as verse; they didn't even rhyme, but some of the words started with the same letters, so it had a kind of hypnotic beat to it, wrapped up as it was in symbolism and metaphor.

'And in that time: the token of the terror shall be thus:
The people of the sea shall come: and bring forth their young that year;
And the young that year shall be great: and their melody music the meadows.
But for jealousy of their joy: evil shall bring forth evil e'en greater
And the sea shall boil: and bring forth a beast to despoil.
Men shall starve and women too: and children cry from hunger,
And the sea-people and people of the sea: shall keen and cower,
While the great White Wyrme: shall devour the dead and despoil the sea . . .'

He paused. 'If it were only that, then we should be lost indeed, for that which was prophesied has indeed come to pass—more of that later. But the prophecy speaks of a deliverance, and this is where I believe you were sent to help us.' He cleared his throat.

'But this shall last only so long: then from the south shall come the seven;
A wight on a white horse: holding for help in his arms
The moon and stars for measure: and the stars shall be green as grass
Blue as a babe's eye: red as rust and clear as river running.
And the seven shall strive: and the White Wyrme shall wither.
And behold! all shall be: as before and better.
Then the people of the sea and the sea-people: shall gift and guard them,
For they go with the gods: and shall take the road west with weal . . .

'So, that is why we have looked for you, for now is the time of our greatest need, and in your company there would seem to be at least part of the promise of our deliverance. A man on a white horse, that is clear enough, but the prophecy foretold of seven. I count but six—'

'Seven,' I said, and plonked Puddy on a free stool.

There was a moment's silence and then Gunnhilde laughed and put aside her sewing.

'Seven it is, seven. We are lucky husband, for in them the prophecy does come true!'

I wriggled on my seat. 'But the bit about the moon and stars?'

Ragnar frowned. 'That I cannot see, but there must be an answer . . .' He glanced at his wife but she was staring at Puddy and then picked up Pisky's bowl.

'Green as grass: the moon,' and she threw back her head and laughed. 'Under our noses, husband, other riddles to be read, I fancy . . . And you and you and you,' she pointed to me, Corby, Moglet, 'must hold the other "stars"?'

I lifted Corby's wing and Moglet's paw and pointed to my stomach. 'And there is another tale. But it hasn't been written yet, 'cos it isn't finished.'

'The riddle is read,' said Gunnhilde. 'Husband, call them to prepare a feast!'

Amidst the bustle, the uproar, the feasting, the smiles, I caught a mutter from Corby. 'First part's easy, all feasting and fal-lals and what-a-pretty-bird: I've an idea the second part will be more difficult . . .'

It was not until the morrow that we realized just what we had let ourselves in for, but that evening it was indeed all 'feasting and fal-lals' for it was obvious the townsfolk were sure we were the answer to all their prayers. We ate and drank our fill and were entertained by their songs and dances until the small hours. It wasn't till all was quiet that I began to wonder what was in store for us. Then I remembered the verses and fell asleep uneasily wondering about boiling seas and great white worms which, together with the cheese I had eaten earlier, engendered weird and disturbing dreams. Twice I woke in a cold sweat, only to be soothed to sleep again by the gentle breathing of my companions and a sort of mournful lullaby that seemed to come in time with the distant rush and suck of the sea.

The next morning Ragnar, with about fifty interested townspeople in tow, took us down to the beach, and there, restlessly milling and turning, were about two to three hundred seals. They were of all ages and sizes, male, female and pups, and seemed to have little fear of humans, allowing us to walk amongst them on the rocks and the greyish-black sand. They became excited when they saw Snowy and gave soft hooting sounds and groans and I realized they were telling him something, recognizing that he was one who would understand. There were more of them bobbing about in the bay, seeming to stand on their back-flippers in the water eyeing us with curiosity. Some porpoised up and down, showing off, others with mouthfuls of seaweed were tossing their heads from side to side, threshing the water, exactly like a housewife beating clothes on stones in a river—another way of drawing attention to themselves, I supposed. All seemed jolly, a gathering of wild animals grown tame and choosing to live in close proximity with man, but there was an unease, a restlessness, a frustration that communicated itself as surely as the ever-moving sea.

Conn questioned Ragnar on their tameness. 'Are they always like this?'

'Not always, but at the moment they have no choice; they are restless because they know the time has long passed this year when they should be at sea. Supplies of food are running low, both for them and us, though we have given them what we could.' He paused. 'You see, we have an arrangement with them; oh, nothing that has ever been written down by us nor agreed with them: one cannot speak with animals.'

I opened my mouth, but Snowy nudged me, and I closed it again.

'The way it works is this: every year the seals are allowed to come to our beaches and have their pups, and then they mate again. During that time we leave them unmolested. Then, when autumn and winter comes we go forth to hunt them, mainly for their skins, for that is our only surplus for trading. By then they are out at sea, and it is an even battle between man and beast. Even then, we do not hunt indiscriminately; each

242

spring the pups are counted. Of these a third will not survive their first year, from natural causes. We only cull a half of the number of adults of the number remaining, the population is kept more or less constant. There are enough pelts for us and enough fish for both man and beast.'

I looked at Ragnar with new respect: a little different from Lady Adiora's method.

The tide was retreating now, making a noise on the pebbles like someone clearing their throat and then spitting. Ragnar waved to the townsfolk not to follow us further.

'We shall go on alone,' he said. Alone? Where? Echoes of last night's dreams made my heart beat faster. 'Of course there may be little to see: if the creature has eaten recently he may not show himself. But if we stay quiet and tempt him a little, then perhaps—' He beckoned to one of the men, who ran back to one of the huts and reappeared with some strips of dried goat's meat. 'Ah, yes: this should do it.'

With the chief leading we made our way round the bay to the southernmost tip, climbing steadily all the way and passing through a small flock of horned sheep, almost indistinguishable from their goat-brothers, so unlike the low-slung fatties Brothers Peter and Paul tended: still, I supposed the brothers' sheep would have been hard put to it to find sustenance on these harsher uplands, while Ragnar's sheep looked fit and well on their poor diet. More evidence of how careful husbandry had made this such a prosperous place. I supposed The Ancient would have a 'clitch' for all this: 'Difficult to tell sheep from goats when both wear horns'?

At last we stood on the edge of the cliff, the breeze from the sea ruffling Moglet's fur and snatching at my mask. The sea foamed and raced beneath us and some twenty feet away was the opposite cliff, crowned by an immense slab of rock that reared precariously over the edge with what looked to me like a dangerous tilt.

'The Look-Out Stone,' said Ragnar. 'The highest point around. We use it for spying out shoals of fish, for posting a beacon if anyone is overdue and, of course, for spotting the forerunners of the seal-cows in April. But there is a suggestion for building a tower on this side instead: that rock can sway dangerously in a high wind and we're not sure how firmly it's anchored.' He sighed. 'It seems we can have little use for either till the Wyrme is destroyed. When the seals whelped this year we had promise of good hunting, for there were more than usual and we only took the born-dead or injured as we always do. Then the Wyrme came, and they could not escape. They lost about twenty cows and pups, before the males arrived looking for them. They only got in by dint of numbers, a mad rush on a high tide. But now of course the beast knows where they are and also knows a mass exit will leave the pups behind. The cows will not risk the pups and the bulls will not leave the cows . . .' He sighed again. 'And it is not only them, it is us also. We have tried to take to the boats and carry on our fishing but the Wyrme overturns them and anyone who swims is immediate prey. We are trapped and the seals are trapped! This is why we welcomed you, knowing that, through you, the second part of the prophecy would come to pass.' And he began to recite.

'And the seven shall strive: and the White Wyrme shall wither.

And behold! all shall be: as before and better.'

'Doesn't he know any nice cheerful little ditties?' muttered Corby. 'Anyway, he's missed out that bit about the road west. And gifts . . . Fat chance! Looks as if we are trapped as tight as the rest. After all that mumbo jumbo can you see 'em saying "Bye-bye, thanks for trying and all that"? No, we ain't going north, south or east, let alone west—'

'Well, then,' said Snowy, 'put your tongue back in its beak, where it belongs, and use your eyes and your cunning brain to see if you can come up with a solution! It could be your turn, you know.'

There it was: 'turns' again. Moglet's turn, Corby's turn—

'Watch,' said Ragnar, who of course had heard none of this by-play. 'Down there, in that wide cleft in the base of the opposite cliff where the water is calmer . . . That's where he rests and watches and waits.' And with that he tossed a strip of goat's-flesh out as far as he could.

Nothing. We watched the meat sink slowly in the clear water beyond where the tide was racing out, until it touched bottom some twenty feet down. Ragnar took another strip of flesh; I was still gazing at the first and the water appeared to be cloudier, as though something had stirred the grey-black sand. Ragnar flung the second piece.

A gull, a yearling with less sense than it should have, flung itself seawards in a dive after the meat; they touched water together and for a moment I believed the bird had won, but there was a boiling beneath us, a great rearing and with the speed of my thought bright blood sprayed between great sharp teeth, teeth like a hundred bone needles, and the blood became the darker colour of the sea and there was a white, grey-tipped feather floating and nothing more . . .

The air was filled with the screaming of sea birds: gulls, guillemots, tern, as they rose from crevices in the cliff upwards from the sea, and the harsh cries of raven, crow and cormorant who banked and wheeled from their perches on the rearing rocks. Bird mingled with bird, and screamed with fright and mourned with despair and watched the feather as it slipped, alone and broken, away with the ebbing tide. Black and white, grey and grey, and the birds calling and Corby answering and trying to fly from my arms on one wing only, and me clasping him tight to save him from further harm, and the stone in my belly hurting—

And then Snowy called, loud and clear. What had been senseless flight settled into a pattern, rising and falling like the midsummer dance of gnats over a pond, and the voices softened and fell quiet. Corby ceased struggling and lay quiet too, except to say in a small voice: 'Those are my brothers—if only I could fly!' I could do nothing save stroke his untidy feathers in sympathy.

Conn nudged me. 'Did you ever see anything so fearsome, Thingumajig?'

Down there, some five feet below the surface, its body undulating with the unseen currents, was a great white worm-like creature. Despite the distortion of the water I could see quite clearly; I suppose it was not a true white, more a grey-tan colour but the green water gave it luminescence. At first, horror made it a hundred feet long and twenty wide at the least, but when sense reasserted itself I suppose it must have been about eighteen to twenty feet in length, including a flat, splayed, scooping tail. It was segmented, but the shell seemed to be soft, judging by the ease with which it arched and bent its spine; there were two vestigial suckers on the foremost segment behind the head, and double gills like fringed curtains. The head itself was the most frightening of all: it looked much as an eel's but the eyes were positioned much closer on the top of its head and the mouth was wider and set, as far as I could see, with a triple row of the fearsome, needle-sharp teeth.

I shivered. 'Do you—' I said, 'do you think it is the only one of its kind—or—or could there be others?'

'Well,' said Conn. 'The sight of that little monster does bring to mind a tale I heard once, told by one who had returned from seas on the other side of the world. He said it had been narrated to him (and I cannot vouch for its veracity, mind, though one of his longer tales about a great grey beast like a mountain with an extra arm in the middle of its head I do know to be true, for my friend Fitzalan had seen such) but, as I was saying, this traveller had been told that in a sea as warm as new milk, a seaman had fallen overboard and by chance bobbed up again where a lucky rope had saved him. But he had come aboard quite mad, babbling of a great forest of worms such as this one, waving beneath many fathoms like a field of sun-white grain. All thought him touched and suspected a knock on the head had addled his brains, but he insisted and it was all written down by the captain in his log.'

Ragnar had been paying keen attention to this story and nodded his head. 'The water you spoke of was warm; hereabouts, even in winter, there is a warm current that brings the fish in close to our bay. Maybe such a worm as you speak of could have lost its way and followed such?'

It all sounded highly unlikely to me, but here it was and here were we, and I was not looking forward to closer acquaintance. Neither were the others, to judge by the careful way they avoided looking at us and each other. There was not even a 'Lemme see! Lemme see better . . .' from Pisky.

Ragnar brought us back sharply to the task in hand. 'Well now, you have seen our monster: you can see our problem. I realize you will have to think about this, so I will leave you to confer.'

'A conference was just what I had in mind,' said Conn, as easy as if he were discussing the weather, and looking Ragnar straight in the eye. 'Of course, you realize that deep magic such as we shall have to use takes a while to conjure . . .'

We watched the chief out of sight.

I turned to Conn admiringly. 'You were great! Just what idea have you got?'

'Not a one, not a one in the world, Thingummy, but I thought we needed a breather. That fellow is not going to let us out of his sight until his little miracle-workers have got rid of that—that creature down there, and I thought we could talk more freely amongst ourselves. Now then, who's got an idea?'

No one, it seemed. I glanced desperately round our circle.

'We cannot dig it out,' said Snowy. 'Nor lead it away.'

'Fire's no good,' said Puddy gloomily.

'We can't spike it or claw it or carve it up,' said Moglet.

'Can't starve it either,' said Pisky, from the bottom of his bowl.

Which left little. I could think of nothing, save drinking the sea dry, and even I knew better than to make that sort of suggestion.

Eventually, aware of an uncharacteristic silence, we all looked at the culprit. We looked so hard that Corby started shifting from claw to claw and muttering to himself.

'Well?' I said.

'Well, nothing! Just don't expect me to come out pat with the solution. Still . . .'

I think we all shuffled forward a pace.

'Still . . .' he continued, musingly, 'there's something a-tapping from the inside of the shell. Probably as addled as the rest of the eggs in the nest, but you never know . . . Tell you what: all right if we go into one of those huddles, like what we used to? You know, when we all held beaks and claws and things under Thing dear's cloak, in the good old days of Her Ladyship? Always felt it concentrated my mind wonderfully . . .'

It was stuffy and warm under my cloak and I was only too conscious of how silly we must have looked as we wriggled together, until I heard Snowy's thoughts through the thick folds and felt Conn's hand on my shoulder.

'Ideas, ideas,' they seemed to say. 'Think, think; concentrate, concentrate. Give Corby your minds, your help . . .'

Deliberately I tried to make my mind go blank, but still a series of pictures flashed across my mind, like the glint of sunlight on metal, seen a long way off. Cliffs; movement of green water; a rock; birds, flocks of birds; pecking beaks; the sky turning over—

'Got it!' cried Corby. 'Leastways . . .'

I flung back the cloak and we all blinked in the midday sun.

'Gorrem-nidea,' said Corby. 'A possibility, anyways. Beaks out: can feel the sun. Now to chip away the rest of the shell . . .' I realized that what I had thought foreign language and complicated imagery merely meant that he had gone back to his nestling days. 'Can't say for certain . . . Still covered with egg yolk at the moment. But, it might work . . .'

'What?' cried Conn in exasperation.

'Not in words. Not at the moment. Lot of thinking to do . . .'

'How can we help?' asked Snowy, practical as always.

Corby glanced up, but his gaze was abstracted. 'Hmmm? Help? Oh—yes, you might at that. I need to get around this bay to the other side. Over by the big rock. Perhaps, if you wouldn't mind like, you could give me a lift . . .'

And so, for the rest of the afternoon, as the rest of us watched and wondered, Snowy or Conn carried him round the bay, back and forth the three miles or so that separated one headland from the other. Each time he reached the other side he was met by an increasing number of birds, many of them crows as ragged as himself. They all seemed to crowd and confer around the base of the great lookout rock that reared up across from us, but no one said anything specific, although Conn looked thoughtful when he came back with Corby the third time, and Snowy was obviously in on the secret too. For secret it was: Corby refused to discuss his idea with the rest of us, afraid, perhaps, that he might look a fool if it didn't work.

The only clue came from Moglet, who at one stage remarked frivolously that it might save time if we ran a cat's cradle between the two headlands, and Corby looked at her so sharply that I thought we were on to something. Unfortunately, I didn't know what.

His behaviour later that day when we returned to the town, also had us puzzled. He first asked Pisky if he could practise

248

dropping pebbles in his bowl, and met an indignant refusal when the first one narrowly missed one of the snails. Then he asked Conn to fill him a leather bucket with sea-water and by dusk was still picking stones from the beach and dropping them in the water until the container was full, then was asking Conn to empty them out and repeating the process until it was too dark to see.

If we were mystified, so were the townsfolk, and in the end Ragnar himself came down to watch.

'This is obviously powerful magic,' he observed, but I could see one hand was stroking his beard and he was frowning.

'Yes,' said Conn. 'And it works better, it does, if the whole world is not breathing down our necks. Some things are meant to be secret, you know.'

And, as everyone retreated precipitately, it was only I who caught his irreverent wink.

Later that night, Corby asleep before any by the smouldering fire, I tried Conn again.

'Can't you tell us?'

'Tell you what?'

'What's this business with the pebbles? Why did you ask Ragnar tonight about the weather and the times of the tides and so on?'

He pinched my cheek through the mask, but his eyes were dancing.

' 'Tis Corby's secret, so it is, and it's for him to tell. Go to sleep, Thingy, and perhaps you'll learn all in the morning.' And he ruffled my hair with an intimate caressing gesture that sufficiently banished sleep. If it had only been the puzzle over Corby's scheme for ridding the town of the White Wyrme I might have dropped off eventually, but what does one do when one tingles and throbs and glows from nose to toes? It wasn't as though he had meant it as something more than the pat he would give Snowy's flank, the tickle behind Moglet's ear or under Puddy's chin—My stupid, vulnerable inside made me want to make more of it, to kid myself that he had a special feeling for me, that he even looked beneath the hunched back, the mask, the hidden ugly face, and saw someone to love. I knew also that it was no good for me, for us, to think this way. Ever since we had rescued him from that ditch, so many moons away, I had loved him. And although the adventures we had undergone had bred an easy, superficial comradeship that sometimes helped me forget my hopeless love, it was at times like these when I lay unable to sleep; at dawn when we woke to a new day; at evening when the night cloaked our familiar forms; when we were nearest in joint endeavour and when we were farthest, like the time when he had conceived his passion for the Lady Adiora—it was at all these times that I held fast in my heart, knowing, hoping, despairing, realizing, the love I knew would never give me peace.

I looked over to where he lay, long and relaxed on the cushions, one hand flung over his head, the other curled close to his body, breathing gently in a deep sleep. If I had dared, I would have leant over and kissed his curving mouth—

'Do stop *fidgeting*!' said Moglet sleepily. 'Got a tummy-ache?'

THE BINDING: CROW

The Sea-People and
the People of the Sea

'WHAT A marvellous idea!' I said, for Corby had at last outlined his plan. 'But surely we can't manage it on our own? Can't we get the townsfolk to help?'

'That's the general idea,' said Conn. 'Corby thinks his friends, the other birds, can do a great deal, but we need some strong men or women, and we've got to get it all exactly right, the timing and everything.'

'Then,' said Snowy, 'as we are supposed to be magic, it were surely best to see that all those details are worked out beforehand. If we ask for aid too early they may doubt our powers and perhaps realize that eventually ordinary brains such as theirs could have worked out such a solution—not to detract in any way from your achievement, Crow dear—so we shall give them a hint, but no more.

'Now,' he continued, 'there are the tides. At low on the slack, I think you said? Then there is the question of light: that from the sun is best. Dawn, or perhaps noon when the sun strikes sword-straight into the flesh of the water. The timings we shall leave to your discreet inquiries, Sir Knight. Corby will coordinate the birds so that they work from dawn till dusk, and the people shall be told that the headland is out of bounds—it would make sense to tell them that we are drawing a magic circle round the beast, or somesuch. I shall accompany the crow and also arrange for the decoy, which is most important, and keep the people of the sea from trying any more suicidal attempts to escape.

'Which leaves you, Thing dear, and Moglet, Puddy and Pisky. As you realize, we shall need two ropes, and at a pinch

251

could manage by binding those available, but I should prefer entirely new ones, so I want you to explain that we need one rope one hundred feet long, with nine strands worked into nine twists—seven or eight would do, of course, but nine is a magic number and that they'll understand—and the other eighty feet long, twists and strands three and three (more magic), and a net the same, to measure three by nine. That should convince them they are being allowed on the fringes of our "magic", but just to add verisimilitude I want you to cast spells on the making, all of you, in full view of everyone. Not real ones, of course, any mumbo jumbo will do. And don't let them know what the ropes are for; let them believe, if you like, that they are to bind the beast when we have captured it. Anything: I'll leave it to you . . .'

It appeared the tides were approaching the midpoint between neap and flood, which meant we were in the Moon of Harvest, and the most favourable time—slack at midday and ideally a sunny day—would occur in seven days. Seven, a magic number, too . . . This made it easier to explain to Ragnar and Gunnhilde about the 'magic' ropes. They fully appreciated the significance of numbers (this is why we made the ropes ninety-nine and eighty-one feet respectively, to fit in with the illusion), but it did not give Corby and his friends much time.

Moglet, Puddy, Pisky and I were so busy supervising and spelling the ropes, we saw little of what the others were doing, though of course we all compared progress at night. Corby said little, beyond moaning that his beak hurt, and indeed he looked more ragged and unkempt than ever. Conn said little either, but ate (and drank) more than he had for some time, declaring that 'opportunity makes gluttons of us all'; Snowy was obviously tired, too, and we had little to report, for ropemaking is, even with 'magic' rope, a very boring business. That is, until it gets snarled up . . .

Ever tried inventing convincing spell-words? Especially a different one for every foot of one-hundred-and-eighty feet of rope and a net? At first it's easy: you say things like 'Shamma-damma-namma-a-do-ma' which doesn't mean anything, as far as I know—leastways it may in another language, but it didn't have any effect on the rope—and then you get bored and think you are clever to say things backwards (I was very proud of 'Der-obots-ra-et' and 'Sra-etot-der-ob'). But eventually I became so 'derob', both backwards and forwards, that I started to say anything. It was on the third day, after the net and the shorter rope were completed, I was half asleep and yawning and gabbled the first thing that came into my head—

'Er . . . Thing dear,' said Moglet. 'Did you mean to do that?'

I thought it had gone quiet. I opened my eyes. Everyone but us had fallen asleep where they were; standing, sitting; upright, leaning; working, idle. Fast asleep. Just like that.

'*What* did I *say*?'

'The instant turned-to-stone-where-they-stand one,' said Pisky, rushing round excitedly. '*Isn't* it peaceful? None of that nasty dust flying around . . . When are you going to wake them up?'

I hadn't the faintest idea. I realized with horror that I had used, all unknowing, one of the Witch's spells. Not one I had ever heard her use, but one I must have read from her books when she was absent—and now, how on earth did I unsay something I hadn't known I'd said in the first place? I went cold all over.

'Puddy . . .'

His slow, quiet thinking reassured me. 'Not to worry; no harm done. 'Tis a weak spell anyway, and needs but a break in the conjunction. Saw Her try to use it once, but She only had me and a bowl of water; need a cat or somesuch as well. You, me, Moglet and the fish's bowl make a filled triangle. Now, if we move a fraction . . .'

Of course the first time we all moved the same way so the conjunction stayed the same, with Pisky's bowl the central point, but we got it right the second time. I looked around fearfully, but all the folk were taking up their tasks as if there had been no break. My heart pounded sickeningly for a full five minutes and I was very careful after that. Not that it did us any harm in the long run, rather the reverse, for whilst the sleepers were not aware that anything untoward had happened, others too far away to hear the spell had seen what had occurred, and we were treated with an added respect and awe after that.

The seventh day dawned misty and damp. It must, it *must* be sunny at midday! The night before, Conn had told part of Corby's plan to Ragnar, who had promised to find the seven times seven volunteers to man the rope and do the pushing. And that was all of the plan he had outlined, on Snowy's advice. The headlands had been out-of-bounds for the last week, and although the increased activity of the birds, wheeling and crying, must have been some indication that something special was going on, no one questioned us— especially after my unfortunate slip—though I could see they were muttering amongst themselves. I had had awful stomach-cramps after the spelling, incidentally, almost as though by remembering the witch's spells in my unconscious I was also subconsciously calling up the pain associated with Her.

'The sun will show its face before midday,' said Snowy, as if he had read our thoughts. 'Come, you laggards: today is the day . . .', and so after a hurried breakfast of oatcakes, cheese and goat's milk we set off for the headland.

Conn and Snowy and Corby carried the beautifully coiled new ropes—well, the first two did, and Corby supervised— over to the far cliff. I left the others on the near clifftop and made my way to the narrow strip of beach below. From where I stood I could see Conn passing the longer rope around the base of the black slice of the lookout rock and tying it off in a complicated knot. Once he nearly slipped on the bird-droppings which whitened the surrounding stones, but eventually the rope was tied to Snowy's satisfaction. Then they made their way down to the beach opposite and I could see them bending over something else on the stones, but knew I must wait. There was a splash! the other end, then nothing for what seemed ages. As I was beginning to think everything had gone wrong, a round head with tearful brown eyes popped up in the shallows nearby and a large seal dragged itself up the beach to my feet.

Round its neck were the two ropes. Swiftly I stroked the seal's head, surprised to find how warm the skin over the skull was, then unlooped the ropes. It—I think it was a he—grunted, a soft moan, its eyes shining. I patted its head again. 'Well done . . .'

I attached the shorter rope to the netting left on the beach with the tie Snowy had taught me, and helped the seal into his net-sling. 'I think you are very brave,' I said, and stroked him again.

Then it was up to my side of the clifftop again, hauling both ends of rope with me and paying it off as I went, puffing and panting with the effort. The longer piece, taut now across to the opposite headland, I tied to a pre-chosen rock, and the other I anchored under a stone nearer to the cliff-face.

I waved to Conn and Snowy. All set.

I gazed down into the dark, green sea, still half-hidden by wisps of morning mist that clung to the columns of the cliffs and wreathed the rocks. I was half-convinced I could see the shape of the White Wyrme, distorted by the water, lurking under the shelf of rock that was its favourite resting-place . . .

The sun brightened, the last wisps of mist blew away like smoke from a camp fire, the tide drew softer and softer away from the cliffs until the pebbles and rocks shone like jasper before catching the drying dullness of sun and breeze.

Behind me I heard the people who were to haul on the rope, twenty-eight of them; across on the other headland I watched Ragnar lead the other twenty-one behind the Look-Out Stone: I hoped someone had got their calculations right. There were onlookers too; I noticed the boy who had led us into the town on that first day sitting on his father's shoulder for a better look. Below us, in the bay, the people of the sea seethed like tadpoles in a drying rut, venturing ever nearer the mouth between the headlands.

Conn came up behind me, breathless. 'Dear God, and isn't it a haul around that bay? Snowy says that when the sun strikes that submerged rock—there—it will be time. I'd better get the haulers briefed.'

I watched the sun creep round, fascinated by the finger of light that probed—so slowly when watched, two inches at a time if you took your eyes away—deep into the waters below. About five minutes before time I glanced back at Conn who had his contingent holding the longer rope, just off the taut, ready between nervous fingers. Too late I wished we had had time to have a rehearsal, had a tug-of-war to test the ropes, had—

Conn was at my side again, this time taking the end of the

255

second rope in his hand and thrusting it into mine. 'Christ! I near forgot—You'll have to help me with this, Thing dear!' I was so astonished I grasped the rope without further thought. He had got my name right again . . . 'Belay it now, round that rock, there's a good girl, and when I say "Pull!" do it as though your life depended on it!'

Two inches of sunlight to go . . .

Below me one after another of the bull seals and a couple of the cows were venturing almost to the gap between the cliffs, and then seeming to think better of their effort were plunging back into the bay with a great slapping of the water with fins and tail.

'Oh, Conn!' I said despairingly. 'It's too soon! Tell them—tell them to go back! They'll be killed . . .'

'Never worry,' said a concentrating Conn. 'Snowy has briefed them; they know what they are doing. Just stirring up a little interest . . .' As he spoke a greyish-white shape stirred under the ledge on the far side of the rocks and the White Wyrme's monstrous head and six feet of his body came into view.

'A minute, a minute! Oh, dear Lord!' Conn muttered from beside me, his lean body coiled with tension. 'Now, my friend, now!'

As if in answer to his fierce vehemence, a solitary seal swam into view beneath us, seeming to test the water, the tide, the creature itself. A foolish, young seal that behaved as though it had never heard of danger . . . Slow, hesitantly, it paddled right through the gap in the cliffs, and the very tide itself stood still . . .

And the sun, the sun, shining clear and true through the slack water, touched the special rock beneath us and the seal swam straight out into the sea, right into the sudden uprush of teeth from the monster below and Conn cried: 'Pull! Pull, you bastards!' even as there was a shrill neigh from Snowy and all the birds in the world rose in the air screaming and Conn's hands closed over mine as we hauled desperately on the shorter rope and the weight below almost pulled my arms from their sockets and—

There was a crack! and groan from across the water and I watched almost unbelieving as the pinnacle of rock, the

256

Look-Out Stone, shivered a little, leaned, hung for a moment at an impossible angle, and then toppled with at first maddening slowness and then faster and faster towards the water beneath.

'Leave go the rope!' yelled Conn to the haulers behind him. 'Drop it, if you value your lives!' They let go just in time for the depth the rock had to plunge was far greater than its length of ninety-nine feet. I watched the end snake and whip over the edge of the cliff. There was an almighty great splash beneath us and then a high-pitched whistling sound. Conn belayed the taut rope we held around a rock and rushed forwards, grabbing my hand.

Through the mist of still-falling spray, the cloud of screaming birds, we peered into the waters beneath. The great black stone had fallen true, just as had been planned. The monster, the great White Wyrme, lay pinned beneath its biting edge, its back broken, a strange whistling noise coming from between its wicked teeth. A great cheer rose from the townsfolk and those with us ran back to join the others, all streaming back to the bay to launch anything seaworthy, mostly skin and wood boats for inshore and bank fishing. The people were armed with spears and short, stabbing swords, and these they waved in the air as they took to the water.

I went forward to check on our seal-lure, the animal we had hauled up with such desperate haste in his netting hammock. I saw him wriggle free, but as he dived the ten feet or so back into the sea I could see a gash on his shoulder, a torn flipper.

The people in their boats were racing across the bay, the bows throwing up steep little waves. The first boats were reckless, came too close, too soon, and one was overturned by a thrash of the dying beast's scooped tail and another's side was stove-in by the still-lethal jaws. But soon there were too many of them and the water oozed with a greenish-white murk as the spears and swords rose and fell; thrusting, tearing, gouging out great clumps of flesh until I had to turn away, sickened with the sight.

Snowy, a triumphant Corby on his back, nuzzled my shoulder. 'The creature is dead: he can feel nothing . . .'

Conn nodded soberly, watching the carnage beneath. ' 'Tis often that way, after long fear and frustration; all a man's

257

tensions build up, and unless one takes the lid off the pot—' He shivered, and a haunted look came into his eyes and was gone, so quickly I almost believed I had imagined it.

'Come on, now!' said the irrepressible Corby. 'Where's all the feasting and fal-lals, then?'

The following morning we stood once more on the headland. The feasting was over, the songs sung, the thanks given, the gifts received. On Snowy's back, besides two panniers full of food and some herb wine, was a fresh-cured sealskin, soft and supple, ready to make into mitts, slippers, leggings, whatever we chose. Conn sported a new cloak, as like the old as made no difference, and our pockets were lined with silver. We were waiting for the great procession, the release of the seals—the people of the sea, and the townsfolk—the sea-people. It had been arranged that at midday, tide-slack, both animals and men would venture beyond the cliffs, past the mutilated body of the Wyrme, now fast disappearing down the throats of the constant sea birds, and out, out into the limitless sea. From then on, after this last day of amnesty, man and seal would revert to their natural roles, hunters and hunted. Until the spring, and the coming of the seal-cows . . .

I shivered a little as my hand crept to the soft hide on Snowy's back: perhaps this skin had come from some autumn killing like the ones that would start soon. I didn't want to think about it, for I had a secret, a secret only Snowy and I and one other shared. For last night . . .

Last night either the feasting had been too rich or my sleep had been too light, but suddenly, in the dark hour before dawn, I had awoken, all my senses keen, aware of far music in my ears. I sat up in the warm darkness of the hall. There it was again, quite unmistakable. Four notes in a descending scale, as though a child stepped down a great staircase, then an upward note as though he had gone back, up a missed step, and then down again to the ground on the last note, and all in a sadness of sound like innocence lost.

The melody was repeated, and I saw the shadow of our unicorn push aside the hangings from the shrouded doorway and disappear into the night. I tiptoed after him—none of the others, even Moglet of the bat-ears, had heard me go.

I followed Snowy down to the beach, his unshod hooves making no sound on the shingle, my stumbling progress plain enough to my ears and his, though he had not turned his head. There, beached on the pebbles, was the source of the song, our brave young seal-lure, his eyes swimming in the light of the half-moon, singing a song of loneliness and present pain. Snowy bent to the torn side, the injured flipper and I felt a shudder of power pass from him.

'There, my friend,' he said. 'It will heal. It *is* healed . . .'

I joined them, and in that dream, half-dream, I looked at the young, royal seal and thanked him again, and the scar on his side and the rip in his flippers shone white and healed. And it seemed to me that he asked whether I would like to try his world and that I agreed, and stripped off my clothes and mask and stepped into the waves and that they were as warm and smooth as new-drawn milk. And I put my arms about his neck, or so it seemed, and with Snowy's blessing we slid into the flooding bay, and the sea closed round us like the finest silk cloth, and there was the taste of salt in my mouth and the waves slid over my back with the gentlest of caresses.

The seal's body undulated like the weeds that waved in dark streamers from the rocks. When we reached the inlet, I felt the sudden great surge of the ocean and I held on tight, breathed deeply and then we were in his world, into the sudden cold beyond the cliffs, and the water sang and bubbled in my ears and lifted me from his back until only my arms held me to his curving, twisting body, and I knew what it was to fly in water and walk in water and live in water . . .

'You helped us,' he said. 'And because of that we shall sing to you when you come to your home by the water. Listen for us . . .'

Now, as we all watched from the headland, the tide from the bay started to flow out from the beach. First came the seals, the people of the sea; the males, the females, the younglings, surging out to meet their natural element, the sea; and after came the sea-people, the townsfolk and fishermen, singing and shouting and brandishing their spears, paddles flashing in the sun. And leading them *my* seal, breasting proudly the breakers that led to his freedom of the seas.

259

My eyes prickled with tears.

Over our heads the sea birds and the cliff birds screamed their victory, told of the long hours spent chipping away at the base of the great, lost Look-Out Rock and above them a lone buzzard spiralled, his call lost in the clamour.

'Shall we go?' said Conn. 'They won't miss us now . . .'

260

THE BINDING: KNIGHT

The Holy Terrier of Argamundness

THE RUINED fortified wall ran just the way we wanted to go, judging by our next marker: the five fingers of rock indicating northwest-by-north that we found on the edge of the moor above the town of the sea-people.

The shortening days were sunny and dry and bramble and hazel yielded a rich harvest. Brimstone (first and last in every year), tortoiseshell and peacock fluttered in ditch and hedge, some of the trees were goldening towards their fall and sheep fleeces were thickening. Folk were hospitable, for harvest was in, and for a time there would be an abundance of fruits and grain, and cattle- and pig-salting was still some way off while there was still stubble for the former and an abundance of acorns for the latter. Thatch was being replaced, wood chopped, peat stacked, preserves jarred, honey collected, grain threshed and stored; everywhere was bustle, harmony, plenty, and we ourselves were in fine fettle, exchanging shelter and food in the main just for a tale or two, a song, some of Corby's 'tricks', but for the most part we just walked the wall, content with our own company and aware that we had in some way 'turned a corner'.

Conn had shown us The Ancient's map and with charcoal had traced the way we had come so far. 'See, 'tis the four sides of a septagon we have done already: over halfway, and not a bone broken!'

'Yes,' I objected, 'but it has taken us at least three months to get this far: at this rate we will be into the Moon of Fogs at least before we finish. And who knows what else we have to face? Snowy got us and the animals out of that prison of a castle,

Puddy reminded me of that fire-spell before we got eaten by tree-roots, Moglet thought of a way to get rid of that spider before we and the bats starved to death, and back there Corby and his friends chucked half a mountain at a sea-monster but—' I stopped. I had suddenly remembered what Snowy had said about it being someone's 'turn', and thought flashed past thought; Snowy, Puddy, Moglet, Corby: they had all had their turns. Which left . . . ? Me, Conn and Pisky. 'Oh dear!' I said.

Snowy gave me a sympathetic look. 'They were not all as bad as each other.'

'Bad enough!' I said gloomily, and spent the next couple of days in fruitless speculation on who would be the next one to save his comrades, and would it be difficult and long-drawn out or just plain scary? And would whoever-it-was prove equal to the task? (I meant me, of course.)

But the sun continued to shine by day, and when there were no hamlets we snugged down on colder nights in the remains of stables, dormitories and officers' quarters along the wall. We built fires against the ghosts that still marched those ramparts and stewed hare and wild fowl and vegetables, drank wine if we were lucky and water if we were not. Soon I forgot my cares and exulted in the peace and companionship and stared north up the steep decline from whence the blue-painted savages had challenged the ordered life and discipline of the Romans. I found a scandal, thongs broken, the haft of a sword, burnt grain scattered among broken shards, a pin without its set-stone, half a helmet . . .

'We turn here,' said Conn. 'Away from the wall, if we are to keep our direction.' To the north the hills were starting to crowd down, though still blue with distance. We were on a plateau, but from now on the way was down, the slopes thickly wooded. It was a clear, pleasant day, but ahead lamb's-fleece cloud banked high on the horizon. 'Leaf-Change will be with us soon, and the way lies through the woods. Corby, your eyes are best.' He took him on his shoulder. 'Is that the sea?'

I squinted through my lashes as he asked the question, but could only make out a haze, a deepening of colour, a glint of sun.

'Two rivers,' said Corby slowly. 'Small 'un and a bigger.

262

Second one's got a wide estuary. Tide's out: plenty of sand.'

'That's our way,' said Snowy. 'We could follow the river from its source, but it would be easier to cut down through the woods and join it nearer the mouth . . . What do you say?'

With the weather changing there was only one answer: we took our bearings and plunged into the forest. The way was difficult, for these woods were old as time and scarce of habitation, and fallen timber and thick undergrowth pestered our way, but I found plenty of mushroom and fungi to supplement our diet, though none of the Magic ones or the Fairies' Tits Tom Trundleweed had shown me. I remembered I still had a little packet of the dried ones in my pack, never used. I checked: they were still there, perhaps a bit squashed and crumbly, but better not to throw them away, just in case.

We descended to the river plain, and here the land had been cleared and farmers and smallholders raised sheep and a few cattle on the sparse, thin grass and fished the banks of the river for salmon and trout. Small, stunted trees bent their backs away from the westerly winds and the fleeced sky brought rain and an uneasy half-gale that gusted and died an instant before it was born. At last the river broadened into a wide estuary where the river Rippam, as it was called, ran fast and wide over great ribbed flats of sand, birds flocked and ran at low tide among the shrimped pools and worm-casts, and the heron flapped slow home with dab and eel in its craw.

We stayed in a fisherman's cottage the night of the Big Storm and lucky it was we found shelter, for the forest and fields of Argamundness, as it was called, were soon roaring with an equinoctial tide and a following gale that had waves leaping twenty feet high over the artificial barriers erected years ago in the little hamlet of Lethum in which we found ourselves.

We had crossed a precarious log roadway over the marsh; the earth and sand packed between the logs were seeping away, and more than once we found places where the logs themselves had disappeared. So it was with a sense of relief that we found the little hamlet tucked away on sand dunes, some twenty feet above the usual tide-level, and protected by an artificial barrier about ten feet high of smooth pebbles, glistening grey, pink and white under the onslaught of the waters. There were also the dunes of sand, bound by spiky marram grass, themselves a natural barrier to the west and north. The hamlet was a poor one, the only livelihood being the fishing that depended so much on wind and tide. Their sturdy boats, broad in the beam, could go out in all but the fiercest weather, and they had nets fine enough for shrimp and tough enough for plaice and dab, which hung pungently from the rafters of the cottages whose shuttered windows faced away from the prevailing westerlies.

Lethum was so poor, it did not even have an inn and the speech of its inhabitants reflected their isolation, being thick and sprinkled with a patois we could not understand. However, our coin they did recognize, and we fed well on fish stew, crabbed apples and goat's milk, and were provided with sacking pallets against the wall of one of the larger cottages. There was no problem with bringing Snowy inside either, for our host's few scrawny hens, a pig and a patient donkey were obviously used to sharing his space. It was warm, if fuggy, and I was more than accustomed to animal smells, so sleeping would have been no problem but for the violent wind.

Suddenly it was upon us, battering and hammering at doors and windows, skirling the rushes on the floor, puffing the smoke from the peat fire in our faces, and ripping great chunks of thatch from the roof, netted and weighted as it was. The mud-and-stone cottage seemed to crouch down upon itself, shrinking into the earth with ears back and eyes closed, a hare in the swirling, shifting dunes. Sand was everywhere; it gritted our teeth, rubbed the sore places in our skin, spun into little shifting castles on the floor. The whole world roared and bellowed and screamed and shouted outside like a huge army of barbarians come to pillage and destroy.

I found myself huddled in a heap on the floor, hands to my ears and eyes tight shut. I only realized I was moaning with fear when Conn took me by the shoulders and shook me.

'Pull yourself together: look at the others!'

I sat up, still shuddering. Snowy was fine, reassuring our host's animals with his mere presence, but poor Moglet was plastered like a dying spider against the far wall, eyes rolling in terror; Corby had his head under his wing in a corner and his feathers were twitching; Pisky had dived right to the bottom of his bowl and hidden his head under the weed; Puddy's throat was gulping up and down in distress and his eyes bulged more than ever. Our host crouched in a corner and was muttering, whether prayers, charms or incantations I could not tell.

I looked up at Conn; his eyes were troubled, and he moved as restlessly as a penned horse who has been used to the plain, but he showed none of the panic of the others. I took courage from his brown eyes, his firm chin, the challenge in his slim taut body.

'Well,' I said, rising a trifle unsteadily to my feet. 'It's going to be at least morning before this thing blows itself out, and I don't feel like sleep. Come, you lot, closer to me so I don't have to shout, and we'll think of a game to pass away the time.' And I staggered over to Moglet and prised her claws from the mud wall, picked up Puddy and put him in my pocket, then made my way to Corby's side and indicated that he should join us by Pisky's bowl. Once there we went into our familiar huddle, all of them under the shelter of my cloak, and there we played 'Going to Market' which Pisky won, having one of those retentive memories that remembers every detail, relevant or no; Corby was runner-up. Then we played it again, with the same result, for by now another sound had added itself to the din outside, and we were all trying our hardest to shut it out—

The sea.

The wind had been bad enough, but now there was the regular beat and fall of waves upon the barricade outside; on the mutable bank of pebbles, on the shifting sand dunes, and with every moment the thrusting, sucking roar came nearer and nearer. I glanced from under my cloak at our host: he was on his knees. I looked over at Snowy: he, too, was listening, poised on his hooves as if for flight. I opened my mouth to say something, I will never know what, and then Conn's arm was about my shoulders and his smile stopped my mouth.

' 'Tis only the tide, Thingy dear. 'Twill soon be full, and then back it will go again . . . Can I join your game?'

Instantly everything was all right again, or very nearly. He must have been as anxious, if not actually as afraid, as we were, but all he was concerned with was our fear, our anxiety, and in so doing, in forgetting himself, he gave us all a courage we had not known we possessed. Suddenly all would be bearable, just so long as we were together. Even death, for surely the frightening part of that is not what comes after but the loneliness of dying, the actuality of leaving the world on one's own. But if we held one another tight and didn't let go, it would surely only be a little jump, like leaping down steps in one's dream and awaking with a sudden jolt into reality. And I supposed that Death must be as great a reality as Life. It must be, for everything, everyone, had once been alive, and would all be dead. So, if it happened to everyone, to everything, it could be no worse than Life, for everyone could manage that, one way or another. And, although Life could be difficult, at least it was never so bad that one wanted to leave it. And yet . . .? Snowy? Had he not spoken of despair, of a longing so great it was a Death-Wish? If so, the Death was to be desired, for if Snowy knew it would bring him release from whatever tortured him, then surely—

'Tide's on the turn,' said Conn. 'And the wind has outrun itself. It's tiring . . .'

From the cracks in the shutters facing east came the first grey, sandy light of morning, and his words were true; the sound of the tide, once advancing so ferociously, was now retreating, but with a sullen roar that spoke of victory lost. The wind still buffeted the cottage but the impetus had gone.

I was suddenly tired, so tired, and I sank down upon the floor, the others huddled to me in like fashion, and now the sea became a lullaby. I felt Conn stretch out beside me, sensed Snowy's relaxation and I slept. We all slept.

It was well into daylight when we awoke, to a grudging bowl of oatmeal and milk, seasoned by sand, and a rind of cheese. The hamlet had suffered badly. Two roofs were blown clean away and the sand dunes, under the driving force of wind and sea, had changed their shape, creeping towards the huts, half-burying the one nearest the shore. Two boats were also lost; one, its sides smashed, had been flung high up the strand to lean crazily against a de-roofed cottage. And sand was in everything: gritty, pervasive, yielding like water and as impossible to shift, for it ran through one's hand and off shovels like liquid, only twice as heavy.

The pebble dyke was in most need of urgent repair; parts of it were entirely washed away where the sea had breached, and all in all it seemed some two or three feet lower. The villagers

266

were working frantically for the tide was at the slack and they had barely six hours to patch things up before high. We offered to help, but even I could see that an inexperienced knight—a novice at building dykes, that is—however willing, and a small hunched female would be of more hindrance than help, so we left our host an overpayment of two silver pieces and set off again.

I could see Snowy becoming anxious, for we were running out of land. Ahead of us the deepening river channel was starting to curve across to the right, directly in our path, and ahead there was nothing but an uneasy ocean. Walking was difficult, for though the sand was firm enough the retreating water had ridged it into tight brown waves some two inches high and it was hillocked with sandworm casts so that I stumbled and stubbed my toes and cursed. The wind had shifted north and though it had lessened considerably it was strong enough still to skim the sand from the shifting dunes to our right and send it wraithing across the firmer beach to redden our legs and arms and grit our teeth. Above our heads tattered, yellow-eyed gulls screamed and slid, tip-winged, into the currents of air and beyond the river mouth we could still hear the sullen roar of surf. Our way was further hampered now by the detritus of the receded tide: uprooted trees and bushes, the carcases of drowned sheep, logs, bales of soaking straw and even a broken chair. One of the Lethum boats was also stranded, its stern shattered. Little brown crabs ran in and out of its broken ribs.

Moglet's ears pricked from the shelter of my jacket. 'Listen! A dog barking . . .'

'Out here?' I said incredulously. 'Don't be daft! There's nothing out here but sea and sand and wind and gulls—' But then I heard it too, a high yapping that seemed to come from our left. We peered through the clouds of sand that swirled round us and saw a sky-ring of gulls circling slowly about a sandbank.

'There's someone out there,' said Conn. 'Come on!'

We came upon an extraordinary sight. On a sand bar, some hundred feet long and half as wide, a tall, thin man was sitting on an upturned fishing boat, reading, his thin hair blowing in his eyes and as calm and unperturbed as if the tide was not already sneaking in behind him, fast and stealthy, scummy skirts brushing the sand to hide its hurrying feet. Between the man and us was a bubbling race of water, widening by inches every minute, and at the man's feet was the source of the barking: a small, dock-tailed mongrel terrier, white, brown and black. He was racing in circles, yelling his head off and now and again tugging at the voluminous skirts of the unheeding reader's habit.

We glanced at one another, then Conn hailed the stranded man. 'Ahoy, there!'

The reaction was not what we had expected; the tall man merely looked up, regarded us, raised his hand in greeting, then fell to reading again, just as if all in the world was perfect and he were not threatened by imminent immersion, or worse.

But the little dog was different. Even as we stared in stupefaction at his master's apparently careless attitude to life, the animal had thrown himself into the channel that lay between us and was paddling valiantly in our direction. The race of the incoming tide inevitably carried him off to our left and he was struggling to reach our position, but Conn moved along the water's edge and, wading out, grabbed him by the scruff of the neck and bore him to safety, gasping and choking with the salt water.

Conn set him down. 'Now then . . .' he said uncertainly. 'Good doggie—'

'Bloody good doggie, nuffin!' hiccoughed the animal and, probably thanks to Snowy's mind-interpretation we could understand everything he said. 'Bleeding salt-water—gets up yer nose, it does . . . Wait a bit, me hearties . . .' He sneezed and coughed and hacked and shook himself in a mist of droplets. 'That's better!' He glanced at us all in turn, brown eyes keen and calculating. 'Well, not exactly the Imperial Guard, are you then? Not even the rearguard . . . Still, *he* says you are the deliverers; more like the unlikely ones, you look to me, but you never can tell . . . What's the scheme, then? 'E can't swim, you know . . .'

'Scheme?' we echoed.

'Yus. How're you getting' 'im orf, then?'

'Getting him off?' We must have sounded like the chorus to a play.

'Orf! Orf!! C'mon then, get the grey stuff workin'!' He really was worse than Corby, who could be difficult enough to understand sometimes. But then, I reminded myself, upbringing and privilege had a lot to do with it; he was obviously a Deprived Dog.

'I can't swim,' said Conn. 'Can you, Thingummybob?'

'I—I don't think so . . .'

'But I can,' said Snowy. 'Leastways, unicorns can and horses can—I've never tried it. But I guess now's the time . . . Conn, can you hang on to my tail and wave your legs up and down? Thing dear, you can ride on my back with the others as safe as possible. The water will be cold, but don't be frightened.'

We got there, but it wasn't easy. Moglet screamed every time she got splashed, Pisky grumbled and choked on the odd drop of salt water and said it was making his snails curl up, Corby rattled his pinions and flapped a wet wing in my face and Puddy made a mistake and shot out a jet of evil-smelling liquid into my pocket, from the wrong end. And me? I was terrified, of course, cold and wet, and hung on to Snowy's mane as if it were a lifeline. It felt so strange to know there was no firm ground beneath his hooves, to know we were at the mercy of the tide, the waves, the water. And it was so cold, that tidal sea, the waters coming sweeping in from the deeps ready to freeze your legs, your arms, your stomach; pulling you gently, insistently, inexorably in the way it would go . . . I tried to remember my seal-friend, and how natural he had found it, and I felt a little better.

We landed on the edge of the sandbank, upriver where the tide had carried us in spite of Snowy's strong swimming legs, and walked back, shivering, to where the man in the long robe was still sitting. He raised his eyes from the page he was reading, still apparently oblivious of the encroaching waters that were creeping up behind his back.

'My friends: welcome!' He closed the book, leaving his finger as a marker. 'I see you have met my companion.' And he nodded at the dog, who was shaking himself again, wetting us even more. 'Now, I am ready when you are. I do not, at this moment in time, see exactly how you will transport myself and my precious cargo—' He indicated with a wave of his fine, long-fingered hand a leather-wrapped bundle at his feet, '—

269

across yon turbulent waste,' (the ever-encroaching tide), 'but as the Good Lord has sent you to my aid, I am confident in our safe passage.' He drew the skirts of his habit absent-mindedly from an early wave, which retreated as if stung. 'We have not long, I surmise . . .'

'I gather you need transport for yourself, the dog and—and those books, to dry land,' said Conn, politely, but breathing hard. 'It has proved a hard task to reach you; perhaps if you left behind those last—'

'And the books,' said the other, firmly. I glanced up at his face; thin, ascetic, with deceptively mild, pale-blue eyes. A strong nose, thin-lipped mouth, long chin, large ears, almost nonexistent eyebrows; a large Adam's apple, unshaven chin whose hairs were whiter than the thin wisps that floated about his head. Pointy fingers, pale-skinned, the index finger of his left hand off at the second joint—not a recent injury—ridged fingernails, long elegant feet in much-mended sandals, with uncut toenails that either curved yellow round the toes or were broken off in jagged points. He smelt quite strongly, too.

'You will be doing the Lord's work, my son . . .' And he sketched a vague cross in the air, in Conn's direction.

I saw Conn bow and cross himself, and knew we were all now committed to getting this strange man and his cargo across to dry land, and Conn's next words confirmed this. 'Any particular part you are bound for, Father?'

'The brothers at Whalley; my associates at Lindisfarne have lent their precious Gospels for the copying, and I have other relics, scrolls and records to convey to our order on the Holy Isle.' He shifted his now decidedly wet feet again. 'I should be obliged, Sir Knight, if we could proceed as soon as possible. The written word does not take kindly to immersion in salt water, and although I protected them as well as I could during the voyage across some two days since, and this morning on our trip from Martin's Mere, I fear that the Sea of Galilee and the Sea of Hirland have little in common. I did indeed try the Lord's commandment: "Peace, be still!", but I fear I was presumptuous, and later said several "Pater Nosters" to atone for this. However, the weather is now less inclement, and by this sign I see that He has graciously forgiven me . . .'

I hadn't a clue what to do next, but luckily that magic cross-in-the-air had worked a miracle on Conn. Motioning the tall monk to stand he upended the boat on which the man had been sitting and scratched his head. The craft was small, bluff-bowed, wooden, and two of the wooden planks in the bows were split. The rest was sound enough, but the mast was missing, snapped off some two feet from its stepping. Conn scratched his head.

It began to rain, quite hard.

'Right!' said the Rusty Knight. 'The sealskin from the pack, Thingy, and the rope . . . Thanks.' And in a moment it seemed he had slit the skin a third, two thirds, and the larger piece was wrapped round the bows of the boat, secured by twine, and the smaller effectually parcelled the books, including the one that was being read. The rope was attached to the stump of mast and a loop at the other end was placed round Snowy's neck. 'Now, Father, if you will sit well back in the stern—the back of the boat—with the—er, books on your lap, my horse will tow you through the flood, letting the tide take us with it until we hit a sandbank or firmer ground. Right, Snowy?'

'What abaht me, then?' asked the dog. 'Bloody swim again, is it? And how do we know our white friend can manage?' He jerked his head at Snowy. 'Beggin' your pardon I'm sure, Your Worship, and appearances are deceptive, so they say, but you look fair knackered already, if you'll pardon the expression,' and he sniggered to himself at the pun.

'Appearances,' said Snowy mildly, 'are, as you remarked, sometimes deceptive. As you should know,' and he shot a glance full of such sharp intent at the dog that if it had had eyebrows to raise it would have done so.

'I see,' said the mongrel softly. 'I see . . .' and when Conn lifted him into the boat by his master's feet he made no further protest at the water slopping around his paws but settled down quietly. On his face, as he looked at Snowy, was much the same expression that Conn had worn when the monk had crossed himself.

With little ceremony Conn put Moglet and Puddy on the monk's lap, bade him hold Pisky's bowl safe and perched Corby high on the bows. By now water was sloshing round my calves, insidiously nudging at me like a dog, turning in little currents about my ankles, and any minute now it would rear

271

up and butt me behind my knees. I dared not look at the increasing expanse of water that separated us from the nearest land. My breakfast rose to the back of my throat in sheer terror and I had to swallow back on the bitter bile.

'Ready?' asked Conn.

I nodded. 'Any time,' I squeaked, wishing I had kept it to the nod.

'Right, then—'

'It's raining,' said the monk gently. 'If you could just tuck the end of the wrapping more securely round the books . . .'

Grimly Conn re-wrapped the parcel. 'All right now?'

The monk nodded, then rose to his feet in the now gently rocking boat and raised his right hand, upsetting practically everything in the process. 'I think a blessing—'

'Sit *down*!' said Conn savagely. 'And *stay* there . . .'

Luckily it was easier than I had expected, for the tide was stronger now and soon Snowy found the main current. We moved steadily upstream, Conn and I clinging to the sides, the better to tip up the suspect bows, gently kicking our legs up and down as Snowy directed. I felt better this time, partly because the exercise warmed me up; indeed I let go of the boat a couple of times, just to see what it felt like, and paddled with my hands. I even turned over on to my back and let the sea sing in my ears the way it had with my friend the seal, and my body unfolded in the water like seaweed and stretched itself, crooked back forgotten, and I floated, a log beneath the racing clouds—

'Thingy!' yelled Conn. 'You're getting lost!' and in a frantic panic that forgot seal and swimming and turned my body awkward and deformed again I threshed my way back to the safety of the gunwhale, my throat and mouth full of choking, salty water.

We landed safely on a spit of land some miles upstream, where the river narrowed and curved to meet the opposite bank. Conn beached the boat, retrieved the rope and offloaded everything and everyone. I noticed how exhausted Snowy looked and slipped a comforting arm around his neck. 'Another half-mile and it's shore and supper,' I said. 'You were great . . .' He nuzzled my neck, and I was aware in myself of an aching tiredness and the pain of cold limbs.

I looked round at the others: all present and correct, if as wet, cold and tired as me. All but our passenger; he seemed invigorated by the cold, revitalized by the water, and now flung his arms in the air and began invoking his Lord. Conn sank to his knees and bowed his head; I thought I had better do likewise, and let the foreign-sounding words flow over my head like a warm, drying wind.

Behind us, in the fervency of prayer, the boat slipped off the bank and rocked on its way upstream, with two thirds of the sealskin . . .

'I shall travel to my brothers at Friarsgate first,' said our travelling monk. 'Will you not go with me part of the way?' He was addressing Conn, who shook his head.

'Thank you, but our way now lies—' he glanced at Snowy, '—southeast.' There was the faintest interrogative lift to his voice.

'Six stones lie half a mile south,' said Snowy.

'So we shall bid you farewell and safe journey,' added Conn. He helped the monk arrange his pack of books—still wrapped in the other third of our sealskin—comfortably on his shoulders. 'God speed you . . .'

'He will, He will,' said the monk fervently. 'He has my project in his care, for He sent you to my succour . . .'

I wished fervently at that moment that He, whoever He was, had thought to ask us first, for I could not remember ever having felt so damp and cold.

The monk hitched up his robe through his belt. 'Goodbye, then, goodbye!' and he strode off towards the dunes behind us, wet robe flapping about his knees. 'Ask for me if ever you come to Lindisfarne. Or the Holy Isle. Or . . . Name's Cuthbert.'

The little dog still sat where he was; at last he stirred, had a good hoof of his left ear and shook out some salt water. 'Oh, well,' he sighed, and rose to his feet. 'Better see the old boy doesn't turn left at Priorstown. Thanks, you lot . . . Still say you're unlikely.'

'Why don't you travel with us?' I asked. 'You're welcome, you know . . .'

'*He* knows,' said the dog, nodding at Snowy. 'He knows as how the old boy would be hopelessly lost without a guide. Sort of thing I've got to do, somehow. Sorry for the old bugger, really: head in the clouds, feet anywhere . . . Oh, well,' and he sighed again.

I pulled out a piece of dried fish from the pack. 'Here.'

'Ta!' He swallowed it. 'Can't live on fresh air like some people I could mention. Likes me nosh, I does.' He burped fishily. 'Don't worry; I'll get him where he wants to go. Keep him snug for the winter, then back to the bloody bogs come spring.' He scratched again. 'Gawd! Anyone'd think all that bleeding water would have drowned the perishers! Well, benny-bloody-dickerty, you lot!' And he was away, jaunty docked tail and ears erect, trotting off in the steps of his master.

'There are saints and saints,' said Snowy cryptically.

'Will he be all right?' I asked, and didn't need to specify whom I meant.

'Of course,' said Snowy. 'They both serve the same Master, don't they? He is a good guide: he found us.' He twitched his ears. 'The unlikely ones: I rather like that . . .'

'Come *on*!' called Conn, by now well ahead. 'I can see the stones, as you said. So we're on the right road . . . Got any dry wood, Thingummy? I fancy a hot drink of something-or-other . . .'

Slinging the others all over me as best I could I followed Snowy's sure steps, while above our heads a storm-driven buzzard or kite or whatever fled our path south.

THE BINDING: FISH

The Face in the Water

PISKY'S ADVENTURE, when it came, was over in a flash of fins.
But there were many days of travel before he had his
moment of glory, and all through the preceding misty
mornings and sharp nights of Leaf-Fall I was wondering, on
and off, whether it would be his turn or mine. Each day was so
beautiful and smelt so of the poignancy of decay as the world
wended its way to the long sleep of winter, that often I
would forget and run to catch a falling leaf, or gather finger-
staining dewberries for their sharp-sweet explosion of taste.
The last flowers were a patchwork of butterflies and moths,
and martlets gathered in soft twittering lines on bending
sprays of hawthorn, their gaze south. Bees fed heavy and
wasps found fallen fruit before I did, angry colours a warning.
Squirrels raced the treetops, younglings not yet the russet of
their parents, and chattered angrily as we plundered the nuts
they would have hoarded and forgotten. We heard wild pig
crashing in the undergrowth in their search for acorn and
truffle, and at night their little prickly brothers wandered
sharp-nosed and blind amidst our sleeping bodies, rootling for
slugs and snails. At night, too, the dog-fox barked his territory
and once, far away, we heard the howl of wolf. Rutting stags
roared and clashed their antlers, owls ghosted through the
twilight to screech threat to every tiny creature that cowered
within range, and mushroom and fungi uncurled and swelled
between dawn and dusk so that we trod a cushion of them,
marvelling at the shelvings and bloatings that shawled and
blanketed the trees with deep, livid colours in contrast with the
other, more muted colours of autumn.

275

Then came storms that shook the trees, bent the brittling grass, drove the clouds so fast they seemed not to know whether to drop their rain or carry it on to another market. On such a day as this I found two martlets and three fledglings locked fast in a cot where the door had slammed shut and the latch fallen. We were seeking shelter ourselves and I was first to the hut—probably some charcoal-burner's—and wrenched open the door. Immediately I was swathed with wings, and even without Snowy's interpreting presence I could understand what they said.

'Thank you, human, thank you: it is late, and we must fly. The children are fat, but little practised in flight. We had hoped . . .'

I listened to their soft trilling and stretched my arms wide so they might light on them. 'Fear not, travellers; the wind is from the west and will carry you all high in its arms to safety. Fly now, and fear not . . .'

'We go, we go . . . And are grateful that you came. We and ours shall bring summer to your eaves when we return, and your home shall be blessed . . .'

And they were gone, the youngsters a little unsteady at first then, escorted tenderly by their parents, flying higher and higher till they were mere specks in the air and turning southeast—

'Gawd! Wish I could stretch my wings like that!' muttered Corby who had joined me, striding and hopping through the undergrowth.

'You will, you *will*!' I promised, bending down to stroke the ruffled feathers. 'Not long now . . .'

But in spite of my optimism—had we not, after all, covered some hundreds of leagues in our quest and taken a whole summer and much of the autumn to do it?—the end of our travels, expected now in every turn of the road for there were only two adventures to go, still seemed as far away as growing up: the nearer, the farther. In the end even I grew impatient, feeling that if it were my 'turn' next I should welcome it; anything would be better than this endless walking. Not that the way was unpleasant; rivers to follow, streams to cross, blue hills to our right, the vales to our left, woods full of the russet, yellow and browns of Leaf-Fall—but there was a sense of urgency in the air that sharpened and quickened with the first frosts and the great skeins of geese that passed swiftly overhead, the way we were going but so much faster!

We ate well enough from wood, river, coppice and field, for the earth gave forth in plenty that year. With our fast-dwindling stock of silver we paused at town and village as seldom as we could, but we exchanged a night or two for the nuts and mushrooms we gathered on the way and luckily did not fall foul of foresters or verderers, for great lords seemed few and far between. The robin began his song again and once more we heard the large voice of the wren and the twitter of sparrow, long silent over the summer.

Then we came to the meres, the pools, the lakes—and, in particular, one lake. We had managed, so far, to keep our direction by sidestepping, cornering, splashing straight through the shallower pools, but now we were faced by a lake whose ends, to right and left, seemed boundless. It was a misty, moist day and the sun shone faint as a moon through a veil of gauzy cloud. Ahead of us the water lay still, unnaturally still, its grey waters scarce rippling though all the while a cold steam rose from it and the reflected sun floated like a blob of yellow fat on its surface. Reeds stood up from the fringes some ten feet distant but they were winter-dying back to their roots and bent in dry hoops to their images, until the edges of the lake seemed looped with them. Ahead, perhaps some half-mile distant, hanging as though suspended above the surface, were trees, land; an island? The farther shore? There was no way of telling.

Conn chucked a stone into the water, as far out as it would go. There was a dull cloop! as though a lazy fish rose for sport instead of food, and a ripple or two ran in faint-hearted circles but disappeared before they reached the shore, as if the water were thick as oil.

'Hmmm . . .' he said. 'A dead lake. Not very inspiring.'

'Dead?' said Pisky's inquiring bubbles. 'Lemme see, lemme see . . .'

I tilted his bowl nearer the water. 'There . . .'

He said something surprising. 'I want to try the water!' He had never said anything like this before, had never ventured willingly outside his bowl except at The Ancient's, and for a moment I hesitated, almost as though I was afraid that once in he would be lost.

'Don't be silly, Thing dear,' he said, reading my thoughts. 'I only want a quick look. Besides, my scales itch. My great-aunt on my mother's side always said that if one's scales felt itchy it was either a change in the weather or mites.'

'Mites?'

'Tickly things that bite like the fleas you humans and animals have. Now, lemme *see*!'

Obediently I lowered his bowl to the still lake and tipped it until he had ingress and egress. He hesitated for a moment and I saw a convulsive shudder run through his little frame, then slowly he moved from the shelter of his weed and I saw what I had feared, a golden-orange shape dim and falter as he moved out into the deeper water. Almost, stretching out my hand, I betrayed his trust, distressfully trying to catch him back before I lost sight, but Snowy nudged me with his nose in time.

'He knows what he does, Thing dear: have faith! And patience . . .'

It nevertheless seemed an age before the orange blur moved back to his bowl again, very thoughtfully. 'I don't know, I just don't know . . . Never seen or felt water like that before. Soft, soft as the robes of a courtesan, the robes they used to trail in the Great Pond at Chaykung . . . Misty on top, but there are clear pools. Bottom's thick mud and tangled roots. Difficult to swim in; slows you down, it does, but it's breathable, just. Nothing living that I can see, but I *feel* that there is some*thing*, or someone, down there . . . Curious. Whatever it is is not unwelcoming, there's just a kind of . . . nothingness. No feeling, nothing positive. Doesn't operate on any level that I recognize.

'Wouldn't do to fall in the deeper bits, Thingy . . .'

'As if I would!'

'There's a sort of boat here,' called Conn and, sure enough, there was a broad-bottomed craft lying hidden under the bank some hundred yards further up. It was built of some tough, greyish wood and looked very old, but when I tried it with my dagger it seemed sound enough. The flat planking inside was almost covered by a drifting of last year's leaves. A long paddle lay amidships, obviously for steering and propelling the boat through a ring in the stern.

'Some sort of ferryboat?' I ventured. 'Is it safe?'

'Seems so,' said Conn, jumping down into the bows. He stamped around for a minute or two, but apart from the quiet ripples that spread in the water there was no other disturbance, hardly even a lowering of the boat's level from his weight. Jumping back on the bank he leant forward and pulled in the broad stern. 'Well, the only way is across, and it seems there's land of sorts over there . . . Shall we risk it?'

'As you say, it's the only way,' said Snowy. 'However, I don't like the feel of this place and I shall be glad when we're across.' He stepped delicately onto the boards and lay down, his hooves tucked close. Somewhere a bird cried mournfully, but there was no other sound save the sluggish lap of water. I went up to the bows carrying Pisky, and the others settled themselves beside Snowy. Conn pushed the boat away from the bank and leapt in after, stepping the steering-paddle.

It was an eerie passage, no sound save the creak and swish of the paddle, Conn's heavy breathing and the 'sss' of the water past our bows. No one felt like talking: it was almost as though we held our breath for fear of waking something. I looked back at the bank we had left but already it was disappearing in mist. The land ahead looked no nearer, although the trees we could see held a dark and menacing aspect.

We were perhaps some three-quarters of the way across when, glancing down, I became aware of a difference in the quality of the water. Where before it had had a thickness, an opacity that made it look like liquid iron, now this seemed to be drifting away, like heavy clouds clearing a rainwashed sky. If it had been real sky then all one would have seen would be an infinite blue, but in the depths there seemed to be tantalizing glimpses of another world, a world in which there were trees, fields, mountains and valleys, an image so immediate and real that I glanced up, expecting to see it was merely a reflection. But no: the mist seemed thicker and, more disturbing, my companions appeared somehow different too; discontented, distorted, disturbingly alien, like the time when I had laughingly viewed them through a piece of broken green Roman glass on our journey. Suddenly they all seemed strangers and I turned from them in discomfort to look again at my prettier pictures in the water.

They had changed also. Where there had been vague landscapes, viewed from a distance, now I could see flowers in the fields, birds in the trees. I leant closer and someone spoke behind me; irritated, I turned back and saw Conn mouthing at me, but he was speaking as though he had a mouthful of rags, and his face and figure were as grey as the mist. Impatiently I turned back. There were other words, other voices still squeaking in my ears but I covered them and leant closer to the water, the better to appreciate the bright colours, the beautiful pictures that were such a contrast to the grim, grey reality above.

Now there were animals and people down there, too. Horses ran through the meadow, manes and tails flowing in the breeze; fair knights armed and helmed were practising swordplay; hounds were on the scent, their bright tongues lolling; birds, fishes, deer, all living in colours livelier than the day. It was like some great new-woven tapestry, but a tapestry that moved and lived and breathed. And there, right in the middle of it all, was a lady, a beautiful dark-haired lady who stretched her arms out to me and smiled a smile that I remembered from times past. Surely my mother must have had a smile like that? I cried out to the pretty lady and she leant up to take my hand and I clasped hers in both of mine and was drawn down, down into the overwhelming brightness beneath.

The waters sang in my ears and I was warm as an infant enshawled. The lady, so like my mother must have been, drew me into her arms and rocked me back and forth and the knights smiled and nodded and clashed their weapons, the horses threw back their heads and neighed and the hounds bayed a welcome, their tails waving like weeds in a stream—

'Weeds in a stream! Weeds in a stream!' came a little voice in my ears, as insistent and annoying as the zinging of a gnat. 'Rocks in a pool! Bones in a bog! Illusion, illusion and death! Come away, Thing dear, dearest dear, before you drown in a dream, before your lungs burst and the Creature nibbles your flesh from your bones in a kiss of death and arranges you in her gallery like the others . . . Look! Look, and *see* . . .'

And I looked, and I saw. As Pisky swam to and fro in front of my eyes I had to shift my focus and the lady's green gaze no longer held mine. Her arms were about me still, caressing and stroking and soothing and I was aware of her smiling, scarlet mouth and the questing teeth—

The knights were bones, the horses were bones, the hounds were bones. Their hair, their manes, their tails waved in the gentle current and they were prisoned by their feet, their hooves, their legs to the floor of the lake to dance and prance and bounce to the Creature's whim. And were long dead and Its playthings, as were the rocks and stones and weeds that made Its landscapes. I saw, too, that It had no heart, no evil intent even, just an overweening curiosity. And that curiosity drew me closer, closer, and I saw that It had drawn from me my own thoughts to create the illusions I had seen, and that It had no real form of Its own, just the locking arms and the open mouth and the teeth, that sought me and my blood and my breath and my being.

All at once I could not breathe and a little orange-gold fish with a pearl in his mouth swam between the teeth that threatened me and down the throat that waited and the Creature choked and gasped and convulsed and spat and loosed Its hold and I shot to the surface and was grabbed and hauled into the boat and all I could think about was a little fish and the sight of him disappearing down that gaping throat—

'Thing, darling, are you all right? Christ Almighty, she's near drowned!' came Conn's distracted, loving voice and even with my tortured lungs and rasping throat I recognized that he had used my right name for a third time while I lay on the bottom boards of the boat, heedless, soaking, abandoned to decency and decorum, and spewed up the foul, cloudy water, murmuring between the violent retchings that Pisky had saved me.

'No thanks to your abominable gullibility!' came a little bubbling voice in my ear, and there was my rescuer, leaping back into his bowl no worse for wear. 'How anyone in their right mind could mistake an apparition like that for the real thing I do not know! My grandmother's cousin, twice removed, was once suborned by one such but her disgrace was never mentioned. By my fins and scales—'

'Pisky you're a darlin' and a hero, and if you weren't in that bowl I'd pick you up and kiss you, that I would!' declared

Conn, and leaving the paddle he stepped forward to cradle my helpless, revolting body in his arms. 'I shall never be able to thank you . . . But unless we get this child to dry land and the water pumped out of her—'

With a sudden jolt—just as I was warming to his utterly unexpected embrace and revelling in both my escape and the sweetness of breath in my lungs and wondering at the supreme courage of Pisky's rescue—the boat grounded on dry land and promptly broke up in pieces. I was shoved and trampled on as the others struggled with me and the baggage over rocks and boulders. Once there I was subjected to further indignity as Conn rolled me over on to my face and proceeded to press the air out of my lungs with the flat of his hand. I consequently threw up the contents of my stomach onto the ground, near choking with vomit and froth, my mask tangled in my mouth.

Just before I died from his ministrations Snowy luckily told him to stop and I was hauled round to sit upright, still gasping for air and shivering uncontrollably.

'Stay with her,' ordered Conn to Moglet, Corby, Puddy and Pisky. 'The unicorn and I will search for wood to make a fire before she perishes from cold.'

'Wanna-come-with-you!' demanded Pisky, and, such was the aura of his recent success, Conn picked him up without demur and carried him off.

I staggered to my feet. I wanted to ask questions about the Creature in the water, about the bones and the hair and the pictures—but at that moment I looked up and saw the shadow of the seven stones and my adventure began . . .

THE BINDING: THING

The Last Giants and Ogres

EXCEPT FOR the seat of my breeches which was still damp against the stone floor, at least now I was dry and warm for the fire was very hot. Not that I was exactly next to it: I lay bound and trussed like a recalcitrant chicken against the woven fence that formed the outer wall of the cave-house. The wind whistled past my ears and outside I could hear the gale that roared and tore at the last remains of the trees in the forest. It was night, for we—me, Moglet and Corby—had been carried here for many miles along twisting, curling paths after our capture.

Prisoners. I had never been physically tied up before and I didn't like it, not one bit. I closed my eyes, looked back on what had happened, wondered if it could have been different.

Conn, Snowy and Pisky had gone to find wood to build a fire and dry me out—so it had been my fault from the beginning. I had started to ask Moglet, Corby and Puddy a question—what question? It had all gone now, was not important any longer—and then had come that sudden crash, a cry from Conn, an unintelligible whinny from Snowy and the awful, hair-raising howl—

I had run, we had run, away from the lakeside, stumbling and cursing over the twisted tree-roots, tearing our way through the shoulder-high ferns, pushing through thicket and briar, and all the while the wild threshing and howling grew louder until—until we came to the clearing, the net and the pit.

At first I thought I had been carried away by the Night-Mare, and fought against the reality I saw, even shutting my eyes tight and throwing my arms wide in an effort to transport myself to another dream or even, please the gods! to awake sweating on some pallet, somewhere else . . .

But no; it was real, and it was horrible.

In front of me, almost at my feet, opened a pit, dark and deep, and the broken branches that had hidden it tipped, crazy and broken, laced with man-high ferns, to the bottom some ten or twelve feet below, where Conn and Snowy were milling about, pulling at the branches which slid down on top of them. Conn's anxious eyes lifted to mine, then I saw him glance over his shoulder towards the other side of the pit. I followed his gaze and recoiled in horror. There, illuminated by branch torches, sputtering with some oily foulness, stood half-a-dozen giants! Ogres. Trolls . . . ten feet high, more perhaps, covered with shaggy hair, their clothing a few skins. Bare-footed, tangle-locked, with long yellow teeth, flat noses and great craggy brows overhanging small, dark, red-rimmed eyes. Legs bowed with the weight of their bodies, hands with hairy backs grasping clubs, a spear, a—

'Thing, look *out*!' yelled Conn, but even as I turned I was meshed in a creeper net, borne down by heavy bodies, smothered in the sharp tang of earth and leaves. I could not breathe, Moglet was nowhere, Puddy was missing, Corby was flapping on his back at my side; we were all panicking, panicking, and we shouldn't panic, we should—

I felt a thump on the side of my head, there were bright lights . . . then darkness.

I awoke to the realization that we were being carried in a kind of sling between two poles. My lungs were not fully recovered from the water, my head hurt, but even greater was the pain from creeper-fastened wrists and ankles. Worst of all was the terror of not knowing how or where, the disappearance of my friends, the awe-inspiring figures of my captors—Not knowing, not understanding what one is facing is far more terrible than facing the most tremendous calculable odds; the Tree-People had been worse than the Great Spider or the White Wyrme.

'Heart up, Thing!' came a hoarse croak above my head. 'At least you're right-way up!' I glanced through tears at the ragged bundle trussed to the pole above me. Corby, poor dear

Corby, was hanging by his bound legs, wing flapping, beak agape, eyes rolling. 'Not as bad as it looks,' he thought quietly at me. 'Least I've got a better view . . .'

'Where are Puddy and Moglet?' I thought back urgently at him.

'Former jumped out of your pocket way back; latter is tied in a bundle at your feet.'

'Thing! Corby! I can't see, I'm frightened—'

'Hush dear!' I tried to quiet her audible wails. 'It'll be all right, I promise. Just lie still.'

There were only three of us left. Somehow we had to escape, find out what had happened to the others. But supposing there were no others? Supposing the frightful creatures that captured us had killed them? Supposing, even now, that my beloved Conn was lying somewhere with his head smashed in by one of those vicious clubs, the bright blood shaming his russet hair, his fierce brown eyes staring up at a darkening sky he could not see? And dear, gentle Snowy? And silly, voluble last-minute courageous Pisky, and stolid, dependable Puddy? Had the one been gobbled in one bite, the other crushed in careless passing beneath some primeval foot? I sobbed again, but not for myself.

I suppose it must have been some half-hour later, and quite dark, when we arrived at the cave. We were untied from the carrying poles and carried roughly over stones, past a wicker fence, into the prison in which we now found ourselves. I had looked round it so many times during the last minutes— hours?—that I knew it by heart.

High-ceilinged with, as I have said, a wicker or wattle fence behind my back protecting about one half of the perimeter. The other half was the stone face of the cave, which extended back into the hillside about thirty feet, in a roughly semi-circular shape. At the far end, in the shadows, was a deep ledge, about twelve feet wide and the same deep, and about two feet off the floor, on which was a pile of skins and three toothless and white-haired creatures with hanging dugs (though men or women I could not tell), who mumbled and waved and shrieked with laughter as the fire was replenished.

This same fire was built high in the middle of the cave, fed by large pieces of green wood which snapped and spat and twisted in sappy fury, belching great clouds of choking smoke up to the blackened roof. Every now and again a lurid flame leapt like a new-drawn sword to be as quickly spitting-sheathed in the scabbard of the dark logs, bejewelled by oozing black resin, before it had time to do more than stab twice, thrice at the darkness.

The torches had been extinguished as soon as we arrived, to conserve them I supposed, and were now stacked upright against the left-hand wall, together with clubs, spears and queerly shaped stone axes, wood-hafted and bound with twine. On the right-hand wall were hung more skins over a stack of roughly chopped wood. Behind this were heaped crudely fashioned pottery bowls and platters, and then a pen containing five or six skinny goats. These were nannies, all of them, who looked as if they had not seen a billy for years. There were no younglings. The floor of the cave was stony, dung-ridden, running with filth; no attempt had been made to sweep away the ordure, both human and animal, and the stench fought an even battle with the smoke.

And the giants, the ogres, the trolls, whatever they were? The flames threw their shadows flickering on the cave wall. They were the creatures of legend: threatening, huge, terrible—until one looked at the substance rather than the shadow. Six of them, that was all, not counting those elders on the ledge at the back. About four feet tall, perhaps a little more; covered with reddish hair and bandy-legged, with low foreheads, jutting chins and wide noses. The youngest I suppose was about fourteen, a boy; two women in their twenties; three men, ranging from early twenties to late thirties: and all of them weak, rickety, with missing teeth, sores on their bodies, arthritic joints. No children, either; where were their youngsters, their promise of a future?

The wood caught suddenly and flared its banners to the roof, and there, silent, vibrant, moving with the firelight, a whole host of creatures was revealed, chased by hunters wielding spears and clubs. A giant striped cat bared its fangs, incisors reaching beneath the chin; deer with mighty horns raced across the plains, hooves flying; a creature such as Conn had talked of, tail both ends, all coated in reddish hair like a shaggy goat, impaled a man with its yellow tusks as the spears

286

in its hide maddened it past bearing. The man's mouth was open forever on a silent scream. Other men, defiant, puny, armed only with spears, managed to herd, pit, snare all these creatures in a magnificent display of primeval bravery and guile. Great fish opened their toothed mouths to engulf; huge lizards flicked their tongues; birds with strange, barbed wings, or ones hooked and spread like bats, flew shrieking from a rain of arrows, and still the hunters advanced, striking, stabbing, flaying, destroying—

They were sketches only, in browns, whites, blacks, greys, ochres, but the sudden firelight made them live and die in glorious movement on the walls of the cave. In a sudden pitying moment, quite divorced from my immediate terror, I could see how these few stunted survivors would spend their last years; drawing their pride, their comfort from the splendid, fierce deeds of their forefathers, those who dead a thousand years had yet ensured their present existence on earth.

My imagination when we were trapped in the pit had given our captors twice their height, three times their ferocity but they still outnumbered us, small, weak and diseased as they were; in this and in one other fact, lay their squalid strength. They had an overwhelming need that our combined strength could not overcome. They were hungry.

Not only hungry: starving.

I knew this because of their staring bones pushing at the skin as if mad to break out; I knew this because of the thin streams of saliva that ran between their bared and gappy teeth; I knew this because the fire had been built higher, higher; I knew this because of the water now boiling in the misshapen pot at the side of the fire. I knew it because I could see the skewers ready to be thrust into the heart of the flames; I knew it because of the animals they had prepared to thrust on those same bone skewers. I knew it because the first of those creatures was my darling Moglet, trussed up in a bundle on the end of a stick, paws together, jaws bared in agony, her pitiful wails half-drowned by the roaring of the flames. I knew it because my friend Corby was hanging by his legs, the next to go, his beak half-open, his eyes closed. I knew it because they had poked and pinched me, licked the salt from my face and hands with

287

eager tongues, made to tear out my hair, pinched my legs until the blood ran . . .

Tears ran helplessly from my eyes and I could see nothing now between the swollen lids except a merciful blur. Then, oh then! something moved under my bound hands, something dry, warty, breathing fast.

'Puddy? Oh, Puddy!!'

'Courage,' said the toad, puffing asthmatically. 'I come from the others—'

'They are all right? Oh, dear one, say they are all right!'

'Yes, yes. They *will* be all right, given time . . .'

'Given time . . .?'

'To get out of that pit.'

'But how—?'

'It is not that deep. When I left them they were pulling down branches to raise the level. Then Sir Knight will climb out over the unicorn's back and throw down more foliage until *he* is able to scramble out. My feet . . . The webs are all stretchy.'

I was filled with instant contrition. 'Poor Puddy! Is it very far, then?'

He moved under my hands. 'The way your captors took 'tis two, three miles, but straight up—toads can climb, you know—it's much less. But Snowy will find a way.' His flanks were still heaving. 'Let me see what's happening . . .' He moved out to get a better view. 'Ye gods! 'Tis as well the fish is with the others, else would he boil!'

Someone picked up the stick on which Moglet's trussed figure swung and pointed it towards the crackling fire. I heard her anguished cry, saw the fire turn to lick at the fur, and then something suddenly clicked in my mind, like fivestones on a stone floor. I found myself remembering.

'Fire cold, flames die, heat go, no warmth . . .' but not in those words, in another language, an older one full of spits and clicks and grunts and as old as the earth. Words I had learnt long ago in another life, in another time than the feared one with our Mistress. Words older even than the creatures painted on the walls; words, not words, sounds only that came with the dawning of time when earth and air and fire and water were still one and four, and apart and together, divisible and indivisible, and Man crouched among the animals and was part of them and Woman was the God . . .

The fire burned blue and cold and died. The painted creatures on the walls faded and disappeared, and an ice crept into the cave. The giants, the ogres, the trolls became small and helpless and frightened and I stepped from my bonds and went to the middle of the cave and gathered the cat to me smoothing the charred fur until it was new, and took the plucked bird from his ties and the feathers grew again under my hand. And I stood in the ashes of the fire and the strength flowed up through the soles of my feet, until my fingertips tingled with the strength of it and I stood straight and tall and unblemished and nursed the creatures in my arms until they, too, were whole—

'Thing, darlin', oh, Thing! Are you all right, then?' And Conn was there, taking me and Moglet and Corby in his arms, while the creatures cowered in the farthest corner of the cave. Suddenly I was myself and glad of his human comfort, and fell in love again with the strength of his arms.

Snowy was holding the troll-men back, dancing on his hooves and neighing, striking out at their slowly recovering bodies.

'Come, my children, come: magic lasts only so long!'

Magic, I wondered, magic? For what I had been, what I had done, seemed of a sudden in another life, far away, and now there was only bewilderment as I glanced down at my chafed wrists. In my arms was a purring Moglet—the purr of relief rather than content—and a once-more sleek Corby. Puddy nudged my toe and Pisky was bubbling away in his bowl dangling from Conn's wrist, telling of dark pits and torches and spears, of great scrambles of wood and a swinging forest, of travel sickness and a lack of water. I looked up at Conn's smiling eyes, his shining white teeth and curling moustache, his sweat-dampened hair and thanked the gods, and his God too, for our preservation.

'Come!' called Snowy again. 'I cannot hold them back any longer!' and indeed the troll-men from the corner were stealing forth again. The youngest seized a spear and hurled it in our direction, but luckily it missed. Conn tucked Moglet inside my jacket and Puddy in my pocket, picked up Corby and resettled

Pisky, then grabbed my wrist and hurried us out of the cave, stumbling and swearing under his breath.

'Which way?'

'Follow your noses and then bear right . . .'

I heard scuffles behind me, howls of rage as Snowy carried on a rearguard action, then we were plunging helter-skelter through bush, thicket and wood, branches whipping our faces and shoulders, stones slipping under our feet and briars and nettles tearing and stinging. Pursuit was not far behind and the thump of feet mixed with the beating of my heart. We had been running downhill but at last the ground levelled out and we were splashing amongst reeds, mud sucking at our feet. Now Snowy went ahead for we were in a quaking bog and heatless fires started at our steps, evil little voices sang in our ears and would have led us astray. All the while the stink of bubbling decay was in our nostrils, but Conn followed the white glimmer that was our unicorn and dragged me in his wake.

I stumbled and swayed from sheer exhaustion and did not even heed Moglet's panicky claws on my chest. At last the ground was firmer beneath our feet and the air smelt sweet and clean once more. We were on rising ground and the wind swung behind us, but it was chill, so that for all my exertions I shivered.

'Are we safe?'

'The men from the cave would not dare the bog,' came Snowy's comforting voice. 'Yes, we are nearly there. Just up this slope and you will see . . .'

I was not sure I could make it. My legs no longer seemed part of me, my feet were numb, my arms locked rigid around a protesting Moglet. There seemed to be a ring of stones—had I seen them before?—then some sort of prickly barrier, a hedge, I could hear a buzzard calling—

And firelight, gentle and warm, a familiar voice, hands taking Puddy and Moglet, a drink of fire and ice, a bed—

THE BINDING: MAGICIAN

Past, Present, Future

I OPENED my eyes to sun shining through the narrow opening to the cave. I was warm, I was refreshed with sleep, I was hungry. The cave! Which ca—

'Easy now, lambkin,' said The Ancient, and pressed me back gently against the pillows. 'Time enough to talk, to question. Here's oatmeal and cream and cheese. Break your fast at your ease. The others are taking the air.'

'But—'

'Food first, buts later. Sufficient that you are safe, well, and finished with journeyings for the time being. Now, eat: there's a pitcher of spring water by your elbow, and if you want to wash there's a bowl of warm water by the fire and privacy and cloths behind that curtain. Oh, and the usual offices are where they were before . . .'

A wren was bursting his heart with sweet song when I at last hurried out to join the others. Conn was lying back in the sunshine, his jerkin unlaced and the dark red hairs on his chest glinting in the light; Corby was preening, Moglet chasing after a scarlet leaf on its breeze-helped progress across the grass, not really interested, but it was something to do; Puddy had his eyes shut, a revolting remnant of legs and wings sticking out of the left side of his mouth; Pisky's bowl was in the little pool nearby and he was housekeeping his weed and the snails, and making little flicking jumps in the air to rid himself of even the suspicion of parasites; Snowy, ungainly for once, pink belly in the air, tail and mane a'tangle, was rolling in the lush grass under the apple trees, where there was the usual bewildering mixture of blossom and ripe apple. I looked for The Ancient:

he was walking some distance away on a rise in the ground.

'Better now, Thingummyjig?' asked Conn, stretching lazily.

'Come and play,' said Moglet.

'Could you just pull my third tail-feather straight?' asked Corby. 'No, from the left . . . *Your* left—'

'Nice morning,' said Puddy, stickily.

'Just look how clear the water is,' said Pisky. 'I doubt if my grandfather, or even his, ever bathed in such as this. And some nice new pebbles, too . . .'

No answers here and it was answers I wanted, so after politely attending to the others I walked up to the hillock where The Ancient was standing, apparently lost in thought. He had one of his more absurd hats on this morning, green, with a white bobble that kept falling in his eyes, and yellow ribbons hanging from the back.

He greeted me effusively, perhaps too effusively, spreading an imaginary cloak on the ground and inviting me to sit down. 'A beautiful morning, is it not? You rested well, I hope?' Receiving no answer, he plucked at his beard, neatly plaited and tied off in a knot. 'You are well, I suppose? No ill effects?' He looked at me again, then shuffled in his purple slippers, the ones with pointy toes. 'No harm done, no harm done—and you completed the quest. Admirably, I might say—Go away!' he shouted, flapping his arms at a large buzzard importuning the air a few feet above his head. 'Come back later . . . Pestiferous nuisance. Now, where were we?'

I shaded my eyes and looked up at the bird. 'Perhaps you should give him his reward now,' I suggested. 'After all, he worked for it.'

'Worked for it?' spluttered The Ancient, then turned the splutter into a fit of coughing.

'Well, he kept an eye on us all the way,' I said, and plucking a stem of grass, pulled at the delicate inner core and nibbled it gently. 'Go on: I can wait.'

The Ancient flustered and puffed, but eventually called down the bird who alighted on his outstretched arm, wings a'tilt and yellow eyes wary at me.

Without concern I rose to my feet and stretched out my hand to the restless pinions and the surprisingly soft and warm breast-feathers. 'Well done, Kiya.' (I knew instinctively

292

the bird's name.) 'I'll vouch that you were there, all the time . . . What has he,' and I nodded at The Ancient, 'promised you?'

'Leave off!' said the old man, his beard coming untied as if it had a life of its own and curling up on either side of his face like lamb's fleece. '*I'll* deal with this . . . Now then bird, what was to be your reward?'

'You know well,' said the handsome buzzard, fluffing his feathers, and I was surprised I could understand. 'For a watching brief—a week only you said, and nothing of the distances, the time-shift, the abominable weather—you said you would find me—'

'Ah, yes,' said The Ancient hastily. 'Now I remember . . . Well, then: fly some seven leagues west-by-south—you'll have to correct with this wind—turn due south by the cross at Isca—now the new-fangled Escancastre, I believe—then another two leagues. Bear west again till you come to the old highway bearing roughly north-south. Two miles further on there is a sudden switch to east-west and there you will find a southerly track. Half a mile on there is a barton in a valley, a stream running east-west on its southern border: can't miss it, the place is full of sheep. In a wood just northeast of the barton—Totley, it's called—you will find a deeper wood, triangular in shape, and there you will find—what I promised you. She has,' and he glanced at me to see if I was listening and, as I was, lowered his voice. I did not realize till afterwards that he was speaking bird-talk, but it didn't seem to make much difference: I still understood. 'She has,' he repeated to the bird, 'been blown from oversea by that last southeasterly and is not used to us as yet. Wants to return to the mountains of Hispania . . . But doubtless you will be able to persuade her to stay. Tell her . . .' and he bent forward to whisper in Kiya's hidden ear. 'That should do it!' And he tossed the buzzard in the air and it rode the wind, balancing delicately from wingtip to wingtip, before taking an updraught and sliding away out of sight above the conifers to my right.

'Now then,' said The Ancient, flicking a lump of bird-dropping from his already liberally marked blue gown. 'Now then—where were we? Ah, yes. You were about to thank me for my hospitality and ask about the next stage in—'

'Sit down,' I interrupted, reseating myself and patting the turf beside me. 'And explain. Please?'

But he remained standing, drawing the edges of his cloak together and becoming very tall all of a sudden.

'And don't,' I said, 'fly off into another dimension or something: we've had enough of that for the time being . . . Just think of me as your equal, for the moment, and, as such, wanting answers.'

'To what?' But he did sit down, rather heavily it's true, and at a discreet distance. 'What to?'

I crossed my legs, comfortably, and selected another blade of grass. 'Lots of things . . . Firstly, how long has this quest taken us? The truth, mind!'

He regarded me under bushy eyebrows like the thatch of an ill-kept house. 'Why—how long do you think it took?'

I recognized the ploy, but went along with it for the time being. 'Well, the others obviously think it took at least six months—'

'So?'

'So why is my hair no longer? So why are my clothes no tattier? So why did we conveniently lose all those things on the way, like the sealskin, that could have proved we actually went anywhere? So why did Kiya still have the feathers of a yearling? So—'

'All right, all right, all *right*!' yelled The Ancient. 'All right . . . I can see you have been talking to that blasted unicorn—'

'Not a word! So, you do admit—'

'I admit nothing! So there . . .' and he grabbed a stalk of grass, just like me, and stuck it in the corner of his mouth. 'Just prove it, that's all! Prove it!'

'So there is something to prove, then?'

'I didn't say so—'

'You did!'

'Didn't!'

'Did!'

'Not!'

I lay back and laughed. 'For an Ancient you are behaving more like a New—no, listen!' For he had half-risen and his face was all red. 'I didn't mean to be rude, you know I didn't. But isn't it time we stopped being childish and started talking like—like adults?' Like human beings, I had been going to say, but I wasn't sure of his claim to this. I rolled over on to my stomach. 'I admit I am being presumptuous, but there are certain questions I should like—more, I think I deserve—answers to. Straightforward answers. Agreed?'

'Agreed,' came the rather sulky answer, but a sharp glance from under the bushy eyebrows accompanied it. 'Shake on it?'

'Good!' I offered my hand, all unsuspecting. A moment later an almighty shock ran through my fingers and palm and up my arm into my shoulder and I was knocked sideways by a sudden strike of power that left me numb. I had not anticipated he would use anything like that: so far it had been a low-dice board game but now he had thrown a double and I was no match for this.

'Thanks,' I said, rubbing my still-tingling arm. 'All right, you're the boss. My strengths have been accidental, yours are calculated. Truce?'

For the first time he smiled, and nodded his head. 'You are an endearing child, Flower . . . I must admit you have called upon powers that I would have thought impossible. Still, a flower may hold a thorn . . .' and he chuckled, shaking his head, and somewhere bells rang.

'You,' I said, 'have had ever so much more practice . . . Perhaps, then, because of what I did accidentally, you will accept that I have a right to some truthful answers? No more evasions? No more—' I rubbed my arm '—games?'

He nodded and his beard replaited itself, even to the knot. 'No more games.'

I studied him; at last we were on equal terms, but only perhaps because he had won earlier. 'Right. Last things first: in that cave . . . The Power. Where did it come from? How did I manage to use it? And was it bad or good?'

'Backwards answer: neither good nor evil. Just there.'

'Explain!'

He considered for a moment, chin in hands. 'Under and over and about and through this old world of ours there flow sources of Power, as aimless as streams and rivers. As I said, they are neither good nor bad, they are just *there*. Clever magicians and wise men and shamans know where and when and sometimes how, but how *you* knew how to use it, I just don't know.'

'But the gods—God—whatever; are they, It, good or bad, or just people like ourselves? Or forces and powers in their own right? And how many are there of them?' I was bewildered.

'I think—but I do not know, child, I do not know—that there must be a Supreme Being, above all others, who wishes for us, for the world as we know it, our good. There are also Forces, name them I cannot, who wish to take all Power for themselves: riches, domination, everlasting life. And they have forgotten the welfare of ordinary people. Just see you use whatever powers you find in the proper way. There is good, there is bad: make sure you choose aright!'

I wanted to ask whether it would make the slightest difference what I did, but then, stealing into my heart as soft as a mouse at dusk, came the answer; a tentative sureness that quietened my fears and gave me breath where before there had been none. It was a sureness outside of myself, borne on the gentle touch of breeze on my cheek, the feel of the crisscross of grass under my hand, the sad smell of autumn, the sweet call of the wren, the taste of doubt in my mouth—

'I will try,' I said simply. It did not matter whether one used the prayer of the peasant or of the enlightened, the supplications of the Christian or the infidel, like smoke they would find their outlet, their goal. The only thing one had to remember was that one's reach had to be towards this goal, this good, and that prayer was the way—not for oneself, for all.

I smiled at The Ancient. 'Thank you. I feel much better.' I noticed him shuffle himself together, as if he had just got out of a tight corner and was now about to obliterate himself from further questions. 'But there are other things . . .'

He glowered at me. 'What things?'

'Time,' I said. 'Time . . . What is time?'

'Time? Time . . . is something man invented to table the night and the day. To explain the good times and the bad. To excuse the wrinkles in the skin. To count the falling of the leaves; to guard against the sudden sun—to know how long to boil an egg . . .'

'And our time?' I prompted. '*Our* time? The days, the

296

weeks, the months we spent on our quest? Why did it take six months by our calculations and nothing by yours?'

'How did—? No, you have answered that question. All right. Time was invented by man: you understand that?'

I nodded. 'Minutes, hours, days—yes. But not the concept in full.' I hesitated. 'We arrived with you in late winter, left on a summer's day when it seemed we had been with you but a week, and arrive back in late winter again apparently not one day older. Some of our travelling seemed to take weeks, some days. Some of the places we visited looked as if they existed now, others had a strangeness we could not account for—'

'You travelled,' said The Ancient, 'in time. As you know it.'

'Explain!'

'Think of a tapestry. It perhaps shows a court scene, a country scene, a hunt; someone has embroidered part of it only. At the sides are the silks that wait to be sewn, the future. Those already in the picture are the past. The threads now on the needle are the present. All there, all at the same time, yet not all in the picture. Not yet. But the picture can be added to at any time without changing the essentials. It will still be a court scene, a hunt . . . And even if the tapestry is complete, or one thinks it is, as the hangings shift and sway in a draught and a candle brightens one fold and then another, one can imagine it is only the lighted corner that is important.' He leant forward and cupped my masked face in his hands. 'So, you found yourselves first in one part of time and then another.' He wagged his beard. 'And don't ask how I got you there and back, because a magician never gives away all his secrets. Suffice it to say that I had the power—' He laughed, and released me. 'No, the knowledge to do it. And you didn't change anything: Time-Travellers are observers. Oh, you robbed the Tree-People of a meal, released some trapped animals, helped a traveller on his way, but you didn't change history; you can only do that in the now, when it is your hand guiding the needle.'

I rose to my feet. I did not fully comprehend, but the image of the tapestry stayed in my mind. So time was a vast picture, never finished, that one could stitch oneself into at any point . . .

'I don't *really* understand,' I said.

He laughed, and rose to his feet also. 'Sometimes I feel I don't either, if that's any consolation!'

Together we walked back down the little hill towards the others, but slowly.

'Snowy? He understands all this?'

'Better than you or I, for he is immortal.'

'Can the immortal never die?'

'No one can kill them, unless it is their choice to die.'

We walked on in silence for a moment.

'Was it necessary for us to go the long way round?' I asked.

'The long way?'

'Yes. Making us suffer all that long journey, making us believe it took so long . . .'

'Maybe it was not necessary. But think how much you all would have missed, how much all those adventures and travelling together taught you of each other and of yourselves!'

'We might have been killed, any or all of us—'

'Not while you five held the jewels and the dragon was still alive in the Now. You were indestructible.'

'And Snowy? And Conn?'

'As I said, unicorns are immortal, with or without their horns.'

'And Conn?'

'Ah, well . . .' For the first time he looked guilty. 'Well, I must admit that there I took a chance. But then . . .' He reached out and squeezed my hand, regaining his composure. 'But then : . .' He winked and tapped his nose, 'I knew you would look after him, you see . . .'

I frowned. 'As far as I can recall he took care of himself, and all of us too, in the end. And it was rather presumptuous of you to suppose that I—'

'Loved him?'

I went all hot under my mask. 'That has nothing—'

'Everything!'

'—to do with it! It was only in the beginning—'

'The Lady Adiora?'

'—that he faltered. In the end he was looking after everyone.'

'Exactly!'

'Exactly what?'

'Your tests came when you were ready for them, not before. The first was Snowy, as you call him, to point the way.'

'I notice I was last . . .'

'So? It was rather a grand finale, wasn't it?'

We stayed in that enchanted place for a week, allowing even for The Ancient's erratic sense of time, grew sleek and mended our gear and healed the last bruises the quest had engendered. And though it was winter away from this place, where we were the sun shone by day and the old man's owl too-whitted us to sleep at night, cosy in the cave. I was given a new comb by the magician and it did wonders for my tangles and for Snowy's mane and tail. I sharpened my little dagger on the honing-stone by the cave entrance till it was as sharp as a dragon's tooth. Conn looked over his spotty armour and pronounced it 'no worse'. Pisky's bowl was cleaned to his satisfaction, Corby's plumage once more lay straight, Puddy had a nice rest and declared his headaches much better, I played with Moglet with twine, leaf and nut till she grew tired, and The Ancient appeared in a different robe and headgear every day.

I didn't tell the others about the Time-Travel bit: it had confused me enough without my having to explain it to anyone else.

On the seventh day I found The Ancient on his hands and knees with a measuring stick at midday, frowning at the shadow it cast.

'One more day,' he said.

'And?'

'Then it's on your travels again. The dragon still waits, or had you forgotten?'

No, I had not forgotten. I had just hoped against hope that perhaps we would have had a little longer . . .

299

THE BINDING: ALL

Journey to the Black Mountains

IT WAS near the shortest day. Away from the shelter of The Ancient's hideaway we found how much the weather had changed in the world outside. In spite of our thickest clothes we shivered in the chill wind that whined down from the northeast and huddled closer as he led us across moorland, past the stone circle where I now recognized we had started and ended our quest, and northwards towards the sea. Across the tumbled grey water of the straits one could see the farther shore, massed and woody on its lower slopes and soaring upward to bare scree and the distance-shrouded mountains, their tops capped like the magician himself with fanciful shapes, in their case of snow. It was both an awesome and an awe-inspiring sight and I was not the only one who drew back and trembled, for Moglet cuddled closer in my arms, Corby blinked and Conn whistled.

'Not easy, not easy at all! How do we get across, Sir Magician?'

For answer The Ancient leant among the reeds that bordered the little estuary in which we found ourselves and pulled on a rope. Slowly, silently, a narrow boat, half a man wide but the length of three and more, nosed its way to the bank. It was painted black but on the bows, on either side, were depicted great slanted eyes in some luminous, silvery substance, watching us from the beaked prow of the boat with a calculating stare.

Silently we boarded, silently The Ancient leant back to fend us off, and silently but for the slap of waves at the bow, we headed for the farther shore. There were no oars, no rudder, no sails and yet none of us thought to question our effortless progress. The Ancient stood in the prow, hatless for once, the wind blowing his white locks into strange patterns behind. It seemed that with his right hand he guided the passage of the boat and with the left gathered the waters behind to aid its progress. But still no one said anything and we moved as if in a dream on those dark waters, a great stillness all around us.

I do not know whether it was minutes or hours we were upon that ghostly passage, but it was with a sense of thankful awakening that I felt the bows of the craft ground upon the farther shore and my feet once more trod upon dry land. If all this had been magic, then I felt more comfortable without. I glanced back at the boat as we crunched up the shingle and the luminescent eyes stared back at me.

We found ourselves in a barren land. The trees were in their winter sleep, only showing they still breathed by the melted circles of frost beneath their branches; they were heavy with years and twisted by wind, and the moss and lichen that licked their roots and slithered down their northern sides only survived by grudging assent. There were no animals, no birds except a couple of gulls who came screaming down to see whether we had any scraps, but we had nothing to spare from our packs, for The Ancient had warned us that our journey would take over a week with no unnecessary stops. He was to come with us, partways as he said, to set us on the right path, and for the next few days, always cold, always hungry, we followed his tall and tireless figure ever higher among the folds of high hill that confronted us.

It was hard going, and even more so because of the hurt our burdens of the dragon's stones gave us. The nearer we came to him, still a mythical idea to me, the more we were reminded of the jewels we had carried so long, though of late they had seemed lighter and easier to bear. Now we were assailed by pains as strong as those that had hindered us while we were still prisoners of our Witch-Mistress. Puddy complained day-long, night-long, of headaches and hid his eyes from the winter sun in my or Conn's pocket. Pisky was always hungry, in spite of the hibernation-cold and rushed around his bowl seemingly lightheaded and losing weight at an alarming rate. Corby dragged his injured wing, lost his cheery banter and grumbled all the time. Moglet could not even put her damaged paw to the ground and had to be carried inside my jacket. And me? The stomach-cramps became worse, I was more doubled-up than ever. Only Conn and Snowy—and, of course, The Ancient—seemed unaffected. Snowy had the restoration of his horn to think about and was impatient—as far as that most patient of creatures could be—of our necessarily slow progress; Conn was cheerful, for now it seemed he was nearing the end of his quest to mend his broken sword and go adventuring again. So, added to my burden of physical pain was an extra heartache. Seeing how optimistic Conn was becoming, I could not but realize that while his mended sword would mean escape for him once more to foreign lands, for me it would mean loss and an eternal worry as to his well-being; I cried a little, but under my mask, and any who saw reckoned it was the hurt of the stone I carried.

It grew colder, and the land became ever more barren save for the occasional green valley sheltering sheep and a few shepherds' houses, and they had little enough to spare for unexpected travellers. Our burdens became heavier even as our packs of food grew lighter, or so it seemed, and in the end Snowy, who alone seemed to thrive on the sparse herbage and icy streams, carried me as well as the remains of our food. The Ancient, too, another member of the Faery kingdom, or near-kin to it, seemed to stride faster, eat less and grow younger as the days passed and the hills grew taller.

We rested up at night, but although the days now gave but some seven hours of travelling light we made good progress. Ever nearer, glimpsed but fleetingly at first but now more menacing, loomed the cone-shaped Black Mountain. Tantalizingly far, ominously near, it was the first thing we looked for at dawning, the last thing at night. At first it had looked smooth, almost like a child's brick placed among the rougher stones of the other mountains, but as we drew nearer we could see the cliffs, gullies, crevasses that marred its surface. Corby swore that he, with his keen eyesight, could even see the cave, high up on the southern slopes, but I don't think any of us believed him. At last the mountain towered above all its fellows, dark, forbidding, looking virtually unclimbable, and that was the day that the magician led us through a high pass, chilly with the grey-sky threat of snow, into a bowl of green grass right by the mountain's root.

Here we were sheltered somewhat from the wind and here we found also a moderate-sized village, some twenty houses and huts, a meeting-house and even the ruin of a once-fortified manor. The priest that had occupied the little chapel—big enough to hold two dozen, no more—had died three years back and had not been replaced, but I noticed a ram's horn twisted with berries and fresh winter-ivy under the half-hidden shrine that held a rudely carved wooden figure that could have been either male or female, so religion of some sort still held their superstitions.

We were welcome in the village, albeit shyly, for travellers in this high valley were few and far between and we were more unusual than most; but over a supper of mutton broth, barley and rye-bread we learnt at first hand that our fabled dragon did indeed exist, and had last been seen in the valley some years back. He could be heard at certain times of the year when the wind was in the right direction, roaring in great desolation from his cave. No, no one had dared the mountain in pursuit but yes, they were sure he was still there, though it was six months back since last Michaelmas or Samain that any had heard him. Yes, once he had been a regular—and welcome—visitor, but since that last feasting some years ago—as far away in time as young Gruffydd here had years—he had not visited them. No, he never did them harm, but had entered pleasantly enough into the spirit of the jollifications they had held in his honour, and it was not many who could boast of a dragon on their doorstep. No, not large, but again not small. Yes, fire and smoke, but not too much damage. And were we really come to seek him out?

'So you see,' said The Ancient, when we were at last alone, with the doubtful luxury of a smoky fire that seemed afraid of standing tall and puffing its smoke through the opening of the meeting-house in which we had been lodged, instead creeping along the floor and curling up among the smelly sheepskins we were to use for our bedding, 'I wasn't telling stories. Your dragon is up there, on that mountain, waiting for the return of his jewels.'

'But no one's seen or heard of him for an awful long time,'

303

said Conn. 'And if, as they say, he's not been down here to feast for some seven years or more, how do we know he's still alive?'

'We don't,' said The Ancient, 'but I think he is. Your stones still hurt, my children, don't they? Well, if he were dead, they would fall away from your bodies like dust, but you have all complained of greater hurt as we approached this mountain, have you not? And I can feel—and I think your unicorn can, too—a sense of latent power, a drawing-forward towards some central point . . .'

'He is still there,' said Snowy. 'But only just. The fires burn low . . .'

'Then the sooner you climb that mountain the better!'

'That sounds,' I said, 'as if you are not coming too.'

'Right. I'm not. This is *your* quest. I am only your guide . . .'

We gazed at one another. Somehow this old man—older in years, but with the single-mindedness and determination of one much younger—had kept us all together without our giving much thought to what would happen next. We had all conveniently forgotten that he was only coming part of the way with us and now, faced with the reality of his departure, I think we all felt rather like that boat we had ridden in, rudderless, sailless, oarless, without the guiding force.

Conn cleared his throat. 'And just how—er, hmmm, sorry; how will we know the right route?'

'You have guides: Corby's eyes and Snowy's good sense. They will show the way.'

'And you? You will wait for us? Watch us go?' I thought perhaps he felt too tired to go further and didn't want to admit it.

But there was a flash of fire from those usually mild eyes. 'And why should I? Think you that you are the only creatures on earth who have a task to fulfil? That you are the Only Ones because you are the Unlikely Ones?' He frowned, those thick eyebrows coming down over the windows of his eyes like snow-laden eaves. 'You are not. But if you come through this—if, I say—I shall see you again. That is all!'

'But I thought—I thought it would be easy once we . . .' faltered poor Moglet.

His gaze softened. 'Easier than your spider, my kitten,

304

perhaps. But it will demand a great deal of physical effort. And you will be cold, very cold . . .'

'But it will be worth it, won't it?' she persisted. 'For then we shall all lose our burdens and be whole again and able to run down the mountain and play!'

He smiled. 'If that is what you choose . . .'

'Hang on,' said Corby. 'Of course that's what we choose. Isn't that what we came all this way for? To lose these wretched encumbrances!' And he flapped his burdened wing.

'Maybe that is what you wanted when you started. But perhaps you will not be of the same mind now—'

'Of course we are!' said Puddy. 'Anything to rest this weary head of mine . . .'

'And I want to eat again,' said Pisky. 'Properly. A feast. Talk right, instead of with a mouthful of pebble. If my parents could see me now they would think I was last year's laying instead of . . . whenever it was,' he finished lamely.

Conn glanced at us all. 'I think you have your answer, Magician. I for one came on this journey for one reason, and one reason only: to mend my father's sword so that once again I can hold up my head and fight with the best!'

'And the armour?' said The Ancient, slyly.

'Oh, that! Well—I can buy fresh armour easy enough,' but he scowled, obviously annoyed at being reminded of something he had patently forgotten.

'And before you ask it,' added Snowy softly, 'yes, I want my horn back, more than anything, and all that has happened will be worth just that. But I think, my friend, you were about to question our motives: and I confess mine are not as clear as I thought. I believed I had made up my mind—but I am not sure, not sure . . .'

I could not understand why The Ancient was sowing doubt in our minds, and making even the always-dependable Snowy have second thoughts!

'Look here!' I said, rising to my feet. 'No one has asked me! I am determined to see this thing through to the finish as I want more than anything, whatever the cost, to rid myself of this accursed burden and walk straight!'

'Well done, Thingy!' applauded Conn. 'We're all behind you—'

But The Ancient had caught at my words—and I suspect that he had chosen them for me even as I spoke. I sat down again sharply. 'Whatever the cost? Whatever-the-cost? *Whatever*?' His voice, heavy and pregnant with meaning, filled the sudden silence until there was no room for further thought. 'Think, oh think, my children of what I warned you, so long ago! You have forgotten, I believe, what I said . . .'

Yes, we had.

'I said then, and I repeat it most solemnly now: whatever we gain in this life must be paid for—'

'But we are about to give something back that we never asked for in the first place—'

He glared at me. 'Did I say different? So—you offer back your burdens, in return for what?'

'Freedom from pain,' I suggested. 'A straight back, mended wing, whole paw, open mouth, clear head—'

'And do you not think that these also must be paid for?' he thundered, rising to his feet and towering above us, his robe drawn close about him. For a breathless instant I caught a glimpse once more of a younger, sterner warrior, helmed and dour-faced. 'How can you have the presumption to imagine that life will then become a bed of mosses, free from trouble? The unicorn here has admitted that perhaps his motives have altered: can you be sure that you will not change also? All of you?'

'All right,' I said, and stood up again. 'Remind us. Tell us again of the cost we shall bear, that once before we said we could discount. Tell us what we have to lose, we who have nothing save pain and burden. What could possibly be worse than that?'

For a moment he glared at me, then slowly his hand came out to pat my head, very gently. 'Why, nothing but the loosing. That is it. The loosing not only of the burdens but also of the bonds . . . Come, sit down. And listen.'

He sat down by the fire and I followed suit, but immediately coughed at the crawling smoke. Almost abstractedly the old man waved his hand and the smoke gathered itself up from the floor, formed a wavery pillar and found the roof-exit.

'That's better . . . Listen well, my children, for I shall say this just once more.' He turned to me. 'You said just now "We

306

have nothing but burden and pain . . ." Now, is that entirely true?' I opened my mouth, but he waved me to silence. 'None of your silly remarks now about being alive, food in your belly, clothes . . . Think, child, think! Look about you . . .'

'What I think he means, dear one,' said Moglet, crawling onto my lap, 'is that we have each other. That we all belong together, after our quest more than ever. That we love each other. That we have been through so much, shared so much, that we are more like one than five.'

'O wise kitten,' said The Ancient softly.

'And not just five,' said Conn, smiling and leaning over to tickle Moglet's ears. 'For have we not, the unicorn and I, shared your travels?'

'I like that,' said Puddy ruminatively, a couple of sentences behind. 'The seven who are one . . . Yes.'

'Mmmm,' said Corby. 'Not bad; never thought of it that way meself. But now as you comes to mention it . . .'

'Comradeship,' said Pisky, bubbling happily, 'is one of the finest gifts one can ever expect, my great-great-grandmother used to say. When I was swimming around in shoals with my brothers and sisters and cousins and second cousins and half-brothers and half-sisters and—'

I dipped my little finger in his bowl. 'Yes, dear one, it is.' I was ashamed. When I had spoken so carelessly a few minutes ago, I had not really meant to sound callous and unthinking. I knew that I loved my companions and that they loved me, but I had been with the idea so long, took it so much for granted, that it was as much a part of me now as—as my mask. As night and day. As loving Conn, in a way that was not quite the same as loving the others . . .

'So you have all this,' said the old man, no doubt reading my mind, 'and you have your burdens. To you these burdens are your greatest handicap, the one thing you wish to be rid of— and once rid, you will be happy?'

'Of course!'

'And once Sir Knight has his sword and the unicorn his horn—then you will all be happy and all your problems will be solved?'

'Well, you know now that I shall be pitifully sorry to say goodbye to my friends, but I shall need to find my way to some indulgent duke or princeling who needs a mercenary—' Conn scowled suddenly. I reckoned he had remembered his armour again.

'And I can join my kindred again,' said Snowy. 'Or not . . . At least I shall have the choice . . .' There seemed to be more to this than I understood, but I could see The Ancient did.

'And we,' I nodded at my friends, 'must find somewhere to live, and the means of livelihood too . . .' I had not seriously considered this before. I supposed I could work at something to keep us all going, but what? Perhaps we could build a little cottage somewhere in the woods and grow our own produce and—and Moglet could catch mice and Puddy and Corby and Pisky would be all right, and I could gather mushrooms . . . No point in working it out in too much detail now. Getting rid of our burdens was the most important thing. It was! I could see the others were following my thought processes and agreeing, but—

The Ancient threw some powdery stuff on the fire and of a sudden it flared blue and a strange, sweet smell stole into—our noses, I was going to say, but it was more like our minds, and the perfume acted like a dousing of cold water, waking us up, sharpening what little wits we had, and I suddenly realized what he had been trying to say.

'The loosing? You are telling us that when—when we are whole again, we shall be so busy being ourselves again—real animals and people—that we shall not need each other anymore? That we shall be happy to split up, each to go his own way?' I knew we should lose Snowy and that I should never see my beloved Conn again, but the others? 'Rubbish! We shall always want to be together, shan't we?'

They all agreed. Of course . . .

'And the forgotten years?' came the creaky, inexorable voice. 'The years you have all forgotten? How long do you think you were with the witch? Now, you live in an enchantment of arrested and forgotten time: what happens when your memories return? And how old will you be? Were you with her five minutes, two days, six months, seven years? That time will have to be paid for, you know: soon, if all goes well, you will be as old as you really are. And those years will have gone and you will be left with what remains of your normal span—'

308

'Golden king-carp live for fifty years and more,' said Pisky bravely, but his voice was smaller than usual. 'My great-aunt on my father's side said her great-great-great-grandfather was over eighty . . .'

'Cats have nine lives—'

'Crows don't do so badly, neither!'

'And toads are noted for their longevity . . .'

'And I,' I said slowly, 'don't know how old I am, but I don't think it matters. And I don't think I have anything to go back to either. There *is* only forwards . . . Oh, why do you have to muddle us so!' I turned on The Ancient in a fury. 'I'd never have thought about all this, but for you!'

'But you had to! You must not believe that just because your burdens are removed all your problems will be solved! You must not think that life will then be yours to do with as you will! I have to warn you—and not only you five jewel-bearers, but the knight and the unicorn too! You think that all your dreams will come true, just as you have planned, *and it may not be so!*'

'I don't care!' I turned to the others. 'Just as we are so near our goal, just as we are about to realize our dearest wishes— don't listen to his gloomy forecasts! After all we have been through—' I turned back to our tormentor '—you don't think we will just give up, do you?'

'No. I did not expect it for one instant. I only wanted to remind you not to expect things to turn out exactly as you planned.' He smiled brilliantly, and his face was transformed. 'Thank the gods that you are all children of Earth! Yes, even you at times, my friend.' He nodded at Snowy. 'The world will never die when there are brave idiots such as you.' He smiled. 'Just remember that you always have a choice . . . And now, my children, my weary travellers, I will give you all one more thing to counter all that wearisome advice.' He waved his hands and the lights in the wayward fire turned rose and green and violet and gold and we fell asleep in a moment, just where we were, and slept dreamlessly and deep.

And, in the morning when we awoke, he was gone.

THE BINDING: ALL

The Black Mountain

THE FIRST part was relatively easy, and the weather was with us. The lower slopes of the so-called Black Mountain—nearer to it was more dark grey, but littered with shiny black rocks that seemed to absorb the light, making it all look darker from a distance—were made up of hummocky ground bisected by small, cold streams that were no barrier to hurrying feet. Now that we were on the last lap, everyone was eager to finish the marathon endeavour as soon as possible. On the second day, however, it began to rain, rain that penetrated our furs and feathers and skins, and by nightfall we were grateful for the shelter of a cluster of pines that clung grimly, roots deep in crevices, to the inhospitable rock. We lit a fire, inadequate barrier to the cold stone beneath and the colder sky. By morning it had begun to snow; fine, thin snow as small as salt with none of the largesse of the patterned crystals that had delighted my eyes as a child—as a child! A sudden memory of stars on my window ledge . . . Gone. But this snow was different. It was hard as hail and ran away beneath our feet, only to circle back behind and around our ankles and paw up the backs of our legs. Before us we could see it form trickles, streams, rivers, sheets, whirlpools in the towering obsidian rocks above, pouring and falling and tumbling down to meet us.

The going became increasingly treacherous, for though Snowy's unerring hooves found a track of sorts that led up towards the top, yet it twisted and turned—one moment edging a crevasse, another stealing behind a buttress and yet again scaling in steps straight up the mountain. Gone were the

310

sheltering trees. Only that morning we had seen our last, a twisted ash bent like an old woman, an incredible last bunch of skeleton keys clinging to the lowest branch, twig-fingers rattling them as if in an ague. Dark clouds raced overhead and no sun shone. Now there was only a lace-pattern of lichen, dank mosses, dead bracken, a few tufts of grass and once in this twilight world we saw five goats, their wild yellow eyes glaring, slanting in single file down the shoulder of the mountain towards the kinder shelter of the valleys beneath.

Only at night did the snow cease completely. Then the moon shone on a scene so desolate, so forlorn, that she would have been better to hide her face. We were halfway up the mountain by now but the climb, the lack of food and the thin air were all beginning to take their toll. That night we scarcely seemed to sleep at all in spite of our weariness, and used the last of our precious store of wood, our fire a brief and brave candle, and as near comfortless.

An inch of ice formed in Pisky's bowl, and in the morning Conn took his pack, unwrapped it and put on his rusty armour.

' 'Tis only a further burden for poor Snowy here, and mayhap it will keep out a few of the draughts, rust and all . . .'

We continued our upward climb, clawing, slipping and stumbling, eyes half-closed from the bitter chill which rimed our eyelashes and made my teeth ache. The last of the food—oatmeal, apple and honey—we had eaten that morning, and the summit of the mountain seemed as far away as ever. My hands and feet ached with cold and the tears froze on my cheeks under the mask. Now Conn had tucked Corby within his cloak and looped a corner of it into his belt to hold Pisky's bowl. I had Moglet inside my jerkin and Puddy permanently in my pocket. Only Snowy seemed unaffected, but the breath from his nostrils came like plumed smoke.

At last we could go no further, although the sun was still a red ball in the southwestern sky. We crawled onto a wide shelf beneath an overhang of rock, too exhausted to speak. Moglet voiced what, I think, most of us felt.

'We're not going to get there! We're going to die . . .'

'Nonsense!' I said immediately, not because I believed what I was saying but because she was smaller and needed comforting. Conn echoed me at once, and much more convincingly.

'Blather and winderskite, kitten! Of course we'll get there!'

'Let me lie down—so,' said Snowy, and positioned himself on the outer edge of the shelf so that he formed a retaining wall. 'Now, if you put the creatures next to me and you, Thing dear, put your feet by me and Sir Knight sits behind you . . . That's better, isn't it?'

And indeed it was. Somehow that wonderful white creature threw out a warmth that thawed the fingers and toes and doubts of us all.

'And now,' he said, 'I think it is time for that little packet in your pack.'

'Little packet?'

'Remember that evening in the forest with Tom Trundle-weed, and the mushrooms?'

'Of course! The Mouse-Dugs . . .' I scrabbled frantically in the almost-empty haversack. At last I found the desiccated remains and held them up to Snowy. 'How much?'

'Divide one between cat, crow and toad, and a sprinkle in the fish's bowl,' he suggested. 'I want none. Take two for yourself and three for Sir Knight. Let them lie first beneath your tongue to moisten, then chew them slowly . . .'

At first there was nothing, then gradually a warmth and fullness crept into my belly. The drug was quicker-acting on the animals. One by one they started talking. Pisky bubbled away of what he was going to eat when his pearl was gone, Puddy explained how much time he would have for constructive thought and philosophy once rid of the emerald, Corby described his anticipations of flight, and Moglet purred and licked her diamonded paw and thought of mice, until all at once they fell asleep. Moglet even snored a little.

I leant back and there was Conn's chest behind me, his mailed shoulder a pillow for my head. He didn't seem to mind, just shifted a little so that he was wedged more comfortably against the rock face, his knees on either side of me.

'They've got themselves all sorted out, haven't they?' he said.

'Mmmm. I hope it's all as instantaneous as they hope. Won't it leave a dent in Puddy's head? And, after all, if one hasn't flown for a while . . .?'

'It'll all take time, I guess, but the loss of pain and inconvenience will be enough for a while, I suppose. Your stomach, fr'instance: that'll stop aching, but you won't be able to stand upright properly for a while. Your bones will have become used to being in a different position.'

'Yours should be easier: one moment two halves of a sword, then suddenly—'

'If it works. If the dragon condescends to help. If he's in a good mood. If he's even there . . .'

' 'Course he is! We'll give him our jewels first, then he'll be in a good mood for you . . . No, perhaps it would be better to give him one, then get your sword mended, give him one more, then ask for Snowy . . . Or perhaps two first, then Snowy, and once he had his horn back he could help to persuade the dragon with his magic and—'

'Stop whittering, child!' and Conn put his arms round me and squeezed. 'God! you're as skinny as a starved rabbit!' And as I protested he shushed me. 'Don't talk too loud, they're all asleep . . .' Glancing round, I saw that Snowy's white lashes, the last to close, were lying in a calm fringe on his cheeks. 'Never mind about planning about dragons: let what will be happen . . .'

'That's not really the philosophy of a soldier, I shouldn't have thought.' I snuggled closer.

He rested his chin on my head and I could imagine him staring out into the dark night, a frown of concentration between his brows. 'No . . . Most military actions are planned, methodical—that's if we are hunting down an enemy, of course—but there is always a hell of a lot of waiting around just polishing up arms, tending the horses, mending gear . . . Of course in an ambush it's training plus instinct. And then there's the awful anticipation when two forces are drawn up opposite one another, each waiting for the other's attack; you spend the days with your stomach a'churn and the nights on your knees, praying, afraid to rest your head in case the other side takes advantage of the dark. You have to wait too for the high-ups to decide when and where: that's how planning comes into it. But it's never your decision. For all you know you may be sacrificed as a diversion, a suicide troop, or may spend your time fuming in the rear as a reserve that never gets used at all—'

'Doesn't sound much fun to me,' I observed.

'It's a way of life. Besides, what else is there for a youngest son with no skills but his sword and a touch, perhaps, of the old blarney?' I could hear the smile round the words.

'Blarney?'

'Aye, there's an old stone somewhere in Hirland, so they say, where they hang you by your heels to reach it and if you manage to touch it with your lips then you can charm the lassies into Kingdom-Come with just words. Me mother said as I had no need to seek it . . . Said it came as natural as a hen laying eggs . . .' The mushrooms made his voice more lilting. He shifted a little to make us both more comfortable. 'And, believe you me, there were times when I found it useful.' He laughed out loud. 'Why, I could tell you such tales! When I attended my first court I had no idea at all what was expected of me . . .

'I had just been accepted in one of the courts of Brittanye on the recommendation of my father's name—for a grand warrior he was, and his name good as a password in all the lands across the water—and there was I, but a scrap of a lad from the bogs of Hirland with nothing to my name save the horse I rode, a second-hand suit of clothes and my father's sword, pitched of a sudden arse-over-noddle into the silks and jewels and soft hands of a parcel of women, the likes of whom I had never seen before! Plucked were their eyebrows and oiled their skins and painted their eyes and lips, and they walked small but tall in their pattens, like cripples, and swayed their hips and fluttered their scarves till I was as helpless as a newborn babe! And if it hadn't been that as a lad of fifteen I had already spent time with the lasses at home and learnt to give them pleasure, I would have had problems, I promise you.

'They all thought, you see, that it would be amusing to sport a little with me. Until I knew what it was all about, I played the innocent and listened to their soft words and pretended I did not know what lay behind them. It did not take me long to realize that they all suffered from the same thing: their lords were so often away at war, and worn out with battling when they returned, and had no time for the soft words, the strokes and caresses, that they were all like pullets without the cockerel. So, when one day they said I had to pass this test they had planned for me, and that six of the chosen ladies were to visit me one night to initiate me into the ways of the court, I knew what was coming.

'For three days I ate lamb's fries, bull's pizzle and herring roe and bathed in rose water till I was surfeited and stank in my own nostrils, but when they came I was ready for them and serviced them all, one after the other, with flattering words and pleasant courtesies between, till the eyeballs fair popped from their heads and they declared themselves worn out!' He chuckled again. 'Took me a week to recover, so it did, but after that I could do no wrong. They declared I was a poet of the bedchamber, so they did!'

I think he had temporarily forgotten to whom he was talking, for he had never disclosed his past so freely before and the topic was not the most suitable for the youngster he obviously considered me. But I stayed quiet and did not remind him, for I was where I had always longed to be, in his arms, albeit as unregarded as a pup or a child's wooden doll. It was only gradually, I think, that I had fully realized my good fortune, for the drug we had chewed, while heightening our sensibilities in some ways, made stranger things as acceptable as they would be in dreams. So, it was only now that I realized the full implications of Conn's arms about me and I had to hide my jubilation, for it was in me to tremble and shake and behave as those women he had spoken of, perfumed and pretty and seductive in silks. Except that I was not like them and never could be, ugly and crooked and poor as I was!

But my love for him was beautiful, more beautiful even than they could ever be, for I loved him without subterfuge. I did not desire him from boredom, or the joy of conquest or in rivalry. I loved him firm and true and plain. Not unquestioningly, for we had travelled too long together for that, but acceptingly and thankfully, for he was a man who deserved to be loved and cherished, even if only in secret.

'I can see you cannot wait to get back to it all,' I said wistfully, and with no hint of sarcasm. 'I suppose the Castle of Fair Delights was a bit like that court?'

'Something like. But do you know, Thingy, the good life can

pall after a while? A man can yearn for the simpler things, he can become tired of trailing across indifferent country through all the seasons to face an enemy he has never met, and would probably drink with instead of fighting if he had the chance. I was bored, for too long, and too often.' He relaxed his arms about me. 'That's why, I suppose, I began to spend so much time with the surgeons—'

'Surgeons?'

'Yes, the fellows who patch up the damage done by sword and axe, pike and spear, bolts, daggers, falling horses; the men who try to cure gangrene and chopped-off limbs, set bones, assuage fever, bandage boils on the bum, scalds from burning oil and give you a cure for the clap. The ones who give the same ointment for dog-bites and pox and saddle-blisters, who gave wine to all and unction to the dying if there was no priest about . . . Horse-doctors, most of them, used to galls and spavin, mange and sprains, but not to humans. But there was one—a little man, dark and pocked from some obscure town in Italia, I think, but married to an English wife, who had a gift with bones. He did not just bind and bandage and splint, he had a full set of human bones, of horse bones, of dog bones, and these he had cunningly strung together with wires so that they held like puppets on strings and he could study the way they moved and were dependent on each other. Also, when a man died of some blow to his head, back, hip, he would lay back the flesh when he could and study the injured bones, to see where and how they might have been mended.' He sighed. 'I learnt a lot from him, Thingummy. That's one of the reasons that makes me suspect that to straighten that back of yours will take more than a sudden dragon-spark. The spine is a marvellous thing, all locked and connected like a necklet of ivory shapes . . .' He settled back against the rock. 'Got any more of those mushroomy things?'

'One.'

'Let's split it. Thanks . . .' He chewed for a moment, then tucked the scrap under his tongue. 'Mmmm, that's better . . . So, I might think twice before committing myself to anything too protracted this time; a short campaign, perhaps.

'And you—what will you do?'

I sighed. 'Try to find somewhere to live, then make a home

of it for the others. Scratch a living somehow, whether by trying to be self-sufficient with food, or by trading mushrooms, or—oh, something or other will turn up, I suppose. It must. It always has . . .'

'Optimist!'

'What else is there to be? Pessimists are always expecting the end of the world tomorrow, so don't bother doing anything in case it comes today instead. Optimists fall flat on their noses often, too often, but at least they don't believe the worst will happen till they've had time to get in the harvest, sow the winter wheat, spin the fleece, set the ram among his ewes, lay in wood, jar the honey—'

'Oh, darling Thingummyjig! You're a tonic for the footsore and heart-weary, truly you are!' And he threw back his head and laughed, quite forgetting I think that he had hushed me a moment since for the sake of the others. They stirred, but it was only to seek a more comfortable position. He hugged me. 'I shall miss you, girl, sure and I will! You're more fun altogether than those fine court ladies with their fal-lals and insipid talk—and if it's more than that I seek, sure a willing trollop from the village is heartier and more honest by far!'

'I shall miss you too,' I said, but I tried to keep my voice light. 'We have had some good times together, have we not, even among the bad?'

'Sure we have!' He seemed to hesitate for a moment. 'You know, I don't like to think of you and all those animals just going off into the wilderness after this is all over without making proper plans. Why, there's no telling what mischief you might get up to, and there's all those dangers along the road . . . 'Sides, you need someone to help build that house you spoke of . . .' He hesitated again, then seemed to make up his mind. 'So—'tis in my mind to stay with you awhile, just until you're all set up. Then my mind would be at ease when I took to the road again.'

I couldn't help the shiver of excitement that started in my stomach and ran out to fingertips and toes and shut my eyes on its way to burning my ears.

'You mean . . .?'

'I mean that we'll be companions of the road that much longer.'

I wriggled inside my clothes like an eel through grass. 'Hurray! I mean—I mean thanks! I suppose I didn't really fancy being on my own, and then having to find somewhere and build a house with only the others to help. A—' I was going to say 'young woman' but changed my mind, 'a person can have a hard time persuading villagers to accept them if they don't appear to have a—' oh dear, this was getting difficult; '—I mean, females do . . . If they don't . . . So you see it will help if they see you around at first: you can say I'm your—your servant . . .'

He didn't answer, so I twisted round in his arms anxiously for confirmation that he had understood, for by now I had a clear picture in my mind of myself, grown straight if not beautiful, dressed in a skirt instead of trews, spinning thread at the doorway of my little hut on the edge of the clearing near the village, and perhaps even leaving off my mask once Conn had gone, and of the villagers accepting me eventually and not even looking at my ugly face after a while, but glad to welcome me into their world because I had arrived with a great knight like Conn.

'I know it's a lot to ask, but if you just said—said to whoever is there that you would be back every now and again—you wouldn't really have to, of course—to see that I was comfortable, then I'm sure they would treat me as—as more normal. More like them . . .'

My voice trailed away, for I was suddenly aware how close we were, now I was facing him. His eyes glittered down into mine, our noses almost touched through my mask and his chainmail tunic rubbed my chin as he breathed. I quite forgot what I had been saying and when his next words came, for a moment they had no context.

'Servant? No, you deserve better than that.' His breath came in little white puffs of vapour and for a moment he closed his eyes. 'Dear Mother of God, she's such a helpless little Thing really . . . Let this be one unselfish thing I do.' He opened his eyes. 'So, Thing dear, as they all call you, before I go off on my travels again, if you're agreeable that is, we'll tie it up all nice and neat in a contract before the priest. I shall give you my name so you'll be the equal of all, and I'll have a home to come back to when I weary of my travels.' He regarded me for a

318

moment, then frowned. 'Well?'

'I—I don't understand . . .' I didn't.

He gave me a little shake. 'Thick, all of a sudden? Well, I'm telling you that my hand is yours, my name will be yours, and my sword to defend, if necessary, when I'm around. Damn it all, Thing—what is your real name, by the way? I can't marry "Thing"—We'll have to find you a name; what would you fancy? How about Bridget? Or Freya? Claudia?'

'Marry?' I faltered, and it must have come out like the silliest bleat in the world.

'Of course. What did you think I had been trying to say?'

'You—you haven't seen my face, and I don't think I want—'

He misunderstood what I was trying to say, interrupting me so I should not get the wrong idea. 'No, no, of course it won't be like that, silly girl! A marriage in name only, I promise you that. We'll be just as we are now, good companions, and you can keep your blasted mask on if you like, though I'm sure I could get used to what's underneath!'

'But supposing you find someone else, someone—well, er, more suitable you wished to marry? Marry properly, I mean. A pretty lady . . . With money?'

'I am nearly thirty years old and I have seen enough "pretty ladies" to last me all my days! They are all alike, believe you me, and the prettier the worse! As for money—I can earn my keep, and if not, I've managed before and can again. And as for—the other—well, I can always find that when I need it, and I promise I would not disgrace you by seeking it while I was with you. No soiling your own front step and all that sort of thing . . . Well, what do you say?'

All sorts of thoughts were chasing through my brain. The first, illogical one: suppose I *had* been pretty? Would he by now have got so used to me that he would still have conferred his request for my hand like a royal order, assuming that I had no other choice—but that thought was so stupid, so illogical that I shocked it into oblivion. The second thought: the man I love above all others has asked me to marry him!! The stars should whirl from their courses, the rivers run backwards, hills grow flat, trees flower in winter and cattle bring forth in threes . . . Why, then, did they all stay as they were and why did I feel like crying? I knew the answer to that one in my

319

rebellious heart, but frantically pushed it away. The third thought: I want to be sick . . . And the fourth? It suddenly burst like an overfull wineskin and I was drowned in intoxication for I loved him so, *so*, and here was my chance to really do something for my dearest knight at last—

I stumbled to my feet, pulling at his hands. 'Stand up!'

'What?'

'Stand *up*! Now, quick: I have something for you—'

'An answer, I hope,' he grumbled and unfolded himself so that we stood, precariously facing one another.

'Now what?'

'Now, say it over again. Formally. But before you do, just say that you realize just what I am—'

'What you are? Oh, come on, Thingy, no time for games—'

'No game. Promise! Listen . . .' I was trembling with excitement. 'Am I or am I not poor and deformed?'

'At the moment, yes, but—'

'And am I not also the ugliest person in the world?'

He shifted his gaze. 'Now, you know I would never say that . . .'

'You wouldn't say it, but do you not truly believe me to be so?'

'A man can get used—'

'Am I not?'

'Well, yes, I suppose you must be. You keep saying so, but remember I have never seen you unmasked.'

'Still, you believe me to be?'

'I told you—'

'Never mind! In spite of all this,' I spoke clearly, slowly, emphatically and could see out of the corner of my eye that Snowy was awake and the others stirring, and there was a hint of a lightening in the sky to the east, 'in spite of all this, you have made me an offer?'

'Oh Thing, you know I have! Why all this rigmarole?'

'Then please ask me again.'

'Ask what?'

'Ask me to marry you!'

'But why—'

'Ask!'

He looked at me impatiently for a moment, then his gaze

320

softened and he smiled so that my heart turned over.

'All right, my dear, all right, have it your way . . . Hey, you lot!' He looked over at the others, all now awake and alert in the growing light. 'Your Thingy doesn't seem to credit what I asked her a moment ago, and I need you as witnesses. So, we'll go over it once again, just so as we all get it right.' Squaring his shoulders, he put his hand to the hilt of his broken sword. 'In the full understanding that Thingy here is poor and deformed and I believe the ugliest person around—though I have told her that does not matter and I could get used to it—I hereby ask, in front of you all, for her hand in marriage. In name only,' he added hastily, 'on that we are agreed. But marriage, none-theless . . .'

There was a gay, tinkling sound.

'And I refuse!' I said triumphantly, as the sun's first rays slanted full on my beautiful knight, glinting on his armour till it almost blinded us.

'Sir Conn,' said the others, more or less in unison, 'your armour isn't rusty any more . . .'

And indeed it wasn't, celebrated with all the 'Begorras', 'Hail Marys', holy shamrocks and all the saints in the calendar (especially St Patrick), and a whooping and hollering that woke all the echoes in that previously God-forsaken spot.

He honestly hadn't remembered about the witch's curse when he had asked me to marry him and it had to be explained to him all over again.

'But you turned me down!' he expostulated.

'That didn't matter! You asked, that was all the curse said you had to do. Don't you remember how The Ancient said you can't face straight up to a curse like that, you had to go at it sideways? You could have broken it any time if you had bribed someone ugly enough to refuse you!'

'To the devil with anyone else! It was you I asked, and you refused. But I'm not taking no for an answer: I shall marry you whether you want to or no. As I told you, you need looking after—'

'Wait till all this is over then. Till we are all whole. You still have a broken sword—'

'And don't you think me still capable of defending you, even with my bare hands? Mother of God, you take some

321

convincing! Very well, I shall ask you once again when all this is over, and you'll not refuse!'

It was a glorious morning. The snow sparkled on the mountain and all around us stretched a chain of hills white and shining, their shadows purple and blue and green. No longer were we hungry, no longer cold, and when Conn set off again up the steep slopes we followed with more enthusiasm than we had shown for many a day. When we were faced with what looked like a sheer wall of rock, Snowy took the lead, slipping and stumbling for all his surefootedness. I felt like a fly crawling up a wall, my hands grasping poor Snowy's tail like a lifeline, Conn panting behind, but at last we emerged on a ledge far bigger than we had seen before, wide and long enough to hold a wagon and two horses.

Even as we gazed out over the ridged carpet of hills below us we became aware of a sound, alien even to our harsh breathing.

There was somebody, something, up there with us— *Snoring.*

The Dragon Awakes

RAISED IN natural steps some four or five feet above the ledge on which we stood, was the dark, triangular shape of a cave mouth, and it was from this direction that the sound came. Instantly we all retreated to the very edge of the ledge, clutching at one another in panic like children caught stealing apples. All, that is, except Snowy, who stood his ground, snuffing the air.

'He's asleep,' he said. 'Or in a coma.'

'Is it . . .?'

'Of course. We were bound to reach him sooner or later. Come, my children, you're not afraid?'

'No! . . . Certainly not . . . Afraid, us?'

But we were, of course we were. It was all right for Snowy, I reasoned, being of faery stock to begin with, but the rest of us were all mortal. Too late I began to recall all I had heard about dragons; immense scaly beings, with leathery wings and huge claws and mouths full of teeth and fire. They ate people, whole sometimes depending on size, and were capable of incinerating entire towns and villages with their flame. They guarded vast hordes of treasure with jealous attention and demanded a sacrifice of seven maidens every year. They hatched from golden eggs and took only a day to reach full size and after that a thousand years to die. They flew in swarms a hundred strong and mated once every nine years, laying nine eggs which took another nine years to hatch—

'Grumphhhh!!'

I jumped back as if I had been punched and fell over the edge of our precarious perch, luckily landing on soft snow only some five feet below, to be hauled back by an anxious Conn. Puddy and Moglet, in jerkin and pocket respectively, had of course accompanied my fall but as I had landed on my back they escaped with bumps but not bruises.

When we were all assembled back on the ledge I looked at Conn. 'I'm not sure . . .'

'Neither am I, neither am I, dear girl, but this is what we all came for . . .'

'Bravo, Sir Knight!' said Snowy. 'Now, shall we—?'

'I'm *frightened*!' said Moglet.

'So am I,' I said. 'But, dear one, Conn is right. This is what we came for. And we're together, so nothing can really hurt us—remember what The Ancient said?'

And so it was that, with Snowy ever so slightly in front, we climbed up the last steps of rock and found ourselves in the mouth of the dragon's cave.

The winter sun was at its highest, illuminating all but the farthest depths of the south-facing cave. Fearfully we peeped: a bare stone floor, stained with droppings; shelves running erratically across the back and sides, and on these humps and piles of metal: shields, helms, coins, a cup or two. In the middle of the cave a few discarded bones—bullock or sheep, perhaps—and a bluish leathery cloak or bag, flung aside from some foray probably, tattered and patched and torn.

But no dragon . . .

Perhaps there was an inner cave. Perhaps—my heart lifted, coward as I was—perhaps he had gone. Perhaps he had never been here. But there were the piles of metal, the bones . . .

'There's nothing here,' I whispered. 'Except rusty metal, old bones and rubbish.'

'Rubbish is rubbish is rubbish,' said Snowy cryptically, who alone of us did not seem disturbed, anxious or disappointed, the sun shining on the hairs on his chin and making his lips pink.

'Well there isn't,' I said. 'If—he—was here, then he's gone, long since. Look! These old bones were chewed years ago.'

'And the noise we heard?'

'Oh—wind in the rocks, I expect . . .' I became bolder and advanced into the cave, while Conn stepped forward and examined the shelves.

'Darling girl, there's gold up here!' His voice was excited. 'Lots of these shields and things are bronze or iron, but there's silver and gold coin and buckles and rings and brooches set with coloured stones . . .'

I put Moglet and Puddy down so they could explore. 'So what? What good is gold on a mountain-top? We need broth and bread. And, besides, we came here to get rid of our burdens, not set up a second-hand armour stall in the market.' I was disappointed now, angry with anticlimax. 'The place is disgusting, that's what it is, and *this* heap of rubbish *smells*!' and I kicked the heap of leathery discard in the middle of the cave.

Upon which the bundle of rubbish stirred.

And opened one baleful eye.

Upon which we beat a fast retreat. I had heard of the phrase 'one's hair standing up on one's head' and now I experienced it. It was horrid! I felt as though a hand had scooped its icy fingers up the back of my neck and yanked my hair by the roots.

Once again only Snowy seemed at ease.

'One doesn't kick dragons,' he said mildly. 'At least, not until one has struck up a friendly acquaintance.'

Helplessly I stared at that yellow eye and, unbidden, a child's rhyme I had learnt—when? where?—popped suddenly into my mind.

'Let sleeping dragons lie;
Tread soft, child, pass him by.
Better not know the power and glory,
Learn it best by myth and story . . .'
Too late! I had awoken chaos, and ineptly too.

The bundle of rubbish stirred again, rearranged itself, snorted, sneezed, and opened the other eye, which was, if anything, more baleful and bleary than the first, and for a long—a very long—moment, we all stared at it, and it at us.

Then the bundle spoke, coughing out an ashy, cinderous breath. '*Who* disturbs my rest?'

Nobody moved, nobody even breathed, then suddenly an absolutely unstoppable sensation rose somewhere behind my eyes, gathered strength behind my cheekbones, ordered itself behind my tongue, pressing its advantage so firmly I had finally to snatch for breath and—

'A—*tish*—ooo!!' The best of it was that I hadn't sneezed for months.

'Bless you!' said the dragon, and suddenly everything was much better, so much so that almost without thinking I wiped my nose on my sleeve and advanced two paces.

'Good-day,' I said, and bowed. 'I regret that we disturbed your slumbers, O—O Magnificence, but I'm afraid it was necessary. Well, not *afraid* exactly: that's perhaps the wrong word.' (It was the right word.) 'But it *was* necessary . . .'

'Why?' Uncompromising. 'And who are you, anyway? From the village, perhaps? Well, if you are, your climb was for nothing. I do not intend to play puppet for your silly games any longer.' He yawned, and a furry yellow tongue curled up like a cat's around stained, yellow fangs. 'Now, go away!'

'But—'

'At once!' He raised himself for a moment and his wings rustled as he half-opened them. A few dry, diamond-shaped scales fell to the floor in dusty disarray, and he sank back on his haunches.

I retreated one step but no further, for Snowy's nose nudged me forward again, none too gently.

'Please Sir, please Lord-of-the-Sky . . .'

The eyes, which had gone slitty, opened wide again. 'What, still here?'

'Yes, if it please Your Eminence. I . . . I—We're not from the village; no, we're from much farther away. Much farther,' I repeated firmly, for now I realized it was no good blurting everything out in one go. It would have to be told in stages, perhaps like a story, for I would have to wake this creature gradually to the reason we were here, lest he lose his temper and blow us over the edge. So, a tale for the fireside . . . 'It all started this way: once upon a time . . .'

When I had got into my story and the dragon was clearly listening, his claws folded in front of him, I sat down cross-legged on the cave floor and made myself comfortable, giving him a condensed version of all that had happened, introducing us all by name at the appropriate moment, so he knew where we fitted in the story. When I spoke of the witch the dragon allowed a wisp of smoke to emerge from his right nostril, but

326

otherwise there was little show of emotion. He glanced at Snowy once or twice and nodded when I spoke of The Ancient, as though they were acquainted, but otherwise he was a quiet and attentive audience. By the time I had finished, the sun's rays cast a fading light on the left wall of the cave.

I coughed heartily for my throat was now dry and parched, but Conn handed me Pisky's bowl and he sank warily to the bottom as I sipped.

'Is that it?' said the dragon, but it was not really a question. 'So . . .'

Slowly he seemed to reassemble himself, taking deep breaths, scales rustling like a long-forgotten pile of dry leaves. Now I could see the shape of his ribs, the heave of his flanks and he seemed to swell to twice his original size before our eyes. Suddenly we all became less cold, as though we had stepped into a room where the ashes were still warm. Indeed little curls and wisps of smoke issued from the dragon's nostrils and when he opened his mouth I stepped back involuntarily, for a small flame licked momentarily between his teeth and then died back again.

'Fear not,' he said. 'I mean you no harm, but when a dragon wakes from as long a sleep as mine the fires take some time to get restarted. Come forward, nearer to me, you and your companions. Show me where the sorceress hid my treasure . . .'

Slowly the others joined me; I pointed to Puddy's head, lifted Corby's wing and Moglet's paw, held up Pisky's bowl and hefted my jerkin to expose my navel.

'It was true, then . . .' Somehow he was changing colour. At first he had been a dull, metallic grey-blue, but now the colour was deepening, brightening, and round the middle of his body assuming a purplish hue. I jumped back again as with a hissing, swishing sound his tail, which had so far been hidden, twitched and curled and unfolded itself, the tip, like a huge arrow-head, curling up against his left flank.

Now he addressed Snowy and Conn. 'Come hither, let me look at you . . . Ah, I see. You both want restored that which you would not use . . .' They both looked puzzled, but he did not explain. 'And what would you give, to restore a horn, to mend a sword?'

327

'What you would need of healing to set you free,' said Snowy, stepping forward and nodding at the discarded scales.

'And I,' said Conn, 'will trim and sharpen your claws that you may take flight and return home without pain.' And he indicated what I had not noted before, the bent and twisted claws on the right front paw.

The dragon nodded. 'A fair bargain, from you both. Stand aside, Sir Knight, stand aside all save the unicorn!'

No need for second telling. We all pressed back against the cave wall as the dragon took several deep breaths and then shot a jet of flame that flared with a gassy roar, like those lumps of blackened wood that one sometimes finds in peat. A thick, acrid smoke curled in our nostrils and I put my hand over Pisky's bowl to save him from the smuts that floated down.

'Sorry,' said the dragon. 'Out of practice. Must concentrate.' And now the flame quietened, burned steady, changed colour from yellow to orange to red to a sort of silvery pink and now we were all very warm indeed. The flame seemed to transmute into a shimmering glow.

Into that glow stepped Snowy, for all that I extended a last-minute hand to stop him and cried out: 'No, no! You will be burnt . . .' and shut my eyes and put my hands over my ears. From her perch on my shoulder Moglet's cold nose nudged my cheek.

'Look! It's all right, really it is . . .'

The shabby little white horse, uncombed and uncared for, stood calmly in the silver fire. As the light streamed over his dumpy body and lifted his mane and tail with the breath of its passing, a curious change took place. The lumps and bumps and tangles were smoothed out and curried and combed and he stood taller, slimmer and shining with the light itself. And suddenly there were golden sparks and a ting! as of a golden bell and there, between his ears, on the sore little stump he had borne so long, there sprouted a beautiful, spiralling golden horn. The silver fire died down and he stepped forth, shining like the moon at Lugnosa, the harvest month; not gold, not silver, but a glorious mixture of both. For a moment he stood, a creature of pure faery, untouched and untouchable, the snow with the sun upon it, and I sank to my knees in awe as he reared and neighed his triumph. Then hooves found the floor of the cave again and he looked over at us.

'It's all right, you know,' he said, and suddenly he was our beloved Snowy again. Going over to the dragon he bent on one knee, his horn touching the floor. 'Thank you, O Master of the Clouds!' and, standing now, he circled the dragon on delicate hooves, bending to touch certain portions of the scaly hide with his golden horn. To my astonishment I saw the parts touched burn with a blue light which gradually faded to leave new scales growing in place of the old.

'Magic,' I whispered. 'Real magic . . .'

'Good magic,' said Snowy, and came over to bend his head and nuzzle my hair, his rippling mane curtaining us both. 'I am whole again . . .'

And now it was Conn's turn. He was told to place the broken halves of the sword upon the ground in front of the dragon. The latter carefully rearranged the pieces, muttering under his breath as Conn retreated to join us.

'Runes,' murmured Snowy, 'and a perfect alignment, north/south.'

The dragon's tail lay straight behind him this time and the fire he breathed was red and hot, so hot that I began to perspire, and the sword itself glowed with a fire of its own. It seemed to me, through the shimmer of heat, that letters of fire appeared on the blade, but if so they were in symbols and words that I could not read. I could not have pinpointed the moment when the two pieces became one; suffice it to say that when the metal glowed as one piece the dragon suddenly roared for: 'Snow! and plenty of it!' Conn and I ran outside, scooped up handfuls and placed them in heaps on the glowing metal. The snow hissed and melted as we watched, and then the blade of the sword gleamed blue and whole on the floor of the cave. Conn, in wonderment, bent to pick it up, but a claw fastened on his arm.

'Not yet, not yet: the metal still burns!'

'But the magic . . .' faltered Conn.

'No magic. Expert welding, that's all. Dragon-fire and snow.'

It was many minutes before the hilt had cooled enough, even with more snow, but eventually Conn wrapped a piece of cloth around his right hand and raised the sword. Blue light still seemed to flow along the blade and it sang in the air as Conn swung, thrust, parried.

'Begorra, 'tis better than ever it was! A power in the hand with a mind of its own! Many thanks, Great Sky-Lizard, for giving me back my right arm!' and he bowed deeply to the beast, sword-point down, both hands folded over the hilt.

'Let's try the edge, then,' said the dragon. 'These pesky claws . . .'

The sun was much lower in the sky by the time his claws were trimmed to his satisfaction. I knew that it was now our turn and my heart seemed to bounce between my mouth and my boots as he beckoned us forwards. I had to carry Moglet, who by now was so terrified that I felt a warm trickle on my arm as I lifted her; Puddy and Corby shuffled forward slowly of their own volition, and the only one who seemed eager was Pisky, who was frisking about happily in his bowl.

'Going to see a dragon face to face, a thing even my revered great-grandparents never did; *their* parents, on the great-grandmother's side, had one drink from their pool, but they hid and were afraid. I'm not! This is a thing I am going to tell my great-great-grandchildren! Wish I could have something special to remember it by . . .'

So did I: instant oblivion.

'Now,' said the dragon, as we arranged ourselves in a semi-circle before him. 'Now, did The Ancient, as you call him, tell you of the possible consequences of relinquishing these jewels?'

I nodded.

'You realize that you must give freely?'

'Yes.'

'I cannot force you to give these jewels up—'

'We understand. But surely—'

'I could take them? No. You yourselves have bound them into a magic of your own, something never envisaged by the sorceress. She merely thought to hide them from me, knowing I should find them difficult to locate if she hid them within living flesh in five different locations. She did not reckon with the bond you forged between you, a bond so strong that, had she tried, she could not have taken them back.'

'She—you—could kill us and rip them away . . .'

'No again. I could kill, she could have too, if you were separate, but even then the jewels would be worthless, dull and insignificant. You were given them to guard, whether you realized it or not, and a gift like that can only be returned freely, never forcibly taken.'

'We—we have travelled many miles, not only to rid ourselves of our burdens, but to return that which is not ours to keep. We are not thieves: the jewels are yours, and we bring them to you through storm and fire, flood and cold, distance and dangers for precisely that reason. It was a joint decision,' and I looked round at the others for confirmation.

'Agreed,' said Puddy.

'Likewise,' said Corby. 'Mind you, I don't think I realized all that was entailed. Still . . .'

'I'm ready, ready, ready!' sang Pisky, happily. 'Great privilege, meeting a dragon!'

'Don't want to,' whispered Moglet. 'Changed my mind . . . Frightened . . .'

'No, you're not!' I whispered back. 'You want a nice painless paw, now don't you? So you can play and hunt properly? Surely my brave Moglet, who wasn't afraid of the wicked spider, won't balk at the last moment when all her friends are willing?'

'Are you?'

'Of course,' I lied, more frightened than I could remember. 'Of course!'

'That's all right then,' said Moglet. 'But you must hold me tight!'

The dragon had missed none of the exchange, I am sure, but he chose to ignore it. 'You do realize, also, that you will regain your memories?' And he looked at me. 'Not all at once, perhaps, but eventually you will remember where you were taken from, your past life, your home . . . And this may be more painful than anything else.'

'We understand. But sometimes the torture of *not* knowing is worse. You should know that . . .' It was daring to speak thus to a dragon, but apart from a hiss and a wisp of smoke he did not respond.

I spoke again. 'We are ready. How will you remove these stones?'

331

'Inspiration.' I thought he meant one thing, but as it transpired he was being literal and physical rather then mental.

'Who will be first?'

We glanced at one another, then Puddy gamely dragged himself forward.

'I only hope it will not hurt too much,' he said mildly. 'Until now the headaches have been bad, but not unbearable. Will the hole in my head hurt worse?'

'I shall take care of that,' said Snowy, stepping forward to stand beside the dragon. 'My golden horn, now it has been restored, will heal your pain.'

'Come,' said the dragon, addressing Puddy. 'Close your eyes and think of nothing save willing me back your burden, my treasure . . .'

The air grew soft, spring-like, and a greenish haze surrounded Puddy where he sat, feet planted firmly on the ground. The light grew brighter and it was now a sharp, metallic green and suddenly Puddy seemed impelled forwards towards the dragon's mouth. Without thinking I leapt forwards and grabbed him, found myself in the green haze and also in a visionless storm of wind sucking me forwards towards the dragon. Shutting my eyes I hung on grimly, my hands cupped round Puddy's frail body, and suddenly there was a pop! as if someone had squeezed a seaweed pod between finger and thumb, a tiny scream, and I was flat on my back still holding the toad, with Snowy bending over us both.

'There,' he said. 'It will soon be better . . .' and he touched Puddy with his horn.

'Sorry,' said the dragon. 'Took more breath than I thought. Been there near seven or eight years . . .'

I turned Puddy round anxiously, looking for the hole in his head, but there was only a shallow depression, through the thin, healing skin of which I could see a throbbing vein. 'Are you all right, dear one?'

He considered, eyes shut. 'Headache's gone. Head feels cold—sort of empty. Much lighter, though.' He opened his eyes. 'Bit like waking up out of hibernation: you feel stiff and cold for a while and have forgotten the taste of a meal. Get used to it. Much better, really; can't grumble . . .' He inclined his head to the dragon. 'Thank you, Your Graciousness. My goodness! Was I carrying *that* around?'

Well might he express disbelief, for the greenish, muddy lump that I had grown so used to on his forehead now lay before the dragon, a shining, glittering clear green stone, sparkling like spring water at the edges, dark and deep as a forest in its depths. Lovingly the dragon curled his claws about it, turning it so that the low rays of the sun caught it with a sudden flash of green fire.

'You were,' said the dragon. 'An emerald from the cloudy heights of a rainforest on the other side of the world, where their gods demand a blood-sacrifice and the suns that shine from the gold they bear are as uncountable as the rays from this stone. Green it is as their forests, deep as their fears . . .'

I shivered, and looked at the jewel with new respect: it was not such as I would care to wear. No wonder it had given Puddy headaches.

'I'll go next,' said Corby, after a doubtful look at Moglet, cowering again under my jacket. 'Can't be so bad . . . 'Sides, I'm interested to see how long it takes before I'll remember how to fly.'

'Well done, bird,' said Snowy. 'I'll be here to ease any hurt.'

'I'd better hold you,' I offered. 'The pull is very strong, and we don't want you a dragon's dinner . . .'

I was only joking, but the dragon made a terrible frown and Snowy hastened to intervene. 'The inhalation, the drawing of the burden, it worries them: the child but makes jest to lessen the fear . . .'

The dragon said nothing but settled down, elbow-joints protruding. I sat about six feet away, holding Corby's wing spread with one hand, the other binding him tight to my breast. 'Close your eyes,' I whispered. 'Remember I've got you . . .'

The dragon intoned: 'Concentrate, bird; will me your burden, my jewel . . .'

'Gawd knows I do,' said Corby. ''Tain't no use to me, Your Worship . . .'

This time the drawing-power was greater, and I found the hair blowing forward round my mask as I hung on grimly to my friend, whose feathers were pulled forward as in a gale. His claws were fastened tight in my drawn-up knees and I had to clench my jaw to stop from flinching. Now the light was a burning, scorching blue, and before I closed my eyes from its intensity it seemed as though great waves were rearing their foaming crests and threatening to engulf us. Suddenly as we hung on there was a crack! as of a breaking branch and once again I was on my back on the cave floor, Corby by my side in a squawking, tangled heap.

Snowy stepped forward and stroked the injured wing with his horn, the bare featherless joint pathetically pink, and slowly the desperate fluttering stopped.

I lay eye to eye with the exhausted bird. 'How does it feel, dear one?'

He considered, getting to his feet and bringing the injured wing gingerly to his side, then stretching it again. 'No pain. Stiff, but it's getting easier every minute. Look!' and he flapped the wing—an awkward effort it was true, but still the first movement of the sort he had been able to make since I knew him. 'Thanks again, Your Worship!' and he bowed to the dragon.

We looked over at the sapphire. Unlike the emerald it lay beside, rectangular and deep, the stone was oval and shallow, yet a blue more dense than I had ever seen. It was deeper than the deepest sea, yet on its edges was a lighter, sparkling fringe, like waves upon a shore. Now the great beast turned it in his claws, murmuring lovingly: 'A fine journey I had for you, my friend: across the warm oceans, skimming the little islands that rose like pustules on the pocked sea; but I found you where others had hidden you, didn't I, left to rot as you were with the other jewels. But you were the prize, my beautiful one, as blue as the eyes of the dead who buried you . . .'

I gazed at the jewel with new respect: dead man's treasure, not such as I would wish to wear. No wonder it had twisted Corby's wing.

'And now,' said the dragon. 'The little cat and her diamond . . .'

'No, no, no, *no*!' howled Moglet, burying her head into my armpit, 'I'm *afraid*! It's going to *hurt* . . .'

'Only a little, I promise,' I said, comforting her trembling body. 'Ask the others, ask Puddy and Corby: was it very bad, you two?'

'Not unbearable, I suppose,' said Puddy. He looked very wrinkly and thin. 'More unpleasant than anything.'

'Felt for a moment as though my wing was coming out by the roots,' admitted Corby, 'but the feeling didn't last long.' I noticed for the first time how grey the feathers were above his beak. Strange how fear sharpened the senses, for I was afraid, just like Moglet, yet for her sake hid it.

'There you are, you see?' I exhorted. 'And Pisky's not afraid . . .'

'Then why can't he go first?' demanded Moglet. 'I don't mind.'

'But I do!' interrupted the dragon. 'You are next, cat, but you must be willing.'

'She is, she is!' I said. 'You are really, you know, dear one: it's just that, like me, you don't like the unknown. I'm next, you know, and I can't get rid of this—this dreadful stomach-ache till you loose your burden.'

'It's very deep,' said Moglet, showing me her paw. 'It'll hurt much more than the others . . .'

'Then it's very brave of you to agree,' I said hastily, sensing her weaken. 'You must show me how to be courageous.'

'I wouldn't really mind keeping it,' she said. 'With you to carry me round. Still . . . If you say your stomach hurts most of the time?'

'Oh, it does!' I assured her, though at the moment it felt both numb and tingly at the same time.

'Right!' said Moglet and, shutting her eyes, she stretched out her burdened paw in the general direction of the dragon, while fastening the claws of the other three firmly in my sleeve.

'You are sure? You will me freely your burden, my stone?'

'Yes . . .'

The dragon gave her no time to reconsider. A roaring, sparkling wind surrounded us and my back bent further in its hunch as I tried to step no nearer the dragon. Stars wheeled and danced around us, there was a blinding flash as of a veritable avalanche of snow falling about our ears and, before I had to close my eyes against the unbearable aching of the

335

light, I saw a rainbow that spanned the distance between Moglet's paw and the dragon's mouth. She howled, an awful sound, her claws tore trails of blood from the outer side of my wrist so that I nearly cried out too. There was a long ripping sound, the light died behind my clenched eyelids, I was on the floor again and Snowy was bending to Moglet's paw and my lacerated flesh.

'Better now?'

The dragon had three stones now and the latest, Moglet's burden, sparkled and spiked with a thousand coloured lights as he turned it in his claws. 'A rare flight that was, the sands burning bright and the sun a molten dagger in one's back. They laboured to bring wealth out of the depths, they died in the darkness that this might have light . . .'

I shuddered: I would not willingly wear such. No wonder Moglet hadn't been able to put paw to ground.

But she was dabbing at my face. 'Let go of me, I want to try it!' Already the healing hole was closing up, the blackberry pads drawing together. She seemed heavier, sleeker, pain now forgotten in the space of two breaths. I set her down, and gingerly at first but then with increasing confidence she set down the once-burdened paw on the ground. 'Look! Look!' she cried with delight. 'It's better! Soon be quite well . . .'

'Now you, little wanderer,' said the dragon. 'You are ready?'

No, I wasn't. Suddenly gripped by irrational fears I sank down again. It was not only the thought of more pain, sharp and quick-over though it might be, it was also the familiarity of the burden itself, like an aching tooth that, however irksome, is still an understood part of one till removed. Most of all, I think, it was the certainty that once I lost it and regained both health and memory, paradoxically this latter might prove a greater burden than the burden itself. I was afraid to be given a future so sudden, so different. Better the devil one knew—

'Come on, Thing darling,' said Conn. 'I've watched you bravely hold the others, now it's your turn to be held . . .' and the words—my name clear and 'darling'—rang so loud in my ears that body was all unresisting as he reached down and lifted me to my feet, kneeling behind me on one knee, one arm across my thighs, one across my breast. He pressed me back against his chest and his breath was warm on my cheek. 'Courage, girl, courage: 'twill soon be over and I'm here, your Conn is here . . .'

My Conn! I felt at least one joint of my backbone click as I tried to straighten. Without further hesitation I pulled my jerkin up with one hand, my trews down with the other and pre-empted the dragon's question.

'Yes, yes; I give freely my burden, your treasure. Take it, take it away quickly, please!'

I was staring straight at the dragon who seemed to grow immensely tall and then there was fire all about us and toppling towers and men and women crying out in fear. The fire blazed stronger and there was a tearing, twisting pain in my guts that I could not bear. I tried to bring down my hands to cover the agony but somehow Conn was preventing me, and I screamed. With a sound like tearing a snail from its shell, but horribly magnified, I felt my burden leave me and there was Snowy's horn to numb the pain and take away the sickness. Strangely the greatest discomfort was Conn's arm across my breasts, which suddenly felt full and tender. I straightened up one crick! more, drew together my clothes and turned, for an instant, to bury my head in Conn's shoulder. He patted my back and released me.

The ruby lay in the dragon's claw and burnt cool as he turned it lovingly. 'The temple held it dear, but it was housed in a heathen idol that crumbled to the touch. The priests in their robes cried desecration and the temple dancers fled into the night as it was drawn from their grasp . . .'

I shuddered, and the stone seemed to wink back evilly at me; if I had known what I carried I would have cut it from my flesh like a canker. No wonder it had hurt . . .

'Are you ready, O King of Fish? You I have left till the last because the burden you bear is probably the greatest, my last and most beautiful gain . . .'

That muddy pebble?

'Of course, Lord of the Clouds, Master of the Skies; all my life I have wished to be acquainted with you and your brethren. It had been my ambition to mount the Dragon Falls that I might join you in the skies, but now that can never be. I shall be content to see you a little closer, perhaps to touch fin to scale. Pray, Thing dear, move my bowl nearer . . . so. It will do.' In his exuberance bubbles broke from either side of the burden in his mouth. I knelt by his side, my finger in the water.

'You are sure?'

'Sure? Why, of course I am sure! I have been carrying this stone safe for a Dragon-Master and now I yield it with eagerness, with pride!'

The dragon bent closer and I flinched. But he did not notice.

'Here, little brother, take a closer look. Look your fill . . .'

For a moment dragon and fish touched, nose to nose as Pisky rose from the water. He looked so small, so defenceless, so like a gulp for breakfast that I leant forward, ready to snatch him away from danger, but he turned on me.

'No, Thing, no! This is *my* day, *my* moment that I have waited for so long and you must not spoil it!'

'I was only—'

'There is no need. We understand one another.' It was the dragon who spoke, but the words might just as well have been Pisky's.

'He is so small . . . the wind of withdrawal . . .' I faltered.

'He is stronger than you think. Watch . . . It is given freely, and you are cognizant of the results?'

'It is,' said Pisky. 'I am. But spare my friends the snails; slow and unintelligent they may be, but excellent privy-servants. And prolific, I hope.'

The air grew thick, like the mist that streams between the trees at shoulder-height on a late-autumn morning; then it was as if the moon rose on this same mist, silvering it until it glowed and shimmered with an unearthly light. I saw clear water running, waves tumbling, spray mounting the rocks, horses of sea-foam . . .

There was no sound when the pearl left Pisky's mouth: it rose like a little moon and hung between them like a sigh. Then the magic disappeared and Pisky sank back in his bowl, his mouth a pained O of surprise and hurt. Swiftly golden horn touched golden mouth and he sank to the bottom, the snails crowding close for comfort.

The dragon had a huge pearl between his claws—how its sheer size must have hurt poor Pisky!—but he was holding it

338

with reverence, for it still glowed and shimmered and shone like a moon behind thin cloud.

'A hard struggle it was for you, my most precious of all; searching fjords and creeks, inlets and rivers; I glimpsed you beneath tossed waters and running streams; saw you in the reflection of the moon on swollen rivers and high tarns; you were the winter sun on ice, a wraith of summer stars; I tasted you on tumbling stones and in the thickness of reeds; sensed you in the flash of scales, the turn of fin; always you called to me and at last you came of your own free will when I had despaired . . .'

The pearl glowed, and it was a stone I, anyone, would have been glad to touch, admire, hold in one's hand, bear on one's breast . . .

'And now,' said the dragon, 'it is almost time for me to go. But, before I do, I would thank you all again for returning my jewels, my treasure. Because of you, because of your honesty and determination, I am now a Master-Dragon, as the little fish so truly observed.' He bowed gravely to each one of us in turn. 'Now, I must try my wings: if you will excuse me?' He went to the mouth of the cave and down the steps flexing his bony, leathery, creaky wings, which gusted a powdering of cinder-tasting snow back into the cave. I gazed at the ring of glowing jewels lying on the cave floor and wondered at their gathering, their binding, their loosing. Lying there like that, now that they were back with the dragon, they still seemed to have a magic of their own, a kinship; they seemed almost like a ring of animals who will turn into a tight circle to meet a common enemy, horns lowered and rear protected against wolf or bear . . . Like us, when we bore them—

There was a humph!! of flame from the dragon, a series of short, staccato bursts from his rear, as one who has dined too exclusively on pease-porridge, and then he turned to where we watched him, smuts on his face.

'A trial flight . . . I think the Lord of the Carp would like to see my world; after all, had he stayed in our country he might well have climbed the Dragon-Falls. This will only be a substitute, of course, but I think he would enjoy it. Would you be so kind as to accompany us and carry his bowl?'

He was looking at me, but I wasn't quite sure what he

wanted. Pisky popped his head out of his bowl, speaking like someone who has had a tooth pulled.

'I should like it above all, Thing dear—please?'

'Yes, but I—' I suddenly realized what was expected. Oh, no! I couldn't, I couldn't! I looked at Snowy, and he nodded.

'It will be all right. You will be safe. I promise.'

So, awkwardly, stiffly, still hunched, I clambered onto the dragon's back, Pisky's bowl clutched in my arms, and lay down, my face to the leathery scales, my heart thudding.

'Hold tight!' There was a slithering followed by a sudden sickening lurch. I opened my eyes and my mouth to yell as I saw the mountainside slipping away from me in a sideways slide. My breath was snatched away by the wind, my face froze and my cheeks blew inward with the sudden rush of air. There was another lurch that left my stomach behind somewhere and then we steadied and the mountain slid by.

'Sorry about that: trailing-edge muscles weren't working.' I could only just hear the words, for the roar of wind and wings in my ears. My eyes were shut once more and would have stayed so but for a little bubbling voice besides my left ear.

'Isn't it beautiful? Just like being in a bigger, lighter bowl. Look, far down below are the weeds and the stony bottom, around us the waters rushing over our fins, and above the deep bowl of air beyond the rim of everything . . . Hold me up, Thing, that I may see and remember!'

'Let the King of the Carp see!' said the dragon, and such was the command in his voice that I obeyed at once, sitting up and holding Pisky's bowl high in my hands, though my fingers were half-frozen: I wound his string round my wrist to make sure he didn't fall. The rest of me was warm enough, for the huge reptile now exuded warmth, and the inside of my calves were, indeed, becoming uncomfortably hot. But all this was forgotten as I looked about and saw what Pisky saw, but with human understanding.

Below, so far as to take away fear, lay the village we had come from. It was dusk down there, for I could see the little twinkling lights of rush and candle; higher the sun still shone on snowy slopes, but to the west great purple shadows showed glen and canyon as they crept forward like a massed pack of wolves towards the lamb's-fleece snow of the nearer slopes.

Black sticks of winter forest covered the lower slopes and iced streams lay like saliva among the black-fanged rocks: but it was all remote, like sand-houses made by children's hands and I was curious, but not fearful. Nearer, the mountains stood like sentinels and I saw great orange fires burst from the dying sun, so that it seemed that pustules of fever opened on a great sore. No bird flew as high as we and all was silent save for the pumping of the dragon's fire-bellows, a gentle thrumming, and the whistle of the wind past my ears. I remembered my swim with the seal: as Pisky said, it was like, very like, an ocean of sky.

With a creak of wings we altered course, and once again I felt the cold air buffet my body and, too soon, we were again at the mouth of the cave. A sudden, jolting landing, a slurp of water from Pisky's bowl, and Conn's arms were lifting me, bowl and all, from the dragon's back.

'You all right, Thingummy?'

I nodded and clung to him, my legs strangely weak. As in a dream I watched the dragon pick up his jewels one by precious one and place them in a pouch of skin beneath his jaw, lastly his precious pearl, which he rolled around his forked tongue for a moment before placing it with the others. He was no longer a blue dragon, he was a pearl-pink dragon, and even the long whiskers on his jaw curled and vibrated as if fired with his new vitality. He gazed around the cave, and then at us, and in his eyes was a remoteness, as if we and the cave were discarded bones and his eyes were on another prey.

'That is all, then. Farewell to my imprisonment, and farewell to you, my deliverers.'

With a scrabble of impatient claws upon stone he moved once more toward the opening of the cave.

'Wait!' called Conn. 'The gold—the silver—you have left it!' He gestured to the shelves round the cave.

'Keep it: it is yours. You deserve it. The jewels were what mattered . . .' and he was gone, launching himself in a clatter of wings into the sunset.

The wind of his passing scuffled the dust in a spiral over the spot where his jewels had lain. When it settled there was no sign of their presence. It was as if they had never been.

INTERLUDE

Dragon-Sky

IN THE country of his upbringing they would have recognized the special corkscrewing rocket-rise with the sideways twist, but all the watchers from the cave and the village below could say afterwards was that the dragon ascended like a reversed shooting star with a noise like twenty hungry bears.

A handful of rustic peasants and the seven weary travellers were the only witnesses of the most extraordinary and accomplished display of free—as opposed to compulsory—figures of dragon skyrobatics since the illustrious Master of the Chrysanthemum had given the Millenium Display for the Many-Titled Emperor-of-the-Thousand-Palaces five centuries past and three oceans away . . .

The dragon swam in the air as if it were water and he an otter, a shark, a seal, a fish. He used the air-currents and therms as an acrobat would use bars and trampolines and springboard, and all the while he played with his great pearl as though it were a ball, an essential part of his act, tossing it in the air so that it described milky arcs, letting it fall a thousand feet and diving like a thunderbolt beneath to catch it again.

For what seemed an hour, but might have been no longer than ten to fifteen minutes, the great beast played like a child in the nursery with its first toy, then as the sun dipped to touch the horizon with its burning belly and as the eastering shadows threw their arms across hill and valley alike, he snatched his pearl from the sky, a pearl now pink as an opened rose, stood on his spade-tail for a heart-stopping moment then clapped his wings together like a vengeful cormorant and dived the depth of the mountain towards the village below, the wind of his passing creating a down-draught like a thousand flocking geese at marshing-time. In a flash of fire he incinerated their alarm beacon and burnt the easterly copse.

The villagers cowered together, the men cursing and shaking impotent fists at the fast-retreating sky-climber, the women flapping useless aprons. Only the children cheered and waved. In their maturity, when visiting other villages, the story would crystallize into legend. They would tell of the thunder-crack of his passing, of a red dragon who soared over their impossibly green fields, until the telling became a symbol recognized by all who listened to a tale: an inspiration, a banner, under which princelings would rise to repel invaders, ordinary men would fight and fall, and a usurper unite and divide . . .

But the Master-Dragon's mind had turned from them all— the past imperfect, the passing present. Taking his bearings from the first stars that winked from the eastern sky, he wiped his memory free of time, of disappointment, of frustrations, tucked away his pearl with the other jewels in the pouch beneath his jaw, spun thrice on his spade-tail and then sang his farewell song.

To those watching and listening, dodging the mini-avalanches and fires set off by his rejuvenation, watching stone clatter down the slopes, regarding with dismay the collapsing huts that disintegrated like imploding puffballs, all they heard was an enormous clash and rattle as of giant metal plates tumbled together, a ringing of bells so huge their peals were as sound-sight, ripples of torturing light-noise in a stone-tossed lake—but to the dragon the cacophony was the best music he had ever made, a soaring passion of release from bondage, a paean of praise.

An ascending rocket-burst of flame, crackling in the still air, a rapid climb to five, ten, twenty thousand feet; a moment's hesitation when dying fires fell like shattered stars to the mountains beneath, and then the Master-Dragon shook free and headed east for Home.

THE LOOSING

Awakening

IN SPRING the young shoots of corn struggle hesitantly from their blanket of earth and poke wary green heads up into the unfamiliar air; too soon, and the frosts nip them black; too late, and they are drowned in the shadows of their bigger brethren, starved of light and nourishment, and shrivel and die. Just as I, the new Thing, was not sure whether I had emerged from the darkness of forgetting to the lightness of an Inbolc or a Beltane. At first I was ill, tossing and turning in fever, waking briefly to moments of lucidity. But before I could reorientate myself, grab hold of life and become better, back I would slide into a haunted black vault of the mind where hope ran down the mazed tunnels of thought, knocking in vain on doors that would not open, with the hounds of Hell baying behind.

They said afterwards it was seven days I was unconscious, sent back into the earth to remember the seed from whence I sprang, but it could have been seven hours or seven years for all I knew. Conn was kept away from me for fear of contagion, for it seemed my skin sloughed away in great strips with the fever. They took away my clothes and burnt them.

When I woke up at last clear-headed, starving hungry, I felt the cold air touch my face with inquisitive fingers: when I put up my own I found my mask had gone, and panicked. Throwing the shift I was dressed in up over my head I screamed: 'Where is it? Where is my mask?'

'There now, dearie, what a to-do!' Strong, warm hands pulled up the covers, covered my hands with hers. 'No need to take on so! Come, take your hands from your face—'

'They'll see my ugliness! *He* will see . . .'

'Now, then! Ugliness is a state of mind, and there's none wrong with that face of yours that fresh air and sunlight and a little extra feeding-up wouldn't cure. Got eyes like piss-holes in snow, you have . . . Now, then: that's better! Let Old Nan (what has been chosen to care for you because she's born twenty and buried all but three, survived four husbands and the phlegm and the sores and the runs and vomits and scabs) let her comb out that nice, thick hair of yours and then Megan—she's the youngest, touched a mite some would say, but a grand girl with the sheep—she will fetch some broth and bread. Been told to make a fuss of you, I has, by that nice tall fellow with the sword. Soon as I lets him know you're better he's to come and see you, he says, and all those animals you brought . . .'

Unlike most chatterers her actions were suited to her words and she had me combed and tidied and fed in no time at all, all the while her strangely accented voice, hovering like a salmon in leap on the vowels until you sometimes wondered whether she would ever reach the smooth waters of the consonants, burbled on like a busy brook, soothing and stimulating at the same time. At my insistence she fashioned me another mask, from kidskin, although I could see she was bewildered by the need. In truth her face was so seamed and pocked that it was difficult to identify any features, except for toothless mouth and red nose, so perhaps my physical deficiencies were not so strange to her after all. I made up some tale about being handfasted to Conn, but having made a vow not to uncover my face until we were wed. This made sense to her, full of superstition like all country folk, who must explain away disaster and joy, gain or loss somehow. Their 'little people', for instance, seemed to have a hand in everything, from birth to death; and they seemed to prefer these household gods to any other, although Conn found a deserted Christian shrine in the woods to say his prayers by.

Once my mask was on I couldn't wait to see the others again, and indeed the next time the door was left open Moglet was on the bed in a flash, and enthusiastically kneading my chest.

'Look! it's much better . . .' She turned over her damaged

paw and now there was only the smallest hollow and increased width among the pink and black pads. 'Are you better, too?'

'Been a bit worried about you,' said Puddy, from under the bed. 'Thought you were . . . Nice to see you. My head is much improved.'

'Caw! Bleedin' cold out there!' said Corby, actually managing a flapping ascent to the rafters, and landing safely. 'Best off where you are . . .'

'Look at me, look at me!' bubbled Pisky, borne in by Conn. 'Twice the size I was already, they say, and eating better all the time. Sir Knight says that if I don't stop I shall have to have a bigger bowl, and the snails are complaining at the extra work—'

Conn sat down on the bed and took my hand. 'How are you, Thingummy? We were all worried about you, but they said it was only a bad fever. Still, you've been away from us a whole week, and had it been but one day longer I should have insisted, infection or no, on taking a turn at minding you. How's the back?'

'The back?' I had genuinely forgotten my other deformity with the trauma of the mask. So much had happened in my feverish tossings and turnings, happened, that is, to memory and understanding, that I had had no recall of my twisted and bent spine. Now I sat up as best I could and eased back my shoulders. There was a little crick! as another knob in my spine straightened its alignment and I found that my eyes were on a level a good six inches higher. With Conn seated so near I could look almost straight into those kind, concerned brown eyes.

I saw him glance down in surprise at my front. 'Why, you've—' He stopped, confused.

'Got a proper front,' said Moglet happily, and pushed painfully against my budding breasts.

'Er—it's better, I think,' I said, and I pulled away my hand, that had gone hot and sticky with embarrassment. I pulled up the covers to my chin. 'Where's Snowy?'

'Here, dear one,' and he stepped daintily through the doorway. A shaft of late sunlight followed him in and ran in admiration down the beautiful spirals of his golden horn and over the waves of his luxuriant mane and tail. 'I only come in the village when there are few about, for I reckon a dragon-memory is enough for these simple folk, without having to get used to a unicorn as well. I can make them unsee me for a while, but it is more convenient to stay out of sight in the forest. Glad to see you are recovering . . .'

'But—isn't it awfully cold out there?'

He lifted his head in an unconsciously arrogant gesture. 'Unicorns don't catch cold,' he said.

I suppose we were there for about another three or four weeks. Gradually I grew stronger in body, although my mind was still full of darkness. When I got up they brought me woman's clothes, for another thing had happened that had sent me cowering to the floor in terror. Until Snowy explained. I had spent the day in bed, with intervals on the stool at the side, and had been feeling grumpy and unsettled all morning with a vague stomach-ache, then suddenly, as I stood up to practise walking a few steps, I was seized with one of the old pains I had thought gone forever. There was no one with me, as Old Nan was busy baking, Conn had gone hunting with Corby, and the others were holed up somewhere in the warm. The pain hit me again and of a sudden a bright scarlet plop! of blood hit the floor from beneath my shift and then another. In terror I flung open the door and rushed out into the snow, instinctively heading for the forest.

'Snowy, oh Snowy! The pain's come back, worse than ever, and there's *blood* . . .'

Another moment and he was there, his warm breath on my face, his mane sheltering us both as he bent and snuffed at me gently.

'No, dear girl, it hasn't, not in the way you think. Listen to me . . .' and he told me how I had become a woman, and that what was happening to me now was something I had been waiting for during the seven long years of the stone's captivity. 'That is why it hurts so much: it means you are catching up on all those years in one go. Now you are girl-child no longer.' He looked sad and I remembered—so many things to remember!—that unicorns appear only to young virgins, never to mature women, and I suddenly understood a whole lot more.

He bent his head and touched my stomach with his healing horn. 'There: the pain is gone, and never will be so bad again.'

I kissed him, suddenly shy. 'I won't . . . I don't mean to . . .'

'I know. I shall be with you till you don't need me any more . . . Now, come: sit on my back and I will bear you to the hut, otherwise you will freeze to death!'

The pain disappeared, but when Snowy turned once more to return to his voluntary exile I noticed a small spot of blood on his otherwise flawless back, like the stain of a trodden berry . . .

At last the snow started to slide from roof and rick, the sun stayed longer with us, fingernails of ice fell with a tinkle from the swelling buds in the trees, and it was time to say goodbye to the village, for we all felt we should move on with the lightening days, though where we had no clear idea. Conn gave the headman three gold coins, a princely sum, for their care of us. He also told him that the dragon had left some treasure in the cave for them—silver and bronze armour, plates and cups (we had the gold coin)—as recompense for burnt thatch and general damage. I could see they could scarcely wait for the snows to melt. The coins and the anticipated treasure were celebrated in our farewell party, which included a roasted steer, mock dragon-fights and much mead, so that it was with a thick head that I turned for my last look at where our quest had ended. The villagers stood a quarter-mile away, still watching us go. I waved once more and then glanced up at the Black Mountain. I could not see the cave, and of a sudden clouds from a warmer air frothed and spilt over the top like scum from a mess of new-boiling bones until all was hidden from view.

The road ahead lay downhill. Once again we heard the tentative song of birds, buds were thick and sticky, and catkins hung like lamb's tails from the willow and everywhere there was promise and hope. Conn sang and the others grew strong and fat, but my heart still lay heavy and full of dread, for I had grown up.

Every day fresh memories arrived with the softening of the days. Sometimes I felt as though my heart would break, for I now knew who I was, where I had come from, some, not all yet, of what had happened in the twelve years before the witch abducted me. I remembered, too, what had befallen my parents and wept the inner tears of one who could only mourn too late. Conn kept glancing at me anxiously but I could not tell him, not yet. And there were the others: I began to appreciate fully what my 'release' meant now for, as The Ancient had predicted, whole and free again, they spent far less time with me and I found my eyes and ears and touch and taste and smell not understanding them as before, as if a veil lay between us.

I think perhaps I realized more was to come, so I was not unduly surprised when one spring day we found ourselves in a countryside of rolling downs and there, sitting on a rock as coolly as if he had only wandered a little way ahead five minutes ago, was The Ancient.

Part of me wanted to run and embrace him, part to refute his very presence, to blame him in some obscure fashion for my private world of misery, so I stood and did nothing as the others crowded round him. Conn's sword, Snowy's horn, Puddy's forehead, Corby's wing, Moglet's paw, Pisky's mouth were all exhibited and admired: he did shoot one piercing glance at Conn's armour and then at me, but had the sense not to make any remark.

That night we spent round his campfire and ate better than we had for weeks. The only question he raised was, where were we bound? Had we thought of this? Yes. Come to any decision? No. It seemed everyone thought everyone else was leading the way . . .

At last Conn voiced all our thoughts. 'We—we all thought there must be something else. What, we did not know. Perhaps it was you?'

'Not me,' said The Ancient, taking off his red-and-white striped hat, decorated with shells, and scratching his head. 'I'm merely here to see the fun . . .'

'The fun!' I exploded, exasperated at last into coherent speech. 'What fun do you think it has been for us? Where have you been, that you think that cold and hunger and fear and illness constitute *fun*? What makes you think that the traumas, the tiredness, the soul-searchings, have been *fun*? You're just a stupid, uncaring, flippant old man who is concerned with nothing but his vicarious pleasures, and has merely learnt

349

enough so-called "magic" to think himself immune from us mortal creatures! You are complacent, narrow-minded, cold—' I ran out of words.

The others, except Snowy who merely looked amused, stared at me in varying degrees of horror.

'Magician,' reminded Puddy.

'Bit strong,' added Corby.

'Special case,' remarked Moglet.

'I really don't think—' Puddy.

'Hang on, Thing dear, moderate it a bit,' from Conn.

More or less all together.

'No,' I said. 'I won't moderate or anything! I meant it!' and burst into tears. Huffily pushing them all aside, I retired to a corner, wrapped myself in my cloak and pretended to go to sleep.

The next morning I arose very early and wandered off among the dunes to where the land sloped away into a haze of forest and fields. It had turned cold again, so the streams were marked by twisting snakes of mist that followed the waters and trees held a shadow-self of clear earth beneath their branches and the rest was tipped and branched and swathed with fingers of frost. I shivered.

'I'm sorry,' said The Ancient. 'Forgive me, Fleur?'

I remembered what he had called me before. 'You knew . . . All the time?'

'Of course. And now you do, too?'

'Most of it. Some of it won't come yet.'

'It has made you sad . . . And bitter.'

Of course it had. To lose your parents, home, nurse, childhood all in one day, to lose your memory for seven years and then to remember everything at once, more or less, was like being forced to swallow huge doses of bitter herb-medicine. I felt disorientated and most of all, alone. Remembering nothing, I had had my friends: the comradeship, their love, and my passion for Conn. Now it was all coloured differently but, in spite of my new knowledge I was not sure who I was, what I felt, where I should be . . .

'I warned you.'

'Yes, I know: but I didn't know it would hurt so much!'

'Don't forget that your friends are in exactly the same boat.'

'The same?'

'Of course the same. As if it were yesterday. Your cat now remembers the home she was stolen from, the warm fire, the loving mother; the toad remembers his pond, the crow his treed brethren and the fish his capture and long travel from abroad while his kin died one by one in neglect . . . Don't you think that they, too, have regrets and memories? Are you unique in suffering just because you are a human being?'

'But they didn't say . . .'

'Of course not. You've been ill. You recover to look like a wet Lugnosa! What did you expect? You have always been something special to them, something that to them was better, more able to cope—of course they are uneasy when you appear to go to pieces.'

'But we no longer talk as we used to . . .'

'I told you that would gradually go as well.'

'But I don't *want* it to!'

'You said a lot of things last night that were true—about me being immune from reality, from mortality—well, I'll say the same to you, but in reverse. You *are* mortal, and being so must accept that mortality, with all it implies. You wished to escape from a painful and confining enchantment, but now you refuse to accept the responsibilities that go with the release!' His tone softened. 'Being a human is hurtful at times but it can also be wonderful, more wonderful than the immortals can ever experience.'

'How can that be? You have life everlasting, if you want it—'

'For that very reason! Quite apart from life itself becoming boring when one has lived it two, three, four times as long as anybody else, it is rather like always having enough money to buy whatever you desire. If you can always have what you want, on demand, it ceases to be desirable. In the end there is nothing left to experience.' He frowned, and his look dared me to probe further.

'But do you—can you—never die?'

'Oh, yes. But only by our own choice, by our own hand. There is another way, but that involves the Powers I told you of once. They are stronger than all.'

'The powers of good and evil, you mean?'

'I have told you, there are no such things. There *is* Power, there *are* so-called Forces. They are like—oh, like a team of strong horses, harnessed and ready for a driver. It is up to their user, whether he or she directs it to plough a field or ride down innocent bystanders.' He nodded. 'Mmm.'

'I still don't quite see . . .' I hesitated. 'This question of immortality: surely the promise of a life eternal, dependent on your own decision to terminate, must far outweigh our little lives, that are bound by the certainty of death?'

'That very thought of mortality adds spice to what you do, don't you see? A summer's day is all the more beautiful for the knowledge that storm could blight the blossoms and frost surely will; a child is all the more precious for the perils of growing-up and the winter of old age; love is all the more glorious for its very ephemerality, the pain of parting or disillusion.' He frowned. 'But perhaps worse than this is when immortal loves mortal . . .' His face darkened, and all at once in his place was a grim warrior standing: illusion, for the image passed and he was once again an untidy old man. 'Ask Snowy . . .'

'Snowy?'

'He will tell you one day, perhaps.'

'I don't understand . . .'

'You will, sooner or later.'

My mind went off on another tack, perhaps inspired by all this talk of love. 'And that's another thing: when I was—was hunched and miserable it didn't matter that I loved Conn, because he was so far out of reach. It seemed right. But now—' and I gestured to my nearly upright stance '—now I am nearly a respectable woman (except for my face, of course). I find I want more, desire more, *need* more. When it was impossible I could bear it: now, I can't!'

'So that's it . . .'

'No! Not *just* that—'

He grinned at me.

'It's *not*!'

'To me it's simple. Then, you loved like an idealistic twelve-year-old; now you are nineteen and a woman grown. At twelve one is allowed to worship from afar, because one's thoughts don't usually encompass anything physical, real . . .

Now you are suddenly grown, the passions you feel are different. You have missed the years from twelve to now that would have made you someone's lover, wife, mistress, and now it is all coalescing into an unbearable desire that you think—'

'Know!'

'—cannot be satisfied, because under that mask of yours lies ugliness.'

'Right.'

'Wrong!'

I stared at him. 'What do you mean—"wrong"?'

But he seemed to change his mind, became a grumpy old man again: even his hands started to dither and fuss among his brooches and fastenings till he seemed the very dotard I knew he was not.

I persisted. 'What do you mean "wrong"? My body may have changed, I can see and feel that, but my face hasn't. I know: I feel it all over every day when no one's looking, hoping against hope, but it feels exactly the same as it did when we lived with—Her.'

He steepled his fingers and considered me under eyebrows like thatches. 'What you need—what you all need—I reckon, is a bathe in the Waters of Truth.'

'And where and what are they?'

'They are in the centre of the world that you know, and they have the gift of clearing your mind, making you see things as they really are.'

I suppose I must have sounded wearily disbelieving. 'And just how do we find these—these magical waters?'

He snorted crossly. 'In order to get you lot off my back and out of my hair I shall lead you there myself. Right away!'

THE LOOSING

The Waters of Truth

WE TRAVELLED by the Secret Ways, the paths known only to sage and faery. Under hedge, by forest path, through tunnels of ancient, gnarled wood, once through caves; and all that while we met none others save shadows, a disembodied greeting, a stirring of windless branches and a bending of grasses, laughter, the sound of dissonant harebells, and yet we knew They crowded us through our journeying, watching, guarding, guiding, enfolding us in their hands so soft we could not see . . . They? The spirits that man has driven from his world to hidden fastnesses among the rocks, the dells, the streams that wind through underground caverns. Listening to their laughter, feeling their mischievous hands I could understand and yet regret man with his earthy, clumsy honesty—but did not Time itself lay aside these Earlier Ones, for They were children of another world than ours, too delicate to survive in ours?

They loved Snowy, climbed on his back for rides, plaited his mane in the night, garlanded him with faery flowers none could see, but picture from their evocative scent. They tweaked The Ancient's beard unmercifully and rode unseen on his shoulders, and he was as indulgent as a father to his children. They pressed fruit I had never tasted and could not see against my lips till the juices ran down my chin, and yet when I opened my eager mouth they were gone, skin, flesh and seeds so that I stood there like a gaping idiot and their laughter tinkled in my ears and I could smell cowslips and rain.

We walked, rode, slept, talked, ate and drank like any other travellers, but of that time I remember less than any other. I do not even remember how long it took, faery time I suppose; all I know was that we left the dragon's village in early spring and it was near the summer of Beltane when we came to our destination. Like all things to do with The Ancient there was a certain dream-like quality about the whole thing, with none of the wear and tear associated with ordinary journeyings.

One evening we couched on soft moss in the forest, the next morning we burst through the thinning trees, breasted a soft green slope starred with day's-eye and lion's teeth, speed-you-well and bright-eyes, and there beneath us lay a secret valley. Behind us the deciduous forest, to the north steep crags, to the east a forest of pines, to the south downs melting misty blue with distance and cuddling a lazy river in their arms. Below us a thin cascade fell like a veil from the crags above onto dark rocks and down to a deep pool of water surrounded by banks stained with flowers. A rainbow arced the falls and from where we stood we could hear the birds sing.

As if in a dream we descended the steep sides of the valley almost as though we were floating, and dropped down by the water and drank deep. And fell asleep, fast asleep, all of us, without dream.

When we awoke the sun was still rising in the sky and we had no way of knowing whether we had slept five minutes or a whole day and night. We stretched, yawned and greeted each other with smiles as if this were one day when all was right with the world. A fire smoked lazily and there were thin pancakes and honey, a mess of vegetable, tiny strawberries and The Ancient in a sparkling robe of purple with golden glints, sleeves rolled up to the elbows, dishing out our breakfast. I moved in a daze, sticky and replete, my nostrils filled with strange, soft smells, my ears full of the rush and fall of water, the song of a blackbird—'veni, vidi, vici, Dubree, Dubree' (whoever he was)—my body warm, my eyes closed against the flicker of sunlight on water. I opened them to roll over on to my stomach and watched an ant climb a stalk of grass until it tilted with its weight against another, which it scaled, busy and full of purpose. My eyes closed again—

There was a slap on my rump that had me leaping to my feet with a yowl of indignation.

'What did you do that for?'

'You were asleep.'

'Wasn't! I was just—resting my eyes.'

'Sounded like snores to me,' said The Ancient, nursing his right hand. ''Sides, that hurt me as much as it did you. What in the world have you got back there that is so hard?'

'My knife.'

'You don't need that now.'

'You never know . . . Anyway, why did you want me awake? To wash the pots? Can't you just wave a wand, or something?'

He ignored my flippancy. 'We're here!'

'Where?'

'Here.'

'Where's "here"?' I was being naughty, for I saw all the others were seated around looking expectant and I knew we were about to have A Serious Talk, and I wanted to giggle instead and run away very fast and pick flowers. I did giggle, then clapped my hand to my mouth over my mask, remembering that I hadn't wanted even to smile for what seemed like months.

Conn patted the grass by his side. 'Come and sit down by me, darling girl. Sure, and I haven't heard you laugh like that in an age!'

But I sat down cross-legged between Moglet and Corby, facing him. I could not trust myself nearer to Conn. Snowy blew down the back of my neck.

'Right,' said The Ancient. 'Now then . . . Well, this is it!'

'What?'

He glared at me. 'Will you let me speak? Good. As I was saying—'

Puddy burped loudly and happily, his eyes closed, a wing or something worse sticking from the corner of his mouth.

'As I was saying—'

Corby bent his head under his left wing then rattled all over, ending with his tail, like a wet dog.

'As I was *saying*—' shouted The Ancient.

Moglet jumped, then scratched inside her right ear, contemplated the sticky mess on her claws, and licked them clean.

'Can't we go in the real water?' asked Pisky. 'I've been waiting ever so long for real water and I am sure there are ever

356

so many good things over there. My blood needs variety, you know, and when one is trying to regain weight after an enforced diet my aunt twice-removed on my mother's side used to say—or was it—'

'SHUT UP!' yelled The Ancient.

'No need to shout, now,' said Conn peaceably. 'We're all listening, you know, and—'

There was a sudden gesture from the old man and the fire jumped into a shower of blue and green sparks as if it had been booted across the grass. Then it died down into pale steady flame.

'Right! Now, can we get on without interruption? Good.' The Ancient seated himself. 'I have brought you here, as I promised, because I think you have all lost your purpose.' He absent-mindedly plaited the wisp of hair above his right ear.

'My way is clear,' said Snowy softly. 'At least . . .'

'I think . . . I should . . . I ought . . . There are places I've never seen. Now my sword is mended . . .' said Conn vaguely, and trailed off into silence.

'Now these headaches are better,' said Puddy slowly, 'I suppose . . .'

'I could go and—' said Corby. 'On the other hand . . .'

There was a protracted silence.

'I don't know!' wailed Moglet.

I hugged her. 'Neither do I, dear one! Except . . .' I looked everywhere except at Conn.

'You see? I was right. This is why I brought you all here.' The Ancient glanced round at us all. 'Do you want to wander around for the next ten years or so wondering who, what, why and when? Or would you rather wash away the cobwebs, rattle your brains into some sort of order, discover again the ability to make decisions—your own this time, not everyone else's?'

There was another silence, all of ten heartbeats long. Then, faint and faraway, I thought I heard music. Not the flute and drum of village dances, nor the chant of monks, nor yet the harsh trumpet of battle, rather a gathering together of sounds from wind and sky and sea, rock and stream, trees and leaves . . . It was gone.

'What do we have to do?' I asked.

'That's my girl! Easy. Go bathe in the pool.'

'Just that?' asked Conn. 'Simple—too simple, methinks.' He got to his feet and yawned. 'Still, I could do with a dip. Wash off some of the grime. Coming, Thingy?'

I wanted to say that I wasn't Thing, Thingy, Thingummy, or Thingumajig, but held my tongue. 'Perhaps. In a moment. You go.'

'Wannagonow,' said Pisky. 'Carrymeover, carrymeover . . .!' Gently I tipped him into the water, so clear, so cold. His little body wriggled delightedly and sank like a stone to the bottom, where I could see him nosing among the plants— trouble was, that pearl had stretched his mouth so that he now ate twice as much as I was sure a fish should, even a starved one: still, I suppose he was making up for seven years—and sucking and spitting, standing on his head, flashing his sides against the sandy bottom as if to rid himself of mites.

'Oh, well,' said Corby. 'Nothing ventured . . .' and he splashed himself into the shallows, claws gripping at stones, ings flapping an arc of spray. 'Corrr . . .'

Beside me Puddy slid into the water and paddled away, bubbling thoughtfully, then shooting off into the reeds with a stretch of legs and a flash of pale belly.

'Can't swim. Don't like water,' said Moglet, but she dipped her paw in and shook off the droplets in a fine spray that diamonded her fur in a million droplets. 'Still, water's warm. I'll soon dry off in the sun, I suppose,' and she stepped delicately into a puddle and wriggled.

I looked around; Snowy had disappeared—strange, I should have thought he would be first into the water—and The Ancient was tending the fire, once more trying to go to sleep.

Conn? Ah, there was Conn. And I blushed and hid my eyes, then peered through my fingers. For Conn stood, naked, right where the cascade of water hit the pool and he was misted with water, his tall, slim body gleaming, the hair on his chest and under his raised arms darker than the hair on his head and the hair at his groin—

I hid my eyes and wished myself desperately somewhere, nearer, farther—

'Come on, Thingummy!' called Conn, splashing happily. 'It's wonderful!'

'In a minute, a minute,' I answered, but I crouched down and held my head in my hands. I did not want—

There was a tremendous shove in the small of my back and I was gasping, drowning, freezing, the water roaring in my ears, my dress floating up past my face, the hair on my head streaming like seaweed. I surfaced, spluttering, to see The Ancient grinning as he fished out my shift and dress with a stick and hauled it to the bank.

'You pushed me in!'

'If I'd waited for you to jump there'd be as much snow on your hair as mine.' He picked up my clothing. 'I'll dry these out by the fire. Enjoy your swim . . .'

For a moment I panicked and tried to climb out, only to slip on the wet grass and fall back in, struggling like a hooked trout, the water filling my eyes, my nose, my mouth once again; but suddenly I realized that the water was not cold, as my frantic mind had told my skin. It seemed now almost the same temperature as my own body. I relaxed, and it caressed me, tickling and stroking, hushing and soothing, a nurse calming her charge. I remembered again how the seal had borne me on his back out of the bay. I turned to embrace the water, and, sliding into the unseen depths, gave myself to the element as though we were indivisible so that I was almost resentful that I had to rise to the surface and take breath. Then, when I surfaced the sun struck me full upon the face. For a moment I did not recognize the significance, but when I did I dived straight back into the water searching frantically, but the mask had gone!

Borne away by the vagaries of the current maybe, tangled in the weed, trapped by a shifting stone: all I knew was that I could not leave the water without it. Why, I had rather stumble naked than bare my ugliness! At any moment now I might come face to face with Conn. Desperately I paddled away into the middle of the stream; perhaps I could ask Pisky and Puddy to look for me: but they seemed to have disappeared. If I gathered a handful of reeds, could I plait them into a square and hold that before my face? But the reeds bent away from my questing hands, slipping teasingly through my fingers, and all at once the water silvered with bubbles, like a pan of water just before it boils, and I forgot I needed to breathe, forgot everything except the shower of brightness that surrounded me.

It scoured my mind free of the stains of bitterness and despair, as it sloughed away all the remaining grime and dirt from my body, until I was as clean as a new-washed child, carefree at last. Now all the memories had returned, but tidied into their proper places; I knew how and where and why and what, and with this came a sort of peace, an acceptance of what I had been, what I was now, so that my face was my face and that was that; no moaning over lost looks, for I had been fair as a child, I had had my mother's silver mirror and my nurse's words for that. So, when the change? The day the raiders came? Had my nurse scarred me to be no longer desirable as a slave? Or had the witch disfigured me? There were no memories for this, but perhaps I had not known at the time. Useless to speculate: I was ugly now, would be ugly for the rest of my life, but at least now I was straight and slim, and unknotted in body as well as mind. Perhaps I could still be of use to Conn, keep house for him while he went off on his adventures. I recognized, too, that the paths of my other companions might take a different direction from mine.

I accepted all this, but it did not mean I wanted it so. No, what had been washed away in those waters was not desire or love or needing, but the worst of my selfishness. I was aware that I must show Conn my face before I lost courage, because this was the face he would have to accept if he were to ask me again to take his name. And if he changed his mind when he saw it, if he did not renew his offer, then I knew he would be gentleman enough at least to help me to find a place of my own. And with that I might have to be content . . .

I surfaced for breath and he was standing thigh-deep in the water, some dozen or so yards away, his back turned, the water running from his freckled shoulders down into the hollow of his back and dropping from his firm buttocks. I stood up and my hair streamed down my back and my face and body were naked to the sun.

Now! Now—or never. Oh, how I loved him, in that last moment before he turned. I should not be able to bear that look of revulsion, I knew that, but I had to, I had to, there must be truth between us. I held that last moment tight as a precious stone . . . I was aware that the water was quiet, the birds had hushed their song, that my friends were nowhere to be seen, except for the flicker of Snowy between the dark trees away to my right. I wished I knew how to pray . . .

'Conn!' I called softly. 'Conn . . .'

And slowly, so slowly he turned and we stood face to face, and then the waters parted and he walked towards me and there was nothing except a loving astonishment in his eyes as he reached for my hands.

'And is it really you? Why, in the name of all the saints, did you hide that away and pretend to be ugly? Sure, and you're the most beautiful girl I've ever seen!'

And suddenly there was music, music that The Ancient had said was Love's Song rather than Love's Death, and all the earth sang until my whole body was filled with it and it spilt from my mouth, nostrils and ears and gushed from my eyes in astonished, grateful tears. For he told the truth. It was in his eyes, and to him, at least, I was beautiful. I freed my hands and put them to my face to discover the sudden difference but it was the same face. Then, how? Was he blinded by the waters? Had some spell diverted him from the truth? And how long would this illusion last?

'I'm not really. It's this place, I suppose. I'm ugly: I saw my face in the witch's mirror and felt it all over and the feel hasn't changed. It was scarred and twisted and blurred and askew, as though someone had ground their heel into the bones and turned it àgainst the flesh. Truly, truly Conn . . .'

He smiled, and the tips of his moustache curled upwards and smiled also. His eyes held laughter-wrinkles at the corners and what I saw in their depths made me conscious that I stood breast to breast with a naked man, naked myself. I lowered my gaze and saw his body, which was more embarrassing still. I blushed, and would have turned away but he reached out and took my shoulders and held them fast. I was intensely aware of the rough callouses on his hands, the puckered scar that ran across his left palm. I raised my eyes to his again, surprised to see the reflection there in miniature of a face I did not recognize.

I had to know. 'Tell me what—tell me what you see?'

'Vain is it now, and asking for compliments? Very well—'

He saw me flinch, '—it's teasing I was. Now, let me see . . .' He stood back a pace. 'Well, the hair is straight, and black as Corby's wings, that you'll agree. The skin is pale, as well it might be, hidden all that time behind that pestiferous mask! But I think it will always be milk rather than ale . . . Cheekbones that stretch the skin high and a chin that bodes ill for anyone that crosses you—No, no!' He leant forward and his hand caressed my cheek. 'I did not mean ill, and if you scowl like that you'll turn the milk of your complexion sour, so you will . . . That's better!' He smiled again, a heart-turning smile, and I shut my eyes. 'And if that's for me to admire your eyelashes, they're as long as grass-spider's legs . . . Look up. I'll tell you that your eyes are the colour of the violets under the hedge and big as an owl's, but twice as pretty. But your mouth . . .'

He frowned, and my heart stopped. Had I fangs like a wolf, a mouth like a fish? Or a beak like a bird? Was it puckered like a tight-drawn purse or sprouting with hairs? Was this last to spoil the whole?

He laughed, and the sun caught his eyes so that they screwed up. 'Your mouth is different,' he said. 'It is the most kissable mouth I have ever seen!'

And he bent his head and placed his lips on mine.

THE LOOSING: UNICORN

The Sleeping Prince

'BUT THEN of course you always were pretty,' said The Ancient.

In utter confusion I had fled Conn's embrace back to the fire, flinging on my still damp clothes with scant ceremony, and combing my hair furiously with my fingers. The Ancient had chuckled, obviously having overseen our dramatic meeting in the waters. Of course I had had to ask whether my new face would last, and he had told me it was my always-face. 'The one you were born with,' he had said, and somehow, even in all the confusion of remembering, the traumas of the quest, the half-forgotten pains, this little consolation was the most important thing of all.

'But it was different when I lived with the witch,' I said, for he had reminded me that my nurse had called me her 'pretty chick'. My father told me that although I had my mother's colouring and eyes, I had his chin, cheekbones and hair. I could recall him well: tall, lean, fierce, with scowling brows yet with a mouth that could smile as easily as it would tighten in determination. And my mother; small, rounded, soft, with hair a little lighter than Conn's, skin like cream and a mouth to kiss and laugh—but remembering was still very painful. It was as though they had died a few days since, and I did not want to think of them as I had seen them last, not yet . . .

'Of course it was different with the witch,' scoffed The Ancient. 'Because you were told so.'

I dragged my mind back to the present. 'She showed me. She had a mirror . . .'

'A magic mirror. You saw what she wanted you to see. She

told you you had a face like the arse-end of a pig with a curling snout, and that's what you saw in the mirror. You were conned, my flower, conned good and proper.' He flung a couple more sticks on the fire and I leant forward to dry my hair the better. 'Not surprising really.'

'Why?'

'Why convince you you were ugly? She could see even then that you would grow into the beauty she could never be, save by sorcery. Number one: jealousy. Number two: even if you were unconscious of your attraction, those morons in the village would soon have sought you out as you grew. Notoriety of any kind she did *not* want. So, you became her hunched and ugly familiar, a Thing to be avoided by outsiders and ignored by her, for masked you were as anonymous as the furniture . . .

'Have you told him who you are?'

I blushed. 'Not yet. We—we didn't have much chance . . .'

'Chance enough now.' He dropped the stick he had been using to poke the fire as Conn came striding up towards us, his hair still darkened and wildly curling from the water. 'Come, Sir Knight, and be properly introduced to your affianced!'

'I'm not—'

'She hasn't—' we said together, and then would not look at one another.

'Come, come now!' said The Ancient, absent-mindedly throwing a handful of some pungent powder on the fire so that we all started back, eyes smarting from the smoke. 'Damnation and pestbags! Wrong one . . . Never mind. Chaudy-froidy then, you two?'

'Pardon?'

But apparently Conn understood his jargon. 'Not exactly. Not as far as I'm concerned. But she—' he hesitated. 'Her, Thingy I mean, er—She's different.'

'Not at all! You agreed to give your name to a person, not a pretty face. You too, flower.'

'That's another thing!' I said, glad to snatch at any excuse to change the course of this embarrassing conversation. 'You knew my real name all along, didn't you? All that business of flowers and flora and fauna and things . . .'

'Flowers?' echoed poor Conn, the only one not in the know.

364

'Of course I did! What's the use of being unusually gifted—' He failed to look modest, '—if one doesn't use the gift? Come on now, tell him your real name . . .'

I remembered my manners and curtseyed formally in Conn's direction. 'My name, Sir Knight, is Fleur de Malyon, only child of the late Sir Ranulf de Malyon of Cottiswode and his wife, Julia Flavia, second daughter of Claudius of Winkinworth . . . So my blood is just as good as yours!' I added childishly and glared at him.

'I never—'

'I know you didn't! But that's not the point . . .'

'Well what is? I still—'

'Not really! *Really*, really . . . It's just like buying a hen that lays one a month and then finding it performs every day instead. Or twinned lambs from a barren ewe . . . All of a sudden you develop a special affection for your liability—'

'I never said you—'

'I know you didn't! But that's not the point—'

'Well, in Heaven's name what is, then?'

'You thought it, even if you didn't say so!'

'I did not!'

'Anyway, I'm *not*, so there!' I left Conn standing with his mouth open and ran towards the river, angry tears rolling down my new-old face, not even sure why I was behaving this way. Was it because everything seemed to be going right, that now I had a reasonable face I also had bargaining power? Had I really wanted to be ugly, to make a martyr of Conn and a victim of myself? Wasn't I glad he would have a pretty face to look at? Did this mean that perhaps he would no longer want me, except as a plaything? Had my ugly security vanished? I didn't know, I didn't understand myself and, blinded by the futile tears, I ran straight into Snowy. 'Sorry!'

'No bones broken, Fleur,' he said mildly, and nuzzled my cheek. 'Come now, no tears: life is for enjoying, my little one, and what seems an insurmountable mountain one day will be a molehill the next. No, don't try to explain—' for I had opened my mouth to sick-up my troubles, '—there is no need. Come, we shall pay a visit together . . .'

'A visit?'

'To a place I know nearby. I have a tryst to keep. Are you too ladylike to ride astride once more?'

'I'm no lady . . .'

'You will be some time, whether you wish it or no. We must all grow up.'

So I vaulted to his back and clung to his mane as we splashed through the stream and moved into the dark forest on the other side. His coat was damp, so he, too, must have bathed in The Ancient's Pool of Truth. He carried me swiftly down a path that snaked among the cool, pale trunks of conifer that crowded in on either side, his hooves making no sound on the deep carpet of old needles. Although here it was dark, and the spring sun seemed far away, there was a sense of stealthy movement, of trees stretching and yawning from their sleep, and the slow stir of sap. Once or twice there was the russet flash of squirrel and roe deer, but for the most part only the soft beat of our passing. We emerged into a bare clearing, where the trees drew back into a circle—winter-blackened grass, a few scrubby bushes, a cloudy sky now visible above.

Snowy halted so smartly that I slid from his back.

'Are we here?' I said, struggling to my feet.

'We are . . . Come, I want to show you something.' He paced slowly to the northernmost corner of the clearing and stopped. There was a bare patch, moss and lichen scraped away but recently, a space surrounded by rock and stone, about as wide and long as a man. Just like a grave—

'Look!' said Snowy. 'Come and look close . . .'

I looked, and saw what seemed like a sheet of dirty ice, but as I knelt down the substance cleared when my breath touched it and it seemed as though I was staring down into a deep, transparent pool.

'Oh, dear Gods!' I cried. 'There's a body down there! Snowy, Snowy, help me drag him out! He may not be quite drowned. See, there is colour still in his cheeks, and—'

'No, my dear one,' said Snowy sadly. 'There is no life there, not as we know it. Do not break your nails, child, it is useless . . .' For I was scrabbling vainly against what I first had taken to be ice, then water, and now knew to be neither. It seemed like some thick, diamond-clear glass, and yet the hair of the drowning boy waved with the weeds and if only I could—I looked wildly round for a rock, a stone.

'It is enchantment,' said Snowy. 'And one of her best.'

'Her?' I questioned, but there was no need for the question. I knew at once who he meant. 'You mean you fell foul of Her, too? But how?'

And then he told me of the dance of death his beloved prince had performed to her bidding, how he and the witch had battled and how the prince now lay in everlasting sleep, locked in the crystal pool. I gazed down at the long limbs, slim hips, broad chest, tapering fingers; at the cloud of fair hair that framed the handsome, perhaps too handsome face.

'But—but there must be *some* way of releasing him!' I said. 'The spell she laid on us was dispelled by the dragon, that on Conn by a twist of words . . .'

'Oh yes, there is a way. But it means death, death to both of us. If I strike the crystal with my new golden horn, the one the dragon restored, then I cease to live in this world; I choose death, as mortals have to die. And my prince? Now, see, he dreams, and could be left forever in a kind of immortality. If I break the spell he dies also, for he is mortal like you. Do I choose that for him, or am I content to leave him to his dreams, and find my brethren in the west?'

'But how can you know what he dreams? See, he frowns, even now, and turns his head . . .'

Snowy reared up, and struck his front hooves hard on the crystal tomb. There was a hollow ringing, but no sign of a crack. 'How do I know whether she locked away nightmares in that living death?' I put my arms around his neck, but what could I say? How could I, with my petty temper and uncertainties, console this faery creature whose agony was so much greater than mine had ever been? How could I reconcile the love of human being and immortal, when apparently I couldn't even manage a mortal affair myself?

When we reached the camp again it was dusk. I slipped down from Snowy's back and joined the others round The Ancient's fire, but no one asked where we had been, or what we had done.

There was a vegetable stew for supper and rye bread, and then a truffle cake, tasting sweet and warm and earthy all at once and we all, even Snowy and Moglet and Pisky, had generous helpings. It was strange, it seemed to answer all the needs for taste in the world. In a way it reminded me—

'Mouse-Dugs!' I accused, sitting bolt upright and glaring at The Ancient. 'And something else . . .'

'Maybe. Maybe not,' he answered mildly, tapping the side of his long nose. 'And then again, perhaps.'

'But you know it makes us all act funnily . . .' I giggled, remembering Tom Trundleweed and as suddenly sobered, recalling Conn's proposal.

'Does no harm. After all, it's our last meal together: you won't need me any more after tonight.'

'Last meal?' said Conn. 'Why, are you going away?'

'Away? Where's away? You knew I could not stay with you once the quest was completed. There *are* other little crises here and there, you know, and also with increasing age I need my sleep. A hundred years perhaps, and then something interesting might turn up . . .' His voice trailed away and he poked the fire until it burned blue.

I looked at him, it seemed for the first time. The trouble was, he kept shifting; like three or four people playing peep-and-hide all at the same time. One moment there was a very, very old man with cheeks wrinkled like a forgotten russet and wearing a silly hat, the next a young helmeted warrior sat there, dark and grim-faced; again, a merry-eyed child with inquisitive eyes and snapping fingers, or a mild-faced middle-aged man with receding hair and protruding teeth . . . I shut my eyes: it was too confusing. Which *was* The Ancient? Or was he all of them? Or they all part of him?

I must have dozed off. When I opened my eyes again the fire was pale green with crackling silver sparks. The Ancient was an old man again, answering some question of Conn's of which I caught the echo but not the sense.

'. . . a question of a different dimension,' The Ancient was saying. 'And only those who have been there could understand. They don't very often come back. It is, I suppose, very much like a vivid dream; you are real and there and experiencing everything as though it were here and now, but when you return you have to re-adjust to now as if *now* were the dream . . . It's confusing, especially if something momentous is involved: sometimes you wish to stay too long, and then you are trapped in that time forever . . .'

Time-Travel. I dozed again, and then someone else must have asked a question—Moglet?—for The Ancient was answering again.

'No, once they have gone, let them go. They have a journey to make and are only confused if you try and call them back, and might lose their way. You would not wake a smiling child from dream, nor yet a peaceful kitten, would you? No, let them go: in peace, and with your blessing.'

Suddenly I did not like all this talk about 'going'—was he talking about death? I sat up, rubbing the sleep from my eyes.

'You say we don't need you anymore, now we have completed our quest—but we haven't.' I tucked my feet under me and glanced round at the others. Snowy's long mane hung down, hiding his eyes; Corby was preening, Puddy's throat moved up and down; Pisky's fins, beautiful now, waved gently from side to side; Moglet was purring with her eyes shut and Conn—Conn was looking across the fire at me, his eyes bright and soft at the same time: I took a deep breath and looked away. 'What I mean is this: we have lost our burdens, thanks to you and the dragon, and you told us that once this was done we should be healed—which we are—' I stretched, feeling with pleasure the way my spine arched back, '—but you also said we should find our own destinies, or words to that effect. And you made us bathe in that pool over there to clear our minds. Well, has it? Cleared them, I mean?'

The fire was now a soft, rosy pink and the cinders gold and purple.

'Oh, I think they all know what they want,' said The Ancient. 'But let's ask them, just to make sure . . .'

'Well, now,' said Puddy, 'let me consider . . .' He made up his mind. 'I have a picture in my mind of a low heath topped by a wood and dotted with broom, furze, gorse and thickets of bramble. There are two or three ponds—nothing too grand, you understand—and there is a jumble of rocks to hide amongst when the sun is too hot or the wind too cold. And there are others there of my kind, to exchange reminiscences with during the long days . . . A toad could grow old there, with pleasure.'

'And I sees a bit of countryside, nothing too grand neither, with a bit of a village with fields and woods behind and cliffs in front,' said Corby. 'Something like that place of the White Wyrme. A place where the wind stretches your wings and there's food when you seek it and company in plenty and shelter if the going's tough. But the great thing is to have the fellers to natter to and the youngsters growing up to be taught to take your place . . .'

'A lake,' said Pisky. 'Full of bright shallows and deep crannies, so you may have the sun and the shadow when you wish it. People to come down and feed you and trail their fingers in the water, which warms at their touch; and they call you by name and there are other, lesser fish, who need a king, a consort. By and by the lake runs with your kind and your children and grandchildren and great-grandchildren come to you for your wisdom . . .'

'A fire and fish and milk and a cuddle,' said Moglet. 'Mice to catch, the run of the rooftops, a length of twine to chase, a basket full of milky kittens . . .'

And they lapsed into their dreams again, dreams that now had a purpose.

I thought, jealously, that I could find them their sandy heaths with pond, cliffs and woods, a small lake, a warm fire; they didn't have to sound as if it would all have nothing to do with me.

'And you, Flora?' said The Ancient. The fire was gold, all gold.

I leant back in the long grass and looked up at the stars, so near I could reach out and pluck them, then blow them away like thistledown . . . 'I want a house, not a big one, but large enough to have separate rooms to sleep, to eat, to cook, to sew and just sit. It must be near enough to the sea for me to hear the seals sing, with a stream that wanders nearby. It would be nice if it were near a hump of hill that would shoulder away the north winds, and I should welcome the martlets in the eaves, come summer. I should grow herbs for the market and we should keep goats and chickens and have a big enough plot to keep us in vegetables . . .'

'We? Us?'

'Me and my husband and the children. Two boys and two

girls. And cats. And a dog, something to guard us when my husband is away, but who will go hunting with him when he is home. Oh, and his horse, a mare so we can breed.'

'And what is his name, this husband-to-be?'

I frowned; I had been able to see all this like a picture, a tapestry of bright colours, but somehow a draught had caught the weave and I could only catch glimpses, no faces, no names. 'I don't know: he won't keep still. Perhaps if I close my eyes . . .' I did, and was drifting off into a dream where I was standing near a gate in the sunshine with a blue butterfly on my finger and the scent of honey in my nostrils, when I heard someone I knew talking nearby.

'. . . and I thought I would go back to travelling, to fighting, the only things I knew, but I have changed my mind. Once, I thought that all I wanted was a sword to be mended and armour to be clean, but now I know there are other, more important things in life than wandering. I, too, want a house, a home; I want a woman to love me and be loved in return, and I want children as well. The sword I was so proud of shall be used no more. I want to mend bones, not break them . . .'

I smiled in my dream: that was my husband talking. I knew who he was now and I turned to greet him and the butterfly flew out of my hands into the sun . . .

THE LOOSING: UNICORN

Snowy's Choice

I AWOKE with a start, clear in mind and very cold, for Corby and Moglet had appropriated my cloak. Puddy squatted on a stone nearby, Pisky was dreaming in his bowl, Conn and The Ancient were huddled under their cloaks, the latter snoring gently. We were complete still, in spite of all the talk earlier, all seven of us, eight with—I knew immediately what had woken me: Snowy was gone. Not just physically, for he often wandered off on his own; no, it was more than that. It was as though he had suddenly severed the ties that had bound us all, cut us from his heart, banished us from his thoughts, and with a growing sense of anxiety I knew what he was about to do. No wonder he had been silent earlier.

Springing to my feet I scanned the far bank of the stream . . . There was a ghostly shimmer of white among the dark trunks of the trees. I should not have seen him at all but that it was the still hour before dawn, when there is an almost imperceptible lightening, as though one veil at least has been drawn back from night's dark window. Without thought I followed him, splashing through the shallows of the stream and scrambling up the bank, running onto the silent pine carpet that aisled its way through the trees, always that pale glimmer tantalizingly far ahead. He was so much faster than I, too, and it was only my desperate desire to catch him before he abandoned us all that lent speed to my stumbling feet.

At last I reached the clearing and there he was, standing before the crystal pool. Stumbling over a fallen log I fell to my knees with a jolt that knocked the breath from me. But with the last of my ebbing strength I called out to him with my mind, my heart.

He raised his head and looked over at me. 'I must,' he said. 'You know that, my little Fleur. Go back, child, to your love, and leave me to mine . . .'

'But my dear one, my dearest one, *we* need you too!'

Crying helplessly now, I buried my face in my hands; only to feel his soft nose against my wet cheek, his mane brushing my hair.

'Peace, peace . . . I loved you, too. Remember us!'

I listened to the soft thud of his hooves, dying away. Then there was silence. Opening my tear-blurred eyes, I started at a terrible crash and a scream of anguish I will always remember. Afterwards all that could be heard was the agonizingly slow tinkle as of thousands of glasses shattering.

I was almost afraid to look up. At the edge of the clearing, where the trees faded into darkness, stood my beloved unicorn, the first light of dawn catching the gleam of his golden horn. Standing by his side, one arm flung around his neck, stood the prince.

'You're all right,' I whispered. 'You're all right . . .'

They did not hear me, they could not hear me! Slowly they walked away from me into the forest, in a world of their own.

The tears were scalding my cheeks, as I watched them go, the most terrible thing of all was that I could see the trees beyond them right through their bodies, clearer and clearer, and the rising sun rose and dissolved them slowly, like mist, until they were merely a twist of smoke that rose into the air, hung for a moment like a frosty breath, and then were no more . . .

THE LOOSING: TOAD, CROW

Six Feathers

CONN FOUND me a little while later. He caught me close and hugged me, not entirely and unreservedly, but with a sort of courteous passion, as though he was not yet quite sure how I should welcome his embrace. 'Don't cry, girl,' he said. 'It's what they wanted. And there are other worlds than this.'

I looked up at last, wiping my swollen eyes. Everything had changed. Where there had been desolation, now the sun struck through the dim conifers, a diffused morning light that candled the wild anemones into pink and mauve and purple, touched late snowdrops into warm white, glowed among the violets, turned the coltsfoot into flame, uncurled the tiny daffy-down-dillies into open-faced wonder and crept like a hesitant visitor among the moss, lichens and first tender spears of grass. A squirrel raced down a tree and hesitated upside down, cocking his head, bright eyes gleaming, russet tail twitching as if timing the full-throated, sweet music of the wren on the branch above. A tiny round vole, furry, sat up and washed his whiskers in the dew.

I stood up. Where the crystal tomb had shattered a tiny spring rose and bubbled in the grass. With a breath that tore in my throat I stepped forward to pick up a scrap of gold that glistened in the clear water, and held it out to Conn.

'It's from his horn!' I said, marvelling at the three-spiralled gold ring.

Without a word, Conn took it from me, and gently slipped it on the middle finger of my right hand.

'Went at early light,' said Puddy, back at the camp. 'Packed up his things and just left.'

'Without even saying goodbye?' said Conn.

'Not exactly,' said Corby. 'Sort of said it was time he made tracks. Said you two would understand.'

'Well, I don't . . .'

''Course you do,' said Pisky briskly. 'He said so last night. Not in so many words, I admit, but I understood him to say that we didn't need him any more now we knew what we were looking for . . .'

'He left you a message,' said Moglet. 'Well, all of us, really. "A direction and some reminders" he said . . . Where's Snowy?'

So we told them.

'Glad for him,' said Puddy.

'Brave thing to do,' said Corby.

'Wish I had seen his prince,' said Pisky. 'Never seen a prince . . .'

'I wish I was brave,' said Moglet. 'When Snowy was here he made me braver.'

Conn looked at me. 'So, now what?'

'I suppose we pack up and go—wherever we belong,' I said slowly. 'Wherever that may be . . .' I would not look at Conn. 'Where's this "direction" you were talking about, Moglet?'

She led us over to a flat patch of ground. There, forming a rough arrow pointing southwestish, were six feathers. A rook's and a martlet's; a sparrow's and a cockerel's; an owl's and a dove's.

Conn took a sighting, then picked up the feathers one by one, scratching his head. 'The direction's clear enough, but what's the reminder? What have any of us, apart from Corby here, got to do with feathers?'

' "One each," he said,' said Moglet. ' 'So as we wouldn't forget . . ." '

I looked at the feathers in Conn's hand. 'Some of them do have meanings,' I said. 'Like flowers . . .'

'Of course! Cock feather for courage, owl for wisdom; martlet's traveller's luck; dove . . . Peace?'

'Or fidelity,' said I. 'Sparrow is for fecundity—Lots of babies,' I explained to Moglet, because we had been talking human-speech.

'And a rook does nothing but chatter, so I suppose that one

is for the power of speech,' said Conn. 'Well, who has what?'

I glanced at the others. 'They could apply to us all, one way and another. Why don't you just pin them to your cloak until we discover which is which? I said to Conn.'

'Right,' he said, twisting the feathers into a badge.

'Fleur, is everything packed up? Puddy, into my pocket! Corby, would you take a scan from the top of that tree and see if the path is clear: in line with the oak and the ash . . . Like a top-up before we go, Pisky? Moglet, you can run on a little until you get tired, then I'm sure Thingy—sorry, Fleur, won't mind carrying you for a while, I'll take the big pack, girl, if you can manage the other?'

I gazed at him in astonishment. Here was a new Conn, very definitely in command. He caught my gaze and winked. 'Amazing what a few feathers will do, isn't it?'

We left that enchanted place in early summer, but when we left its shelter we found that the world outside was still in early spring and none too warm.

For the first few miles I missed both Snowy and The Ancient, maddening magician that he was. Sometimes I would look up, half-expecting to catch a glimpse of our unicorn. But I knew in my heart that he had gone for ever, and gradually his loss became less hard to bear. But Conn kept up a fast pace with Corby calling out the route from overhead. Moglet continually got lost in the bushes chasing inviting smells. Pisky demanded to stop every time we came to a likely pond. We also had to buy provisions in the first village we came to, and I had Conn's shirt and my shift to wash as well as a rip in his hose to mend.

We travelled the way The Ancient had indicated, and were happy in each other's company as every day the light grew stronger, the sun rose higher and the land burgeoned. Every day the animals grew stronger, braver, more capable of providing for themselves, and every night they slept nearby and every morning I found it easier to talk to Conn than to remember their speech, and forgot to remember why . . .

Until one day, just after Conn's Easter Feast. It had been cold at night and sharp during the day for a week. Spring had held back her buds, but that morning we awoke to a change of wind; a warm southerly breeze shook the pale catkins and ruffled my hair. We had been climbing a small escarpment under a hazy sun, and at midday I suggested we sit under the trees for bread and cheese.

'Can we go just a little further?' asked Puddy, restlessly shifting on webbed feet. 'And a bit to the left?'

'What's "a little further"?'

'I don't know; just a feeling. Can we?'

If only I had said no—but would it have been any different in the long run?

Instead I picked him up in my hands and followed his directions, the others trailing behind. The land dropped away into a sandy slope, rock-strewn and gorse-covered. Beyond lay scrub, marsh, two ponds—

'Oh, Puddy,' I said. 'Not yet, not yet!'

'But this is the place,' he said simply. 'My home.'

'You can't! We belong . . .'

'Yes. We belong, and always will. But I had a picture in my mind, and this is it. Sorry, Thing dear, but this is where I want to live out the rest of my life.' He looked up at me. 'You wouldn't want to deny me this?'

I shook my head, not trusting any other form of communication.

'Glad for you,' said Corby. 'Hope it's as easy for the rest of us . . .'

'Nice ponds,' said Pisky. 'But too shallow for me, I suspect; a king-carp wants a larger territory. Still, I'm pleased you have found your destiny so soon. May luck go with you, my friend: cool summers and warm winters and food and company whenever you need it.'

'Happiness!' said Moglet.

'Good place for toads, I should think,' said Conn. 'Shall I carry him down to the nearest pond?'

'Next one's best,' said Puddy. 'Doesn't dry up in a drought, as I remember . . .'

But I had to carry him, not anyone else. Making my way down between rocks and yellow gorse I trod upon the soft sand where all about me were the tracks of other creatures: water-birds, lizards, frogs, newts, grass snake, and I saw several toads bound on the same journey as Puddy. A brimstone butterfly brushed my cheek and joined another dancing towards the bright waters. Midges patterned rhythmically above our heads.

Gently I set Puddy down, looking for the last time at that warm, warty little body, the bright eyes, the tapered toes, the gulping throat, and the slight, light scar where the emerald had lived for so long. The wind was soft, the water ruffled with cat's-paws, and all around bird-song, the calling of frogs late, toads early.

'Oh, Puddy,' I said. 'I didn't realize how much it would hurt!'

Conn came over and tickled his finger under Puddy's chin. 'Goodbye, old comrade: it was fun travelling together. Now, go and find a nice young lady toad . . .' I doubted if Puddy understood, for Conn was speaking human. 'Come on, girl, he'll be just fine now.'

But I knelt and cupped Puddy in my hands once more. 'I love you,' I said.

'Me too, human.' He nodded at Conn. 'I understood . . . Our ways are different now, but I shall not forget. It was good, was it not?' And he jumped from my hands and waded into the pond, turning at the last moment. 'May your destiny be near,' he said formally, 'and me and mine will always live in peace with you.'

'And I with you,' I answered, equally formally. 'And all creatures that share water and land shall be my concern and that of my children and theirs for ever more.'

'Thanks. Can I have my feather? The rook's, I think: I have rather got out of the way of speech, of gossip . . .'

My fingers trembled as I unfastened the feather from Conn's jacket. 'I'll stick it here, so you can see it when you come out of the pond . . .'

'Remember me!' he said, and I watched the gallant little form, moving a little stiffly, for he was well into middle-years, toad-time, swim down and down into the depths until he was hidden from view.

From then on it was as if I had forgotten how to speak to his kindred. I could never again, as long as I lived, converse with them as I had once done.

But Moglet snuggled up to me and whispered: '*I'll* never leave you . . .'

* * *

It was Corby's turn next.

After three days the wind changed yet again and came gusting in from the northeast, and farmers were looking anxiously at their orchards as the trees tossed and troubled, blossom falling too soon. One morning Corby declined breakfast, but stretched and flapped his wings, rising a few feet, then sinking down again, his eyes bright, his head restless.

'It's no use,' he said at last. 'I shall have to go; the winds are calling . . .'

'Oh, no, Corby! Not you, too!' I cried.

'Me too, lass. You knew it had to come.'

'But so soon!'

'Human years are not crow years; I'm not a youngster any more, you know.' It was true: around his bill, and under his wing where the sapphire had been, the feathers were greying. 'The winds tell me of that village I was speaking of, remember? And I know my brethren are waiting: I can hear them call down the wind. You wouldn't deny me that, now would you?'

What could I say? But I tried to put him off, till tomorrow, next week—

'The winds are right and I can smell my way home. If I wait . . .'

'But—I shall never see you again!'

'Who knows, who knows . . . Better choose a feather, I s'pose . . . Give us the martlet's: traveller's luck, that's what I need.' And he tucked it under his wing, where it blended with the rest of his feathers.

I wanted the others to help me to persuade him to stay, but once again they played me traitor.

'Fly the air like water,' said Pisky. 'And may you have food a-plenty, comradeship, and your choice of the ladies.'

'Happiness!' said Moglet.

'Fare you well,' said Conn. 'Enjoyed your company, bird . . .'

I sank to the ground and held out my arms and he waddled to my lap, his beak nibbling my ear. 'Now, come on then, human: your life lies ahead of you too, you know . . . We all knew this had to happen sooner or later, didn't we? Me and mine will always live in peace with you . . .'

'I love you,' I said, and he walked from my lap and rose into

379

the air, at first clumsily, then as a gust of wind caught him, riding the currents easily.

'Me too!' he cried. 'It was fun, wasn't it? Remember me . . .' and he spiralled upwards and then headed northeast into the wind, and the sun hurt my eyes so I could not see for the tears.

'The winds be with you,' I said unsteadily. 'And all creatures that fly the air shall be my concern and that of my children and theirs for ever more . . .'

But from then on it was as if I had forgotten how to speak to his kindred and I could never again, as long as I lived, converse with them as I had once done.

For days after, whenever I saw an untidy bundle of crow on the ground, or heard their harsh cry or watched their erratic flight in the air, my heart beat faster, hoping against hope that it was Corby. But it never was.

There was no bright destiny waiting for me that I could see. But I had Pisky still, trapped in his bowl, and my beloved Moglet.

And every night now she snuggled up to me and whispered: 'I'll *never* leave you . . .'

THE LOOSING: FISH

The Lake by the Castle

DURING THE next six weeks I was lulled into a sense of false security, for the four of us travelled undisturbed and undivided. There seemed no change in anyone although there was, so subtle that I did not note it at the time. Every day, imperceptibly, Moglet's and Pisky's voices dimmed to me and more and more I heard Conn's. I grew stronger in body, more capable of walking the distances he demanded and, in secret, I bought a mirror at the first opportunity and it was as The Ancient had said: I was pretty, or at least not ugly. I begged silver from Conn for a new dress, sandals, a fillet for my hair and he indulged me without quibble, for we had plenty of dragon-gold to spare.

Once or twice I asked where we were bound, but he only answered that he followed The Ancient's directions. Still, it was pleasant travelling, for the weather was warm and I did not have to decide anything. There was one puzzling factor: Conn had never again referred to the contract between us; at first I was glad not to have to think of an answer, then I became a little uneasy, and at last I became downright anxious. Had he forgotten? Did he think, perhaps, that my metamorphosis from masked hunchie to presentable female absolved him? Was the new me—because less pitiable, less dependent—less attractive to him also? I longed to ask and almost succumbed once or twice but held my tongue. I had rather anything than be rejected, for my love, dimmed and almost forgotten sometimes in the trials we had endured, nevertheless had always burned true and clear.

Every day when I woke I checked first to see whether he was

awake, perhaps to dwell on his sleeping, unprotected face, mouth calm under the curling red moustache; to watch the fluttering lids, so white against the lean brown cheeks; to touch, perhaps, the unruly curls that framed his head; and then, when he was awake before me, to note with delight the flash of those red-brown eyes, so clear, so positive; and all the while to watch the taut grace, the economy of movement, the sudden, fierce aggression. Had he some goal in mind that did not include me? I tried to remember what he had said that last night round the fire with The Ancient, when we had all eaten those tongue-loosening mushrooms, but could recall very little—something about healing instead of fighting? Memory teased at the fringes of consciousness, a cat's paw under the curtain.

The beginning of the Month of Maying, Beltane was warm, very warm, and it was with relief that we crested a hill and saw a castle off to our right, the town beneath us.

'Cool ale,' said Conn. 'And a fresh shirt. This one is in tatters.'

'I need more needle and thread,' I said. 'And more provisions all round.'

'Houses mean mice,' said Moglet. 'And things . . .' She did not specify what.

I looked at her. My kitten no longer, she was grown of a sudden to a full-size cat, small maybe, and dainty, but nevertheless mature.

'Did you say there was a castle?' asked Pisky. 'A real one? Lemme see, lemme see . . .'

He was growing out of the bowl I obligingly raised, and he now had twelve snail retainers. His fins were bright red, not gold, and they waved like the pennons on the litter we saw being carried down from the castle towards us.

Pisky contemplated the castle and gave a bob of satisfaction, then his eyes slid sideways. 'Is that gleam over there a lake by any chance?'

'Er . . . yes, I believe it is . . .'

'With trees all around, and a sunny bank covered with flowers?'

'Why, yes: but you can't possibly see—Oh, Pisky . . .'

'I only asked—'

'I know what you asked! And I won't let you! You can't walk over there, and I'm not going to take you, and besides the castle probably belongs to someone important and they will chase us away . . .'

I had been standing on the bank to let the litter go by. It swayed with white and gold curtains and was accompanied by six men-at-arms riding before and behind. Conn bowed courteously as it passed, the dust from flying hooves powdering his boots. I was so busy reprimanding Pisky that I shook his bowl, to emphasize my displeasure, and water splashed over my bare feet and I had to rescue a snail. There was an unseen command and the litter came to a lurching stop, and twelve unprepared horsemen reined in their skittish mounts with difficulty on the narrow path. The curtains of the litter parted and a dumpy little lady with her grey hair drawn back in an optimistic bun leant out. She spoke to one of the escort and he beckoned to us.

'The Lady Rowena wishes to speak with you!'

Conn held out his hand to me and slowly I descended the bank, Pisky's bowl in my hands, Moglet keeping pace safely from beneath my skirts. I curtseyed then looked up at the lady shyly. She had merry eyes, a round red face full of fine wrinkles, a generous mouth, and surprisingly looked all-over untidy. The gown she wore, though of stiffened silk, did not sit prettily on her overweight figure, the rings on her fingers were either too tight or too loose, hair wisped about her face because the pins in her bun had come out and she was eating sweetmeats out of a box and dropping the crumbs in her lap. But her voice was surprisingly young, clear and sweet.

'My dears . . . You did not mind me stopping you to have a word?' She didn't wait for a reply, but first dabbed at her sticky mouth with a linen cloth, then ineffectually flicked at the crumbs. 'Oh dear, oh dear, I am so . . . Now, what was I saying? Ah, yes. Stopping you . . . You *did* say you didn't mind? But I thought it was—yes, it *is*!—just what I have been looking for all these years! I send my men far and wide, and seven years ago I was all but promised . . . He said it had been stolen: probably kept it for himself, if the truth were known . . . Inferior ones I have been offered from time to time, but this!' She tumbled out of the litter, all skirts and grey hair and crumbs, and clasped her hands round Pisky's bowl. 'A king! A king Magnus golden carp! And in *such* condition! A youngster, not more than twenty years old—they take an unconscionable time a-growing, my dears—and this one has fifty—nay, seventy or more years to go and may end up as long—as long as my arm! And who would have thought ... It's my birthday, you see, and I had meant to treat myself to some more ... But no matter. Just to see *him* is sweetmeat enough! Here, my handsome fellow: a crumb of something special ... There!' And she dropped a sliver of sweet stuff from her sleeve into his bowl.

'What does she say, what does she say?' said Pisky excitedly, between further offerings.

I translated the relevant bits, adding: 'And she talks more than you do, even!' in human speech, but luckily she was casting about for the combs to fasten her hair at the time and didn't hear me. The combs and pins were all scattered in the dust, and she and Conn bumped heads companionably a couple of times before they were all retrieved.

I put my nose up against Pisky's: 'And she's not having you,' I added, but he was not listening either.

'There now, that's better!' said Lady Rowena, at last, patting a precarious pile. 'And now—why, I don't even know your names! A handsome knight and a pretty young lady, a king among fish and—ah, yes! I thought so: a little cat, and *so* dainty, too ... There must be a story to tell here ... Now, come: I have quite lost interest in a trip to town; we must all go back to the castle and have some refreshment. My husband must see the fish! You, dear child, squeeze up beside me in the litter ...'

And so, without going willingly at all, resisting her blandishments in my mind, I nevertheless found myself being carried back to the castle among the crumbs and scattered cushions, with a suspicious Moglet on my lap and Pisky's bowl cradled in hers. She chattered all the way to the keep, and although she asked questions she never quite waited for all the answers and by the time we were introduced to her husband, the lord of the manor of Warwek, she had twisted our names to Connie (me) and Flint.

Sir Ranulf was as tall, thin and cadaverous as his wife was

short, plump and rosy, but his eyes were brown and kind. 'Now then, Rosie dear, don't bewilder the young people . . .'

'Now, *would* I! But see here, Ranny darling, what the young lady has brought with her!' She exhibited Pisky, who was now beside himself, aware that all eyes were admiring. He pranced and danced, curved and pirouetted, rose and sank, fluted his fins and tail and pouted and gasped, till I muttered that he would run out of air.

'Shan't! But I want to see the water she talked about. Ask them, ask them, Thing dear! Please!'

I knew I had lost the battle as soon as they led us to the lake. It was large and calm, its northern side some hundred paces from the castle, shallow, reed-fringed waters dipping to a deep centre. On the eastern side were thick trees, to the south a smooth hillock and to the west the land sloped gently away. There were water lilies, a little artificial island, an arch of rocks, again artificial, and the water was warm and clear. A moorhen with her half-grown chicks swam away from the reeds at our approach and two black swans, younglings, curved to their high-winged reflections.

'Down in there,' said the Lady Rowena, pointing down into the water, 'there are twenty-five assorted fish, including three young golden carp princesses. My collection . . . It is mating-time now, and the water is the right temperature . . .' and she knelt down and pulled up her sleeve, testing the lake with her elbow, just like a nurse trying the water for a babe.

Sir Ranulf stood watching her, twirling the ends of his moustache. 'Loves 'em, you know. Never had any children . . . Pity. Spends all her time caring for the fish. Feeds 'em every evening, rain or shine. Designed all this herself. Been looking for one like yours for years. Pride of her collection and all that. Still . . .'

'Now then,' she said, 'I should love him above all the others; I can't help thinking of those carp princesses waiting too . . . They are a little larger, being females, and they usually spend their time near the western bank, under the lily-leaves, just hoping . . . But I could never try to persuade these darlings to part with him against their will!'

'It's his decision,' I said, knowing all the while what that decision would be, for he was leaping about now like something possessed. 'Oh, Pisky, dear one, is this what you really want?'

'Lemme see first,' he said, and gently I lowered his bowl to the waters and with a flash of silver belly he was gone. We waited for five minutes, for ten, for twenty . . . Oh, Pisky! I prayed for his return, I prayed for him not to like it, for disillusion to overcome the invitation of the lake. Conn looked at me, and in his expression I read that I was wrong.

'It's right, Fleur love,' he said, and at that moment Pisky's head popped out of the water at my feet.

'Oh, Thing dear, you've no idea how beautiful it is! Everything laid on! There are waters deep and cool, waters shallow and warm and a veritable underwater garden to exclusive design, with tall spawning-trees just to fin! And I found them, the lady fish: they are a beginning, a beginning! Oh, dear one, my father, my grandfather, my uncles, my great-grandfather—they never had it so good! A fish could be happy here for a hundred years, he could found a generation that would last a thousand . . .'

I turned to Lady Rowena. 'He wants to stay,' I said, and my throat tightened on the words, thick with unshed tears. 'A gift for your birthday.'

Her face lightened with joy, and she bent to tickle Pisky's chin, very gently. 'Bless you, King Carp!'

'Can I?'

'Pisky,' I said. 'You don't have to ask . . .'

'Good manners . . .'

'Yes,' I said. 'You always had those . . . Oh, Pisky, are you sure?'

'Sure as snails . . . Which reminds me: can I have them, please?'

I submerged his bowl in the water. 'There; let them crawl out in their own good time.'

'Now. I *am* king of the lake!' And, sure enough, the bowl was empty in double-quick time as I teased out the last of the weed.

'There, dear one . . .'

'Thanks . . .' He whirled away, but in a moment he was back, balancing on his tail. 'It was a tremendous experience, wasn't it? I rode the winds with a *dragon* . . . Bless you both, and you, cat. I love you. Remember me!' and he was away, lost forever to me beneath the water of his lake. I plucked the sparrow feather from Conn's jacket and stuck it in the earth at the water's edge.

'I love you, too,' I said unsteadily. 'The waters give you peace . . . And all creatures that swim the waters shall be my concern and that of my children and theirs for evermore . . .'

But from then on it was as if I had forgotten how to speak to his kindred, and I could never again, as long as I lived, converse with them as once I had done.

They asked us to stay at the castle that night, and the Lady Rowena found me a gold pin and a pearl necklace she wanted me to have, but we pleaded urgent travel and refused both hospitality and gifts, and left them with her searching for ant's eggs for her 'children' and spent the night in the nearest hostelry. I could not bear the thought of being so near to Pisky as to want to go and scoop him back into his bowl . . .

'Do you think he's all right?'

'The best of them all, so far.' I didn't like the last two words. 'He's found his kingdom. Be glad for him!'

'Oh, I am, I am!' I said, the stupid tears pressing hard behind my eyes, all the while cuddling my beloved Moglet, who had whispered earlier: 'I'll never, *ever* leave you!'

'But I do miss him!'

'That's not what you said when you had to carry him all those miles without spilling!' said Conn.

'That was different.' And it was. 'He will—he will live for seventy years?'

'*And* found a dynasty. All of whom will be exactly like him, down to the smallest tiddler who, in hundreds of years to come, will bore *his* great-great-great-grandchildren with the tale of his great-great-great-grandfather who spoke to dragons and, for a little while, carried a Dragon-Pearl . . .'

'You're laughing at me!'

'Perhaps just a little . . . But think of it rationally, Thingy— sorry, I just can't get used to the "Fleur" bit after all this time—if you can. Three creatures: a toad, happily basking in the sun in the company of his friends, and probably already having contributed to the increase of the toad population, is

387

sitting with his eyes shut digesting some horrible insect, and remembering happily his moment of glory with the Walking Trees; he's home, and has no more headaches . . . Then there's that great crow, soaring happily over the cliffs somewhere, enjoying the feel of the wind under his once-crippled wing; remembering, too, his part in the White Wyrme adventure; beneath him, somewhere, his mate is on the eggs that will produce other Corbys. He is fulfilled. And Pisky: his own kingdom, able to eat what he wants, when he wants, a harem attendant on every wish, and memories of a dragon, and of rescuing you from that thing in the water—Dear Christ, girl, let them be! It's just selfishness to want them back!'

'I know,' I said, cuddling Moglet tight. 'I know . . .'

THE LOOSING: CAT

A Gain and a Loss

IN THE morning Conn declared his intention of going to buy a horse. 'We're travelling too slowly.'

'To where?'

'How should I know? The way The Ancient pointed us.'

'But why the haste?'

'I don't know that, either. I just feel that something is waiting. And . . .' He hesitated again.

'Well?'

'Today I am going to buy a horse.'

So we went to the market, held in the square. How he knew, I do not know, but it was the monthly horse-trading fair and we dodged hooves as they were trotted up and down, some still shaggy with winter. There was no other stock; on inquiry I found that apparently one week it was fowl and pigs, the second sheep and goats, the third cattle and the fourth horses. I left Conn watching the trading and wandered among the other stalls, Moglet under my cloak, buying eggs, salt, cheese, bread, honey and my needles and thread. I found some excellent cured pork and bought a small sack of oatmeal; it would hardly fit in my hard-pressed haversack, but I reckoned if Conn found a horse we should have saddlebags as well.

I reached the pens where the last of the horses were being held; there were a few left, the dregs by the look of it, but I glanced at them all, nevertheless. One never knew—Perhaps, that one in the corner . . . A pale mare, filthy dirty, with matted mane and tangled, soiled tail, her ribs sticking through her coat; unclipped, uncared for. I moved over, pushing the others aside, and pulled a tuft of grass from the stones outside the pen.

'Here, girl . . .' She did not raise her head. I coaxed. 'Here my beauty . . .' The Roman nose lifted, dark brown eyes regarded me steadily, warm breath blew in my face. 'So it's Beauty, is it? Here, take it . . .' Gently she lipped the grass, no snatching. I studied the collar marks that had seared the skin, the missing slashes of hair on the rump where the switches had bitten deep. 'Here, Beauty, let's see . . .' I took the jaw and opened the mouth; six, seven years old, no more. She blew at me again, searching for response. 'I can't talk your language, sorry . . .' But I blew back gently and brushed aside the ragged forelock, then slipped into the pen beside her, to run my hands down her legs, lift the hooves to look for rot, try the lameness test, legs held bent tight for a minute. She was basically sound, as far as I could see, but had been badly neglected, was weak with winter fasting and hard work. I had hooked my haversack over the nearest post, now I popped Moglet on top. 'Keep an eye open; I'll be back in a minute.'

Conn was watching a rangy chestnut being run up and down, all rolling eyes and flaring nostrils, ears laid back.

'Mettle, yes, but temper too. Did you find anything?'

He turned. 'Was outbid on quite a nice grey, but I decided I would only pay twenty silver pieces top, and he went for twenty-two. You don't think this one . . .?'

'No,' I said firmly. 'All fire and no heart; short-winded too, I shouldn't be surprised. Come on, I've found one to show you.' I dragged him back to the pen and led him over to the corner. 'See? There's a good horse lost under all that hair. She's been hard-used, but with a little feeding-up . . .'

'She wouldn't carry your kitten, let alone you or me! She's clapped-out!'

I leant forward and pulled at her halter. 'You're not, are you, Beauty?'

'Beauty?' He managed to make it sound utterly ridiculous.

'Yes, Beauty.' The mare gave a soft whinny and lipped at Conn's sleeve. He moved back, frowning, then suddenly leant forward and pulled aside her forelock.

'I don't believe it! I-just-don't-believe-it . . .'

I pulled at his sleeve. 'Don't believe what?'

'Look here—there, on her forehead. Yes, there . . .'

There was a silvery patch arranged in a peculiar radiating whorl.

'Is that special?'

But Conn was dancing around like a mad thing. 'Special? I'll say it is! And of course she's Beauty, you were right there. When I got her in the Low-Lands she was booty, and that's what I called her: "Booty" or "Beauty". Seems she still knows her name. She ran off when—' He stopped abruptly.

'When the witch . . .?' I prompted.

'Yes. Well—The horse got frightened by her fireworks and I never thought to see her again. Yet, here she is. I'm sure of it.' He snatched a wizened apple from my pack and offered it to Beauty, who again took it gently and scrunched it happily, allowing him to pass his hands all over her. 'Hmm . . . a bit of muscle strain in the right shoulder. No problem. Well, well, well . . .'

'You're sure it's her?'

'Quite. Here's the little knot in her shoulder where she was nicked by an arrow just before I got her. How's my old Booty, then?' and the beast nuzzled his shoulder only to start back nervously, flinging her head up, as a diminutive man came and perched himself on the pen rails.

'Thinking of buying 'er, then?' He had a cold. 'Shouldn't. Not with 'er 'istory. Three owners already from 'ereabouts she's 'ad, and not a one satisfied. No good to none of them, she's been. Some feller east of here found 'er eighteen months back, tried 'er with the plough—'

'The plough!' snorted Conn.

'No good,' continued the snuffly little man, nodding his head. 'Got a good price for 'er though, none knowing 'er 'istory. Second feller, Wyngalf, tried putting her in shafts: no good. Still got a decent price, 'cos she were a looker, then. Peterkin's 'ad 'er overwinter—couldn't even put 'er to 'is stallion, she weren't 'aving none. No good for anything, if you asks me . . .'

'Perhaps not round here,' said Conn, sarcastically. He ran his hand over the scarce-healed weals on her quarters. 'Doesn't look to have been well-treated.'

'That Peterkin's a violent man, 'e is. 'Eard 'im say as 'e'd carve 'er up for meat 'imself if she didn't fetch ten of silver . . .'

'Well,' said Conn. 'In spite of what you say, I've a mind to her.'

The man jumped down from the rails. 'Don't say as I didn't warn you, then.' He shuffled off, then looked back. ''E'll ask fifteen, but'll take ten . . .'

Conn tossed him a coin. 'Thanks for the advice. Get something for that cold of yours . . .'

We got her for the ten pieces of silver: no one else was interested beyond knacker's price. Afterwards Conn brought second-hand bridle, saddle and saddle-bags cheaply and led her to the nearest stables to give her a rub down, clean and file her hooves, curry her mane and tail and bed her down with oats and a bran-mash. 'We'll spend another night here,' he said cheerfully. 'Give her time to get used to the saddle again tomorrow. See if the inn can put us up again, will you?'

'I'll leave the haversack with you, then,' I said, setting it down. 'And come back and let you know. Come on, Moglet . . . Moglet? Oh, Conn! I've lost Moglet!'

He stopped rubbing Beauty down, hearing the anxiety in my voice. 'She was with us at the pens, because she hopped off the haversack when I gave Booty that apple. Don't worry, she can't have gone far. Just got lost in the bustle, I expect. She'll turn up.'

Frantic, I ran back to where the horses had been corralled: no kitten-cat. I wasted time asking passers-by whether they had seen her; some were sympathetic, others just stared or tapped their foreheads significantly. I asked at every open doorway I could find, but still no cat. There were a couple of tabbies, a black and white, a ginger tom, but no multicoloured striped/brindled/spotted cat like Moglet. At last, almost crying, I went back to the stables, where I found that Conn had spread out some sacking in a corner and laid out bread, pies and ale.

'No inn tonight. Too late to get a decent lodging,' he said, seeing from my face how miserable I felt. 'We'll have a bite to eat and then I'll have a look with you for that wretched animal of yours.' He was only teasing with the 'wretched', I knew that, but I couldn't stop myself.

'You don't care about her!' I sobbed. 'You don't care about me, either! Now you've got that—that wretched horse of yours back again all you can think about is going off adventuring! You don't need us anymore . . .'

'Don't be silly!' He was quite sharp with me, a fact that set me wailing again. 'Of course I care; but she'll be back—and, if not, don't you think she might have found something *she* wants to do, somewhere *she* wants to go? She's got the use of her paw back now and this town is full of nooks and crannies where mice hide out. She's probably out hunting her dinner—'

'She may have been stolen!'

'Why on earth would anyone want to steal a scrawny little scrap like that? Be sensible!'

But I didn't want to be sensible, all the more so because although he had been quick to assert that he did care about Moglet, he still hadn't mentioned me . . .

I ran out into the street, darkening now, with shadows deep in the alleyways. 'Moglet! Moglet!'

A little figure, tail high in greeting, came running down the centre of the road. 'I'm here: stop shouting!'

I scooped her up into my arms, my heart beating more wildly than hers, and now that I had her safe I scolded her like a mother who has snatched her child from under the hooves of a runaway horse, anger proportionate with relief. 'You're naughty! Where on earth have you been? You had me worried sick—didn't you hear me calling?'

'I was hunting . . . Two mice! And I was invited into a house for supper. Such *nice* people! They fussed over me as though I belonged to them and had been lost, and in truth it *did* feel like some place I had been before. There is a girl there, younger than you perhaps, and she can't walk properly—like me when I had the stone in my paw. The back of their house leads down to the river and it's there, in their mill, that I caught the mice. And the miller's daughter, the one who is crippled, was watching him work and and he saw me catch the mice and put me on her lap for a cuddle. And he has a little cart to wheel her in, because she can't walk, and I went back to their house in the cart with her, and they gave me a bowl of cream, real cream! Then they let me out, and the girl was sad. And then I heard you calling and I came . . .'

I had never heard Moglet talk so fast, so excitedly, nor had I been able to understand her so well for ages. At first I was so glad to get her back that the implications of what she was saying didn't register, but at last I understood: Moglet had found a family, a home—

She was the one of them all, perhaps, that I had loved the most, because she had been, then, like I was: small, crippled, female, frightened and tatty. Now she was a full-grown cat, quick, alert, loving and whole, and she wanted a fire to dream by, mice to catch, a bowl of cream and a basketful of kittens to croon over and tell how once she had been on a quest and had carried a dragon's diamond in her paw. And the kittens would not know what a dragon was, but would listen just the same. But she would be able to catch a spider for them and tell of the one that was as big as a house . . .

But I could give her all that! She could come with *me* and I would give her cream and shelter. She didn't need this—or the crippled girl who had to ride in a cart. I opened my mouth and my mind to say all this, to explain to Moglet that she mustn't be misled by the first family who fancied a mouse-catcher, to tell her that I needed her because I had no one else, but instead I listened to myself say: 'Well, I'm glad you're back, 'cos I've saved some pie. Tell you what, we'll all go back and see these people tomorrow, shall we, and you can see that crippled girl again. I'm sure she'll be glad to see you.'

And Moglet purred, and lifted her face to my hand and showed her teeth and half-closed her eyes and opened her mouth to take in all my scent, the greatest show of affection a cat can give, and the back of my throat ached with the effort not to cry.

Magdalen was actually a very nice girl; small, pale, with a twisted and shortened leg, but eyes that were loving, and hands that gentled Moglet with a skill I had never achieved. Her parents had married late in life and obviously adored their only child. The home they lived in was one of the more prosperous in town with a large kitchen and eating room on the ground floor, with a solar and three bedrooms above.

I began by resenting the whole idea of the family and ended up by liking them, although I confess I was surprised by the way they had taken to Moglet, until the wife explained.

'It's like this, my dear; when that little cat appeared it was just like seeing a ghost! You see our mother cat, bless her, lived to fifteen years and only passed away last winter. She hadn't had kits for seven years and the last one she had was stolen off this very doorstep when our Mag was seven years old, and this one is as like as two peas, even to the one white whisker. My husband says she's a champion mouser, like our Sue that died, and Mag just fell straight in love with her! She cuddled her like she never did with dolls when that kitten was stolen. It were she, though, as knew that the cat belonged to someone else, and insisted we let her go, otherwise I'd have shut that door tight last night, bless me if I wouldn't! As it was, she cried fit to flood the meadows when the little thing slipped out and was away . . .'

I looked across the solar to where the sun shafted through the windows; Magdalen had rolled a scrap of leather into a fair imitation of a mouse, ears and tail and all, and had attached it to a length of her sewing silks, and now Moglet was playing catch-as-catch-can among the rushes, eyes intent, body totally involved. I realized with a pang that I had never played with her like that . . . At last the girl drew the toy up onto her lap and Moglet followed, to settle down in the sunshine with a yawn of delicious tiredness.

'Would you let her have kittens?' I asked.

'First thing,' said the father (I never did find out their proper names). 'I could do with a good mouser or two in the mill and there's plenty of the neighbours as could do with one too; been a shortage of good ones since our Sue died.'

'There's a nice ginger tom down the road,' said the mother. 'He might do.'

I glanced again at Moglet; she was purring. Yes, the ginger tom 'might do' very well.

The girl glanced across at me, but her hands did not cease their caressing, I was glad to see. Her speech was slightly impaired, but I could understand her well enough. 'But you love her too: we can't take her away. It wouldn't be right.'

'She is not mine, nor yet Conn's,' and I nodded in his direction. 'She is her own creature, and as such is free to choose her own destiny. And if you will care . . .?'

'Always,' and she gently stroked Moglet's ears the right way so that she sighed happily and settled deeper.

I plucked the cock's feather, emblem of courage, from Conn's jacket and gave it to the girl. 'Let her play with this sometimes . . .'

But we had not reached the turn in the street when there was a cry behind us and Moglet was in my arms.

'You are leaving me!'

For the last time I hugged her. 'But you want to stay. So, we were only leaving you without saying goodbye because we thought it was best. Besides, I hate goodbyes . . .'

She looked up at me. 'You don't mind? I thought . . . I thought . . .'

'Of course we mind! Don't be silly!'

'But I always said . . .' she hesitated.

'That you would never leave us,' I supplied. 'But—but *she* definitely needs you. She—she hasn't a dragon to cure her of that poor leg, and because you were crippled once you will be able to understand her better. And I am cured, and I—I have Conn.'

'I still promised never to leave you . . .'

'And I said all sorts of things. And meant them, at the time. Circumstances change, my dearest one, and so do we.'

'You won't cry, and call me back?'

'I can't promise not to cry, but I will try not to call you. But if I do, and you hear me, just ignore it . . . You may miss us too, you know.'

'Oh, I will, I will!' and the little wet nose touched mine. 'Always . . . But it was fun, wasn't it?'

I nodded, not trusting myself further.

'Even the bad times . . . I'll never forget!' She purred anxiously. 'Are you *sure*?'

'Oh Moglet! You're grown-up now, so am I! Yes I'm sure. Go, and live your life, and kittens and mice and cream be yours always!' I spoke the formal words. 'And all creatures that walk the earth shall be my concern and that of my children and theirs for evermore . . .'

She licked my right ear, briefly, rough-tongued, and then sprang down and away, back to where her new mistress waited hopefully by the open door.

'I love you!'

'Me, too,' I whispered.

'Remember me . . .' and tail up, little pale dot-and-dash under her tail the last things I saw, she went happily to her new life.

'Oh, I will, I will!' and I turned to Conn and cried into his leather jacket until the front was all damp with my tears.

But from then on it was as if I had forgotten how to speak to her kindred, and I could never again, as long as I lived, converse with them as once I had done . . .

The Journey Home

IT WAS a long journey, that last one, the longest he had ever made in one haul. At first the very flush of enthusiasm, the knowledge of his quest ended, the eager thought of Home, carried him hundreds of miles with ease, helped by a fresh westerly. Initially, too, it was easy to forget the hunger, the thirst, the scorching heat as he flew nearer the sun by day, the searing cold of brittle nights, but he had forgotten how low his reserves had become over the bitter seven years of waiting. At first he had thought the sudden dizzy drop of a thousand feet or so, the giddy turns of a hundred-and-eighty degrees, the retching and nausea, were due to the weather and his inevitable weariness but at last, after an unplanned and disorientated plunge into the black cold of a northern fjord, which almost extinguished his fires forever, he realized that part of his trouble was lack of nourishment. Then, also, he remembered Precept No. 137 of Dragon-lore: never forage in a northern winter.

There was no food: berries, a pitiful few; nuts, a mere clawful; moss and cones a bland taste, no more, and the icy waters of the tarns and rivers gave him stomach-cramps and hiccoughs. Vainly he searched for frog, toad, newt, fish: they were all hibernating and sifted easily through claws grown desperate with famine as they scooped the silt of scummy, half-frozen ponds. And all the animals were crowded too deep in safe burrow or fled too fast to catch, and the domestic ones were close-byred or cottage-stabled for the winter.

Somehow he kept going, though his flights became shorter and lower, so that fanged mountains with glaciered saliva reached hungry jaws to scrape his belly. His tired eyes were forced to follow the slow, silver snake-wind of rivers instead of a higher scan for the headwaters and a shorter route, and all the while a north-falling dragon-shadow kept pace on the earth beneath, sometimes ahead, sometimes behind, depending on sun or moon. And then came the snow, borne in from the north in goose-feather flakes, striking across his path in cruel, blinding flurries that weighted his back and iced-up the trailing edge of his wings till he was forced to lie-up in a convenient pine forest for a few days, pondering his mistake in not taking the longer, southerly route home; but it was too late for him to change his mind for the detour would cost him precious weeks, and he doubted whether he would now have either the strength or the memory. His enforced stay in the forest brought him some sort of luck, however, for he found a cache of frozen meat left by some hunter, and managed enough heated breath to thaw out the chunks to an acceptable chewy stage, though he suffered from indigestion for days afterwards.

But there were many, many hundreds of miles still to go and the weather, if anything, grew worse. It was a mere shadow of a dragon that turned due south for the last few leagues and drifted down like a spent leaf into his own, welcoming valley. There was a cessation of singing wind in his ears, no more rattle of sleet on his stretched skin, no creak and flap of shedding wings. His breath no longer rasped painfully in his throat. It was suddenly warm in this sheltered valley, though the towering mountains that surrounded it seemed to touch the sky, their snow-covered tips tapering to the sun.

The sun! The golden sun that tinted the yellow skin of the villagers who crept out to look, to touch him, to wonder as he lay at last in the dusty square under the green Heaven-Trees that sheltered the temple. A tonk! tonk! of bells heralded more people still and there was the smell of cedar and sandalwood. A silken robe was slipped beneath his tired limbs. Warm, scented oils washed away the crusted tears of effort from his eyes and the dried saliva from jaws grown strangely slack. There was rice, too, in flat wicker baskets, but suddenly he was hungry no longer. Hunger and tiredness had no place here. All he wanted was the friendly scrape of scale against wing-tip, the intimate caress of spade-tail, the warm, ashy smell. He opened his eyes and there they were: gold upon silver upon red upon green upon yellow upon purple, breathing a fiery welcome from the steps, the walls, the doors of the temple. He lurched forwards crying his greeting, a clashing of cymbal and rattle of drum—

But there was no answering greeting, no surging forward to welcome him. The dragons were not real dragons, they were stone, they were wood, they were plaster, they were paint. He tore his claws reaching for them and swung round and round in his dismay until he was circled by his own disillusionment. The villagers fell to their knees at the sight of his distress, their pigtails bobbing in the dust. At last there was one brave, or wise enough, to come forward and explain: an old, old man with a moustache that hung like white string to his knees, and who lisped in the faded, once-familiar sing-song that the dragon remembered from his childhood. He told how the last of the dragons had left the valley in his father's father's time, taking their treasure back with them to the mountains from whence they came, but leaving gold to gild the temple and memory to make their likenesses.

And the tired dragon lifted his eyes to the distant peaks and he sighed.

After a little while he took out his pearl and looked at it for a long, long time. Then he took out the diamond, the ruby, the emerald and the sapphire and looked at them. He rolled the pearl on his tongue and then he put all the jewels back in the pouch under his jaw and sighed again and then seemed to fall asleep and all the people tiptoed away, shushing each other to let him sleep in peace.

But in the morning he was gone, leaving only the shallow depression where he had lain and several baskets of uneaten rice. So they painted his picture on the temple, in the one space above the doors that was left: a small blue dragon with a red belly and a pearl the size of the moon curled on his tongue. And they pointed out to visitors the high peaks where he must have gone and told of his last visit, until the paint faded from the temple in the time of their children's children and the dragon passed into legend.

THE GLEANING: DOG

Wolf-fog

'WHERE THE hell are we?' said Conn.

'How do I know? You're the one who's supposed to be guiding us.'

The fog lay like a dense, muffling blanket all around. When we stopped all we could hear was our own breathing, the chink of Beauty's harness, the stamp of her hoof.

'I'm sure I heard . . .'

'What?'

'Something. It sounded like a dog howling. Yes, there it is again!'

'I can't—'

'Shut up, and listen!'

We were near to quarrelling. Over the past few days our relationship had worsened, and now, with the added uncertainty of direction, the baffling fog, the hint of something crying in the mist, I felt I hated everything and everybody, including Conn.

For nights I had lain awake mourning my lost ones and he had wearied of my sullenness and misery and told me so. And I had snapped back at him that he was unfeeling, uncaring, a man without sensitivity—and so it had gone on. Vanished was the comradeship, the warmth there had always been between us; instead there was a tension, a bitterness, a resentment on my part and irritation and arrogance on his. No longer did I wake early from sleep just to wonder at his resting form, nor watch his lithe movements during the day, nor tease a smile from those curving lips. No longer did he pay me little compliments, pick me a flower from the hedge, glance at me sometimes with an unfathomable look in his eyes that made me turn away, suddenly embarrassed. No, it had all gone as sour as yesterday's milk and every moment we spent together drove us farther and farther apart—

There it was again, a high, plaintive keening, a dog mourning. I shivered. Conn sighed with relief. 'We must be near a farm, a village, some habitation. That dog is tethered, not roaming. Come on.' He pulled at Beauty's bridle and started off in the direction of the sound, me trailing miserably behind, damp and cold. Who would have imagined weather like this in high summer?

The howl came again, but apparently from another direction, more to the left. We stopped.

'This damned fog,' muttered Conn. 'It distorts everything . . .' We listened, and again came the keening. 'Left it is,' said Conn.

We found the village, if you could call it that, after another half-hour of tripping and stumbling. The fog, if anything, was worse. There were some half-dozen hovels, single-roomed, and a somewhat larger farmhouse. Doors were closed, tallow-dips flared at midday through chinks in the shutters, but no one, not even dog or cat, was abroad. We groped our way towards the gate to the farmyard, for none but funerals or weddings went to the front door, and all the while we heard the keening of the dog grow louder.

'What the hell—!' I stopped behind Conn, fighting to control Beauty, who was doing her best to dislodge his hold, puffing and snorting and stamping her hooves, trying all the while to sidle away from whatever it was that hung threateningly from the tall farm gate. Peering past Conn's shoulder I saw snarling teeth, grey hair—'Thank the Lord!' said Conn. 'It's only the skin . . . Still, one of the biggest I've ever seen.'

It was a wolf-pelt, torn with rents as if from sword or spear, and those teeth were fighting even in death. 'Poor thing,' I said. The eyes had gone long since, probably pecked out by birds. I lifted one of the huge, bony feet and the dry claws rattled.

'Poor thing, my arse!' said Conn. 'A great brute like that could even take a pony, let alone sheep or pig. Villagers were well rid of him. Shouldn't like to come up against such myself, without weapon.'

But still I held the lifeless paw, remembering the wolves at the Castle of Fair Delights, so long, long ago . . . Had he forgotten so easily?

The gate was firmly bolted, and Conn rattled the latch. 'Hola! Anyone at home?' For a long while it seemed as though the fog itself held breath, then a door opened and shut and we heard uncertain steps across the yard.

'Who's there?' It was a woman, the voice thin and quavery with a hint of fear beneath.

'Respectable travellers, Ma'am,' said Conn in his most reassuring voice. 'Me and—' he glanced at me, '—my wife, seeking shelter and a bite to eat. And with pence in their pocket.' He jingled his purse.

'Go away!' came the uncompromising reply. 'We want no strangers here!'

Conn glanced at me again, a quick frown on his face. 'Strange: a poor village that needs no company and no copper . . .' He raised his voice again. 'Bring your lantern nearer and see that we pose no threat to you and yours. We have but one sword and two daggers between us.'

There was hesitation, the steps retreated then advanced again, and now I could hear clearly the click of dog's claws on the stones. I peered through a knot-hole in the thick wood of the gate and saw a middle-aged woman, some forty years old, advancing across the yard, lantern in one hand, a great bitch-hound on a leash in the other. She was an old dog, with thick curly hair, a long, lean body and small ears, obviously built for speed. I wondered if it were she we had heard howling earlier. They arrived at the gate and the woman thrust aside a looking-panel and gazed out at us.

Conn returned her gaze steadily. 'We mean no harm, as you can see. Just shelter for the night, for 'tis miserable cold and dripping out here. And perhaps a bowl of broth and bread and a handful of hay for the horse?'

'There's no hay and no broth neither,' said the woman, her eyes fearful in the wavering lantern-light. 'And no letting-in of strangers. And hasn't been since that great devil came to the village at the turn of the year.' And she indicated the great wolf pelt. The bitch hound reared up, as tall, taller, than the woman, and put her muzzle to the dried pelt. Gently she blew through her nostrils, stirring the skin, making a strange growl-snarl-wail in the back of her throat. Conn started and cursed. The dog turned her brown yellow-flecked eyes on him, considering.

'By the Saints! 'Tis one of the Great Ones!'

'Great Ones?'

'Aye, the Great Dogs of Hirland.' As always when he was excited his voice held a singing lilt. 'By all that's Holy! Here, girl . . .' and he placed his hands on either side of the great muzzle that poked out through the looking-panel. The woman gasped and dropped the wildly flickering lantern, as the dog growled softly in her throat but did not move her gaze from Conn's nor pull away from his hold.

The woman retrieved the still-burning lantern. 'She's supposed to bite!' she whispered, her eyes large with distress. 'She's supposed to kill!'

'Not this one,' said Conn confidently. 'Not with me. She's a princess, this one, and princesses know their own . . .'

The great dog still regarded him steadily, then whined softly and turned to look at me, her muzzle still in Conn's hold.

'She wants something,' I said. 'More than anything ever before . . . I don't know what it is.'

'She's after that pup of hers,' said the woman, and I could see by her guilty expression and the hand she clapped to her mouth that she had not intended to speak of it.

Conn released the dog. 'What pup? Oh, come on now: you started to tell us.'

She hesitated, then made up her mind. 'You'd better come in.' She unbolted and unlatched the gate. 'He's away hunting . . .' She nodded back at the house, and I presumed she was speaking of her husband. She led the way into the yard and Conn looped Beauty's reins over a post, loosened her girths and offloaded the saddle-bags.

Inside the hall a cheerless fire burned fitfully, adding smoke to the fog that curled under the door and through the ill-fitting shutters. 'You see? Even the fire won't burn true!'

'Insufficient draught,' muttered Conn out of the side of his mouth, then he put some coin on the table, addressing the woman. 'Some bread, perhaps?'

She put the coin back in his hand. 'What I can give you will be a gift: we have tempted the Gods far enough.' From a

404

cupboard she brought stale bread, a rind of cheese, and from the barrel in the corner two horn mugs of sour ale. "Tis all we have since—' She shivered.

'Since?' Conn prompted, making a face as the liquid touched his tongue.

'Since—What harm can the telling do now?' She was persuading herself. 'None, I reckon . . . Well, it was like this . . .'

Like all tales it had grown in the telling and now was so twisted and twined with her own thoughts and local superstitions that it took two or three times as long as it should, but the bare facts were these. It had been a late, cold spring and just before lambing a number of wolves had pestered the village, setting the sheep and cattle to uneasiness and the dogs to singing the night long. This was not unusual, for many outlying villages were used to wintering packs like these, on the scavenge. What was unusual, apparently, was that their leader was a giant wolf, more cunning and ferocious than any seen before, who had led his inferiors in raids of such daring that the villagers had lost three tups and two swine before they had had time to organize themselves.

All efforts to drive the wolves away had failed, until the woman's husband had a bright idea. His hound, now old but still fertile, had come into season and he had staked her out one night and watched from the safety of a tree. It appeared that the giant wolf had not been able to resist this lure, and on the second night the husband had gathered all the able-bodied of the village together and when the wolf returned they had rushed in and slain him on the spot, though he had not given up without a fight. The pelt had been borne home in triumph and nailed to the gate. The village had celebrated, in anticipation of the routing of the wolves and a return to normality. Not so: from that moment the cattle had suffered from a murrain, the ewes had slipped their lambs, the hay crop had been blighted, blossom had not taken, milk went sour between udder and pail and the women had miscarried.

Apparently, the wolves had disappeared, but their presence was still felt. Paw-prints were spotted in the village street, chickens and a goat went missing, yet never was there clear evidence. No one ever *saw* anything . . . Added to this, the hound was now clearly in pup, and her behaviour so peculiar that it was suspected she was suffering from wolf-bite. She was short-tempered, skulked in corners, cried at night and would not hunt anymore. Eventually she whelped, one pup only. The husband and wife were not allowed near her nest in the barn, so it was only after the pup was able to crawl out into the open that they could see what had happened: the pup was part hound, part wolf, and the bitch was so intensely protective that she would still not let anyone near. Twice the husband, fearing the wolf blood, had tried to kill it and twice the bitch had forestalled him. But when the pup was some seven or eight weeks old, he had lured its dam with fresh-killed hare and had tied her up; he was about to hit the pup over the head when thick fog swirled in about them and they had heard the howling of a wolf at noonday. The wife had warned him against shedding the pup's blood in the face of these obvious signs and he had said: 'Let his kinfolk have him then.' Hurrying across the fields to the great pit where all the village rubbish was dumped, a deep gash in the earth with unscalable sides and a deep pool at the bottom, he had tossed the pup down. He had heard a yelp, a splash, then silence. He wasted no time in making for home, lantern swinging wildly, breaking into a run when he imagined he heard the padding of feet behind him.

This had happened only the night before last. Since then, the bitch had howled constantly, driving all distracted, and the unlifting fog was full of wolves, grey and vengeful.

It was a strange enough story. I looked over at Conn for his reaction, but he was frowning. The hound stood quietly by the door, now and again scratching at the lintel and whining softly. The wife jumped to her feet. 'I shouldn't have let her loose! My husband said to hold her fast, lest she go after the pup!' She rose to her feet, but Conn forestalled her.

'Wait a moment . . . Fleur—Thingy dear—what's to do?'

For a moment I was so flummoxed with him calling me 'dear' again that I could only stare, then I pulled myself together and went over to the hound. Lifting her chin in my hand I looked into her eyes aslant, avoiding the threat of out-staring, and although I could no longer receive her thoughts in my mind, nor give her mine, yet I could read puzzlement, hatred, yearning. I put my hand on top of her head and my fingers tingled, and all became clear.

I beckoned to Conn and he came to stand beside me, putting his hand over mine on the dog's head, then snatching it back and shaking his fingers. 'Like touching iron in a thunderstorm! What is it?'

I kept my voice low, looking over my shoulder at the woman, who had backed away from us. 'I don't want her to hear, otherwise they might destroy this one too . . . Somewhere near here is a Place of Power, where the lines cross—Oh, you know!' I said impatiently. 'Don't you remember The Ancient saying that power sometimes lies beneath our feet, neither good nor evil, just waiting to be used?' He nodded, his eyes grave, his fingers fiddling with the little silver cross he wore about his neck. 'Well, this one, without knowing it, has tapped the power. She grieves for her lost pup, she mourns the great wolf that was its father, and it is she that has cursed the village, albeit without conscious evil . . .

'You said she was a Great One?'

Conn nodded. 'In Hirland her line is royal.'

'Then would she have the greater power . . . Poor lass!' And I kissed the wide brow while the woman cowered behind us in terror. 'You don't know what it's all about, do you?' I whispered softly to the dog. 'What's her name?'

'He bought her from traders, ten year back. Deirdre, they called her . . .'

'Deidre of the Sorrows,' said Conn. 'I'll tell you the story sometime, Fleur.'

My heart jumped and I reached for his hand and held it tight, for all the good was suddenly back between us. 'Right now this princess is sorrowing for her pup. Coming?'

He nodded and turned back to the woman. 'We are—we are going to lift the spell. But we shall need the bitch. All right?' Without waiting for an answer he lifted the latch and we slipped out into the fog, now denser than ever. 'Which way?'

'Follow the dog . . .'

Out through the gate, down the narrow street, up on to the downs. I stumbled and fell once but dragged myself to my feet, for the great bitch was outrunning us. Instantly Conn whistled and she turned, ears pricked.

'Wait, girl, wait!'

After that we moved more easily, for she kept turning, to accommodate our slower speed. Behind us the fog closed in and I, too, could hear the pad of paws keeping pace to our right. I looked at Conn, but he had not heard it as clearly as I. 'You are going to have to help me.'

He misunderstood. 'Not far now, I shouldn't think. Here, take my arm: I won't let you fall again, I promise.'

I smiled to myself. Darling Conn, so eager to help even if he didn't understand . . . We were panting up a slope now and ahead of us the bitch had stopped and was whining softly. We reached the brink of the pit and gazed down together at the precipitous sides, the jagged boulders, the bushes clinging with precarious roots to the few pockets of earth.

Conn dropped a stone into the depths and counted under his breath before we heard the splash. 'It's deep: we'll need a rope.'

'You go back for one. I'll stay here.'

The instant he had gone I felt the wolf-fog close in about me. 'I'm going down,' I said steadily into the mist. 'He shall be brought up, never fear. Just wait, and do not harm my friends.'

Hitching my now-cumbersome skirt into its waistband, longing for the once-despised trews and jacket, I lowered myself over the edge, clinging to a rowan tree as I did. I looked up at the bitch; she whined, and paced the edge of the pit. 'It's all right, old girl; stay there. Conn will know where I've gone down. I'll bring your pup back if he's there, never fear.' Slowly, cautiously, I lowered myself down, grabbing at whatever prominence or crevice I could for a finger- or toe-hold. It was nearer fifty feet than forty, and looking up, I realized I could never manage the ascent without help. By a miracle, I completed the descent without falling, and at last felt firm ground beneath my feet.

My arms and shoulders ached intolerably, my exposed legs were badly scratched and my nails broken, but at least I had made it. The fog was slightly less dense at the bottom. Piles of stinking rubbish, old bones, a broken wheel, shards of pottery, droppings, torn cloth lay around me. Behind me was a scummy pond, dancing with midges. Every now and again a plop! disturbed the surface, but there were no fish here. The borborygmi from decaying matter were eructating spontaneously from the foul depths. If the pup had fallen into that—! I moved forward and heard, just ahead, a whining snarl. So, he was here!

Forgetting caution, forgetting that I no longer held the power to communicate, I stumbled in the direction of the sound, to be brought up short by bared teeth and a definite growl. I peered through the murk; there, back against a rock, was one very hungry seven-week pup, stomach cramped, paws thrust hard against the earth to keep him upright, determined to fight to the last!

I crumpled to the ground, fighting a desire to laugh. I could have eaten him for breakfast! But still, the courage of the little thing! Recollecting myself, I feigned the surrender position, carefully avoiding looking him straight in the eye. 'Come, little one, I mean you no harm . . .' I edged forward, my hands held for him to sniff. As if to help, I heard his dam's whine from up above and so did he; absurd ears cocked, he gave a little yelp, all the while keeping his eyes steady on mine. This time the teeth were not bared, although he shrank back as far as he could. I used all the powers I could remember to reassure, to comfort. At last I was near enough to reach out without the smell of fear on my fingers and stroke his muzzle.

'Come, little Great One: I am here to take you back. It's cold and lonely down here, and up there the world awaits you. Be brave, and let me take you back where you belong. I promise you no harm: my man and I will keep you safe, and you will grow into a great hound whose fame will travel far and wide. You are hungry, and your dam waits to feed you. Come to me, and show you are my friend, as I am yours . . .' I patted my lap. I do not know how much he understood but two seconds later I had a lapful of tired, desperate pup and a tongue sought my face and two very dirty paws were around my neck.

Luckily he appeared uninjured by his fall into the pit, so I wrapped us together tightly in my shawl, and when Conn's rope came snaking down I made a loop in it and he hauled us seemingly without effort to the top, using the rowan tree as a belayer. He embraced us both and I released the pup, who immediately rushed over to his dam, two days of deprivation emptying the two rows of teats in record time.

409

Conn watched him, still keeping his arms around me. 'You all right?'

'Fine,' I said. 'Just fine!' I leaned against his shoulder, burning hands, scarred knees and aching shoulders forgotten for the moment.

Suddenly there was a low yipping from the other side of the pit. Peering through the fog, I thought I could see grey shapes and the glint of yellow eyes, a prowl of wolves reminding me that all was not yet well. I shivered for a moment then walked over to the pup: the concave stomach was now rounded and full and as I picked him up he once more smelt as any pup should, of fur and sunshine, warm milk and hay.

'Come on, you two,' I said. 'Time to get things sorted out . . .' And I led the way back to the village, the pup in my arms, Conn's hand round my waist, the bitch at our side. But keeping pace, just out of sight, something moved beside us in the fog.

Halting outside the gate of the farmhouse I hooked the pup's paws over the top bar and motioned to the bitch. 'Up, girl!' She stretched to her full height so that now the pup was between the pelt of his father and the head of his mother, his body against my chest. I sensed rather than saw the woman on the other side of the gate and knew that eyes and ears in the village were pressed against gaps in the doors, chinks in the shutters. I took a deep breath and, summoning up memory and instinct, spoke clearly and slowly so that all who wished could hear and remember. Clasping the pup firmly with my right hand I raised my left, the sinister, the magic hand, to pass from pelt to pup to bitch.

'Father, son, mother; dog, pup, bitch; each of each and one of both; wild one, child, tame one: here I lay the spirit of the father to rest, nevermore to roam: may he give the little one his courage, his cunning, his hunting skills. I release the spirit of the bitch back to her owners. May she give the little one her speed, her wisdom, her devotion. I take this pup for me and mine. He shall be ours to take away, ours to keep, ours to cherish. He shall never come nigh this village again, and the curse that was laid upon this place shall vanish with his departure, never to return . . .'

I was exhausted: all this meant nothing in real terms, just

410

reassurance for the villagers, the farmer's wife. Conn slipped an arm about me and the pup, his other hand through Beauty's bridle.

'Well done, dear one.' What the others used to call me . . . 'We've done all we can here. Give me the pup, and do you mount and ride for a while.' He had no idea that this was only the beginning . . .

We progressed slowly down the main street, conscious that the skulking villagers spied our every movement. The great bitch trotted at our heels, her eyes fixed on the pup Conn was holding. I had a moment's unease; supposing . . .?

We came to the edge of the village and I looked back; already the fog was thinning behind us. I slipped from Beauty's back and held out my arms for the pup. 'Let me have him, Conn.'

I put him to the ground and he gambolled over to his dam, nuzzling at the empty teats, and biting teasingly at her ears. Elbowing him aside I knelt to the bitch and used all the powers I had left to try to communicate, voicing the words to myself as I tried to remember the nuances of thought communication I had once so easily used with my friends, such a little while ago . . .

'He is old enough to leave you now, and if you take him back *they* will destroy him. Let us take him, Great One: we will care for him as one of our own and he will grow to be the greatest hound of his time and his children's children shall hunt with kings. Go back to your people, who have loved and cared for you over many years, and live out your life in peace . . .'

She was listening to me, but I could feel the power still rising through her, confusing thought.

'Give me your hatred, your bewilderment, your fear— Conn! Pick her up in your arms high above the ground, when I give the word—Now!' And as he did so, staggering under her weight, I flung myself directly beneath her and covered the Power, pressing it back to flow once more beneath the earth where it belonged. 'Back, back!' I heard my tongue use words in a language I do not remember. Slowly, reluctantly it seemed, the tension eased. At last I nodded to Conn to put the bitch down; she whined, looked puzzled for a moment, shook herself all over from ears to tail, then turned towards the village.

'Back then, girl; but first say your goodbyes to the pup. He is in good hands: make him understand that he must not follow you.'

I watched as she gently licked his head and under his tail. Then, as he jumped up, snapping playfully, she raised her head to us, eyes full of sorrow, then snapped back at him and growled. He shrank bewildered into an uncoordinated heap. I longed to pick him up and comfort him: not yet, not yet! The bitch turned and trotted off purposefully towards the village, and after a moment the pup gathered his feet together and stumbled after her. Conn started forward but I clutched his arm. 'It's all right: wait . . .'

The pup reached his mother: she checked and turned. For a moment I feared, then as he attempted to nuzzle her she growled again and nipped him sharply in the flank. He yelped, and for a moment did not know where to turn, then came pelting back to us, ears back, tail between his legs, the whites of his eyes showing. I picked him up. 'He has chosen . . . Conn, a rind of cheese from the pack!' I cuddled him, feeding him a scrap of cheese from my fingers, then deliberately walked on up the down, Conn following with Beauty. Once, I looked back. The bitch stood, just within misty vision, gazing at us. 'Go on, girl,' I willed. 'Back home. And forget . . .'

She turned, and went her way.

We reached the top of the down and the fog was still with us. But now it had a different quality; before, it had blanketed all in still, grey anonymity, now it had shape. The pup shivered in my arms and Beauty flung up her head fretfully. Only Conn was steady as a rock at my side, asking no questions, trusting me.

I halted. 'This is the place.'

'The place?'

'The boundary between the village and *their* world. Listen!'

All around us the fog was advancing and retreating; paws rattling, tails swishing; whining, yapping; ears laid back, eyes yellow; teeth bared, tongues lolling—

'Dear God!' muttered Conn. 'Are they real?'

'More or less. Take Beauty up to that small hawthorn and tether her tight, otherwise she will panic. They won't hurt either of you: they are only interested in the pup. I'll be all right . . .'

412

Brave words . . . Now I was alone with them. The pup lay quiet in my arms but now and again a shiver ran through him and a little trickle of warm wet ran down my arm. But he was trying hard to hide his terror and in that moment I accepted him as one of us.

The wolf-fog swirled closer and now I was truly alone, for no longer could I see either Conn or Beauty, some hundred yards away. The beasts were becoming braver, encroaching on the unwritten empty space that humans keep between themselves and other creatures, beyond which none may come unless invited. A tail brushed my leg, a muzzle snatched at my skirt, a paw struck my arm.

'Enough!' I said, and used a Word of Command, one that our Mistress had used.

The fog hesitated then steadied, and I had my space again. Remembering the witch's spells, The Ancient's commands, the bond that had existed between me and my friends, and now, most of all, the memory of Snowy, I summoned up all my strength. 'I am not calling you back, dear one,' I said in my mind, 'for that I know is forbidden, but please give me what help you can . . .' Instantly, or so it seemed, the middle finger of my right hand itched intolerably. Absentmindedly I reached to scratch and touched the golden band around it. I felt a charge go through me. Touching the pup on the head with Snowy's ring, I boldly set him down at my feet.

'Once, long ago,' I said to the fog, 'you and yours said you were mine to command until a certain debt was repaid. The debt is still owing. I was also promised that when my need was great, one would come. I have him here: the answer to a need, the repayment of the debt.' The words were only in my mind, but I felt their meaning ring round the circling mist. 'This pup before you is not of yours; he is neither dog nor wolf, and as such is only acceptable to such as we. Let him go! His dam has released him: now it is your turn! This pup before you, sired by your dead leader, now belongs to me and the man who—'

The man who now strode urgently through the mist to my side, wading carelessly through tails and muzzles, to stand with sword drawn, his other arm encircling my waist.

'You're not tackling this on your own! We may be outnumbered, but my sword can bite as sharp as their teeth!' He

413

never knew how near he came to upsetting everything, even while my heart sang with his 'rescue', for as I let my attention turn to him the thread that kept the wolves at bay nearly snapped. In time I recalled myself.

'No need, I think, my dear Conn . . .' I touched Snowy's ring to my lips and concentrated again, willing a visual impression of that strange flight from the Castle of Fair Delights. I tried to project that last meeting with the three wolves, the bitch's last words . . . I felt the wolves about me grow still, then there was a pause, as though they were considering. The mist thinned a little and I could see a silent, watchful ring of animals. They sat or lay where they were as if waiting for something to happen. A young wolf, scarce six months, became tired of the delay and crawled towards the pup. Instantly an old bitch snapped it into submission.

We waited. And waited.

At length, trotting proudly through the pack, came the largest of the wolves. In its jaws were the dangling remains of a fresh-killed hare. He halted in front of me, eyes blazing. A pledge. I held out my hand and he laid the limp body of the hare in front of the pup, who immediately sniffed at the still-warm body. Kneeling, I took out my knife and, slitting open the body, brought out the liver, steaming in the cold mist. Quickly I sliced at the meat and handed a piece to the leader-wolf, who snapped it from my fingers. Quelling my nausea I stuffed a bit in my own mouth and handed a piece up to Conn.

'But—'

'Eat! and don't argue. It's important . . .'

The last piece I gave to the pup, who took it delicately and chewed likewise, his eyes never leaving the wolf. The body of the hare still lay before the leader: in one swift movement he snatched it up and tossed it over his shoulder, almost like a game, and immediately the whole pack fell on it, growling and snarling till there was not the smallest scrap of fur or bone left. The new wolf-leader looked at me, at Conn, then slowly, deliberately, he lifted his leg and urinated on the pup and then wheeled round into the thinning mist without looking back. One by one, in correct pack order, the other wolves got up and followed him until at last we were alone.

A fresh breeze blew from the west.

'Suppose,' said Conn, 'you tell me what all that was about?'

I picked up the pup. 'Pah! You smell, you poor little so-and-so! Let's find a stream and get you cleaned up . . . Yes, I'll tell you, Conn, but shall we get out of here? I'm hungry, and cold, and tired . . .'

Without a word he picked me up, pup and all, and carried me over to where Beauty was waiting.

Journey's End

AFTER THAT it was different. We were back to the easy, gentle relationship we had had when first setting out on our journey, when Conn had plucked me flowers from the hedge and I had gazed at him when I did not think he would notice.

But that was all: we were back where we started, but no further. It was just like going to all the trouble of preparing a meal, smelling the delicious aromas as it cooked, tasting to see that the juices blended right, preparing the table, sharpening the knives, wiping the bowls, even putting the serving spoon into the stew—and then, no food. Just the tantalizing smells, the salivating mouth, the stomach-turn of anticipation, the growing hunger. And surely, just like a meal that is kept too long, the meat would dry up, the bread go mouldy, the wine sour, and the chief guest disappear? I was hungry for love, real love, desperate to taste what I was sure would be the finest nourishment I had ever been offered, sure that it would fill me to satiation: but the guest at the meal was too polite to invite himself to dinner, and I was too proud to ask, lest I be refused.

That was the worst of all, I suppose, not knowing. When I had been ugly he had promised to take care of me; when I was pretty he had tried to renew his offer but I had sidestepped, and since then he had not referred to it again. I knew he had a journey's end in mind where everything would suddenly be right, why else had we hastened all these miles? But I was not so sanguine. Had I dreamt those moments round The Ancient's fire when he had talked about laying down his arms? Did I imagine in dreams that he had said he wanted to settle down with wife and children? Or had he some other person in mind? To me, love didn't wait on destinations—if, indeed, this were love, this funny, aching, irritating, lovely, despairing longing that I felt.

But thankfully I could not be introspective the whole time. We were travelling through countryside rich with late summer, through forests where the leaves hung heavy and the birds were almost too drowsy to sing, across streams and rivers where the trout lay in somnolent shoals, through villages where it was too hot to do anything but laze in the sun. Beauty grew sleek and plump, Conn and I became almost as tanned as the Dark People and the pup grew tall and strong. We had discussed what to call him. None of the names I tried—Misty, Silver, to do with his colour; Hero and Speedy (hopefully his attributes)—seemed to fit. Then Conn told me how, as a child, he had tumbled on the floor of the Great Hall of his father's home with all the hounds and dogs and terriers, and how he had had a chosen animal he had later hunted with and loved above the rest, one of the Great Ones named Bran. I looked at the pup. 'Bran?' I said. He wagged his tail. So Bran it was.

He was already showing promise. Every day Conn, firm and dedicated, taught him obedience and exploited those skills in which he showed promise. For an hour at a time man and dog worked like teacher and pupil, both wearing frowns of concentration, both throwing all they had into the lessons. Then would come a break; Conn would relax, lie back with cheese and bread and the pup would come running to me, all smiles and wagging tail, and I laughed with him and we tussled on the ground together until we were both exhausted. He would roll onto his back, ears flopping in the dust and his hairless belly gleaming in the sunlight and I would kiss his nose and pick the burrs out of his coat . . .

'You spoil him,' grumbled Conn. 'He's a working dog.'

'Not all the time. You weren't a soldier every minute of every day. He's only young: he's got to relax sometimes, just as you are doing now.'

'I'm eating.'

'And resting . . .'

'At least I'm not playing about!'

'Children must play sometimes; he's still only a youngster.'

And then Conn would relent and come and join us, playing

417

with the great paws and scratching him behind the ears. 'He's going to be a beauty, just like his dam!'

But the pup would slide his slitted yellow eyes round to mine, eyes slanting back along his head that were pure wolf—

And so the promise they had made, all that long time ago when they escaped from their prison in the Castle of Fair Delights, was fulfilled . . .

And then we came to Encancastre, that the Romans before us had called Isca, through fields heavy with harvest and sickle Lugnosa moon at night. The town stretched away in front of us up narrow, winding streets, a roof-pattern of thatch and wood and tile—and the river ran away at our feet. A haze of smoke drifted down to our nostrils and somewhere was the merry sound of pipe and drum and all the usual hubbub of people living on top of one another: shouts, hails, laughter, complaint; a man singing, a cow bellowing, a dog barking, a child crying—

Civilization.

Part of me welcomed this, looked for the close intimacy of person to person, the comfortable proximity of my own kind; part rejected the whole idea and wished for the loneliness, the open spaces, the close communion that was possible between humans and nature—or was it that I was frightened of giving myself unreservedly to my own kind? Perhaps this had something to do with the gulf that still existed between Conn and myself? I knew, by that extra sense that all women have, that he was far from indifferent to me and even desired me, but I also knew that he was ignorant of the full extent to which his feelings were involved. I knew also that unless he was reminded fairly soon we should just drift farther and farther apart, until—

'—so I thought it would be fair if we split it two-thirds to you and one to myself,' said Conn, arranging the gold pieces on a convenient tree-stump. 'That means twenty for you and ten for me. I can earn my living easily enough now that I have Booty back and sword and armour. I'll leave Bran with you for the time being anyway, because you need some kind of protector and, although he's by no means full size yet, I'd not like to—'

'What are you *talking* about?'

He looked across at me, puzzled. 'Weren't you listening? I said that now we had reached journey's end—'

'Journey's end?'

'I don't believe you heard a word I said!' He frowned. 'A long time ago, or so it seems, I said I knew of an army surgeon and bonesetter from my Frankish days who had settled with his English wife in Isca and that I had a mind to learn his trade—'

'But you just said you were going back to fighting—'

'I said that now I had horse and armour I could earn my living, yes, but I intend to learn the trade of surgeon, to travel to where the battles are, fight if needs be, but to offer my services initially as mender rather than breaker.'

I was silent. My insides had settled in a doughy lump and my head felt as if it were stuffed with uncombed fleece. He was really going, then: I was to be left on my own.

I tried to keep my voice steady. 'I—I remember you saying you—you would see me settled . . .'

'Of course, of course!' He looked uncomfortable at the reminder, was speaking too heartily, would not look at me. 'Well now, I've given the matter more than a little thought in the last few days—' (I'll bet! I thought bitterly) '—and the best idea is that I leave you with my friend's wife, who I am sure will prove an excellent chaperone until you get settled. You will have the gold as a nice little—dowry, or somesuch, and when you find someone—somewhere that you want to settle— What's the matter?'

He had said once that I had a stubborn chin: I stuck it out. 'You said *you* would! I don't want just any old female looking after me, either! Besides—' I had had a sudden, saving thought. 'How do you know she'll agree? In fact, how do you even know they are still there?' I warmed to the theme. 'Hadn't you better make sure that this *is* journey's end before you start dividing up the dragon's gold?' And our lives, I added silently. 'Why don't you take Beauty and go up into the town and find out? Bran and I will wait for you here.' It sounded thoroughly reasonable, yet I thought he might detect the guile that had prompted my words.

He didn't. 'Very well. You are sure you want to stay here?'

Oh yes, I was sure, very sure. Even if the animals conspired

419

against our parting, Beauty turning her head twice to look back at me, and Bran whining to see them go.

'Traitor!' I murmured, and stroked his ears. 'Now, it's long past noon already, and there is a lot to do . . .'

Further into the woods behind the town I found what I wanted and spent a very busy two or three hours. It was already blueing into twilight when I heard Beauty's hooves on the track. On one edge of the world a thin silver reaper's knife peeked over to counterbalance the gold-plated platter that was sliding away over the other side. Between them a star blinked and yawned, ready to blaze the night, and the air was very still: earth, sun, moon and stars in perfect conjunction and the paths of Power beneath my feet. All boded well and it must be near, or on, the actual feast of Lugnosa, when all good things ripened and fell to the knife and were gathered for harvest. Not the painful, cold birth of Inbolc, nor the frenzied coupling of Beltane, nor yet the haunted darkness of Samain, but still a time for magic . . .

'Did you find him?' I asked Conn as he tethered Beauty to the rowan where I had already tied Bran. Pretending to fuss I looped the garland I had prepared over her neck and turned for Conn's answer.

'After a fair bit of searching, yes. His name is Hieronymus, but he is called Jeremy here, so that complicated the search. But he is just the same, and his wife's as charming a lady as you could hope to meet: makes three of him but still handsome enough, and she's more than willing to take care of you—'

'And what does he say,' I interrupted, 'about you learning the trade?'

'He agreed at once! He wants us to set up in business together for a while, and says that after a year or so I shall be able to start up on my own if I wish, or buy him out, because he wants to return to his birthland and—'

'Well, isn't that nice!' I said. 'Just what you had hoped for!'

'You'll like them too, darling girl. And now shall we—'

I was temporarily sidetracked by the 'darling girl' but not so much as not to try and divert him as he moved back towards Beauty, obviously wanting us to go back to the town straightaway. 'Let's just have a last, quiet supper on our own tonight and go and see them tomorrow first thing. I made a stew, just in case, and baked some bread, and I saved some of that mead you liked . . .'

The smoke from the fire drifted upwards in a careless spiral, the air was lazy and warm, and all the scents of the earth mingled and thrust at one's senses; great hawk-wings fluttered on teasel and late foxglove, bats swung low, and the ground was dry, the heath springy beneath one's feet. Such a perfect, sweet-smelling night meant unsettled weather for the next few days, especially as tabby-stripe clouds were rising slowly in the west, but now it was perfect.

As was the place I had chosen.

Once there had been a circle but now only the postholes were left for those who cared to see. A minor place of power, else there would have been standing stones instead of rotted wood, but the rowan, ivy, holly and hawthorn were still there. There were paths of Power beneath our feet, and Conn had seated himself unknowingly on the old altar stone, a slab of rock half-overgrown by the ubiquitous ivy.

He stretched back, his arms behind his head. 'What a perfect night! Just right for—' He stopped abruptly. 'Er . . . Dinner ready, Thingy?'

Fine, it was going as I had planned.

'Nearly. Why don't you go over to the stream, down there in the hollow, and wash off the grime of the day? I have a clean shirt waiting for you. I'll just add a pinch or two of salt to the stew and cut the bread and then it'll all be ready.'

If he thought it was a little odd having a dip at this time of day he made no sign and disappeared behind the bushes. Good. It was necessary to be cleansed.

I added the special touches to the stew, inhaling the pungent, earthy smell of the mushrooms before crumbling them into the bubbling pot, then laid the bowls and horn mugs ready, unstoppering the mead to let it breathe the night air. I had bathed earlier and now, in these few stolen moments, was the time to tune myself to the Power.

I was about to step into the circle to begin the incantations but suddenly there came the hoot of an owl, as out of season as The Ancient's Hoowi. Without thinking I looked across the clearing at Conn's discarded jacket, where the owl's feather and the dove's still blazoned the right breast. The owl's, wisdom; the dove's, peace and fidelity. The owl hooted again, urgently it seemed. Was that, then, my feather? Wisdom? And surely what I was about to do was the only wisdom: lulling Conn into an acceptance of what he really felt, make him declare that which was hidden—

My right hand spasmed as if it were cramped, but only for an instant. I opened the fingers again and stretched them: strange, for one's toes sometimes cramped, but not one's fingers . . . I stepped towards the circle, the owl hooted, my hand spasmed once more and this time the ring on my middle finger, Snowy's spiral of magic horn, bit into the palm of my hand. I pulled at it, tried to unwind the coil, but it was as firm as a fingernail yet still soft and malleable, and as like my own flesh as if it had grown into it, and it wouldn't shift.

Once again I stepped forward, once again my fingers clenched involuntarily. So, I was doing something wrong. Had I mispronounced one of the correct words, mispaced one of the steps, forgotten one of the essential herbs? Quickly I ran through them in my mind, but everything seemed as it should. Then through the soft night air came stealing a strange, alien odour, compounded of so many different things that were foreign to the time and place. There was a warm, sweaty horse-smell, like but unlike Beauty; a scent of singed horn, fresh spring grass; water bubbling over rocks, summer hay; moss, trampled pine-needles—Snowy!

Forgetting, I turned to look for him, but the traitorous moon showed only emptiness. My eyes flooded with tears, aching for one more sighting of that beloved form, my hands reaching in vain for the soft curtain of his mane, my ears for that quaint, gentle speech. At this moment he was nearer to me than he had ever been since I had seen him pace away into oblivion with his prince, the prince he loved without subterfuge or dissembling or magic—

Oh, Snowy! Of course. Real love was either there or it wasn't. No need to conjure it with runes, bind it with ivy and hawthorn, induce it with mushrooms and mead! Love thus forced was as bad—worse!—than our Mistress's Shape-Changing that had seduced an innocent village-lad and near-trapped Conn also. What was I doing, what was I thinking of? If Conn loved me he would tell me: if he didn't then I had no right to drug him into believing he did!

Running over to Bran and Beauty I tore off their garlands, untied them from the rowan and tethered them again to an innocent oak sapling. Picking up the heavy cooking pot I attempted to heave away the contents into the bushes, but some of the scalding fluid tipped down my dress; panicking both from the heat of the liquid and from some imagined contamination I ripped it off and stood naked. Quickly I circled widdershins to counteract any lingering spells, then raced away to the stream to rinse my dress, without thinking further than that a great load was off my mind: I was free of power, spells and enchantments forever. Now I was me, myself, and never again would I be tempted to use a magic I was not entitled to!

Running through the bushes barefoot I stumbled more than once, but the knowledge that I must wash away all traces of my foolishness spurred me on. Splashing at last into the clear, cold water, I held my dress under and scrubbed away all traces of the magic between my fingers and looped it over a bush to dry, then turned to wash all fever from myself.

'Whatever in the world are you doing, Thingy dear?' There was a lilt to his voice like the turn of the water over the stones, and once more we stood face to face in running water, birth-naked the pair of us, but this time there was no shame on my part, no coyness, no hesitation. I had to know, I had to know right there and then, and convention and a few scraps of cloth, or rather the lack of them, were irrelevant.

'Oh, Conn! I had it all planned but it wasn't right, it was wicked and Snowy told me so and I think The Ancient's owl did too, but I spilt the supper down my dress and had to get myself clean and please say you don't mind, but I must know!'

'Darling girl, you're talking scribble again! Spilt the supper, have you? No bother: there's a tavern not a half-mile from here—'

'You don't understand!' I wailed. 'I'm unclean, I—'

'Then that's soon remedied. Just stand still, girl dear, and I'll scoop some water over you . . . So.' The water poured from his cupped hands over my shoulders, between my breasts and down my flat stomach to the cleft between my thighs. He lifted more, and this time the tips of his fingers accidentally brushed my breasts and I felt as though I had been kicked in the

423

stomach. Looking down, I saw that my nipples were hard and firm like two wild cherries.

Looking down revealed something else, as well.

'Is that—is that because of me?' I asked wonderingly and put out my hand to touch, but he leapt back as though he had been stung, hands over his crotch, and all but lost his balance.

'Don't—don't!' he said. 'You don't know, you don't realize . . .'

'I'm sorry,' I said, but there was no consciousness of shame, only a lively curiosity. 'I just wanted to touch. You see, that sort of thing has always frightened me before; there was Broom, and then the swineherd: they only wanted to attack, to hurt . . . But yours looks rather nice and friendly, not threatening at all. I have seen it before, you know,' I added. 'When you were ill, or bathing or getting dressed.' I was going to say something about the Lady Adiora, but thought better of it.

'If you try and touch me,' he said unsteadily, 'knight or no, I won't answer for the consequences . . .'

'Do you mean—you would make love to me?'

'Just that!'

'Then—Oh Conn, I must ask! Does that mean you love me, just the littlest bit? Or is it only what they call lust? You see, I have to know. I've loved you so much all this time, ever since we found you in that ditch, in fact, and at one time I thought you might—Then you didn't ask again, and I thought you didn't . . . I know ladies aren't supposed to ask things like this, and it doesn't matter if you don't, I won't mind—well, not much anyway—but I must know, —'

He stepped forward and kissed me then, quite hard, and I fitted nicely into his arms and everything was very interesting, because although my feet by now were cold from the stream and the skin was going all washerwoman-wrinkly, the rest of me was warm and smooth and tingly.

'Does that mean you do?' I asked, when I had got my breath back.

'Does it mean . . .! Dear Christ, girl, I've worshipped you ever since I first saw you properly in those Waters of Truth! I loved you before, poor helpless little Thingummy that you were, but when I saw that beautiful face on you and the body to match and I knew you were born a lady it was just like your

424

dull pebbles turning into the dragon's jewels: I felt you were way beyond my reach and would never consider an ageing, well-used adventurer!'

'But I *love* you—'

'But I wasn't to know, now was I? You never said . . .'

'Neither did you!' I thought back over the wasted miles. 'You're not really well-used . . . Can I now?'

'What? Oh. Well . . .' He seemed a little disconcerted, but I looked down and saw that his body was still keen. Perhaps he was hungry. My mother had always made sure my father was fed and wined before she asked him something special, especially if she was afraid he might say no.

'Perhaps we could have supper first,' I suggested. 'There's bread left and a bit of cheese, and the mead—'

'Blow supper!' said Conn. 'Hang supper! To perdition with supper!' And he picked me up in his arms and carried me all the way back to the fire.

On the way I tried to explain what I had intended to do and he kissed me in all the nicest places and told me he didn't need magic and moonlight and mushrooms to know that I belonged in his heart for always and then he laid me down and took me in his arms again and the earth stretched beneath us like a dreaming beast, and the sickle of the reaper took the last thread that bound me to my past and gathered me and tied me to my love and I heard the music again, the music The Ancient had called Love's Song, and the air sang with it the whole night through . . .

'How about breakfast?' said Conn.

'Breakfast?'

'Yes, breakfast: making love always leaves me with an appetite . . . Now you are to be my wife I shall expect all the comforts of home, you know: meals on demand, and all the rest of it . . .'

'Your wife? Am I really to be your wife?' I looked at him. He was laughing, his moustache curled upward, his eyes sparkled, and on his face was a look of love and contentment and on his jacket our two feathers: wisdom and fidelity. Yes, he meant it.

'Just as soon as we can say the right words in front of the right person.' He reached over and spanked my rump. 'Now, lazy one, get some clothes on and we'll go up to town.' He followed the spank with a kiss on the offended portion. 'And then if you'll bear with me learning the surgeon's trade for a while, we'll go on afterwards and find that home you dreamt of: sea, hills and a stream, wasn't it, with martlets in the eaves and seals to sing us to sleep? And we'll settle there and have children and love and quarrel and then kiss and make up. I'll cure the people and you will tend to the hurts of the animals, and we'll live happily ever after . . .'

And so we did.

> *And so the soldier: hung up his sword;*
> *The hands that had hewn: turned to heal.*
> *The loves she had lost: became different loves,*
> *And the martlet made: his mansion in the eaves.*
> *The wolf-cub waited: by the wall of the house*
> *And the people of the sea: sang them to sleep.*